Dr. Strudelbert von Hexenschluss

THE DISCOVERY OF LEFT WORLD

Part One

of

A STORY NEVER TO BE TOLD

An Almost Completely True Fairy Tale

[7] *cf. Lux Mundi XI* Publishing

The Song of the Radiator Sprites

Once upon a time – right about now actually – there was a skyscraper on the Isle of Dogs in London taller and more magnificent than any other. It stood right at the southern tip of the huge letter U the River Thames makes on its way out of London and it was the headquarters of a big company called Advanced Computers & Games.

The ACG skyscraper dwarfed all other skyscrapers around it, even the famous towers of Canary Wharf. It resembled a pyramid at the base but transformed into a needle at the top, giving the impression that it tickled the underbelly of the sky. On cloudy days, when half of it disappeared in low-lying clouds, it was as if Earth had extended a hand to heaven, and heaven grasped it in a display of warm friendship. There were rumours that on windy days heaven liked to give Earth's hand a shake, but that could be felt only on the top floors which were populated with the top management, who knew better than to go around telling foolish stories about the hand that fed them.

The lobby of the tower was as big as a cathedral, with video games and consoles lining the marble floor instead of pews, occupied at all hours by throngs of teenagers. Everybody liked to go there because it was the policy of ACG to allow unlimited and free access to all. And on one particular morning in March when this tale began, the lobby was particularly busy because many more had come to take part in a widely advertised testing of new games equipment.

Mehdi was impatient. He was one of many teenagers queuing in the lobby to interview for a games testing position. As usual, he was dressed in a neat and unassuming way, but stood out from the rest of the crowd on account of his height and tousled hair that imparted an impatience wholly of its own, as if it was about to jump the queue and leave Mehdi behind. It was the one thing on him his father could not manage to control – and not for lack of trying. Either the hair had its own character or it reflected that part of his character that still refused to grow up. The strongest part.

For Mehdi, a position in the ACG games testing project would be a dream come true: not only would he get a chance to play new games and try new consoles if he got the job, but his school would accept the position as required work experience for his final year – and a paid one at that!

He was so impatient that he could not help being irritated by the man standing in front of him in the queue. He was rather out of place – his clothes looked shabby and covered in black dust – and he seemed totally uninterested in the games around him. What was he doing here if he did not want to play games? Then again, maybe he was just more disciplined, he was older than most of the crowd, well into his twenties it seemed – maybe even his thirties! And his clothes were so scruffy and full of black dust – was it soot? – that even Mehdi noticed it. Oh, no! – that was the kind of remark reserved for the mouth of his father. Was he really going to grow up to be just like his father? The thought unsettled him.

Mehdi made an effort to think about something else, when his attention was drawn to the weather outside. Although London's weather had seemed stable that morning, now the sun had lost its brightness, the shadows were starting to blend into the background and the colours were dull. It was clear that a storm was brewing.

Suddenly a huge white limo pulled up in front of the glass entrance doors. Mehdi could see ACG staff jostling around it, straining their necks in expectation of something. The excitement peaked when a well-tanned, blond man in his forties emerged from the limo wearing an immaculately tailored white suit.

'Welcome, Mr. Pingvarsson,' said a middle-aged woman with a wide smile grafted on an otherwise stern expression as she stepped forward to greet him. 'Welcome to ACG!'

Mr. Pingvarsson could not help noticing her incredibly voluminous dark hair with just a few strands of grey and a pair of thick glasses with elaborately shaped frames that looked like the back end of a 1957 Cadillac, shrunken and mounted on the woman's nose.

'Delighted to meet you – '

'Edna Edwards, Chief of Human Resources,' she said, cutting him off. 'Our chairman, Mr. Furthermore, is awaiting you on the upper floors. And may I say how delighted and honoured we all are to have you here, Mr. Pingvarsson.'

'I, too, am delighted to be here. Looks like not even good old ACG can get ahead without some expert help,' said Mr. Pingvarsson.

A hum of chatter began to grow in the lobby as queuing candidates and assembled staff spied the man in the white suit. 'Ingvar Pingvarsson, the greatest motivational consultant in the world today!' 'Will we have a chance to meet him?' 'Is he going to interview us?' 'Is he going to designate our unit the *Group Selection Pool*?' 'Will *I* get to work with him?' 'Will he change my career as he changed so many others'?'

'Don't mind the youngsters,' said Edna Edwards leading Mr. Pingvarsson into the lobby, 'they are here to interview for our new interface testing program.'

'I prefer a hands-on approach, Ms. Edwards,' said Mr. Pingvarsson. 'You know my motto, don't you? *Tell me what you do and I'll tell you how to do it!*'

'Of course, Mr. Pingvarsson, of course! I read all your books!' Edna Edwards squeaked with excitement.

'Then let's jump the queue and see what it's all about,' said Ingvar Pingvarsson.

Mehdi was becoming less and less impressed with the sooty guy in front of him. First, he stared at the ceiling for the whole of eternity (and Mehdi had checked it out; there was nothing of interest on the ceiling – unless four huge chandeliers with a myriad of crystalline lights in endless numbers of colours were interesting to him). Then he acted like he fell asleep queuing, and when it was his turn, he just waited, speechless like an Egyptian mummy, wasting everybody's valuable time. 'I mean, let's move it, the consoles are waiting!' thought Mehdi, as if urged on by his hair too. 'Look, some important-looking people are walking to the interview desk – but just look at him answering the questions!'

Mehdi could not hear everything that was said, but he heard that the guy's name was Pim Pergamon and that he was twenty-eight – way too old in his opinion. This Pim guy pondered over every question, took deep breaths, scratched his head before answering – in other words he was totally unfit for the job. He couldn't answer anything about computers *or* games – what a moron! 'Why did he bother to apply in the first place?! And why is this funny guy in white suit behind the desk nodding?' thought Mehdi.

His impatience grew into anger when he realised that this Pim was accepted for the job – despite the soot! They told him to fill in some forms and wait by the desk where he continued to look lost in both space and time. Mehdi eventually calmed down, realizing that if such a totally unsuitable blockhead as Pim Pergamon had been accepted, it would be a piece of cake for him to get in. There was no doubt about it – they would give him something very sophisticated to test!

Mehdi's enthusiasm knew no bounds when it was his turn to talk to the people behind the application desk. He showered them with his knowledge of ACG and its technology, gave them a long (expanded and embellished) list of the equipment he was familiar with and explicitly stated that he could master any game they gave him – first person shooter, first person slayer, morphs and shapeshifters – you name it! It took some time before the clerk had diligently typed all this into her computer. Once she had finished, she turned towards the woman with the 1957 Cadillac glasses and the man in white suit standing behind her. The Cadillac looked at the white suit who shook his bleached head. The clerk typed something and then raised her eyes from the screen.

'I am sorry, but you are not suited for our testing program.'

Mehdi was so shocked that he could not find the words to argue.

'Thank you for applying and we wish you success next time.'

'Yes, I wish you a great success, young man. Some day you will be a tremendous asset to this company – but not today,' Ingvar Pingvarsson said to Mehdi with a big smile and then walked away with Edna and her suite, keeping the smile on all the while.

Mehdi wanted to move, but his legs would not carry him away. He just remained there, stunned, so the clerk felt compelled to lean towards him and say in a confidential tone now that others could not hear her, 'I suppose they are looking for someone a little bit more average, you know.'

Mehdi turned and walked away. The last thing he saw was a technician who came and escorted the moron who stole his internship through security and towards the lifts that led to the upper floors – that hallowed place where things which meant so much to him were made.

'You must be Pim Pergamon,' said a young man with an Eastern European accent standing on the 57th floor when the lift opened. He was wearing a white overcoat and holding a clipboard, trying his best to look and sound important. His purpose was somewhat defeated by his thick lips which, especially in combination with the white overcoat, made him look like the proverbial nerd.

'Are you a doctor?' said Pim.

'No, I am a Research Director. My name is Gustav and I will lead today's testing. Come this way, please.' There was something reassuring in Gustav's mild manners.

Gustav led Pim along a long corridor, past one more set of security barriers and ushered him through a large door, trying rather conspicuously not to brush his neat white overcoat against Pim's sooty clothes. They found themselves in a spacious room with black walls and black ceiling and no windows. The ceiling was high, with several wires suspended from it. A young Chinese woman dressed in a grey overcoat with the ACG logo was busy in one corner with some machinery. Pim could not see her well but she seemed attractive.

'I can't offer you a seat because, as you can see, we have no chairs and no furniture in this room,' said Gustav. 'This is Laboratory 21. The main goal of the experiments we are conducting here is bringing human and computer sensory perception closer together.'

'Computer sensory perception? What's that?'

'Switch it on, Lia!'

The Chinese assistant – who was, on second thought, definitely attractive despite her glasses – pressed a button on a control panel and the whole room was all of a sudden criss-crossed by a myriad of infinitesimally thin green rays of light.

'It's a completely new interface between humans and computers,' said Gustav. 'The world's first Supraquantum Laser Motion Sensor! Isn't it magnificent?'

'What does it do?'

Gustav loved explaining things. 'ACG has long been in the forefront of gaming industry, since before the days of Pacman, always coming up with new games, one more exciting than the other,' he said sounding like an excited press release. 'This would have been impossible without one very important thing – constant reinventing of the way we communicate with the computer. I would like to tell you more about the invention of the mouse, the webcam, the smartphone – not to mention the kinetic software – but I am prevented by certain patent agreements. Similarly, what you see here you are not permitted to describe to anyone else, you've just signed some papers downstairs to that effect, remember? Anyway, this is what you will be testing today. I don't want to burden you with technical details, so suffice it to say that the supraquantum laser motion sensor – as the name implies – will be recording your motion in real time. Each supraquantum laser ray is nearly invisible – yet capable of recording not only the positions along the x-y-z axes, but velocity and acceleration as well. And if we feed all this into a computer, it will know where you are and where you're going – '

'You mean no more keyboards and consoles.'

'No more clicking, no more tapping, no more voice instructions with silly outcomes. Whatever you do with any part of your body in your world, no matter how small – hand, finger, nose, even belly button! – our computer will transpose into its world.'

'The computerworld.'

'Exactly! It will be as if you are inside the computer.'

'Gustav, what's that dust on his clothes? It could be a problem,' said Lia.

'Oh, this? It's soot,' said Pim Pergamon somewhat embarrassed. Actually, doubly embarrassed in front of a girl as attractive as Lia.

'The lasers might pick it up. What happened to you?'

'I had an accident this morning. I don't normally go out in the street like this.'

'You might be right, the lasers might pick it up,' said Gustav. 'Lia, switch off the lasers and get him a brush or something. *An accident?*'

'Actually, an explosion.'

'Terrorists?!' Lia could be heard from the corner rummaging for a brush or something.

'No, nothing like that,' Pim was eager to reassure Lia.

'What was it then?' asked Gustav.

'It's a long story,' said Pim.

'Well, we can't start with the supraquantum laser motion sensor until we've cleaned you up a bit,' said Gustav looking at the reticent young man in front of him.

'And I love stories,' Lia was heard from the back.

'Alright,' Pim's face brightened. A guy with his ordinary looks and his anything but muscular body could use this sort of female attention. Or to be more precise, any sort of female attention. 'This morning, just before dawn, I was asleep in my room when I heard noises from downstairs. Normally I like to sleep long and Uncle Pohadka dislikes it very much – '

'Turn around, I'll do your back first,' Lia came holding a big brush. Pim decided that the glasses were her strength.

'But this morning some strange noises woke me up. So I went down to the workshop where we keep all sorts of powders and chemicals. I work – I used to work at Pohadka's World Famous Fireworks and Novelties shop in Brick Lane. He's my uncle and tormentor – I mean mentor. The noises were coming from a radiator in the workshop. When I came close, I thought I heard tiny little gurgling voices inside – as if a swarm of little imps were quarrelling inside the radiator.'

'Imps. He heard imps inside a radiator,' said Lia. 'Turn.'

'That's how they sounded to me,' said Pim. 'But of course, I knew that it was just air in the system. When air gets into pipes and radiators, you hear such noises from inside. Everything in Uncle Pohadka's house is old and the central heating is no exception. Anyway, we often had air in the system and after some time it would stop working. Not only heating, hot water for the shower too. So I decided to bleed the air from the system, as Uncle Pohadka had taught me, before going back to sleep. I hate to wake up in cold and with no hot water. But then, when I opened the valve on the radiator – whoosh! A whole host of little vaporous creatures hissed out, still quarrelling in their gaseous way. They were all airy, a bit plump, each of them of a different colour – something like beach balls, except that they were almost transparent. When they saw me they stopped quarrelling and started giggling. Then they held their hands together and began singing and dancing all over the desks and cabinets and shelves. And they sang a beautiful, enchanting song.

> One for a boy, two for a girl.
> Three for the fire inside a pearl.
> Then four for Abdals and five for Rubalkals,
> Six for a hero righteous and bold,
> And seven for a story never to be told!

'Squat down,' commanded Lia. 'Only your shoulders left.'

'And then they kept repeating it faster and faster, and dancing around faster and faster. I tried to stop them but they evaded me and laughed mischievously until in the end they knocked over a big Erlenmeyer flask. The moment it hit the ground there was an explosion – calcium azide is a very volatile compound, you know.

When the dust settled, the radiator sprites were all gone and I was all covered in soot – and then Uncle Pohadka came fuming and threw me out of the house.'

Pim gloomily stared into the distance. The distance was a meter away and it was occupied by Lia, more specifically Lia's lovely tummy.

'Stand up, you're done,' she said.

'That's why I signed up for this testing. I have no job and no home now – Uncle Pohadka was so angry he wouldn't even let me explain what happened.'

'Maybe it's for the better,' said Gustav having heard the story.

Although Ingvar Pingvarsson could hardly wait to be introduced to such a legendary character in the computer business as Alexander Benjamin Lawrence Furthermore, CEO of ACG, he halted for a moment after getting out of the lift. Not even World's Most Famous Motivational Consultant™ had seen anything like this before. Mr. Furthermore's office was on one of the last floors of the ACG skyscraper, close to the point where the building stopped being a building and turned into a needle. Ingvar entered a perfectly round space with glass walls that extended 360 degrees around the floor, offering breathtaking views of the Greenwich Observatory and the Thames Air Line on one side, all the way across Canary Wharf and the City towers to Westminster and London Eye on the other.

Ingvar quickly pulled himself together and firmly shook the hand of the Chief Executive Officer of Advanced Computers&Games. Mr. Furthermore was a sprightly lean man in his early sixties with a small moustache and in his three piece dark striped suit presented quite a contrast to the flashy Ingvar Pingvarsson – apart from the fact that both suits were expensive.

The two men quickly struck a rapport around one phrase – Increased Efficiency. It happened to be the title of both Mr. Furthermore's presentation at the Leading Business Leaders Conference last month and Pingvarsson's best-selling book.

'There is one secret to Increased Efficiency, as you undoubtedly know,' Ingvar said to Mr. Furthermore's enthusiastic nodding before continuing along his favourite line, 'and that's the hands-on approach. My assistants from Shelwood, Iberd, Tubston & Eaglestone will be arriving here in the coming days. But I, myself, like to start on the hoof, so to speak. I like to acquaint myself with the work process from the inside.'

'Sure, Ingvar, be my guest. That's why you are here. ACG is yours for the taking,' said Mr. Furthermore, his moustache quivering with excitement.

'You won't be seeing me much in the coming days, but I'll be watching you, all of you in ACG – from the inside,' said Ingvar Pingvarsson and disappeared into the lift, all the while smiling.

Outside, the wind was strong and getting stronger, and the sky dark and getting darker. The storm was rising and people in the streets sought shelter inside. Street vendors who were not quick enough saw their stalls blown away as they tried to dismantle them. Newspapers joined popcorn and hotdogs in the air in front of the amazed eyes of the ACG staff as high up as the fifth floor. Darkness descended upon the city. Television stations were quick to interrupt the scheduled programming with special storm updates, and the first one to come up with a satellite picture showed a rare phenomenon to its startled viewers. The familiar storm pattern, a giant white whirlpool of clouds spiralling outwards from the eye of the storm, was centred on the Isle of Dogs. Only, the spiral was not white. It was black. And the eye of the storm sat right on top of the ACG tower.

Deep inside the building, in laboratories shielded from all external influences, Pim Pergamon and his two technicians were just one of the testing crews working that day who did not even notice the change of weather. Their experiment was just beginning.

'Before we start, we are going to dim the lights,' said Gustav. 'The room is covered with non-reflective black paint and the darkness during the experiment should be pretty much complete. It is also covered with soft energy-absorbing foam in the unlikely case that you bump into a wall.'

'What makes you think that it will be an unlikely case?' said Pim.

'Because I am going to control your movements. Here, put on this earpiece,' he gave him a small device that fitted perfectly inside Pim's ear. It was similar to a hearing aid, even the colour was the unnerving pale pink – except that it was smaller and fitted so snugly that after only a minute Pim could not tell which ear it was in. Until he heard Gustav's voice in his right ear. 'It's very sophisticated. It works both ways simultaneously.'

'Without a microphone?'

'It's both a microphone and a headphone. It picks up whatever you say directly from your skull bone and thus eliminates the need for a separate mic. They developed it all the way back in the Apollo program, imagine! And now Lia and I are going to leave you and move over to the control room,' Gustav said and closed the massive laboratory door with a powerful Mbang!

Pim was left alone inside the huge empty space which seemed to have no boundaries now that all other objects and people were gone. It was hard to distinguish the floor from the walls or the ceiling. He couldn't stop thinking about the thick-lipped East European geek and his lovely Chinese assistant. There should be more pairings like this in life, he thought, even if those two just happen to work together. In fact, he should ask her to show him out of the building when this is done. And then they should get lost. That part at least shouldn't be too difficult. And then –

'We are going to use the lasers to project a holographic image of a system of paths and tunnels all around you, and you will have to find your way around,' the East European accent in his earpiece went on.

'Like in a maze?'

'Yeah – only, here you can't get lost, OK?'

'Copy, mission control.'

'OK, here we go. Lights out.'

With these words the world around Pim disappeared and he found himself in complete darkness, devoid of a single ray of light.

'This is what we call a zero-photon situation,' said Gustav. 'Now, I am going to enable the holographic surroundings.' Laser rays appeared all around Pim, rotating faster and faster until they merged together and a new world materialized in front of him.

A very simple world it was. He was standing in a green corridor.

'What do you want me to do?'

'It's very simple. Just walk slowly down the corridor and try not to bump into a wall.'

As Pim moved forward, a crude, jagged human image on the screens that Lia and Gustav were watching in the control room moved forward as well.

'Excellent, I have you here on the screen and I can see your body moving. You are still a bit sketchy, but that's why we are doing these experiments, to improve on the resolution,' said Gustav.

Pim stopped at a T-junction.

'Simply keep walking wherever you want to go. Just play along and don't try to lean on a wall.'

'What would happen if I went through a wall?' enquired Pim.

'Nothing. You can stick your hand into a wall if you want to. It's just that we want you to follow the rules of the simple environment we created for you so that we can tally your results with others.'

Pim stopped and extended his arm to touch the wall but there was nothing there to touch. The wall was made of green light and his arm just went through it.

The darkness outside was now total. It was two o'clock in the afternoon but it felt like midnight. The wind howled through deserted streets. Weathermen on all television stations warned people not to venture out of their houses or they would be swept away by a wind so fast and powerful that nothing like it had been recorded ever before in London.

The warnings were superfluous. The primordial combination of one part common sense and nine parts fear, which had accounted for the survival and evolution of human race for aeons on end, kept people off the streets. Whole sections of the city were left without electricity one after the other, until only the ACG skyscraper with its powerful backup generators remained a beacon of light in the darkness, its lights stretching between earth and the sky. Suddenly, a bolt of lightning dived from the sky and touched the ground with colossal thunder just a few streets away. Those watching from the ACG building were struck speechless because the gigantic spark remained suspended in air, twisting and pumping millions of amperes of electricity through the incredibly hot arc that extended high into the black sky. Then another flash of lightning touched down on the opposite side. All the staff on all the floors ran up to the windows and pressed their noses in awe – Finance on the 36th floor, Research&Development on the 42nd, Human Resources on the 53rd, Security on the 59th…

'What on earth….?' Edna Edwards peered through her glasses and bolted out of her office when she realised that no one was at their desks.

'Look!' someone beckoned her to the window, but she could see it herself across the open-space floor. A third bolt of lightning came down from the sky with tremendous thunder and joined the two that would not go away. For the first time in her life, Edna Edwards felt small.

When another two thunderbolts struck, this time closer to the ACG building, people started to run away from the windows. The storm had turned day into night, but now the persistent bolts of lightning transformed that night into a most brilliant day. They were closing a circle around the tower. When the sixth bolt touched the ground, the ACG found itself in the centre of a hexagon of fire, resembling the seventh lightning inside the lattice.

It was precisely at that moment that Pim felt a slight 'puff' all around him. Gustav and Lia could hear it on their loudspeaker. They were all oblivious to the forces of nature that raged outside. Pim serenely walked left and right in the experiment which he had started to enjoy – until the strange sensation that could only be described as a 'puff' jerked him to a stop. The next moment, the six bolts of lightning disappeared and darkness descended again on the Isle of Dogs.

'What was that?' said Pim.

'What?' came the reply through the earpiece.

'That – did you feel it too?'

Gustav and Lia looked at each other, not sure how to respond.

'Feel what? We heard something in your channel, but we don't know what.'

'Never mind. I don't know what it was either. It just felt like a gentle puff of air.'

'Now, that's negative,' said Gustav. 'There are no air currents in the laboratory. It's a fully controlled environment – now, look at that! Look at the resolution!'

The big screen in the centre of the control room did not show the crude and jagged human figure from the beginning of the experiment. A myriad of lines now gently curved around a human shape delineating Pim's body with surprising precision.

'You look almost real! That's the greatest progress I've ever made on my shift!' Gustav happily shouted into the microphone.

'This is good news! This is definitely good news for the project,' Lia kept patting him on the back. 'Do you think the soot had something to do with it?'

'I want you to keep walking now,' Gustav said and briefly squeezed Lia's hand. 'Let's see how it holds in motion.'

'OK – hey, what's that?' said Pim.

A strange little creature, a screeching hairy ball, appeared on the floor in front of him from one of the side corridors. It tumbled, quickly swooshed past Pim and disappeared somewhere behind him.

'It seems that your simple holographic world is not that simple after all,' Pim said to Gustav. 'What was that?'

'What are you talking about? What was what?'

'That strange squealing ball of tumbleweed that just went past me.'

'Nonsense! The laboratory is empty and locked. There's no tumbleweed in there.'

'It only looked like tumbleweed, it wasn't really a tumbleweed. But it didn't look like something from the laboratory, it looked like something generated in your computer – look, there goes another one!'

Gustav and Lia stared into their monitors, but there were no fast-moving hairy balls on any of the screens – only the image of Pim drawn with what Gustav thought was incredible precision. He switched off his microphone. 'Damn it! Why did this happen now that we have achieved by far the best resolution any of the testing teams have managed so far?' Then he switched it on.

'Listen, just stand still until I save your parameters. Yours is the best resolution so far.'

'OK, I'll wait,' Pim's voice came through the loudspeaker, when suddenly he shouted and a sound of commotion filled the control room. Gustav looked at the main screen where the human figure now lay prostrate on the floor.

'What're you doing? You interrupted the save! I lost the data!'

'That stinking hairy ball just knocked me over!'

'What are you talking about? There's nothing in that room with you. You must've tripped over something,' Gustav replied impatiently.

'You told me yourself there was nothing here to trip over! I was standing still and this thing just ran into me!'

'That's true,' said Lia, 'he was not moving when he fell.'

'Well, then he just lost his balance – you lost your balance, Pim!'

'Here comes another one! And another one!' Pim said as the screeching sounds grew louder in the control room and the figure on the screen moved to dodge invisible balls. 'Stop it! Stop it!' Pim cried out.

'That's it! I am terminating the experiment. I am coming over and you'd better explain yourself!' Gustav kept talking into the headphones as he left the control room angry. 'You've ruined the best experiment we've had so far – by far the best!'

'Well then, come and take me out. Energy-absorbing foam or no energy-absorbing foam, my butt hurts! It did all the energy absorbing, as it usually does!' Pim was shouting back when suddenly a strange sound caught his attention. It was not the screeching of the little hairy balls; it was a cold metallic sound, reverberating through the maze in regular intervals.

'C'mon, switch on the lights and stop the charade,' Pim shouted into the air around him.

'Hold your pants. I'm on my way.'

The metallic sound was getting louder. It reminded Pim of ironworks, of some huge metal press in action – and it was getting unmistakably nearer.

Then he saw something appearing from the corridor on the right. It was yellow and round, like a huge wheel of cheese lying flat and sliding forward, with a gaping hole in front, opening and closing sideways. The metal sound was coming from the incessant clapping of the huge jaw as it moved forward.

'Hey, Gustav, are you there? What am I supposed to do? This corridor ain't big enough for the both of us,' Pim managed a laugh. Then one of the hairy balls tumbled from a side corridor at exactly the wrong moment. The huge jaw opened without changing its rhythm, and the small hairy creature disappeared inside with a long, painful screech. The jaw closed with a metal clang that muffled the screech, and when it opened again, the little creature was not there.

The yellow monster did not stop moving for a second. It was coming right towards Pim.

'This has definitely stopped being funny, Gustav, do you hear me?' Pim turned around and began to briskly walk away. 'I don't trust your holograms any more. Game over! Do you hear me?!'

Gustav pushed against the massive laboratory door and it slowly opened to let him in. He slammed the switch to his right and the big room was bathed in light again.

Apart from a thin white smoke that filled the air, Laboratory 21 was completely empty.

The Head Called Harry

The black storm dissipated quicker than it had arisen. After the six lightning bolts had disappeared, the wind died out almost instantly and a refreshing light rain poured down from the sky. People warily ventured out on the streets again, casting their eyes suspiciously towards the dark clouds. But the clouds appeared to change as well, getting brighter, and the suffocating darkness that had enveloped London gradually transformed into an ordinary rainy afternoon. The good people of the city set out to clear the streets. Afternoon editions of newspapers with descriptions of the extraordinary storm would soon be hitting the stands.

Lia had run out from the control room when she heard Gustav scream. She found him running around Lab 21, shouting and frantically grabbing at walls as if he expected to somehow extract Pim Pergamon from the black foam.

'What happened? Where is he?' asked Lia.

'I don't know. He just vanished!'

'How could he vanish? The laboratory doors were locked, he couldn't have opened them from inside.'

'I know that!' Gustav yelled at Lia. Then he stopped and raised his finger.

'Hush! I hear something.'

The two of them listened carefully until they realized that a sound was coming from Gustav's headphones which hung loosely around his neck. He pulled them up again. The expression on his face quickly changed.

'Yes, I can hear you. Where the hell are you?'

Silence.

'No, *I* am in the laboratory! You are *not* in the laboratory. Where are you? Come back right now!'

Lia was trying to read the other side of the conversation from the grimaces on Gustav's face. His eyes rolled up and down in exasperation.

'Where is he?' Lia cautiously uttered. Gustav pulled down one side of the earphones and said, 'He says he is in a pacman maze.'

Pim's first instinct was to just move aside from pacman's path, to cross through a wall, but when he tried to do that, he discovered that it was not possible any more. Suddenly the light green wall was a hard, impenetrable surface. He abandoned the experiment and started to run in earnest. The experiment came after him in the shape of a huge yellow pacman whose clanging jaws were getting nearer and nearer.

Wherever he went in the maze, whichever turn he took, the yellow menace was behind him. It occurred to him that he was acting unreasonably, and that he should stop and face the imaginary holographic monster. But the heavy, metal sound of the closing jaws which sounded so real, coupled with the fact that the walls were suddenly not the optical illusion they were supposed to be, made him vote against this option.

The vote thus being one hundred percent for running away, Pim kept running and shouting to Gustav to switch the whole thing off and get him out.

Gustav had in the meantime returned to the control room, where Pim's image could be seen running along a corridor. To Gustav's great surprise, there was something moving behind Pim.

'A pacman!' exclaimed Lia. 'He is telling the truth.'

'How can that be?' Gustav was bewildered, looking at the round yellow thing that kept snapping its jaws behind Pim. 'This is not a game routine, this is a simple hologram generator routine. Where did this thing come from?'

'Never mind where it came from! Tell me why is he not in the laboratory?'

'Pim, can you still hear me? Listen carefully. Where are you?'

'What do you mean – where am I?' said Pim. 'You should know that better than me, you brought me into this laboratory.'

'I was just now in the laboratory and it's empty. Pim, you are not in the laboratory. Where are you?'

A loud shout came from the other side. Gustav and Lia could see why. The image on the screen was in a dead end corridor.

Pim stopped and turned round. The corridor behind him was empty, yet the sound behind the corner was getting closer. He tried to think, but nothing that he experienced in his life so far had prepared him for this situation. He moved a few steps into the corridor and stood with his back against the wall. The sound was getting louder and nearer. Let's just hope this thing doesn't notice me, he thought. After all, it doesn't have eyes.

But as soon as the round yellow shape appeared at the other end of the corridor it changed its course and went after Pim without the slightest hesitation. It's as if it was programmed to go after me, Pim thought.

'Do something!' he said to Gustav, but Gustav could not muster a word.

Then Lia shouted, 'Jump! Jump over the wall!'

Pim could not see the edge of the wall, or if there was an edge at all; the only thing he could see was the pacman coming towards him. He took a step back, towards the great jaw, and then thrust himself upwards. He expected to hit the wall, but the moment he left the ground an invisible force took him away and propelled him to what felt like an incredible height. The pacman, the maze, the clanging of the jaw, all this was left far below in an instant and Pim Pergamon found himself in a peculiar state of weightlessness.

He hovered in the darkness, helpless and disoriented. Despite the warnings against looking down from great height that he remembered from countless action movies – he looked down. What he saw was not the maze from which he was ejected so forcefully. Instead, he seemed to be floating in a state of weightlessness above a perfect rectangular grid of thin white lines that stretched out into infinity on all sides.

He kept shouting to Gustav, but his earpiece was dead. He had stopped hearing Gustav the moment he left the maze.

A twisted streak of blue light resembling the long beak of a bird then appeared out of nowhere and jerked him sideways. The next thing he knew, he began to fall head first towards the grid. He helplessly flailed his limbs, as if trying to delay the moment of collision. Then a thought flashed through his mind – that he might miss the ground, that he might fall through an opening in the grid and continue to fall forever into the darkness.

But before he could think of an even more terrible fate, Pim saw the grid below him bend into a hollow that got deeper and deeper until it became a well that swallowed him.

He slid along its curved sides, and soon found himself flying through a long, winding tunnel. It was made of thin bright lines which seemed to possess an invisible force that guided him along, even at the sharpest bends. 'What is happening to me?' he barely had the time to think when, just as suddenly as he was lifted from the pacman maze, the tunnel spat him out and he hit a hard ground.

His bones hurt but a sense of relief flooded his body when he felt firm ground under him again. It wasn't any energy-absorbing foam, it was plain reddish dirt, and he was at the bottom of a shallow hole.

'Gustav, there's dirt in your laboratory,' he said when he pulled himself together. Nobody answered. How did dirt get into their precious Lab 21?

Then he heard a whirring sound from above. He raised his head and looked up. What he saw was a towering, shiny metallic robot walking right towards him pointing a huge gun. Pim's sense of relief was replaced by a sense of horror.

'Gustav, there's a robot in your laboratory,' said Pim. 'And he's got a gun!'

But before he could say anything else, the robot disappeared in a loud explosion that deafened him and showered him with tiny pieces of hot metal.

'Whooaah! This is not a simulation! Gustav! This hurts – ' Another loud explosion cut him off. 'Don't do it! Do you hear me?'

He crawled to the edge of the hole and looked around. What he saw froze his breath. Dozens of robots were advancing relentlessly towards each other from left and right. This did not look like Laboratory 21 – this was a vast open plain! It looked like a field re-enactment of some old gallant battle where two lines of soldiers unflinchingly advance towards each other while shooting – only the soldiers were made of stainless steel and their eyes were glowing blue. They walked steadily through a flat reddish landscape as if under a spell, firing salvoes of incredibly bright laser rays at their advancing adversaries and causing explosions which brought more destruction to the already desolate terrain.

Pim was caught in the middle – if there was such a thing as a middle in the madness of the battle around him. As far as he could see, there was nothing but blasts and explosions, constant firing of cannons, and hordes of robots blindly advancing towards each other, oblivious to the destruction that invariably awaited them.

When hot pieces of metal fell on his clothes he could smell the burning fabric. And when they burnt through, there was nothing virtual nor holographic about the sensation on his skin – it was as real as the heart pounding in his chest. He needed shelter. He took off and started running across the desolate plain towards the only rock he could see.

Missiles whizzed past his ears. Laser rays cut blackened troughs in the ground before him. He ran as fast as he could, zig-zagging, not so much out of intention as out of confusion. It was only sheer luck that he wasn't hit. And then, just when he reached the rock, an explosion thrust him to the ground. Unable to stop, oblivious to his surroundings, he rolled past the rock and fell into a chasm that lay beyond the edge of the landscape.

And this chasm turned out to be another tunnel.

He almost sighed the proverbial 'Phew!' when he realized that he was in a tunnel again. The sense of weightlessness, which a minute ago caused him deep unease, now felt like a comfortable refuge from the madness of the robotic Armageddon.

He did not care that he had no control over his flight, meandering left and right, up and down through the tunnel with no end in sight. It was much better than anything else that happened since the experiment began. Although, it did not compare with being at home in bed.

As he pondered on how all this was going to end up, a strange apparition emerged from the opposite side of the tunnel. It was a witch on a broomstick. She looked very much in a hurry. Before Pim could do anything she swerved around him, an expression of endless surprise on her face.

Then, just as he decided to focus on the tunnel in front, he heard a gallop. Six horses were trying to overtake him, harnessed to a gilded carriage on golden wheels. The horses were running at the limit of their strength although there was nothing below them for their hooves to tread. The carriage was driven by a headless coachman who showed no sign of noticing Pim, except maybe that he didn't run him over. The carriage quickly left him behind and disappeared around a sharp bend just ahead.

It was out of one such bend that a green ball of light appeared, coming straight at him. Suddenly the tunnel looked too narrow to pass. Pim did not have much time to think about what to do before the ball of light smashed right into him.

There was no physical sensation of crash, but Pim sensed that his motion through the tunnel had stopped. He became enveloped in a green whirlpool of light. He looked at his hands. He was able to see through them. That's it, he thought, I am disappearing. I will dissolve and stop existing and become just another flash of light – a dot on Gustav's screen – someone's screen – somewhere –

He felt a jerk and looked around him. He was not in the tunnel any more. He was sitting on a rock that was rough and cold. There were no laser guns shooting around, no fierce battle and no pacman to worry about. Indeed there was nothing around him but black stony ground disappearing into a vast darkness far away. There was no sun, the sky was black but there was enough light to see around. Except that there was nothing to see.

He looked at himself again. He was not transparent any more. But something about his legs caught his attention. Something very peculiar.

There were four of them. Two were clearly his, but there were two more, with funny long pointed shoes on them. And they came out of his body as well!

Then something about his arms caught his attention. There were also four of them. He raised his left arm. One of the arms duly moved. He raised his right hand. One more arm went up. But there were still two more arms with hands cradled in his lap.

'Well, don't look so surprised now!' a voice could be heard very close to him. He slowly turned his head and, right there on his shoulders, he saw – another head!

And the head was not amused.

Pim felt the blood stop in his veins. Before the head had time to speak again, Pim fainted.

When he came to, the surplus arms and legs were still there. Pim turned his head very slowly to the right and, to his despair, saw that the extra head on his shoulders was also still there. The head belonged to an older man and had a funny-looking long thin moustache, twisted and sharp at both ends. Its lively eyes were scrutinizing Pim.

'I dare say, young man, what an awful way to make acquaintance!'

Pim remained silent. He noticed that he was now wearing a strange brown waistcoat that he'd never seen before in his life.

'I did say, just the other day, that a Bedel's job is a lonely one. And I have been known to yearn for company, that much I will grant you. But this? Troglodytes of Hernia! My dear fellow, this goes beyond – or should I say above – my most rampant expectations!'

'What is this?' Pim finally responded in a faint voice. 'What happened to me?'

'To you? What happened to you – Heavens to Betsy! Never mind what happened to you – look what happened to me!' the head shouted indignantly, the sharp end of the moustache poking Pim's face. 'You ended up in my body, boy!'

Pim's recovery from shock was greatly aided by a natural reaction to the wholly inappropriate verbal abuse from an alien head which could only think of itself.

'What?' he said. 'From where I stand, it looks like *you* ended up in my body.'

'Now, does it? How is it, then, that where you stand, I stand as well? Surely this peculiarity could not possibly have escaped you "over where you stand"?' the head sneered at him.

'If we both stand where I stand, it means that what happened to you happened to me as well,' replied Pim. 'And I don't see what makes you think that you are in a worse situation than me, and that we should "never mind" what happened to me.'

'Well, whose fault was it in the first place, ha?' the head quickly changed the subject.

'How do you know it wasn't your fault?' said Pim, to which the head responded with a loud and offended 'Ha!' as if the very thought that it, the head, could have had anything to do with the whole situation was an affront to reason.

'Do you know where we are?' asked Pim.

'Ha!' came the answer in a higher pitch.

'Can you explain what happened?' continued Pim.

'Ha!' came back in an even higher pitch.

'I can't,' said Pim, to which the head triumphantly responded, 'A-ha!'.

'A-ha what?' said Pim.

'A-ha you can't,' the head replied, 'and I can. What happened is that you were travelling through Median Tunnels without proper transport. What happened is that I was travelling through Median

Tunnels on official Bedel business. What happened was a Median Tunnel collision – which was your fault. What did *not* happen is that you did not succeed in getting us both maimed or killed or completely disintegrated! It's a miracle that we still exist.'

'I would have thought that it's a miracle that we exist in the same body,' said Pim.

'Ha! That's nothing. I assure you, my dear fellow, I have heard of worse – much, much worse.'

'Such as?'

'Such as travellers who were transformed into a plasma discharge outside the tunnel. Or Cuthbert de Barks, who was thrown off course and, instead of Star Central, ended up right in the crater of a volcano in one of the outer worlds. Or Gira Tzutzuladze who, through an incredible twist of misfortune, landed straight inside a giant spider's stomach. Didn't even have the time to shout. Or – '

'Alright, alright, I get the point!'

'Although, I often wonder if it was maybe a twist of fortune. After all, he did not have to go through the jaws, hmm … what do you think?'

'Who are you?' said Pim instead of pondering on the technicalities of passing through giant spiders' jaws.

The head was thrown off course for a moment but quickly regained its pompous posture.

'I am Sir Henry Grenfell-Moresby, of the Grenfell-Moresbys, and I am the Royal Bedel of Zandar, the only remaining holder of the Royal Warrant. With whom do I have the dubious honour?'

'My name is Pim Pergamon and I want to go back!'

'Hah! And I want to see the Towers of Billbalirion!'

'I wasn't supposed to leave the laboratory at all. I don't know what happened.'

'He doesn't know what happened – it's a rather feeble excuse, is it not? Which world do you come from?'

'I beg your pardon?' said Pim. The head rolled its eyes in response, sighed and asked again:

'What dreadfully under-educated place breeds dimwits who not only wander into Median Tunnels without a transport, thereby exposing selves and others to mortal dangers, but then think it is enough to say "I don't know what happened" when asked to account for their ill-mannered behaviour?'

22

'You don't understand,' Pim started to realize that it would not be easy to explain to his other head what happened. 'I was taking part in an experiment. One minute I was in a laboratory, and the next minute I was in the middle of some robot war. I've never heard of something like that happening to anyone else. I really cannot explain what happened – nobody can.'

'Oh, I am sure somebody can! And that somebody will be brought to justice just like you.'

'What justice?'

The head made another, deeper sigh of exaggerated exasperation with questions whose answers should be obvious to anyone.

'Trespassing in Median Tunnels is not only dangerous, young man, it is also against the law,' said the head. 'As I suspect you very well know.'

'What? What law? What tunnels?'

'Look, if you think that you are going to earn my sympathy by feigning ignorance, you are plain wrong. But if you think you are going to earn Mamluks' sympathies with that same unbelievably transparent approach, you might be fatally wrong. Absence of remorse would be an aggravating circumstance before any court of law. Before Judge Corpus, it might be a fatal circumstance.'

'Judge who?'

'His Honour Judge Corpus Juris of the Lower Bench of the Courts of Star Central, of whom it is said that he is stern like Hera, but wise like Pallada Athena.'

'This – is – too – much!' Pim said emphasizing each syllable. 'I don't believe a word you say – and why should I? Gustav! Beam me out of here right now, do you hear me? Gustav, you bastard! I will sue you and the whole ACG the second I am back! Get me out of here!'

The other head tut-tutted disapprovingly. 'This won't get you anywhere, my dear fellow.'

'Don't call me fellow, and especially not dear fellow, OK?' Pim snapped back. 'I am fed up with all this. You don't exist and I am going away.'

Pim moved his legs in an attempt to stand up, but the other two legs would not budge. After a few seconds of trying, it became obvious that Pim's own legs were not enough to move his strange new body.

'Where do you want to go anyway?' the other head continued to be annoying. 'There is nothing around here and I haven't got the faintest idea which world we are in. It could even be a Rubalkal.'

'And what's that?'

'Why, an Empty World, of course.'

'What's wrong with you? What's this obsession with worlds? And what are these tunnels you keep mentioning?'

'Median Tunnels? They really don't teach you the basics in your world,' the head said disapprovingly, but then seized on the opportunity to be didactic. 'Nobody knows any more how the name came about. It must have been the Builders of Tunnels themselves who bestowed the name on their masterpiece. Before they began work on the first tunnel, people could travel between worlds only if they chanced upon a natural gate. There are many natural gates scattered around, but they are hard to find and they only connect with one other world. That's why travel between worlds was almost impossible in ancient times. You would have to pass through one gate to jump into another world; then, once inside that world, travel on foot, so to speak, until you found the next gate, jump again, and repeat that many times until you reached your destination. Given the state many worlds were in – and some still are, might I add – it was not only tedious, but dangerous as well. The Median Tunnels changed all that.'

'It's a nice story,' said Pim.

'It surely beats the hell out of climbing beanstalks. But the 'story' doesn't end here,' the head continued in a voice suggestive of an unpleasant moral coming up. 'Once traffic was on the increase, it became obvious that certain rules had to be introduced to govern the interactions between worlds. That is why the Builders left behind them the Builders Code and Mamluks to enforce it. And one of the basic articles of that Code is that travel through any of the Median Tunnels without proper transport is strictly prohibited.'

'What is a proper transport?'

'A proper transport,' the head continued impatiently, 'is any device or creature that enables you to travel safely through a Median Tunnel.'

'You mean, if I was on a proper transport, we would not have collided?'

'Ha! He finally understood something!' the head exclaimed theatrically. 'Entering Median Tunnels without transport is like walking on a subway track instead of riding in a subway train – except that the latter is dangerous only for you, while the former is dangerous for both parties who find themselves in the Median Tunnel.'

'And I am somehow responsible for that?'

'That will be for the Court to decide.'

'Ha! That's just great. The day that started with an explosion I didn't cause is going to end with a prosecution for a crash I didn't cause.'

'Are you saying that I caused it?!' the head got agitated.

'It was just something that happened, it was nobody's fault. I didn't know I was not supposed to be in that tunnel and I certainly don't know how I got there. There are no gates where I come from and no Median tunnels. Nobody travels between worlds. It's nonsense. There is just one world and that's it. Period.'

'That, my dear boy, is not only the shoddiest defence you could possibly put up, but also a complete and utter nonsense!' the head responded resolutely.

'And I think not only that it is completely and utterly sensible, but also that you are the grumpiest old man that could possibly have invaded me!' Pim held his ground, for a change.

'Ha!' said the head.

'Ha!' replied Pim and they continued to sit in silence in the dark, desolate landscape.

The pacman stopped at the end of the tunnel. His jaw was empty. The creature that was supposed to end up in it had disappeared. If pacmans had faces, this pacman would have had a very disappointed expression on his face.

Then something unusual happened. The pacman did not do what pacmans are programmed to do. It did not go back to chase the tumbleballs. It stayed in the tunnel where Pim disappeared. First, it slowly moved back to the beginning of the tunnel. Then it dashed towards the same dead end where Pim was last seen. Nothing happened.

The pacman repeated the move several times. And again nothing happened. It seemed that it was unable to accept that Pim managed to escape. If pacmans had nerves, this pacman would have been quite furious. He kept dashing towards the dead end faster and faster.

This strange behaviour did not go unnoticed. First one, then two, and then a whole crowd of tumbleballs appeared in the adjoining corridor to observe their pacman go mad. Every time the pacman went back, they would hastily retreat, and every time he made a run back in, they would quickly follow to see what was happening.

This dance went on in the eternal night of pacman's maze until suddenly a bright light flashed at the end of the corridor. The pacman dashed forward one more time and was consumed inside a brilliant blue ball of light. The next second, the light was gone – and so was the pacman.

Pim Pergamon found his position annoying as well as absurd. He could not move, but even if he could he did not know where to go. And even if he knew where to go, he did not know how to get there. The head on his right shoulder, on the other hand, seemed to be perfectly at peace with what Pim considered to be the most bizarre conceivable set of circumstances. It was probably not the best idea to wait for Gustav to get his experiment back on track and rescue him from sharing his body with a fruitcake called Henry Grenfell-Moresby (of the Grenfell-Moresbys!)

'Do you know where we are?'

'Yes,' the head replied curtly.

'Are you going to tell me?'

'Only if you ask,' came another curt reply.

'OK, I am asking.'

'Politely.'

Pim took a somewhat noticeable deep breath and decided to make a sort of an effort.

'Would you mind terribly sharing with me our present whereabouts, Harry old boy?'

'*Nobody* calls me Harry!'

'That's odd, Sir Henry. You know, back where I come from, you would surely be known as Grumpy Harry!'

'In that case I presume I should prefer your theory about there being no gates in your world,' the head replied.

'It's not a theory, it's a fact.'

'Then how do you account for your presence here and now?'

'I was taking part in a computer experiment when this happened, and I suppose the experiment is still going on.'

'And where did this experiment take you?' the head demanded to know.

'I have a feeling I'm not in Kansas any more.'

'What?'

Pim hesitated before answering. 'Well, if you need to know, I think I somehow ended up inside the computerworld.'

'That's absolute rubbish!' the head exclaimed. 'People do not get inside computers.'

'I know that,' said Pim defensively. 'But look: first I was in a pacman maze – that's a computer game. Then there were robots fighting each other – that also looked like a computer game.'

'Robot machines with laser cannons?' the head wanted to know.

'Yes,' said Pim.

'Spitting hot metal?'

'Sort of.'

'That's Robogeddon,' said the head.

'Exactly! It even sounds like a game.'

'It is not a game, it is a world. A world inhabited by fighting robots. They engage in endless combat until total annihilation and then begin anew.'

'Definitely a game.'

'Young man, let me elucidate here,' the head went didactic again. 'What you described are just some of the many, many worlds that exist in Zandar, or Left World, as some prefer to call it. I know most of them, as I am the Bedel, the Royal Messenger, the mouthpiece of the Master of Zandar, a most ceremonial Usher and Master of Royal Ceremonies, Bringer of Royal Warrants, Official Decrees and Important News In General, Royal Proclamator Extraordinary and Plenipotentiary ...'

'Wait, wait, wait!' interrupted Pim. 'Do you know anybody called ... say ... Lara Croft?'

'A rather ebullient young lady, I'd say.'

'How about, say, King Arthur?'

'Spends all of his free time helping Jack grow beanstalks.'

'Odysseus?'

'Currently at sea.'

'Scheherazade?'

'Ah, lovely Scheherazade!' Harry swooned at the mention of that name. 'The girl who truly stole my heart. Funny that you should mention her – of course, I was much younger then, I had just been appointed Bedel, and I often used to visit King Shahryar's court – '

'That's it! It's all fiction! You are all unreal,' said Pim with agitation.

'Unreal! Ha! Look at him! Comes from a world with no gates and no tunnels and tells me that I am unreal!' the head scoffed. 'And pray tell, what is your definition of a real world?'

'I am real. And all this around me, it's fiction because – ' all of a sudden Pim was startled by a loud, metallic shrill from the darkness that surrounded them.

'You are very easily disturbed by fictional sounds, I dare say,' the head observed wryly, but pricked up its ears all the same. There was a silence and then the sound was heard again, louder.

'What was that?' asked Pim.

'It could be anything,' the head gave a noncommittal answer as the strange sound was heard again, this time closer.

'Don't you think we should at least stand up?' said Pim, trying to see into the darkness.

'That may be the first sane thing you've uttered today,' the head answered in a hushed voice, adding to the eeriness of the situation, 'but I am not at all sure we can do it with all these legs. Plus, somebody just told me this was all fiction.'

The metallic sound was heard again. It reminded Pim of many jaws clasping at once.

'I refuse to discuss existential issues while being chased by a pacman or pacmans,' Pim announced and tried to stand up.

It was not an easy task. The human body is built for amazing functionality and mobility, but doubling the number of its limbs does not lead to doubling of its locomotive capacity – on the contrary, as the two heads immediately found out.

Although nothing could be seen in the dark barren landscape around them, the metallic sound was undoubtedly approaching as they were trying to stagger away. Harry suddenly lost his grumpiness and tried to reassure Pim, saying that any pacman would most probably recognize him, as he was the Royal Bedel. 'Actually, I was on my way to serve summons on Barney when I ran into you in the tunnel.'

'On Barney?'

'That's his name.'

'So why are we running away if you are on first-name terms with that creature?' said Pim.

'I wish we were running,' replied Harry as they almost lost their balance trying to coordinate their four stumbling legs, 'because I am not at all sure it's him.'

'No? Then what is it? Where are we anyway?' said Pim.

'I wish I knew, my dear boy, I wish I knew!' replied Harry.

'But you told me that you knew!' Pim shouted at his other head as they made their way through the darkness.

'I was make-believing!'

'You hypocrite! I just had to ask politely, ha? Here, I am asking politely: Where are we and what is coming at us?'

'Your fictional guess is as good as mine!' Harry replied when their legs finally lost their coordination and they toppled over.

A powerful flash illuminated the landscape around them. The shape of a tremendous black metallic creature as tall as a house was visible on the horizon against the black sky. It resembled a giant spider with scorpion claws and the head of a praying mantis. But it was no mutant insect.

It was made of metal. Its many limbs moved in perfect coordination. And it was coming their way.

Pim turned to his other head looking for help. He was dismayed to see that the other head did exactly the same.

'What is this?' he yelled at Harry.

'I am afraid I don't know,' Harry replied, 'but I think it's dangerous.'

'Oh, really?'

The creature let out another shriek in the darkness. They could feel the ground tremble from the pounding of its many legs as it drew nearer, and hear the sound that could most closely be described as thousands of bayonets being sharpened at the same time.

'You wouldn't happen to have any matches on you, would you?' said Harry and pulled a thick hair from the inner pocket of his waistcoat. 'Here, hold this hair. Don't let it drop!'

The many-limbed mantis was getting nearer and nearer while Harry searched his pockets – how many pockets he had!

'What's this for? Shouldn't we at least try to run?' said Pim.

'There's no running away from this creature, not in this state,' replied Harry. 'I am trying to summon my hippogriff!'

'A hippogriff can fight this thing?'

'No, but it can take us away from here. My Hipp is a Median transport. Here, give me the hair,' said Harry and lit up a match that he found in what must have been the thirty-fourth pocket. The metallic mantis let out a shriek louder than anything Pim had ever heard before when the Hippogriff's hair finally caught fire and began to burn. Harry looked all around – but there was no mythical being anywhere to be found.

'It's all your fault!' said Harry. 'Had you not run into me in the tunnel, my Hipp would be here now. Oh, who knows what happened to him when you struck!'

'Never mind him, what's going to happen to us?' said Pim looking at the approaching mantis. Its many limbs were made of thousands of hexagonal segments that slid on top of each other in quick succession, which made it look like the limbs were moving by constantly rebuilding themselves. There was not one single feature on that monster that did not look razor sharp.

'What's going to happen to us?' said Harry. 'I'd rather not describe it.'

The mantis stopped right in front of them and began to raise its head. Hundreds of metallic teeth could be seen inside its jaws – and they were moving. The mouth of the metallic monster was one big horrible metal saw. Harry said something but Pim could not hear him from the blood-curling noise of shifting metal in front of them.

Then a piercing sound split the air. A brilliant red ray of light came from behind them and struck the black monster. The creature shrilled and shook violently but stood its ground. Another red ray of light came from behind, and another. This made the metallic monster close its jaw and begin a retreat. But before it could get away, another red ray struck it just below chin and the hideous creature burst into a myriad pieces. A rain of small hexagonal black crystals poured all over shocked Pim and Harry who frantically tried to shake them off.

The little crystals, however, continued to move even as they were falling. Instead of scattering on the ground, they gathered in swarms. The swarms then moved off as if by a command and swiftly disappeared in the darkness.

Just a few seconds later, there was no trace left of the frightful metallic creature.

Then a group of armed men appeared from the darkness behind them. Each of them was carrying a shiny, tremendous looking weapon. They looked human, except that they were all very big and unnaturally muscular. Each of them had a tremendous mane falling from the back of the head, neatly tucked into their orange and black armour.

'Mamluks!' exclaimed Harry. 'It's a miracle that you chanced upon us!'

'Not at all, sir,' replied the one with the biggest mane and an enormous muscular chest. 'We set out as soon as Tunnels Control notified us of the collision. We knew we would find you in this Empty World.'

'So we *are* in a Rubalkal.'

'But this world is not empty,' said Pim. 'There's a monster in it.'

'Not any more, it isn't.'

'But – '

'We are here in official capacity, sir,' the Mamluk with the biggest mane said to Pim. 'I am Sergeant Flagg. It is my duty to inform you that you have committed the offence of unlawful passage through Median Tunnels in contravention of the Builders Code. This is an apprehension. You shall be detained and taken to the Courts of Star Central, where you will appear before a judge.'

'You saved my life only to arrest me?' remonstrated Pim. 'What kind of sick joke is that?'

'The law must be obeyed,' said Harry. 'You have to go with them.'

'The arrest warrant applies to you as well, sir,' the leader of the Mamluks told him.

'That cannot be! I am the Royal Bedel!' Harry exclaimed, his moustache quavering in anger.

'With all due respect, sir, you ceased to be the Bedel with the passing of Master Propp, the last Master of Zandar,' the Mamluk replied.

'He trespassed in the Tunnels,' Harry nervously pointed at Pim with his moustache. 'He is the criminal, not me! Take *him*!'

'That may be so,' said Sergeant Flagg, 'but it is impossible to separate you now.'

'You cannot arrest a person who has committed no crime! It's against the law!'

'Be that as it may, the duty judge authorized us to detain you as long as you are amalgamated with the offender, as you are in a position to aid his escape from justice,' the Mamluk explained.

'Duty judge? Which fool is the duty judge this week?' asked Harry.

'The Honourable Justice Corpus Juris.'

'Ha! That old sack of poppycock!'

'Really?' Pim interrupted, 'And I thought he was supposed to be the epitome of justice!'

Harry turned towards Pim and said, 'Oh, shut up!'

The Courts of Star Central

The City of Star Central was a true metropolis. There was no countryside outside the city and no hinterland. The suburbs led to more suburbs and more suburbs brought you back to the centre. It was a whole world by itself – the only way to leave Star Central was through a Median Tunnel, or a natural gate.

Its downtown was imposing. The skyscrapers competed with each other to reach higher and higher and it was not unusual for a building to grow many years after it was originally built. Many among the tallest buildings in Star Central grew not only upwards, but sideways as well, to intertwine with their neighbours and create endless Escherrian bridges and stairwells teeming with hurried tenants. Downtown looked like a colossal forest whose canopy allowed only a small portion of sunlight to reach the streets below. Street lighting was the main source of light for residents of lower floors. True daylight was a valuable commodity there, affordable only to those who were willing to join the constantly whirling life in the upper reaches of the canopy of concrete and steel.

Star Central had enjoyed something of the status of unofficial capital of Left World ever since Median Power Station which fed the Tunnels was built here and the traffic between worlds became regular. Before Median Tunnels, only fugitives and the curious would search for naturally existing gates in their worlds and then chance entering them, never knowing where they would end up. Many worlds had imposed prohibitions on entering such gates, prohibitions rooted in religious or administrative lore, depending on the nature of the world. When Median Tunnels were built, the restrictions slowly crumbled away with time and their only remnants today were some strange rites and rituals required to enter Median Tunnels in some of the worlds. Crossing between worlds was otherwise as mundane an affair as taking a bus (except in Hernia, where buses were used as mallets by local giants who lived in perpetual bus-to-bus combat). Every now and then, word would come of some world where Tunnels were still forbidden and it was still taboo to leave, but the inhabitants of the many worlds of Zandar were generally not inclined to meddle in affairs other than their own. Although, Harry would probably tell you, this was changing as well.

Star Central had never really finished its formation. The city kept growing away from the Median Power Station, leaving its older parts undisturbed for those who wanted to live there. There were always enough humans and other less usual beings who came to Star Central and continued to inhabit surroundings that they were used to: mediaeval castles for knights warriors, nineteenth-century industrial revolution suburbs with steam-powered bridges for eccentric inventors, hyper-tower futuristic complexes for rocket scientists and, most amazing, a whole forest in the middle of the city for trolls, sprites and fairies.

But not all sprites wanted to live in a forest and not all knights wanted to live in a castle. Star Central was thus truly a cosmopolitan place where you could meet rocket pilots who lived in trees and sprites who inhabited power stations. At the time when Pim Pergamon was first brought to Star Central, a well-to-do dragon occupied a magnificent penthouse with a superb view of the southern skyline of the downtown. He was so attracted by the apartment that he signed the lease despite the strict fire regulations in the building which prohibited any open fire on the premises. As a result, he had to go out three, sometimes four times a day to spew fire in a nearby quarry (also superbly centrally situated), just as other people would take their dogs out for a walk. 'I am taking my throat out for a walk,' he had to explain to his startled neighbours when he would run into them in the lobby in the small hours of the morning. But the view was worth it, he would say, and proceed to explain to anyone who cared to listen that dragons were particularly keen on open spaces and magnificent views, having spent aeons in caves, waiting to be awakened by wicked wizards or impulsive heroes.

The seat of the city government was in the City Lair, but there was another, even more important institution in Star Central. Early on in the post-tunnel history, the presence of a great many different beings from all over Left World made the city an ideal place for meetings and business. Making deals and closing contracts was a natural breeding ground for disputes, and it was not long before the first Master of Zandar had to step in and mediate in a controversy. Litigation was thus born in Zandar and the first Court was established in Star Central for those who were willing to subject themselves to its jurisdiction. That was in ancient times. Today, the Court has grown into the famed and feared Courts of Star Central and their jurisdiction is now deemed to include all known worlds.

The Courts have sat in judgement on many renowned feuds, such as Grendel v. Godzilla (title of most fearsome ogre disputed), Faust v. Mephisto (default on contract), Mephisto v. Faust (breach of contract), Big Bad Wolf v. Three Piglets (building permits), Tiny Helpless Little Creatures v. Amalgamated Vicious Warriors (disturbing peace), Ali-Baba and Forty Upright Citizens v. Scheherazade (libel) and others.

The Court Complex had been the biggest and most prestigious building in Star Central, until recently Kutlurg Corporation, the biggest mining corporation in Zandar, built an imposing white skyscraper 777 floors high on the other side of the river. The new construction aroused much curiosity among the citizens and they came in throngs for the opening. Everybody was impressed by the new building, by its magnificent lobby and by the huge holographic sign above it visible for miles around showing the motto *Kutlurg Corporation, Miners of Ore&Lore*. The friendliness of the staff on the inauguration day was surpassed only by the congeniality of its president, a great thaumaturge called Otokarr Gnüss, who personally greeted each and every visitor that day.

Many were surprised to find out that contrary to the prevailing stereotypes about mining and miners, Otokarr Gnüss was not a dwarf but a perfectly ordinary wizard in human shape, despite his illustrious title of thaumaturge, which basically meant just a magician of sorts. The word on the street was that he also owned vast farms of words and numbers in the outer worlds. The story never got more elaborate because Star Central was used to visits from the strangest possible characters who came from the oddest possible settings.

One fine evening, as the sun was casting its last warm rays of the day, the city looked far more amiable than on any given morning. Loud giggle could be heard across the meadows in Botanical Gardens as sunrays tickled *Laughinia Tittilatensis*, a very sensitive specimen of flower from Bou Regreg.

The streets and open spaces were snugly wrapped in the colour of the pastel red dusk, teeming with city dwellers attracted by the sun. The curious architecture of the metropolis meant that this was the only time of the day when even the remotest pavements deep inside the belly of the skyscraper jungle could receive some reflection of warmth and light. They were full of strange little folks who every day interrupted their measly tasks to soak in the few minutes of warmth and light. The city paused, as if it were a cat stretching in the sun.

It was in this very moment that Pim Pergamon, still bound to Harry very much against his will, arrived for the first time in Star Central.

The Human Resources Department on the fifty-third floor of the ACG Tower was certainly the first place in the whole London to recover from the morning's storm. The huge building had not been touched by the tempest and it was only the general sense of excitement that kept people milling around the corridors and open space floors. Everybody was talking about the freak show of nature they had witnessed – but not for long. As soon as Edna had recovered from her freak sense of humility in the face of nature, she swept through her floor to make sure everybody was back at their desks.

She also had the custom of going to the parts of the building which were outside her formal sphere of influence. Her role in promotions and disciplinary actions made her a bit of everybody's boss and she liked to reinforce that perception by materialising again and again all over the ACG.

Besides Edna, there was one other person in the building whose day had not been significantly interrupted by the storm and the ensuing confusion. It was World's Greatest Motivational Consultant™. Utterly uninterested in natural phenomena and completely unperturbed by thunder and lightning, by the time the storm was over Ingvar Pingvarsson had almost finished setting up his new office. First, he carefully unwrapped a framed photo and put it on his desk, thus marking the territory. Since Ingvar was a bachelor, it could not be a photo of his family. If asked, he would say that it was his father, but it was in fact Ingvar himself, in a high school production of Sherlock Holmes, suitably disguised as Professor Moriarty.

He proceeded to make his office look a busy place, by carefully depositing memos and folders, and by rearranging the few chairs that were inside and drawing the curtains to the exact spot he deemed appropriate. He pulled the desk drawers half open, switched on his computer and set it to 'Never Hibernate'. He took out another computer from his briefcase, and positioned it right next to the desktop. Its function was to constantly show a screensaver in the shape of a rising sales chart.

When he was finished, anybody who would care to look could see that it was the office of a busy person who was about to come back any minute from his inside observation of the work process. Which he fully intended to do.

Only not very soon. He had other companies to observe from inside – and invoice from outside.

When he sat down he proudly concluded that he could now go – everything was just the way he wanted it. Except the chair he was sitting on. It wasn't higher than other chairs in the office and that would not do. He often lectured about how important it was to establish a playing field on the subconscious level – and not a level one. Which meant that he had to sit higher than anybody else in the office. So he set out to adjust the chair he was sitting on.

Five minutes had passed, ten minutes had passed and fifteen minutes had passed – but the chair was still not high enough for Ingvar Pingvarsson.

He pushed the knobs and pressed the pedals, he clicked the latches and rotated the shafts – but could not make the chair yield to him.

It was obvious that there was only one way out of this situation. He would have to steal someone else's chair.

Luckily, only a few doors away from his office Ingvar found a whole storage room with several new chairs still wrapped in plastic. Let's take this for the sign of an auspicious beginning, he thought. The first of *Ingvar's Seven Signs of a Successful Project*™.

He of course knew that to just wheel away the new chair would be asking for too much – but an inconspicuous swap would preserve the chair count and cover his tracks forever. He went back to his office and brought his old chair.

As he was entering the storage room, Edna appeared round the corner. His flashy white suit caught her eye and she came into the storage room just as Ingvar was savagely tearing the plastic cover from his chosen chair.

'Hello, Mr. Pingvarsson – oh, what are you doing?' said Edna. Ingvar responded with a magnificently feigned, 'Who, me?' and proceeded to explain. 'Oh, me, you see, well, I was, it's just ... '

Whether it was the expression on her face, which she could not lighten enough even in the presence of a consultant celebrity of his calibre, or the Cadillac on her nose that kept distracting Ingvar's attention, World's Foremost Motivational Consultant™ could not come up with a credible explanation for his actions. Instead, he started retreating step by step, all the while trying to explain himself.

'It's the chair, I wanted to requisition a chair, I mean, I understood that I could – Oooops!'

While he was mumbling, he stumbled and fell backwards, toppling a stack of carton boxes. He turned to Edna and laughed awkwardly. She started towards him to help him stand up, but then something moved on the floor among the boxes.

Ingvar's gaze was fixed at Edna. He did not look behind him. It was only when Edna shouted, 'Oh, my goodness!' that he turned around to see a huge yellow jaw coming towards him. He tried clumsily to get away, but instead got himself right into the spot for a perfect bite. Edna could only scream as the jaw closed around Ingvar with a loud metal 'clang!' And when the jaw opened again, there was nothing inside it any more – no Ingvar and no white suit. Only a faint tumbling echo came from deep inside the jaw – Ing … Ping … Ing … Ping … Ing …

And that was the last anybody ever heard of Ingvar Pingvarsson, World's Greatest Motivational Consultant™.

'You will be released to the Courts Custody Sergeant now,' Sergeant Flagg informed Pim and Harry upon their arrival to the Courts of Star Central.

'Released into custody!' Pim could not help remarking. The irony was lost on his captors, but not on Harry. He added his own sarcastic 'Ha!' in a newfound solidarity with Pim, and raised his eyebrows unbelievably high so as to be able to look down on the Custody Sergeant. The Sergeant was a wide and short old man in a grandiose looking uniform, not unlike a senior doorman of a luxury hotel in Gstaad. The moment he saw Harry in his double captivity, he started to chuckle.

'Well, well, what have you gotten yourself into this time, Sir Harry? Or better, who have you gotten yourself into?'

The Mamluks laughed as Harry struggled to maintain both dignity and balance at the same time, although it was obvious that one had to be sacrificed at the expense of the other.

'Sergeant Gschwendt, it has been a long time since I had the pleasure of your company, has it not?' Harry replied, unfazed, all the while on the verge of losing both balance and dignity.

'Indeed, Sir Harry, indeed. But I never would've imagined that you'd have changed so much!' Sergeant Gschwendt replied gleefully to another roaring laughter of the Mamluks.

'It's not me,' said Harry. 'This other head and limbs belong to a gentleman by the name of Pim Pergamon, into whom I happened to run in a tunnel on the way to Barney the pacman. He found himself in the tunnel without any transport and so we collided. That's how we amalgamated. I actually think we were extremely lucky to survive it.'

'You survived a collision in the tunnel?' Sergeant Gschwendt's demeanour changed into a mild awe. 'You were more than lucky, Sir Henry. The Builders themselves must have been protecting you.'

The Custody Sergeant took them through a long corridor lined with windows, bathed in the same warm sunset that shone outside. At the end of the corridor, he opened a small door and let Pim and Harry through. He did not follow. He told them to wait there and locked the door. Pim and Harry found themselves in complete darkness.

When the light came on again, Pim and Harry finally lost their balance despite all their best efforts and landed flat on their bottoms. There was no floor beneath their feet, and no walls and no ceiling. They were lying in mid-air, as if supported by some invisible force. But they were not alone. Other people (and not only humans) were standing or sitting spaced at regular intervals in the air all around them. As far as they could tell, left and right, up and down, the space was filled with small invisible cubicles stacked on top of each other, and each cubicle housed one prisoner and his belongings. This was the notorious Gaol of Star Central.

Like any newcomers, Pim and Harry first cautiously groped around to determine the bounds of their cell. It was not big, but the open space around it made it feel much more spacious. The ceiling was beyond their reach, maybe for the better, because they could not quite make out whether the strange silhouette straight above them was human or not. It seemed to be asleep and Harry observed that it would be best if it remained asleep as long as they were there.

'If somebody had told me this morning that things could get even worse after the explosion in Uncle Pohadka's workshop, I certainly would not have believed them. Now, I think I am prepared to believe just about anything,' said Pim, looking at the strange characters suspended in space like molecules in a crystal lattice.

A flurry of voices rose throughout the prison on the mention of Harry's name and Pim quickly concluded that he was a kind of celebrity around here.

'No wonder,' Harry said by way of sullen explanation, 'I served the court summons on some of them.'

'You mean you arrested them?'

'You have absolutely no notion about the workings of the Law, do you?' said Harry. 'Mamluks are the arresting authority. I merely deliver the summons to appear before the Court.'

'No good did that do to me either,' said somebody in a cell behind their back. 'Glad to 'ave you with us, guv! Never thought I'd live to see the day!'

When they turned around, Pim could not quite judge what he was looking at: was it a lovely bespectacled granny with a body of a spider, or a spider with the face of an old lady?

'Who's the lad with'ya?' she enquired and winked at Pim. Now she looked more like a granny than the other way round.

'None of your business, Spidergranny, none of your business at all,' Harry replied grumpily, but this only drew more laughter all around.

'Fancy this, Sir 'arry in the slammer with the rest of us, would you believe it?' said Spidergranny. 'Mamluks've got themselves very busy these days. Next thing I know, they'll nick one of them Warriors!'

'Or Pan Kratohvil!' said another voice as more laughter came from all sides. As Harry's spirits were sinking, the mood in the prison became decidedly cheerful.

'Who are the Warriors? Who is Pan Kratohvil?' asked Pim. Harry was delighted at the opportunity to answer so that others could hear him too.

'Pan Kratohvil, the greatest wizard of our age, is the Chief Scientist of Star Central, currently serving as the Potentate-in-Spe. He is the most upright citizen I know,' here he made a pause and continued emphasizing every syllable of each word, 'and a very, very dear friend of mine.' The last sentence so spoken injected him with new vigour, so Harry continued. 'Ever since the passing of the last Master of Zandar, and until the new Master appears, *my friend* Pan Kratohvil is acting as the highest authority in Zandar.'

'But not for long, matey. The Fair of Zandar is in a couple of days,' a voice countered him.

'The Fair of Zandar, which is to be held soon, is the occasion on which the new Master will be revealed. I have no doubt that the new Master will hold Pan Kratohvil in highest regard, just as the old one did, and I look forward to serving him as his Royal Bedel.'

The lesson on constitutional matters of Zandar would have no doubt continued, but in that moment the nasal voice of Sergeant Gschwendt announced lights out – and the lights went out in prison.

With darkness came silence and Pim and Harry soon found a position to sleep which was not altogether uncomfortable. They lay on their back, looking up at the mysterious silhouette which did not take part in the discussion, each of them preoccupied with his own thoughts.

'Good night, Sir Henry,' said Pim.

'Good night,' came the reply, from which it was not possible to discern Harry's mood.

Overwhelmed with everything that had happened to him that fateful day, Pim quickly fell asleep.

And he dreamt about long brown hair.

Inside a storage room somewhere high in the ACG Tower, Edna Edwards had made a mistake. In the panic that gripped her when she saw what happened to Ingvar Pingvarsson, she rushed towards the door – and fell and slammed it shut. When she tried to open it, she discovered that she couldn't. She scrambled for her ACG pass but there was no card reader on any side of the door. The emergency circuit breaker was for the time being just a hole in the wall with a few wires sticking out of it.

The yellow thing that ate World's Greatest Motivational Consultant™ made a few more clasps and swallowed a couple of boxes. Edna Edwards stood in front of the door, shouted 'Help!' and pounded on the door. The thing stopped. When Edna shouted for help again, the yellow thing started moving again, but this time towards her. Edna froze in silence. The thing kept moving. The chair that had cost Ingvar his life was snapped in two and followed him into the great jaw. Trying not to move too much, Edna quickly grabbed one of the telephones from a pile neatly stacked on a nearby shelf and threw it away from her.

The telephone broke into pieces at the other end of the room. The yellow pacman followed the sound and turned 180 degrees in a physically impossible instant, just as if he was still in his unreal maze.

Now he went after the new sound, swallowing whatever stood in its path: chairs, boxes of staples, whole computer monitors, fax machines, boxes of toner cartridges, new printers.

Edna stood with her back against the door unable to move or make a sound. The sight of the yellow jaws swallowing, coupled with the metal clang that accompanied each item of office equipment on its journey into oblivion, had paralysed her. As more and more items disappeared inside the pacman, she realized that her turn was getting nearer.

Then the pacman suddenly stopped. It turned towards Edna. It was then that Edna noticed a pair of little black eyes on top of its pie-chart body. The eyes were looking at her.

The pacman opened its jaws wide, left and right, paused for a moment – and let out a loud burp.

The two little eyes then slowly closed.

Edna Edwards remained motionless for a long time, standing tight against the door, trying hard to make her breathing inaudible. But her precautions were unnecessary.

Overwhelmed by everything he had eaten that fateful day, pacman Barney had fallen asleep.

'All rise for the morning session!'

'Case number IT-79-97, Zandar versus Pim Pergamon and Sir Henry Grenfell-Moresby. The charge of unlawful passage through Median Tunnels in contravention of Builders Code, Section Five, Article Twelve. Honourable Judge Corpus Juris presiding.

'Please be seated!'

The courtroom was quite spacious but almost empty. There were a few seemingly empty black robes fluttering around as court clerks and lawyers and a couple of uniformed Mamluks in orange and black uniforms whose manes were smaller than usual. The mahogany-clad walls were decorated with bronze heads in various states of distress, reflecting the ability of justice to bring suffering to those who find themselves in its path. Today it was the turn of Pim and Harry to glance around the courtroom with jitters up their spine. But there was also the judge himself. Only his head could be seen behind his elevated desk, but it was an incredibly big head and it bore an incredibly stern expression. His spectacles, on the other hand, were incredibly small, as if specifically made to cover only the pupils.

'May I have the appearances?' said the head of the judge towering above the accused.

'Your Honour, Counsellor Knarrpanti appearing for the Prosecution,' said an amiably looking man with rather flamboyant blond hair in great contrast to his red robe. 'Bleached,' Harry managed to whisper to Pim.

'Defence?' the judge turned to Pim and Harry.

'Your Honour,' Harry began, but was interrupted by the judge.

'It is the custom in this courtroom to address the court standing.'

Pim and Harry clumsily stood up.

'Your Honour, if I may be permitted to explain,' Harry began again.

'No, you may not,' the judge cut him off swiftly. 'You may only introduce yourself to the court. These are the appearances, not merits.'

'Sir Henry Grenfell-Moresby, Your Honour.'

'I know. And?'

'My name is Pim Pergamon, sir.'

'I am Your Honour to you, Mr. Pergamon, not sir.'

'My name is Pim Pergamon, Your Honour.'

'Yes. You may be seated.'

Pim and Harry sat down.

'Before we proceed, are we dealing here with one or two defendants?' the judge asked.

'If I may be permitted to explain, Your Honour ...'

'On your feet, Sir Henry, on your feet.'

Pim and Harry laboured to stand up again and Harry continued.

'If you permit me to explain ...'

'This time I invite you to do so,' declared Judge Corpus Juris.

'You see, Your Honour, the real defendant against the charge in this case – that is the unlawful passage through Median Tunnels – is this other gentleman with whom I have the misfortune of sharing my body. Only temporarily, if I may add. It was the fact that he entered a tunnel without transport that occasioned the collision between the two of us, as I was on my way through the very same tunnel on official Bedel business.'

Here Harry made a short pause to let the fact that he was an official on official business sink in, but the judge made no sign that it impressed him one way or the other.

'It was only through that collision that we became – ahem, amalgamated – if you permit me to use the word, Your Honour.'

'Granted.'

'Therefore we are two separate individuals amalgamated against our will, sharing our bodies in this most clumsy of fashions. That is also the reason, Your Honour, why we had trouble standing up. It was not meant as a discourtesy to you or this honourable Court. At this moment, Your Honour, we can hardly walk together.'

'I see. Let the record show that you are both excused from standing in this courtroom until such time as you are decoupled,' said the judge matter-of-factly and Pim and Harry at last sat down in peace.

'Do you have anything to add on this issue?'

'No, Your Honour,' said Pim.

'But I have, Your Honour' said Harry. 'I did not trespass in the Tunnels and I should be released at once. I did not break the law! I demand that you set me free!'

'Sir Henry, this is a court of law and you are required to temper your utterances, despite your personal feelings in the matter, which, as I can see, are quite considerable, and understandably so, considering the circumstances.'

The judge turned to the prosecution.

'Counsellor Knarrpanti, we are faced here with a somewhat peculiar situation, both from practical and legal standpoint. One of the defendants makes a good case for his immediate release. Would you care to address the court in this regard?'

The prosecutor sprang up to his feet like a loaded gun, the expression of infinite deference pre-installed on his face.

'May it please the Court, Your Honour. The Prosecution indeed has no intention of pursuing a case against Sir Henry Grenfell-Moresby at this point in time. However, we maintain that he should be included in the indictment as long as he is amalgamated with the defendant, since one cannot be released without releasing the other.'

'How about releasing us both then?' Pim interrupted him, to the visible displeasure of the judge.

'Mr. Pergamon, you will not interrupt the proceedings in this courtroom. You shall be heard in due course.'

Judge Juris then turned to the prosecution.

'Counsellor Knarrpanti, what are the reasons, if any, that both persons named in your indictment should not be provisionally released pending their decoupling?'

'Your Honour, it is our position that it would be contrary to the applicable provisions of law and not in the public interest to release both Mr. Pergamon and Sir Henry Grenfell-Moresby until such time they are decoupled. Moreover, it is not within the purview of this Court to surmise how or when such decoupling were to occur, should it occur at all, bearing in mind that such a feat of magic is in the power of only one person – the Master of Zandar himself or, in his absence, the designate Potentate-in-Spe.'

'So what is it exactly that you require from the Court?'

'Your Honour, we move that the Court proceed upon the indictment, find the defendant guilty and impose a penalty of imprisonment in Kutlurgian mines.'

The judge looked impassively at the prosecutor. 'You are aware, are you not, Counsellor Knarrpanti, that that would mean punishing the innocent party as well?'

Counsellor Knarrpanti was unmoved.

'Your Honour, it would still be open for Sir Henry Grenfell-Moresby to sue Mr. Pim Pergamon for damages arising from the sentence suffered.'

'I think our worlds are much less different than I thought,' Pim whispered to Harry, but Harry was not listening. If looks could kill, Harry would have been guilty of murder – and the victim would not have been Knarrpanti, but Judge Juris. Instead of letting Harry spew bile at the prosecutor, the judge simply said:

'You are opposed to the motion, Sir Henry, that much I gather. Let us then hear the other defendant. Mr. Pergamon?'

Pim's first reflex before the stern judge was to stand up, but after some shuffling of his feet against the floor he remained firmly seated. He looked around him. The four sides of the courtroom clad in heavy mahogany already looked like prison walls to him. The empty robes that hovered behind some of the desks offered no hint of understanding. His eyes finally rested on the eyes of Judge Corpus Juris. The face around them looked almost theatrically severe, but the eyes remained uncommitted. It was impossible to determine what was going on inside the head of Judge Corpus Juris.

'Your Honour, I did not know that travelling through Median Tunnels was forbidden,' said Pim. 'I wish I could say that, had I known it, I never would have done it – but I cannot even say that.

'A strangest thing happened to me yesterday. Something that, to the best of my knowledge, has never happened before to anybody in the world. Or, at least, the world where I live. Something happened that took me, against my will, from a room where I was and transported me, literally beyond the bounds of my wildest imagination to a place that does not exist – to this place.

'I did not come here because I wanted to come. I certainly did not have the slightest intention to break any law, in any world. Or to cause problems to Sir Harry. And for all that, I apologize.

'I recognize that now I am in the power and at the mercy of this Court and I wish for only one thing from Your Honour – to send me back home.'

Before Corpus Juris could speak, another voice was heard in the court. It belonged to a man with intense blue eyes and a short, styled pointy beard, dressed in a purple velvet shirt and velvet trousers who appeared at the door of the courtroom.

'I request to appear as *amicus curiae* before this Court,' he said as he entered the courtroom accompanied by a murmur.

'Pan Kratohvil!' Harry whispered to Pim. 'He came to save me! Didn't I tell you he was a friend of mine?'

'*Amicus curiae* means friend of the court as far as I know,' said Pim.

'On what grounds does the highest executive authority in Zandar seek to appear as *amicus curiae* in my Court?' the judge asked Pan Kratohvil, seemingly the only one unmoved by the presence of the high dignitary.

'On the grounds that one of the defendants may be speaking the truth, which may have serious and far-reaching consequences for the Government of Zandar.'

Harry and his moustache started to smile importantly. Pim even thought he saw a mischievous wink.

'Which defendant are you referring to, Pan Kratohvil?'

'I am referring, Your Honour, to the defendant known to this Court as Pim Pergamon.'

Just as quick as Harry's self-important smile turned into a veritable surprise, Pim's expression turned into one of utter puzzlement. This detail was not lost on Judge Juris.

'And what would those consequences be?' he asked Pan Kratohvil.

'Your Honour, I myself am not aware at the present moment of the full scope of those consequences. Suffice it to say, though, that I believe that defendant Pim Pergamon may have in his possession – ' here Pan Kratohvil made a pregnant pause ' – information about the possible existence of Right World.' This was enough to jolt even Judge Juris.

'Mr. Kratohvil! You cannot just walk into my court with any wild supposition and interfere with rules of criminal procedure.'

'I never would dream of doing such a thing, Your Honour. My learned friend Mr. Gator from the Star Central Bar is here to take care of the procedure,' Pan Kratohvil said and gestured behind him.

The door opened to let in a dazzling figure in a shiny metallic robe and an old-fashioned barrister's wig. He strode in carrying a silvery buckram-bag and immediately took up his position in front of the bedazzled Pim. Before the door closed again, a few photographers who were assembled outside managed to steal a couple of photos of this flamboyant figure and annoy Judge Juris. The press then rushed to the public gallery to see what would happen next. But what happened next was that Judge Corpus Juris closed the gallery for the public.

'Mr. Gator, I presume. 'Your fame, unfortunately, precedes you,' said Corpus Juris when the last spectator left the court.

'May it please the Court, Your Honour, Lee T. Gator appearing on behalf of the defendant Pim Pergamon.'

'Who the hell is that?' Pim asked Harry.

'It's your lawyer, you idiot!' Harry hissed in response. 'And not just any lawyer. He's a Warrior Lawyer.'

'A what?'

'Oh … he is like Lara Croft, only he fights in courts!'

'Your Honour, the prosecution most strenuously objects to this turn in the proceedings!' Counsellor Knarrpanti was trying to make himself heard. 'There is no basis either in law or fact – '

'I am afraid I have to contradict my learned colleague on both counts, if you will allow me, Your Honour?' Lee T. Gator quickly manoeuvred to nip in the bud any attempt of prosecutorial resistance. From his buckram-bag he produced an enormous bundle of documents, much bigger than the briefcase itself in fact, and placed it on the clerk's desk. He continued with the well-oiled routine of an old courtroom fox.

'Here we have an affidavit signed by the tunnel maintenance technician who was on duty when the alleged collision in the tunnel took place, attesting that he is, and I quote, "unable to attest"' – here Mr. Gator's voice rose together with his right eyebrow – '"unable to attest the origin of the longitudinal field disturbance known as the Krauterkrafft Pattern in the tunnel sector Lambda X at the level of the fourth scalar field," etcetera, etcetera, and that "the given tunnel metrics at that point does not allow for retro tracking of virtual scalar fields" – or in layman's terms, Your Honour, at this moment, we truly do not know where Mr. Pergamon really came from.'

Mr. Gator's voice and his eyebrow now returned to normal.

'And as for the point of law, Your Honour, I have taken the liberty of compiling several authorities on the subject of executive authority appearing as *amicus curiae* before the Courts of Star Central, and they are all contained in the bundle I have just handed over to your clerk. Could I have the exhibit number?' Mr. Gator sent a sleek smile to an empty court robe which sat perplexed with the documents piled in front of it.

Judge Juris took a deep breath and said, 'Let us have the exhibit number, then, Madam Registrar.'

The robe stood up and coyly said:

'This shall be the defence exhibit number one.'

'Counsellor Knarrpanti, you will no doubt want to study these submissions?' said the judge and proceeded without waiting for the prosecution to answer. 'Very well, we shall adjourn and reconvene in seven days, which will give you the opportunity to respond in writing.'

'On the question of continued detention of both defendants,' Mr. Gator continued unabated, 'the *amicus* respectfully proposes that the defendants be released on his recognizance and undertakes to bring them both to court in seven days' time, or any other period stipulated by the court.'

'Your Honour, I really must most strongly – ' the prosecutor began, but was cut short by a single word from the judge: 'Granted.'

The Theory of Moving Gates

'As dignitaries from all over Left World gather in Fairybury for this year's Centennial Fair of Zandar, the organizers are working round the clock to ensure a successful Procession,' a TV rumbled on in the corner above the bar. 'This is the first Fair after the passing of the last Master of Zandar and the preparations are taking place amid tight security, as it is expected that the new Master of Zandar will be revealed during this year's Procession. Our Ron Butler is in Fairybury coming to us live.'

A cat on his hind legs dressed in a trench coat, with the belt squeezed firmly around his waist to withstand the strongest of winds, appeared on TV, standing on a balcony. It was a very warm and sunny day in Fairybury but, for some reason, Ron Butler, the cat reporter, seemed to be prepared for a dramatic change in weather. A wide avenue stretched behind him as far as the eye could see. Giants dressed in blue overalls were busy erecting grandstands on both sides, while dwarfs hurried everywhere setting greenery around.

'Ron, what is the atmosphere like in Fairybury today?'

'Don, what you see behind me is just a small part of a gargantuan effort which has been going on ever since the flags went down on the last Fair, almost exactly a year ago. As you know, the Fair of Zandar is not only the engine of Fairybury's economy and its biggest source of income, but also the single most important event in the annual calendar for all the worlds of Zandar, a unifying catalyst if you will. And this year is no exception – on the contrary! The anticipation of the new Master to be revealed this year makes this occasion all the more important. Don?'

'Ron, are there any clues as to who will be revealed as the next Master of Zandar?'

A bout of ersatz laughter ensued on both sides.

'Well, Don, it could be me, it could be you, it could be somebody brought into being especially for that job. As you know, no one is able to guess the outcome. Not only that, no one knows exactly how the Master is found among the many inhabitants of Zandar. All we know is that, when the Procession begins, the Master will be there, under a veil, flanked by the Elders of Fairybury – only at the end of the Procession will his identity be revealed. So, until the veil is removed from the new Master in a little less than 24 hours from now – all bets are on. The excitement is almost palpable here in Fairybury and it has been impossible to find a hotel room already for weeks. Delegations are arriving amid stepped-up security and many of the famous sights of Fairybury have been cordoned off. At the same time, we are told, more celebrity hunters are expected to arrive, attracted by the prospect of running into just about everybody who is somebody in Zandar.'

'Objection on grounds of relevance!' said Lee T. Gator in his deepest courtroom voice and proceeded to lower the volume of the TV set above the bar without waiting for a pronouncement on his objection. Then he joined Pim, Harry and Pan Kratohvil seated around a table in the corner as the two reporters happily continued their contrived babble in the background.

The lawyer warrior wasn't wearing his shiny metallic court attire any more but still looked formidable, at least a head taller than anybody around. They were all in the basement of a bar called False Witness, his usual hangout not far from the Courts of Star Central, and Harry was in the middle of fuming at Pan Kratohvil: 'Where were you so long? First you let me spend the night in prison, and then you come to save *him*, not me!'

'Do you think I would have been more effective in obtaining your release if I had just walked into the prison and said to that Gschwendt person, "Harry here is my friend, would you let him go, pleeease?"'

'Alright, alright. But did you have to invent this whole story about Right World just to get me out, ha? How are you going to get us out of that?'

'Why do you think I invented it?' said Pan Kratohvil.

'You don't mean to say you really think he came from Right World, do you?' Harry replied, astonished.

'Would somebody here explain to me, what is this Right World?' said Pim looking at the strangely shaped bottles lined above the bar, some of which seemed to be more alive than bottles were supposed to be.

'A myth! A fiction!' said Harry. 'In the past, some people used to believe in the existence of a parallel universe, a counterpart to Zandar and all its worlds. Since the worlds of Zandar are collectively called Left World, they called this fantasy Right World. And that's all there is to it, a legend.'

'You are right, it probably is just a legend,' said Lee T. Gator. 'But still, I am intrigued by all this. You see, I went and talked to Ludo Ludbert, the Chief Engineer of Median Power Station. I checked all their operations logs and I spoke to a professor of Tunnel Mechanics at the University of Star Central. The fact is, nobody can explain where Mr. Pergamon came from. I did not make that up just to impress old Corpus Juris.'

'Alright, those nitwits in Tunnels Operations short-fused something again. But there's no need to invoke old wives' tales to explain it!'

'I think there is more to it than that, Harry,' said Pan Kratohvil with excitement in his blue eyes. 'You heard it yourself – they recorded the Krauterkrafft Pattern at the point where you and Pim left the tunnel. It would take the passage of a sun to create the Krauterkrafft Pattern in a Median Tunnel, that much I know.'

'My mum used to call me the sun of her life,' Harry replied without batting an eyelid as the barman brought their cocktails.

'Here you are – False Witness, the choice of the legal profession!' said Mr. Gator with a big grin.

'Mmmm,' Harry told the barman after tasting the cocktail. 'You know your trade, young man.'

'Thank you, sir,' said the barman. 'Actually, I am just filling in for a friend, mornings only. I am not really a barman. I am a junior superhero over at the Battles of Zdombia. I hope to get promoted soon to principal superhero, when Crushogator Rex leaves.'

'Oh, old Crushogator is leaving?'

'Yes, he got a job as a megahero opposite Shockasaurus Smash in Brutal Terror Five. The pay is the same, but in Brutal Terror the conditions are better.'

'I still cannot comprehend,' Pim turned to Lee T. Gator, 'how could that prosecutor ask for Harry to be jailed if it was me who committed the crime. What kind of laws do you have here that make something like that possible?'

'Justice rests on laws as much as on the people chosen to enforce them,' said Lee T. Gator. 'And Counsellor Knarrpanti just happened to be the duty prosecutor this morning.'

'That hack!' said Harry. 'A provincial wannabe who should have stayed put in Boondongla. He'd do anything to catch a bit of limelight, no matter how idiotic. Remember that time when he tried to enact the ordinance forbidding the use of coarse language within 250 meters of a school? Or the one about breaking wind within 250 meters of a perfume shop? He's nothing but a – '

'It's not something that you should worry about, Pim,' said Pan Kratohvil. 'In fact, Knarrpanti was probably more after Harry than after you. My friend here has a way with people that leaves some of them with a desire to – how should I put it? – well, you have to love him to like him.'

'Harrumph!' said Harry.

'But tell me, how did it happen that you two collided?'

'I don't know really, to tell the truth,' said Pim. 'I was taking part in an experiment in a computer factory, walking in a simulated maze, they were measuring something. And the next thing I know, this big yellow pacman came around the corner and started chasing me. I didn't know what to do, so I jumped over the wall.'

'Jumped over the wall in a pacman maze? That's interesting.' said Pan Kratohvil.

'Why?'

'Because that's impossible. Pacman's world is a two-dimensional world. You cannot go up or down there.'

'Well, I did.'

'That reminds me of something,' said Harry. 'When you crashed into me, I was on the way to the maze to serve a summons on Barney. And the reason why he had to go to court was that he – and I remember I thought at the time it was a bit strange – he apparently tried to eat his way through a wall and he damaged some maze property. The owners were furious. His is a leasehold maze, you know.'

'Does he do that often?' asked Pim.

'Surely you jest! Barney never leaves his maze, serving a summons on him is as easy as serving a summons on a cauliflower.'

'Well, legend or not, I want to go back to where I came from,' said Pim. 'Not only is this very uncomfortable,' here his eyebrows made a slight gesture towards Harry, 'but I also simply want to go home. I don't belong here!'

'There is only one thing we can do,' said Pan Kratohvil. 'We will go to the maze and pay a visit to Barney. I think there lies the answer to our questions. And your way back home, Left or Right.'

The bleached blond figure of Counsellor Knarrpanti appeared at the side door of the Courts of Star Central. He looked left and right and then blended into the crowd. It was a cold and overcast morning, in contrast with the warm sunset of the day before. The wind was picking up and people on the streets walked briskly in expectation of rain. Knarrpanti hurried without stopping past the house where he lived, Villa Sycamore, and turned into Blumenthon, one of the main avenues of Star Central. The grey light coming through the low clouds was fortified on Blumenthon with the vibrant colours of giant neon signs and shiny screens playing commercials 24 hours a day: *Nivea Body Moisturisers – Now With Dragon Sweat for Added Strength; Listerine Undead™ – Use No Other Mouthwash for the Fateful Bite (as recommended by Nosferatu)* or *Quasimodo Hump Polish – Will Make a Beauty Out of a Beast.*

Vacations in far-away romantic worlds with tropical settings dominated this morning, just as wet, green and wooded destinations would take over as soon as the sun shone again. Knarrpanti noticed a special offer for the Pirates World, *Come and meet the swashbuckling handsome heroes of the warm and sunny southern seas!* garnished with the sights of white beaches, blue seas, palm trees and pirate ships. As he thought of himself lying in hot sand far away from his office, the ad seized on his attention and quickly rolled out the following text:

Terms and conditions apply – May also meet one-legged foul-mouthed rum-guzzling sea captains – Sea temperature variational and may vary – Heroes sweaty and may smell – Photos non-depictional – Contract non-contractual.

As Knarrpanti walked along Blumenthon, a beautiful tree-lined street opened to his right. Median Power Station was on a hill at its far end. Barely visible in the mist behind it was the Master's Castle – locked, silent and empty now that Zandar was without a Master. Closer to Blumenthon, both sides of the street were lined with overgrown gardens that accommodated old villas and stately mansions behind the greenery. The buildings seemed to embrace the green cloak of grass, bushes and trees lovingly provided by their gardens and, if you walked further, the gardens became bigger and lusher and the houses shyer and more reclusive until they were no longer visible from the vegetation. Only the oldest of old families of Star Central lived in the street that Pan Kratohvil liked to call Advanced Decomposition Street, to Harry's great annoyance as some of his uncles lived there.

Knarrpanti crossed a bridge over the Sassandra river, one of the few crossing it on foot. In fact, the only one: coming from the opposite direction were three creatures from Bou Regreg crossing it on hoof, two junior robowarriors crossing it on force field, and Spidergranny, just released by Sergeant Gschwendt, crossing it on eight footless wobbly legs after her first good shot of buckwheat whiskey as a free spider.

On the other side of the river, the traffic from the bridge split into two wide boulevards that spread out in the shape of the letter V as far as the eye could see, Avinbeda East and Avinbeda West. Right in front of the bridge, at the source of the two boulevards, stood the tallest edifice of Star Central, the headquarters of Kutlurg Corporation. It was one of the most prestigious addresses in town, One Avinbeda Avenue. Knarrpanti crossed the aptly named Kutlurg Plaza, replete with fountains carved in white stone and black granite blocks, and ascended the wide, gently sloping marble stairs which led him to the innumerable grandiose doors encircling the base of the building. One such door opened for him.

The question of transport arose as a crucial point when Pim and Harry emerged into the light of day from the dark bowels of the False Witness with Pan Kratohvil and Mr. Gator. Harry insisted, unsuccessfully, on his own hippogriff. Pan Kratohvil reminded him that he could go nowhere without Pim.

'It's just a horse, after all, Harry! And you two cannot ride a horse while you are together – especially not a winged one.'

'I am not going to be seen travelling through Median Tunnels on a common broomstick! I am the Royal Bedel!'

'Alright, then, we'll use my official transport. I am entitled to a few of Master's perks during the interregnum.' He turned away and spoke a few unintelligible words to cast a spell. The next moment a splendid six-horse gilded carriage appeared around the corner.

'I saw that carriage! Yesterday in the tunnel, just before the collision!' said Pim.

'I know, I was in it,' said Pan Kratohvil. 'And I saw you, tumbling along, looking rather bewildered.'

'And you immediately jumped to the conclusion that he came from Right World!' said Harry.

'No, it was something that Headley said that – ah, there he is!'

The carriage stopped, accompanied with much neighing and snorting, and a headless coachman jumped down to open the door for them. 'At your service, sir!' a disembodied voice came from the direction of the missing head.

'Why, thank you, Headley, that was quick,' said Pan Kratohvil as he helped Pim and Harry to climb in.

'I am pleased to please, sir,' the voice responded. Pim peeped from the carriage in what Uncle Pohadka would have disapprovingly called a morbid curiosity, to see the exact point where the head would normally join the body. But its neck was surrounded with a majestic ruff, eerily flat on top, almost like a tray on which the head used to stand before it was removed, probably by one of the two principal causes of headlessism in Zandar – accident or authorities.

As soon as the door of the carriage slammed shut, the whip was heard cracking and the carriage jerked forward. The next thing Pim saw – they were in a tunnel.

Compared to his previous experiences in Median Tunnels, this was indeed a smooth ride. The carriage glided effortlessly, guided by the gently curving tunnel walls. It was far more pleasant to be sitting on its red plush seats watching the walls whizz by than flying alone, head first and nauseated. Plus, this time they knew where they were going. He, he was going home – away from that unsympathetic egoist on his right shoulder.

The carriage stopped almost instantaneously and yet smoothly. Pim's spirits rose at the sight of the neon-green colour that he disliked only yesterday. He was in Gustav's maze again and he could not wait to find his way back to Laboratory 21.

Harry, on the other hand, was decidedly less energetic. The last thing he wanted to do was to hop around on four legs around the maze until they found a gate that did not exist in the first place! Whoever heard of gates in pacman mazes anyway?

'Fourth Detachment Tunnels Security at the scene, Agent Askew reporting,' a Mamluk appeared out of a corridor. He was taller and more muscular than the rest, his jaw almost a square, and looked more like a superhero than a simple Mamluk Agent. 'The investigation is almost complete. If you'd follow me this way.'

'What is it that you are investigating, Agent Askew?' asked Pan Kratohvil.

'We are acting on a criminal report filed by the owners of the maze, Godforsaken Properties Ltd., specifying repeated wilful damage to the maze and naming the leaseholder, one Mr. Barney Pacman, as responsible.'

'Have you spoken to him yet?'

'Actually no, sir. We have not been able to locate him yet.'

'What do you mean?' said Pan Kratohvil. 'Even if he is hiding, this is not a big maze. And pacmans normally do not hide – on the contrary!'

'Indeed, it is a rather small maze. You know, the kind of slum Godforsaken specializes in. We swept the whole place already once, but could not find him, and I ordered a second sweep just to be sure.'

'No need for that, he's not here,' said Harry. 'Look!'

'The tumbleballs!' said Pim. 'Yesterday they were running away, today they are just running around.'

'Exactly. The Shtchees are not afraid – ergo, Barney is not here.'

Of the wilful damage there was not much to see. If it were not for the criss-crossed plastic tapes saying *Mamluk Line, Do Not Cross, Do not approach, Do Not Touch* and just *Don't!* and the multitude of curious Shtchees assembled around it, they would have hardly noticed any damage. At first sight, it looked as if a small firework went off at the end of the corridor and left faint traces of soot.

'The wall is slightly damaged,' said Pan Kratohvil after examining it, 'but I can't find any sign of a gate.'

'I told you so,' snapped Harry whose naturally limited supply of patience was already running out.

'OK, then how do you explain that I am here and Barney is not?' replied Pim in exasperation. 'There's got to be a gate in this maze – look, I wasn't born here!'

'Your birthplace is none of my business! But don't worry, the investigation is going to find out soon enough who you really are and what you are doing here!'

'The gate is not in the maze,' said Pan Kratohvil, 'or to be more precise, it's not here *any more*. But it didn't just disappear – I think it moved. We have to find where it moved.'

'We can't do that, it's impossible!' said Harry.

'Impossible? Not at all,' said Pan Kratohvil. 'Tomorrow is the Centennial Fair of Zandar. It means that at least one representative of each and every world of Zandar will come to Fairybury. Think of the news they'll bring, Harry! Think of the gossip they'll exchange after the Procession is over and the celebrations begin. And think of all those who will be there – if we need strength, we'll go to Shockasaurus Smash. If we need courage, we'll go to Sir Lancelot. If we need wisdom, we'll talk to Pallada Athena. And if we need authority, we'll get it from the Master of Zandar himself. This time tomorrow, we'll have the whole of Zandar helping us!'

'I would feel infinitely more comfortable,' said Harry, 'if I was led to believe that this moving gate theory is not something you just invented to reassure us, Pan Kratohvil.'

'I thought you were better versed in Theory of Gates, Harry.'

'It is an arcane science capable of arousing much passion among experts, but with little practical application for us ordinary fellows,' Harry turned to Pim. 'My friend Pan Kratohvil is considered the foremost expert in the field. What got over him to devote so much of his life to gates I will never understand.'

'Because they're there,' Pan Kratohvil replied unblinkingly and continued. 'You see, not many people remember this, but long time ago all natural gates were also moving gates, I know that from my grandmother. Every natural gate in Left World was unstable and shifting after it was created, just like Pim's Right World gate. Only when two objects were exchanged between two worlds through a gate connecting them did such a gate become stable, or *anchored* in the parlance of my theory.'

'The natural gates of Zandar are now fixed because of the objects that passed through them?'

'Correct,' said Pan Kratohvil. 'It is now impossible to retrieve all the objects that have passed through various gates and return them to their original worlds through their original gates. That's why Left World gates never shift, not even those that are completely forgotten.'

'Does that mean that it would be possible to anchor my gate and make it stop moving simply by taking something from Left World into Right World and the other way round?'

'Unfortunately, according to my research – not quite. Things get complicated with a Right World gate, other conditions are necessary, I won't bother you with all the details. Anyway, it's an old hypothesis of mine that I just might call a theory if I test it. Right now I am simply trying to convince my friend the Bedel that a moving gate is not something unknown to science – just to him.'

When Pan Kratohvil and his entourage were gone from the maze in another blue flash, agent Askew raised two fingers to his ear.

'Yes, sir,' he said. 'They were here.'

A pause ensued.

'Certainly, sir. Just as you predicted. Yes, we followed your instructions to the letter.'

Agent Askew raised the eyebrows listening to the incoming communication.

'Are you sure?' he said. 'But that's less than 24 hours from now.'

'Harry, you look awful!'

'Dreadful!!'

'Frightful!!!'

Three old witches had opened the door. One was tall and skinny, another very tall and very skinny and the third one was maybe even taller.

One wore small glasses at the tip of her long nose, another wore thick glasses and the third one's nose was maybe even longer.

One looked shocked, another perplexed, while the third one was simply bewildered.

'Good evening, ladies!' said Harry. 'How very nice to see you again. I happen to be amalgamated with this, ahem, gentleman for the time being, so allow me to introduce him. His name is Pim Pergamon. Pim, meet my aunts.'

'Gertrude, charmed to meet you, sir.'

'Gwendolyn, delighted!'

'Guinevere, enchanted!'

'The pleasure is all mine, ladies,' countered Pim. 'I hope I am not intruding.'

'Oh, no!'

'Not at all!'

'On the contrary!'

'Talk about intruding!' said Harry poking Pim with his moustache. Pim turned to him and said, 'Sometimes I think it would be just so awful if you were anybody else.'

'Oh, you are so charming!'

'Oh, you are so delightful!'

'Oh, you are so enchanting!' the witches screeched enthusiastically

'Troglodytes of Hernia!! He is enchanting and I am frightful?!' Harry protested but the aunts had already descended on Pim, ignoring Harry altogether.

'Harry always stays with us when he is in Fairybury,' said Gertrude.

'Harry often brings guests for the Fair,' said Gwendolyn.

'Harry's friends are always welcome here,' added Guinevere.

'He is not my guest!' muttered Harry.

Pan Kratohvil appeared at the door, causing three more gusts of excitement. The aunts were very pleased to see him in their house. When he announced that he could not be a guest at the dinner, they were disappointed.

'Oh, what a pity!'

'What a shame!'

'What a tragedy!'

'I could not possibly agree with you more, ladies,' Pan Kratohvil joined in the register, 'but you will surely understand that I have to attend to some urgent matters arising from the peculiar happenings which led to – '

'Oh, yes, we heard!'

'Oh, yes, we know!'

'Oh, yes, we understand!'

'Collision in the tunnel!'

'Mysterious stranger without transport!'

'Royal Bedel on bail!'

'I am not on bail – *he* is!'

As it turned out, the aunts were fully informed about this morning's events in the Courts of Star Central. For them, Pim was already a sort of a mini-celebrity and their curiosity quickly aroused a maxi-envy in Harry.

Later that evening, after he had patiently answered as few of the aunts' questions as it was polite to do, Pan Kratohvil announced that it was time for him to attend to the yet unspecified 'urgent matters'. Before he left, he went to see Pim and Harry on the terrace.

Gertrude, Gwendolyn and Guinevere lived in a spacious three storey Grecian house overlooking Elfindor Park, the largest park in Fairybury. Eight slender Corinthian columns rose from the grass covered ground to support its white walls. The roof was flat and had been turned into a terrace ages ago by a previous owner, a certain

Helen, before she was compelled to move to Troy by circumstances that were later the subject of much press coverage.

Cheerful songs and laughter could be heard in the distance, coming from the celebrations in the streets and from the pilgrims' tents erected in almost every park in Fairybury. The Centennial Fair of Zandar itself was a rather ceremonious occasion, but Pan Kratohvil was right. The eve of the Fair was one long party, an opportunity to drink or smoke a pipe with folks from many worlds away – and to listen to stories of moving gates if such stories could be had.

Pan Kratohvil found Pim and Harry half asleep on the terrace – i.e. Harry was fully asleep and Pim not at all. He was looking at his new companion. Even though faced with spending the rest of his days in the inescapable embrace of that grumpy old fellow, Pim had to admit that the nap brought an affable, baby-like quality to the face of the Royal Bedel.

He and Pan Kratohvil watched from the terrace as Snow White joined Candide in a karaoke version of *I will survive*, while the Seven Dwarfs provoked bursts of laughter impersonating each other (or that's what they thought they were doing). Then Hiawatha, in a moment of inspiration, challenged Shockasaurus Smash, the nation's foremost authority on senseless violence, to play a tune on musical glasses with his gigantic fingers. A bet was made, and Shockasaurus unexpectedly won because he managed to play full two bars of *Eine Kleine Nachtmusik* by Mozart before smashing the glasses with his unwieldy hands.

'Listen to them,' said Pan Kratohvil as the wind brought more cheers and laughter to the terrace. 'Knights and wizards, superheroes and warriors, sprites and goblins, ordinary people and ordinary dwarfs, everybody wants to be the first to see the new Master of Zandar. They come from so many different places and yet they all bow to him.'

'Where do you come from?' asked Pim.

'Oh, it's hard to define, really. We moved a lot when I was a kid,' said Pan Kratohvil stroking his pointy beard with short, measured strokes.

'Your father was in the army?'

'No, not at all,' laughed Pan Kratohvil and allowed himself to unbutton his purple velvet shirt. Underneath was an equally purple undervest. 'I was brought up by my grandmother, Baba Yaga. You may have heard of her, she is a famous witch. She started as the witch who puts the spell on Sleeping Beauty, but that was only part time, as she would be out of work for the next one hundred years while everybody else slept. So she also worked as the Mother of All Calamity in A Thousand and One Nights and as Mother Muggosh in the Tales of Long Ago. And all the while in private she was actually the nicest and the sweetest granny you could imagine! She used to live in a house on chicken legs in Stribor's Forest when she took me in, and that's where I spent most of my childhood. She began to take me to work with her as soon as I could come along. So we would be away from home for long spells at a time – because she disliked Median Tunnels and preferred to travel through natural gates, like the one that you came through.'

'Except I didn't come from A Thousand and One Nights – I came from Advanced Computers&Games.'

'Whenever we travelled, Baba Yaga's falcon was never far away, always hovering majestically above us,' Pan Kratohvil continued. 'His name was Buckminster Platt. To this day I think that his only purpose in life was to hover majestically. He would only ever land on Baba Yaga's hand. Nobody else could tempt him, he would rather exhaust himself flying until Baba Yaga appeared. I haven't seen Buckminster in years,' he sighed.

'To get back to gates ...' said Pim.

'Yes. You see, throughout history, in their incessant search for ore, miners in all worlds would sometimes find underground passages which led to unknown places. Gates are similar to caves, you know. So it was always easy to move through Left World – if you knew your way around. I liked these journeys in the beginning, travelling through all those enchanted forests and visiting all the accursed castles, but you don't get to see many different worlds if you don't use the tunnels – you spend most of the time trekking from gate to gate. I suppose that's why I became so fascinated with Median Tunnels later on, as a teenager. That and the Median Continuum, the mysterious space that lies outside the Tunnels but does not belong to any world. So when I again became interested in gates, much later in my career, and studied their anchors and developed the Theory of Gates, it was as if I had gone the full circle – back to the bosom of my grandmother.'

'She sounds like a major influence in your life,' said Pim for want of better thought.

'My granny taught me my first steps in magic – she wasn't a witch for nothing – and I naturally followed in her footsteps. When I finally chose to study science, I had a natural advantage.'

'I don't understand – how can the knowledge of magic be an advantage for the study of science? The two things are quite opposite,' said Pim.

'No, no, no!' Pan Kratohvil replied with great incredulity. 'On the contrary, magic and science are two sides of the same coin! Magic tells us how to do things, while science explains how they are done. If you don't know how it works, it's magic. When you find out how it works – it's science! But it's still the same thing.'

'Which one do I need, then, to get back home?'

'A little bit of both and quite a bit of luck!' said Pan Kratohvil, his blue eyes again open with excitement. 'Yours is a moving gate, Pim. This means two things: first, we need to find out where it moved. Then, you have to get there before somebody else gets in and the gate shifts again. But,' whispered Pan Kratohvil, 'when we find your gate, if it really turns out to be the Right World Gate – I am coming with you!'

The Centennial Fair of Zandar

'Good morning, time to get up, you two!' Gertrude opened the doors of the bedroom without waiting for an answer. 'It's the Procession Day!'

The morning of the Centennial Fair was warm and sunny, like all mornings in Fairybury, and indeed all afternoons. Pim and Harry lied half-asleep in their immense guest bed. Before they could even prop themselves up, Gwendolyn threw the doors open:

'– 'ning! Rise and shine! The Procession won't wait!'

A little later, one more witch rushed into the bedroom and yelled, 'Up! Up, you lazy two! Time to go! The Procession's almost started!'

By the time they had left the house for Place Bayard, where the VIP lodge was erected every year in the shade of a big bay tree, the streets were already swarming with people of all shapes and sizes. But when they arrived at Place Bayard, there was no VIP lodge. Not only that, there was no big bay tree either. The only thing left was a shrivelled stump, some dry branches and a notice informing members of the public that the VIP lodge had been moved to Fulworth Square, courtesy of Kutlurg Corporation, due to the fact that the big bay tree had recently withered.

Harry was furious that Pan Kratohvil had not thought of telling him that the lodge was moved, but the aunts chided him for such a reaction, reminding him that Pan Kratohvil had other things to do besides arranging VIP seating for him.

'Even if there are two of you,' added Gertrude.

'Especially if there are two of you,' added Gwendolyn.

'Precisely because there are two of you,' added Guinevere.

'I mean,' she said after all heads had turned towards her, 'he called to say that he could not come to take Mr. Pergamon and you to the

Procession because something had come up. There was something else to do. Something very important, I gather, something to do with a gate.'

'You mean, my gate – *the* Gate?'

'Troglodytes of Hernia! Forget about the gate!' Harry cut in. 'We need to get to Fulworth Square or we'll be late.'

Harry was right. The Procession was about to begin, and the oval space of Place Bayard was already brimming with those unconcerned by the lack of shade and eager to take advantage of the fact that the best spot to watch the Procession was now available to them.

'We could also stay here …' Pim began to say, but Harry looked at him so ferociously that he chose not to finish the sentence. 'If you want to stay here with him,' Harry gestured at Counsellor Knarrpanti who had appeared out of nowhere and stood in the crowd with his eyes fixed on them, 'you'll have to get out of my body first.' Pim reluctantly agreed. He had no desire to be anywhere near people who came from Boondongla to advance their careers over his back. 'Besides, Pan Kratohvil will be looking for us at Fulworth Square after the Procession, anyway,' Harry added in a more pacified tone.

A taxi then appeared at the entrance to the square and Harry quickly pulled Pim towards it. He was suddenly pretty good at walking for both of them. The aunts followed and Pim more or less dangled along. But, as it turned out, it was a Star Central taxi and the driver was adamant that he could only take a ride back to Star Central.

'I am only licensed for Star Central traffic, not for commercial traffic inside Fairybury,' he said. Harry tried to explain that he was the Bedel of Zandar on official business.

'Everybody is on some official business today. It's driving me crazy!' the driver replied. 'But my point of departure or point of arrival has to be in Star Central. It's in my licence.'

'But, young man,' Gertrude said, 'It would be frightfully nice of you if you could take us just to Fulworth Square?'

'Fearfully jolly!' said Gwendolyn.

'Awfully good!' rounded up Guinevere.

Faced with such semantics, and the prospect of a large tip, the driver relented and they all quickly crammed into the back of the car.

The streets were swarming with tourists all going to the Fair: fairies, goblins, grand caliphs, kings' sons in groups of three, small thieves and great warriors, shockworkers and bureaucrats, simple dressmakers and ambitious vezirs, wolves in top hats with doctorates from the University of Koenigsberg and dragons with T-shirts from the Far Side.

The taxi was making slow progress through the crowd. Harry was impatient and nervous, the aunts were excited and full of enthusiasm, while Pim felt just plain uncomfortable. Not only was he cramped tightly in the back seat with one grumpy Bedel and three overly merry witches, but there was something under him on the seat that kept poking him in all the wrong places each time they made a turn. He could not extend his hands far enough behind his back to reach the offending object, while Harry did not seem bothered by it at all. There could hardly be a more unhelpful person to share your bottom with than Harry, thought Pim and kept wriggling, but to no avail.

They passed through a small square with a bronze relief of two knights riding a horse sideways. 'Knights Templar?' said Pim.

'Knights Theranal. Knights Templar never ride sideways,' said Harry.

'Oh, look, the Shockasauruses are here this year,' said Gertrude, pointing at something. Pim looked in the direction of her finger, but could only see a group of dwarfs setting up a better viewing position for themselves with various kitchen pots and utensils. Their grandstand looked great in the sun, as it was made of polished copper, but they could hardly be related to Shockasaurus Smash, observed Pim. Or was there more than one Shockasaurus family?

Then he realized that her finger was pointing at something much farther away. Out in the distance, on the outskirts of Fairybury, a group of giants was sitting on the slopes of a nearby hill.

'Oh, yes, the whole family is here because their youngest is taking part in the Procession this year,' said Gwendolyn.

'It feels as if it was only yesterday when we used to change young Master Bash's sails, doesn't it?' said Guinevere, to which all three sisters let out a joyful sigh.

The Shockasauruses were comfortably seated in their lodge, actually a quarry on the side of the hill, wearing cool sunglasses and sipping from cocktail barrels. There were old bearded Shockasauruses engaged in a conversation about politics, with young Shockasauruses playing around them, tickling each other behind their ears with small trees.

'Will you stop that!' Harry suddenly bawled at Pim in the taxi.

'Help me,' said Pim, 'I am sitting on something here.'

Harry looked around with an innocent look. 'I am not sitting on anything.'

'Well, I am!' Pim snapped back. So Harry inserted his right arm behind their common back and, after some wriggling, out came a small shiny, metallic device of some sort.

'It's a computer! Is it yours?' said Pim.

'Certainly not!' replied Harry.

'Then it means that somebody forgot it in the taxi,' said Pim.

Harry was about to come up with a sarcastic reply when he noticed a friend outside. The taxi was by now driving so slowly, through a cluster of elves, that the two of them could converse through the open window. The aunts, on the other hand, noticed a group of Bouregregians, which got them carried away in a discussion on this season's garbs, very much approving the choice of flowery patterns in a world containing mostly flowers, as Bou Regreg does.

All that meant that Pim was left with the small computer in his hands. As soon as he turned it over, his attention was captured by a plethora of shiny holographic stickers on the back proclaiming various hardware and software loyalties. One of the stickers caught his eye. It contained a barcode and three red letters: ACG.

He paused. Then he switched it on.

When the computer finally came to, its screen displayed a document titled 'Unaccounted Encumbrances: Interpersonal Competencies in Cross-Competitive Environment of Lavatorial Stratification'. A closer look revealed that it was a memo informing the reader that he was granted access to the ACG Senior Management toilets as of Monday next week.

Suddenly, Pim's eyes were glowing. This was an object that came from his world – *the right world*.

He tapped the screen to see what else was on the computer. He went through many files and tables before stumbling across something different: 'X9 Demo'. And right underneath it, the word 'Connect'. Pim did not hesitate for one second. He clicked on it.

'Excellent!' Harry turned to the aunts. 'Eukuleles, my friend the Hawaiian philosopher, will be in Star Central next week, on a conference, something about the meaning of all existence, and we will meet for dinner. I haven't seen him in ages!'

'Wonderful!'

'Marvellous!'

'Staggering!' said the aunts.

'Or was it the existence of all meaning?'

A message appeared on the computer screen: 'Connecting'. Pim felt his excitement rising.

But then the taxi stopped in front of the security barrier at Fulworth Square and before Pim could do anything, Harry opened the door, jumped out and dragged him away, leaving the computer overturned on the back seat.

'But, Harry –'

The taxi driver shouted, 'Hey! Hey, you!!'

'Now that we haven't paid, it was a non-commercial service and there was no breach of license. Your problem solved!' Harry replied smugly while the aunts discharged themselves from the other side incredibly quickly. The driver simply could not believe the audacity of the jaw-dropping explanation he'd been offered, while his passengers were quickly whisked away by big men in dark suits with wires growing from their ears. The line of Mamluks from the Ceremonial Detachment closed again.

Inside the VIP tent the aunts were directed to their seats in the back, while Pim and Harry were discreetly carried towards the front.

'It is quite out of the question to go back, even if that was an object from your world! I am here in my official capacity and I may not leave until the Procession is over!' Harry was saying.

'Harry, that computer came from my world! I need to find out where exactly in Star Central it got into the taxi,' Pim was still trying to turn back. 'Star Central – that's where the gate to my world is! It shifted! We need to go there!'

'We don't need to go anywhere. We need to wait for Pan Kratohvil,' Harry dug in his heels. They almost fell. Then they realized that they were the centre of attention. Harry attempted to look straight and nudged Pim with an elbow.

Lara Croft and Dr. Zhivago, Snow White and Black Dwarf, Aladdin, and even Aladdin's lamp on the seat next to him, all had turned to see what the commotion was all about. Captain Nemo sent a distinct look of disapproval. Pim and Harry stretched one big polite smile across both faces, then continued to hiss at each other until they were seated next to Judge Corpus Juris who gravely looked at them and said, '*Pendente Lite*'. His head was even bigger than in the courtroom, precariously perched atop a puny, unsteady body.

When the judge looked away, Harry hissed dismissively, 'Going to Right World? Now, *that* is a story never to be told.'

Pim opened his mouth to reply, but in that moment the loudest fanfare that he had ever heard pierced the air above Fairybury and left him open-mouthed. The sound was coming from the orchestra just below the VIP lodge. The musicians blew their lungs out in a series of triumphant notes to announce to Fairybury and the whole of Left World – that the Procession had begun.

Out of the echo of the fanfare came the hissing, expectant sound of snare drums, joined by the heavy beats of bass drums. Soon other, more energetic drums joined in the beat, and the momentum kept rising until it sounded as if the orchestra which a moment ago was composed entirely of fanfare trumpets, now contained only drums, dozens and dozens of drums. It was the sound of the famous Zandar Marching Band.

Pan Kratohvil then appeared from the left on a magnificent, brocaded horse. He wore a blue velvet robe with golden hems and carried the massive ceremonial lance of the House of Kratohvil. He looked different from yesterday and the gaze of his otherwise intense blue eyes was lost in the distance somewhere far away. When he approached the lodge, Pim waved and called out to him.

'The gate! It's still open! I found – '

Harry slapped him on the wrists as the distinguished guests in the VIP lodge scoffed discreetly at such breach of etiquette. Harry was deeply embarrassed. The majority of guests, however, interpreted it differently and suddenly the tribunes around the VIP lodge burst out in cheers for Pan Kratohvil, just as the Band began playing the Potentate March.

Despite the fact that it all began quite unwittingly, the enthusiasm quickly spread ahead until the whole Procession Route was up in ovations, standing and cheering, clapping hands, hooves and tentacles, neighing, scraping, snorting and plain banging metal on metal in unison. Harry and his moustache disapproved immensely at first, but as he kept looking on all the beings from all the worlds of Zandar cheering together in front of him, his face softened somewhat.

'You seem to hold quite a sway in Left World, Pim Pergamon. I hope you use it wisely in the future.'

The parade continued as the Band transformed into a veritable Red Army Orchestra, fervently playing the most uplifting marches the reeds in its instruments would bear. Now you could really see uniformed musicians, red in the face, beautifully adorned with medals and decorations across their enormous blowing chests.

The music was very fitting for the Procession. The representatives of many worlds of Zandar proudly marched on, some of them on floats, coming out of the staging area in D'Orby Park, passing by the VIP lodge and continuing along Procession Avenue. At Liosalfar Square, at the far end of the Avenue, Table-Be-Set was sumptuously laid out for the new Master.

Dwarves traditionally marched first. It considerably slowed down the whole Procession, but you could not argue with dwarves, who were by and large notoriously bad-tempered folk. There were dandiprats and manikins, goblins and hobgoblins, gnomes and trolls, many of them proudly wearing medals of the Petite Order of Itsy-Bitsy with a Silver Cat's Hair, the highest decoration a dwarf can obtain. Dwarves are all crazy about medals and honours for some reason, that is, all except the Goodmen of Zandar, or Brownies, as they are also known, who are warm and friendly, probably the friendliest of them all. They received a warm welcome from the crowds, although there were almost none of them among the spectators, as the Goodmen firmly believe that more than three is a crowd.

There followed a long cortège of lively chess figures. One of the black knights was restless, the nostrils of his horse steaming even in the warm air of Fairybury. The White Queen sent a long look to Harry, something that did not go unnoticed by Snow White.

Superheroes and megaheroes marched escorted by shiny metallic robowarriors. An awesome amount of armour and sheer firepower filed past the VIP lodge, accompanied by powerful, almost menacing music from the Band.

Then came elves and fairies, sprites and angels, jinn and corposants. Cacodemons, banshees and gremlins were seated on a float drawn by Valkyries, followed by imps and orcs in their best Sunday outfits. A great white light enveloped the Procession route as witches and wizards rode out on white unicorns and a sweet scent descended on the audience, something Harry called a cheap trick. But everybody else loved it, at least those with nostrils in the audience.

A huge aquarium right next to the VIP lodge housed some of those who were not bothered by wizards' smells. The stands inside the aquarium were crowded with mermaids and water sprites, while a great white whale nested in the back, blowing off lazily. Lady of the Lake sat in the front row, separated from the Little Mermaid by

Poseidon and Neptune, their mutual rivalry being a well-known fact in the VIP aquarium.

Just as the vampires were driven past the VIP lodge in their own VIP coffins, a sudden squall of wind came from the east. The first gust behaved mischievously and took off Judge Juris' enormous hat from his enormous head, which greatly amused Pim and Harry, then inflated the canopy above the lodge and finally shook one of the coffins on the parade. A muffled grumble could be heard from the inside.

But then the wind picked up and soon not only hats, but parasols and even corposants were swirling above the crowd. That was unusual for a Procession day, Corpus Juris observed in the VIP lodge.

Then lightning struck out of the clear skies. That was unheard of on a Procession day! A murmur arose among the spectators, while those taking part in the Procession remained undisturbed. Especially those in the coffins.

But not for long. A series of lightning bolts struck the Procession one after another, each one striking closer to the VIP lodge. The last, sixth bolt of lightning struck right into the Marching Band, shattering the instruments. The Band let out its last short agonizing squeal and the music suddenly died. Silence hovered over the VIP lodge for a moment.

The Procession halted, cut in several places. Judge Juris rose, as much as he could on his scrawny legs, to appeal to everybody in the lodge to remain calm. Mamluks from the Ceremonial Detachment and security personnel in other guises began murmuring short, sharp responses into their communication sets, mostly about Charlie and Oscar going to Lima in November.

Pim, on the other hand, could not help feeling relieved, because suddenly he was spared waiting the whole day before he could talk to Pan Kratohvil. Interesting as it all was - except the Bedel bore - the key to ending this whole bizarre episode of his life was now in Star Central. And finding the taxi did not look like an insurmountable problem. Pan Kratohvil only needed to set the Mamluks in motion. Pim even remembered the beginning of the taxi registration number - H8.

He could see Pan Kratohvil riding back towards them through the crowded Procession Avenue. To Pim, impatient more than ever before, it seemed that Pan Kratohvil was positively crawling. There was much commotion on the route itself which probably explained his slow progress. Harry had not said a word since the Procession began, but now he looked into the distance and said, 'It's not him.'

'What is not who?' said Pim.

'You know who I am talking about,' said Harry. 'That's not Pan Kratohvil. Look!'

Pim looked again and noticed something he missed before. The commotion around the horseman was of his own making. People were trying to get out of his way, but it was not easy as the Procession Avenue was lined with densely packed spectators. The black horseman was wielding a long black sword and cutting down anybody who stood in his path. It was most definitely not Pan Kratohvil.

'Harry, is this how an average Procession looks like?'

'Don't be stupid,' came the short response.

The black horseman now galloped through the line of vampire coffins. It was the black chess knight Pim had noticed earlier. As he charged forward, one by one the coffins fell off their gilded carriages. One of the coffins opened in the fall and a terrible shriek could be heard from the inside as its occupant disappeared in a thin puff of smoke in the blazing sun of the Procession day.

The voices of TV commentators seated in a row of booths not far from the VIP lodge could be heard restlessly chattering away. Words like 'Un-be-lie-ve-able!' and 'Out-ra-geous!' feverishly mingled with the ubiquitous '… remains to be seen.'

The knight stopped in front of the VIP lodge. Before the Mamluks from the security realized what was happening, he spurred his horse and jumped in an unbelievably long leap, landing among the panicked occupants of the lodge. A couple of Mamluks from the Ceremonial Detachment who tried to offer resistance were beheaded in an instant by his black sword.

Everybody now rushed to get out of the lodge. The knight turned his horse towards Pim and Harry, who were unable to follow others as quickly through the sea of upturned chairs and tables. Captain Nemo was the only one to come to their rescue, but before he could draw his kirpan he was crushed under the black hooves.

Pim and Harry now stood frozen right in front of the black horseman. He raised his sword high up, slowly and deliberately, so high that he tore the canopy above their heads. Bright sunlight suddenly flooded the VIP lodge. The last thing that Pim saw were the horse's nostrils. He had been wrong. They were not steaming. They were smoking.

The knight brought the sword down with full force, striking the hapless two right between their heads. They fell, cut in two, and remained lifeless on the ground.

The black knight victoriously raised both hands high in the air and let out a long, chilling cry. The Mamluks from the Ceremonial Detachment surrounded the black horseman and ordered him to surrender, as was their usual procedure. But this was no usual Procession emergency, and two more Mamluks lost their lives before the commander issued the order to fire.

Several powerful ray blasts from Mamluk guns criss-crossed on the knight and threw him off the horse. He smashed into pieces when he hit the ground, as if he was made of brittle stone. His horse let out a deep neigh and followed its master to the ground. Although it had not been hit, the horse too crumbled into hundreds of pieces. The Mamluks, who have seen much stranger things happen in the many worlds they patrolled, thought nothing of it and contentedly began to murmur reassuring ten-fours into their wires. The black pieces remained on the ground, but just long enough for Mamluks to turn away. And then, before any of them realized what was happening, the remnants of the horseman and his horse miraculously rose from the ground and formed a new shape. In an instant, they had combined into a terrifying winged reptile which swept another Mamluk to death with its spiked tail. The reptile then rose into the air and flew high above Procession Avenue, bellowing the same bloodcurdling cry as its predecessor. The TV commentators paused to let their audience hear the scream.

'Morph!' the Mamluk commander barely managed to shout, his voice chords paralysed with fear. 'He's a morph! Run! Run for your life!'

As if the cry of the beast high above Fairybury was a battle call to its hidden kin, other morphs suddenly began to appear. They were everywhere – among spectators, in the Procession, even among the Mamluks. A warrior morphed into a monster and attacked other warriors. A dwarf morphed into a black troll and began devouring dwarves around him. A hotdog stall not far from the VIP lodge morphed all of a sudden into a knight in dark armour and attacked the poor hotdog seller with a hotdog that morphed into a heavy mace. Then one of the fairies morphed into a vicious warrior-maid covered in blood and started cutting down elves around her.

Mortally wounded elves did not fall on the ground. In death as in life, they remained detached from the ground and just drifted away carried by the force of the fatal blow. It was a sad and terrible sight. The colours of life drained from their bodies quickly, making them ever more transparent until they literally disappeared into thin air. As the morph warrior kept shooting all around her into the crowd of elves, the ripples of death spread outwards until she stood in an empty circle.

'Watch out!' shouted a witch on a spectator stand in the middle of Procession Avenue. The scaffolding holding some one hundred terrified spectators shook violently. Before any of them could get off it, the aisles opened up below their feet and swallowed all of them in one go. The giant jaws snapped once or twice more into the empty air and then morphed back into scaffolding. The benches stood clean and empty as if nothing had happened.

Mamluks fought back as much as they could but they only managed to slow down the onslaught. Morph warriors rarely died when hit. They transformed from one shape into another, from humans into beasts, from live beings into objects, even into weapons themselves. And when one of the Mamluks turned into an orange and black morph warrior and mowed down a score of his surprised colleagues, the little success the Mamluks had had began to melt away.

The whole Procession Avenue was in chaos. Tourists ran in all directions looking for cover in the pandemonium. Screams and cries for help were coming from all sides. The initial panic now turned into despair. Even the TV commentators were lost for words.

There was only one person still fighting. Pan Kratohvil was at the head of the Procession when the attack began and was now trying to fight his way back towards Fulworth Square. His horse was still draped in ceremonial robes but they were getting tattered. He fought with skill and determination. His lance, although only a ceremonial one, seemed to be more effective against morphs than Mamluk high-tech weaponry.

A small group of warriors rallied around Pan Kratohvil bolstered by his success. Fighting together, they managed to create a circle free of morphs, a miniature liberated territory. When other, defenceless creatures saw it, they started moving towards it. One by one, they sneaked past the morphs engaged in combat outside the circle. Less fortunate ones were caught in a swing of a blade or pulse of a laser, but many of them succeeded in breaking through. The circle began to fill with allies. Pan Kratohvil began to turn the tide.

When his horse suddenly reared, Pan Kratohvil firmly pulled the reins and managed to remain in the saddle. He leaned forward and whispered something into the horse's ear. But the horse reared again. This time he was just barely able to stay in the saddle. Finally, the horse shook violently and threw him off. A friendly banshee ran to him and helped him get on the feet. The horse shook again and shed the last remains of the brocade. What remained was not a horse. It was a giant snake, hissing as it uncoiled. Unbeknownst to him, Pan Kratohvil had been riding a morph.

He started towards the lance which he dropped. The banshee tried to raise the heavy lance herself but, being a banshee, paused instead to wail. Before Pan Kratohvil managed to grip the lance, the snake swung its razor-sharp tail and stabbed him in the chest. Its poisonous tip came out in the back. Pan Kratohvil dropped to his knees, paralysed. The snake pulled the tail out and Pan Kratohvil slowly folded to the ground. He was dead.

The Last Ship Out

The Procession had always been the TV event with the largest audience in Left World, but when the screens in Star Central started showing scenes of the attack live, there was hardly anyone left in the streets. Just about every goblin tram driver, gnome liftboy and pixie baker whom duty had originally prevented from following the Procession was dragged to the nearest available television screen to see for themselves what was going on. By the time Pan Kratohvil was killed, literally the whole of Star Central was glued to TV screens. All creatures, big and small, rich and poor, friends and foes gasped in horror and disbelief wherever they happened to be.

Sitting in a cheap downtown bar, Spidergranny took another shot of buckwheat whiskey to help her face the facts.

The live transmission from Fairybury went on for a while, until the link was lost and white noise filled all the screens. Then the message 'Stand By For an Important Announcement' appeared. Star Central, still in shock, remained glued to the screens.

Minutes passed without any change. Streets remained deserted, with driverless trams stopped in the middle of intersections, empty, all doors wide open. Food stalls were left unattended, steam still rising, but there was no one interested in stealing. Nobody dared move away from a TV screen.

The stand-by message faded into black and a group of uniformed men, elves and dwarves appeared, standing around a man seated at a desk in a bare room. The camera zoomed in on him.

'Brothers and sisters of Left World! This morning, the vile morphs, enemies of everything that is good and sacred, invaded Fairybury and attacked the Centennial Fair of Zandar. They struck not only at the envoys proudly carrying their colours in the Procession – No! They attacked the Honourable Pan Kratohvil, Potentate-in-Spe, and the new Master of Zandar as well! It is my sad duty to inform you that they are both dead.'

The silence in front of millions of TV screens across Left World gave way to cries of distress. The tension exploded into shock and anger, bypassing sorrow altogether. As vows of revenge reverberated throughout Left World, the announcement continued.

'The attack has now ended. The morphs have withdrawn. But I assure you, citizens of Left World, that this outrage will not pass unpunished. I promise you that all those responsible will be brought to justice, wherever they may hide. I give you my word that the collaborators of the morphs will be hunted down, whoever and wherever they may be.

'Citizens of Left World! The Crisis Staff of Zandar, assembled here behind me, was activated as soon as the first news of the attack reached Star Central. Effective immediately, the Crisis Staff will begin taking steps and introducing measures to protect Zandar from any further attacks. Firstly, an investigation is already under way to find and punish the perpetrators of this heinous attack. Furthermore, to assist the security services, and to prevent the escape of morphs and their collaborators, we hereby proclaim the State of Mondial Emergency and general curfew, effective immediately. We also hereby order the complete shutdown of all Median Tunnels until further notice.'

Immediately after the announcement, the streets of Star Central and many other worlds of Zandar began filling with people. They were scrambling to get home before the curfew was fully enforced and to find the nearest Median Port before the shutdown was complete. Any taxi, limo or rickshaw that could be found quickly filled with people desperate to reach home while they still could.

Spidergranny was suddenly left all alone in her watering hole, that is, not counting many friendly bottles of buckwheat whiskey that also chose to stay. It seemed that the Median engineers were the only people who remained at their posts as they began with the preparations for the first shutdown of Median Tunnels in history.

Almost all TV stations soon replaced the sombre music transmitted from the Crisis Staff headquarters and found a new angle on the situation. The music quickened and a flashy logo at once splashed across the screens: 'Shutdown Live!'

Later that evening, in a small deserted street in Fairybury, a broken figure slowly rose from the ground. The sky was low and gloomy, lit at places by strangely warm red light from the fires still burning on the Procession Avenue. The whole right side of Pim was hurting like hell, but when he opened his eyes and looked with dread to the right – he only saw his right leg and right arm. The other two legs and the other two arms were gone – as was the horrid head!

Three thoughts crystallized slowly in his head as he stood up propping himself against a burnt-out wall, bathed in a strange blue light that contrasted sharply with the fire at the end of the street.

First, that he was himself again. The strike calculated to kill had somehow spared him and severed him from Harry. There was no sight of the Royal Bedel anywhere around.

Second, that he was not in the lodge at Procession Avenue. Somehow he got here while he was unconscious.

And third, that there was an open gate somewhere in Star Central. A gate leading back to London.

The pain on his right side gave him a slight limp. He began to make slow progress through the narrow streets full of rubble, if progress it was, because he did not really know where he should go. He wanted to get out on a bigger street where he could try to find the way to the Median Port. All around him the houses looked empty, abandoned in haste, scarred by bullets, tetrablasters and, at places, uncomfortably large claws. He seemed to be enveloped in a bubble of strange bluish light as he walked. After about ten minutes spent wandering through a maze of small alleys, the only thing he found was a piccolo flute lying in the middle of the street on a pile of rubble. It looked so forlorn amid the devastation that Pim took pity on it. He could not get a sound out of it, but he put it in the pocket anyway.

He came to a small square at the intersection of two streets. It was getting dark. A fire was burning at the far end of one of the streets. Just as he was trying to decide which way to go, several ugly looking silhouettes appeared on the background of the fire. He quickly moved to hide but it attracted their attention.

'Hey, you!' one of them shouted, accompanied by the ominous sound of reloading of a weapon. 'Come here!' Pim stopped.

It was a group of hairy three-legged trolls. They were big for trolls, almost as big as Pim, and they had red burning eyes. One of them was limping and they were all armed. 'Identify yourself!'

'My name is Pim Pergamon and I am with the Bedel of Zandar.'

'No, you're not. Here you're on your own. Are you a morph?'

'No, of course not.'

'Yeah? And why should we believe you?' said the limping troll.

'Don't you try to play any of your morph tricks on us, or we'll blast you to pieces,' said another troll, bigger and nastier than the first.

'I am not a morph,' Pim repeated. He realized that they were not only trolls and not only armed, but drunk as well. One of them stepped towards him and poked him in the ribs with the barrel of his gun. 'Leave me alone!' Pim shouted but it only acted as a signal for the others. 'How does it feel, morph? Why don't you morph, morph?' they pushed and shoved him as they closed a circle around him sliding effortlessly around on their three legs, apart from the limping troll who couldn't move fast.

'Call the Mamluks, I want to talk to the authorities!'

'The authorities? The useless Mamluks who chickened out when morphs attacked! Look at this,' the troll pointed at his injured middle leg. 'Who needs authorities like that?'' The trolls laughed at these words, deeper than any man could laugh.

'What shall we do with him, Duane?' they turned to the limping one who seemed to be in charge.

'The same thing we did with the others.' There was a rumble of satisfied grumbling among the trolls.

'Wait, who are you anyway?' said Pim.

'We are the Provisional Resistance Committee of Fairybury,' said the troll called Duane. 'And you are under arrest.'

Just my luck, thought Pim, a bunch of politically conscious thugs. 'You can't arrest me, I'm not a morph!'

'We'll see about that.'

'I want to talk to the authorities!' Pim demanded after yet another vicious shove.

'I'll show you who's the authority around here right now!' Duane roared furiously. 'Stand against the wall! Put your hands behind your head!'

'Wait, what's going on here?' Pim protested. 'You can't just – '

'Shut up!' another troll shouted at him. 'Turn against the wall!'

In that moment a big green flash of light knocked them all off their feet. Headley's carriage, horses and all, sprang out of the flash and with lot of screeching and neighing stopped right between Pim and the vigilante trolls. Harry opened the door and pulled Pim inside.

'Go, go, go!' he shouted as the thugs tried to grab the other door of the carriage. Headley cracked the whip and the carriage jolted so forcefully that both Harry and Pim fell and found themselves folded atop of each other on the floor. In an instant the square in Fairybury was empty again, except for a few dazed trolls bowled over by yet another green flash.

Somewhere deep in the bowels of the Median Power Station in Star Central, a technician walked up to the manager and said, 'Ready to disengage, sir.'

The last of the daylight coming through tall windows high under the ceiling cast long shadows of twelve colossal conical shapes inside the cavernous generator hall.

'Never in my life did I think that I would hear these words,' said Ludo Ludbert, the Chief Engineer of the Power Station. 'And I've been around this station for quite a while.' He was a middle-aged elf. He was talking about several hundred years at least.

'I know, sir,' the technician said. 'It's a strange feeling to do exactly what we've been preventing from happening all these years.'

'Gentlemen, you are under direct orders of the Crisis Staff now,' a high ranking Mamluk said nervously pacing next to them. 'And the order is to shut down the Tunnels.'

'I know,' replied Ludo Ludbert. 'But it's not an easy thing to do for me. How is Zandar going to look without Median Tunnels? What will you Mamluks do without your *raison d'etre*?' he said rather firmly for a translucent being.

'Never mind that,' said the burly Mamluk. 'There are more important things to do now. The security of the whole of Zandar is at stake. Are you ready?'

The elf looked at his assembled staff – people, gnomes, elves and two cats in blue overalls – and nodded.

'Call the Tunnels Control.'

The Tunnels Control responded through a crackling loudspeaker. 'Stand by to shut down.'

'Begin the shutdown sequence,' the elf instructed the technician on the other side. The cathedral-like inside of the enormous Median Power Station was pierced by a loud klaxon which marked the beginning of the disengagement sequence. One by one, twelve huge generators began to decrease power accompanied by the nervous chatter of technicians ready to take them off line. A loud, dramatically impassive pre-recorded voice began to say: 'Twenty, nineteen …'

'Call the Tunnels Control,' Ludo Ludbert melancholically said to himself in the cacophony of the shutdown. 'Tell them to go home.'

Pim and Harry quickly disentangled themselves in the carriage. The last thing they wanted was to be close together again. They were in a Median Tunnel once more, flying away from Fairybury. This time the flight was accompanied by a halo of blue light and an energetic music inside the carriage that gave the whole situation a strange sense of urgency.

'I need to go to Star Central,' was the first thing Pim said.

'That's where we are going. Headley! How are we doing?' Harry shouted through the window and a head would have appeared through a small opening in front if only Headley had one. Instead, only the ruff pressed against the window and Headley's voice could be heard saying:

'I am not sure we have enough time, Sir Henry. Ever since we picked up Mr. Pergamon, we are much heavier than usual.'

'Heavier than usual? This carriage is made for six and there's only two of us!'

'I can't explain it, sir.'

'Headley, we have to get to Star Central!'

'The shutdown of Median Tunnels has begun. If we hadn't stopped to get Mr. Pergamon out of trouble, we could have made it to Star Central, but now …'

'You see? We can't make it to Star Central now because of you!' Harry said to Pim.

'Sir Henry, allow me to point out that it was your idea to jump out of the tunnels to save Mr. Pergamon from the ruffians in that alley,' said Headley.

Suddenly, the ambient music quickened as if announcing a heightened suspense. Just as Pim was about to ask where the music was coming from, a big hairy arm smashed through the window of the carriage, grabbed Harry around the neck and began to pull him out.

Pim tried to get him loose but the hand was pressing with great force. Harry tried to wriggle his way out of the grasp, his eyes bulging, but the hand was too strong. Pim called out to Headley to stop the carriage and come and help.

'I can't Mr. Pim! There is not a second to loose!' replied Headley. 'The shutdown countdown is well underway! If I stop now, we may never make it out of the tunnel!'

The music quickened again. Behind the hand, on the background of the tunnel wall which seemed to be flying past faster than ever, appeared the red burning eyes of an angry troll. He was holding on to the carriage from the outside and trying to get in, still cursing morphs.

Harry was choking and could not speak but his eyes were literally calling out. So Pim bit the troll's hand as strongly as he could. The troll let Harry go, but he would not let go of the carriage. He even managed to push a leg through the window. Harry pulled himself together quickly and struck the troll's leg. The troll whacked him with the foot and Harry folded on the floor again.

'Listen!' shouted Headley from the outside. He turned up the volume of the Tunnels Control: 'Thirteen, twelve, eleven ...' The countdown was going fast.

Headley cracked the whip again and again in a desperate attempt to get them out of the tunnel. The horses neighed in pain and pulled even faster. The troll was now almost half inside the carriage. As he turned to put the second leg in, the ambient music shifted into an even more dramatic gear.

'The door!' shouted Pim. 'The door!'

'What?' said Harry still dazed from the masterly wallop, unable to hear Pim because of the loud music.

'Nine, eight ...' the countdown went on.

'Open the door!' Pim shouted over the mad music.

'Get him off the door handle!'

Pim was looking around for something suitable to attack the troll when the trilling clarinets in the music gave him an idea. He pulled out the flute from his pocket and poked the troll in the burning eye.

'Six, five ...' said the voice from Tunnels Control as the troll shrieked and grabbed his head. Harry unlatched the door which swung open and dropped the three-legged troll into the long green abyss behind the carriage where he disappeared out of sight.

'Hurry, get up here!' shouted Headley. Pim and Harry quickly climbed out to join him. They could see a green light in front of them at the end of the tunnel.

'You've got to jump,' said Headley as the countdown reached number three.

'Are you coming with us?' asked Pim.

'Look for *De Rectorum Cineris*! And don't worry for me,' answered Headley. Then the last words from the Tunnels Control came through: 'Two, one – zero!' The carriage suddenly slowed down and Headley shouted, 'Now!'

Pim and Harry jumped together, holding hands. Enveloped in a bubble of blue light, carried by inertia, they flew in an elegant long arc, leaving the carriage and Headley behind in the fading tunnel. The music reached the climax as they disappeared in a blue flash in front of the carriage which slowly ground to a halt in complete darkness.

Pim was still holding the flute when they fell out of nowhere on a clearing in the middle of a forest.

It was some time before one of them slowly sat up on the ground. 'Where are we?' said Pim looking at the tall silver firs that surrounded the small clearing. The forest lay dark and impenetrable behind.

'I don't know,' Harry replied massaging his neck. He had landed a few feet away from the bed of leaves which softened Pim's fall. 'I didn't exactly have time to discuss it with Headley after we picked you up.'

'What is going to happen to him now that the tunnels are shut?'

'I don't know,' said Harry and looked away. 'I really don't know.'

Pim fell silent at Harry's listless words. There was not a hint of the usual grumpiness or bad temper in the old Bedel.

'Thank you for getting me out of trouble, Sir Henry,' he said.

'Never mind,' Harry replied quietly, looking glumly at the shadows of the forest around them. Pim had never seen him like this.

'Where are we? Which world is this?'

'I don't know, I told you,' Harry replied in a tired voice. 'I just don't know.'

Pim realized that it was now up to him to be cheerful. 'Look, we are finally separated now, but we are again together in the same mess – I would say that's almost funny.'

Harry did not reply.

'OK, it's not funny that we are in a mess – but boy, am I glad to be with you! Now, that's funny, don't tell me it isn't! If anybody'd told me this morning that I'd be saying anything like this before the sun was down, I would've told them they were mad. And you, too, admit it. But the way things are now –'

'Look, there is a footpath. Let's hope it leads somewhere,' Harry interrupted him. A narrow strip of slightly trampled ground could be seen winding between the trees and disappearing in the forest behind. Harry set off without uttering a word and Pim followed him.

It was dark. The sunlight barely reached the ground through the dense canopy formed by the tallest trees. The path wound left and right on the soft brown bed of fallen needles between many smaller firs that crowded the floor of the forest yearning upwards, towards a greater share of light.

It was the first time that Pim had a chance to take a good look at his other half – as a separate and distinct person, that is. Harry was tall and thin. His long face somehow made him look even taller. Despite his advanced age he was very agile, capable of sudden bursts of frenzied activity, but only when it suited him. He wore long pointy shoes and a tight brown waistcoat, always buttoned up, that must have gone out of fashion even before he was born, whenever that was. Both ends of his long thin black moustache were carefully twisted to the point of being dangerously sharp, yet Pim couldn't remember ever seeing him touch his moustache with fingers. He was prone to extreme outbursts of agitation but could, within a split second, turn into a composed high-dignitary capable of the highest order of detachment. It was hard to tell what was true and what was feigned in Sir Henry Grenfell-Moresby.

'If I knew we were going to end up in a forest, I would've brought some breadcrumbs to find our way back,' said Pim after several minutes of walking in silence.

'There is no way back, Pim. From now on, there is only forward for us.'

'Hey, this is the first time you called me by my name!'

'It's not. But I suppose one can be on first name terms when one is stuck again with one's former half.'

'I suppose so too,' agreed Pim, glad that Harry was talking again. 'So why are you going to Star Central?'

'You and I were not the only ones attacked today. The whole Fair was attacked. As you probably gathered by now, there were many dead in Fairybury.' Harry paused. 'The new Master and Pan Kratohvil are among them.'

'My goodness!!'

'That's why I have to return to Star Central. I have to join the Crisis Staff and help Otokarr organize the defence.'

'Who's Otokarr?'

'Otokarr Gnüss is the president of Kutlurg Corporation. He's a friend of mine, a good and able man. He set up the Crisis Staff of Zandar while the attack was practically still underway. His swift reaction and decision to close Median Tunnels probably saved Star Central from the same fate as Fairybury. He will do everything to protect Left World, but he can't do it on his own. Without the Master and the Potentate-In-Spe, Zandar needs a Bedel now more than ever. That is why it is imperative that I reach Star Central as soon as possible.'

'I am sorry about Pan Kratohvil, Harry,' Pim replied quietly, suddenly drained of all cheerfulness. 'My condolences.'

'Thank you.'

They walked in silence for more than an hour, each of them immersed in his own thoughts about what the future would bring. Although it was now a long time since they woke up in that big bed in Fairybury, the fresh scented forest air made them forget that they were tired and that it was actually very late back in Fairybury. Birds were singing and every now and then a ray of sunlight made its way through the canopy high above their heads to tickle them on the cheeks. They pressed on.

The path meandered between old tree stumps and rocks covered with moss and lichen until it suddenly brought them over a ridge and into a hollow dominated by two colossal pine trees. Comfortably nested between the pines was a small white cottage with a moss-covered thatched roof. A rusted sign above the door read: *Spiridon Mekas – Rare Books*.

'Ohh, distinguished gentlemen, welcome! Welcome to my humble establishment,' said Spiridon Mekas when they opened the door. 'We have old books, we have very old books and we have rarest editions! Welcome! If books is what you want, you are in the right place!'

Spiridon Mekas was the epitome of an antiquarian – dishevelled grey hair, small wire spectacles perched atop a small nose, fingers long and arthritic yet able to hold even the heaviest tome, and a passion for his trade which radiated from his old but lively eyes.

'And if books is not what we want?' Pim said just for tease.

The smile and the passion evaporated instantly. 'Then why are you here?' Spiridon Mekas responded coarsely, the look of an old viper darting toward Pim. 'And why do you bring blue light into my shop? What is it? It's not good for my eyes!'

'Dear Spiridon, is this a way to greet old clients after such a long time?' Harry replied.

'Who are you?' Spiridon Mekas strained his eyes towards Harry.

'It's me, Henry. Henry Grenfell-Moresby.'

'Ohh, Master Henry, I didn't recognize you, my eyes are not what they used to be. Thousand apologies! Oh my, oh my! Here, sit down, make yourselves comfortable.'

He quickly removed some books and blew off what seemed like a century worth of dust from a couple of ancient leather chairs to accommodate the guests in the cramped space between overladen bookshelves. 'But what brings you here if not books?'

Harry explained the events of the past day to the appalled Spiridon Mekas who sank deep in his chair. 'You don't say! Six lightning bolts – you don't say!' he kept repeating as Harry finished the description of what happened at the Fair of Zandar. Then he sprang up and locked the entrance door.

'The Tunnels are down, Mr. Mekas, you will not be getting many visitors now,' Pim said to reassure him.

'Ahh, you never know, young man. Dark days are ahead, dark indeed. And the Forest is full of creatures, old and new. I keep some very valuable books here,' said Spiridon Mekas and repeated, 'Very, very valuable books.'

'Anything on Rectorum Cinerum, per chance?' Pim remembered Headley's last words.

Spiridon's eyes narrowed into suspicion again. 'Who are you? Are you mocking me? And how do you know – '

'I'm not mocking anybody, Mr. Mekas. And I don't know – '

'You have to excuse my young friend here, Spiridon, and me as well,' said Harry. 'It was not our intention at all to disrespect you. If we have offended you in any way, we apologize, and beg for clarification.'

'*De Rectorum Cineris* – that's the proper declination – is a rare and valuable book of which I happened to have the only known copy in circulation outside the Academy Library – until it was stolen. Somebody broke into my shop with a spell more powerful than mine – more powerful than what I could afford, anyway.'

'What kind of a book was it? Was it very valuable?' asked Pim.

'*De Rectorum Cineris* is a book about an ancient ruler called the Ruler of Ashes – Rector Cinerum in Latin. I've had it on the shelf for ages, and then about a month ago, all of a sudden, it was stolen. I have no idea why.'

'Must have been a particularly keen historian who nicked it,' Harry's face widened into an ironic grin.

'And it was the only copy of that book?' said Pim.

'The only copy that ever went on sale in Zandar. There is only one more in existence, the legal deposit in the Academy Library.'

'Only one copy on sale?' said Pim. 'How can that be?'

'You should write to the publisher, perhaps,' Spiridon Mekas said drily. 'In the meantime, may I interest you, gentlemen, in a rare little tome that I happen to have in stock? I think you will find it more useful than *De Rectorum Cineris*, given the new situation in Zandar. It's called The Book of Gates.'

Spiridon Mekas went to one of the shelves and scanned the books murmuring to himself. 'Now, let me see. I have the entire stock inside my head. And I happen to know that I have two books with this title … Ah, here's one: the Book of Gates, published in Redmond, Washington in 2012 – but who would want to read that … And the other one should be … let me see … Aha! Mr. Pergamon, would you be so kind to fetch it for me?'

Pim stood on a small stool and looked at the strange titles: Irish Swordsmen of France; Cawdallor, the King of Rats; Acanthus Leaves; Mousetraps and their Influence on the Character and Achievement of the Feline Race. Many of the titles he didn't understand because they were in Latin. 'Harry, do you understand Latin?'

'Of course I understand Latin. I am the Royal Bedel, the Proclamator Extraordinary and – '

'Most of the books with Latin titles are not actually in Latin. Latin titles are popular because they sound more learned,' Spiridon Mekas explained. 'Yes, up there! The small one right next to *Frogborg and Other Ikea Stories*.'

It was a small leather-bound book with well-worn covers. Pim read out loud the golden print on the front page: '*Book of Gates*, by Arne Saknussemm, Upsalla 1721.'

'Yes, Mr. Pergamon, that's the book you are looking for.'

'And why would we be looking for this book?' Harry said distrustfully.

'Because this is the only remaining compendium of natural gates between worlds of Zandar,' Spiridon Mekas replied.

'Troglodytes of Hernia!' Harry jumped at hearing these words. 'We'll buy it. How much is it?'

'Ninety-nine thalers.'

'Whooaa! A hundred thalers?!'

'No, ninety-nine. And that's with cash discount already applied,' replied Spiridon Mekas unfazed. 'My credit card machine is dead now that the Tunnels are down.'

'It was dead every time I remember coming to this shop,' said Harry.

'Yes, but now it's really dead,' said Spiridon Mekas matter-of-factly.

It took Harry a couple of minutes of wriggling and extricating silver thalers from every imaginable pocket and recess of his clothes to put together the ninety-nine thalers necessary to buy the book.

'Thank you gentlemen. I am sure a time will come when you will need this book,' said Spiridon Mekas.

'We need it right now, we need to get to Star Central,' said Pim.

'You don't need it just yet. There is only one way out of here now that the tunnels are closed and I can show it to you. Come here, help me move this.'

It took the combined strength of Pim and Harry, and lots of coughing in the dust, to move aside a cupboard full of old books. Behind the cupboard was a small door. Spiridon Mekas opened the door. There was nothing behind, just darkness.

'If you want to make use of the book you just bought and eventually get to Star Central, you have to pass through here first. This is the only other natural gate in the Forest that I know of. My great-great-grandfather built the cottage around it, so it fell out of use and is almost forgotten today. I bet it's not even in the book.'

'I'll write to the publisher,' said Harry. 'Where does it lead?'

'I don't know. I never left here since I was born. Never needed to, never wanted to. But it's the only way out of the Forest that I know now that Median Tunnels are closed.'

'I've always said, the service you get from independent booksellers – simply incomparable,' said Harry. Pim looked at him. They exchanged brief glances. Then they bade farewell to Spiridon Mekas and crossed into the darkness.

It seemed at first that the antiquarian had played a joke on them and locked them into the cupboard. When they passed through the doors, they found themselves in complete darkness. But when Pim turned around, the doors were not there any more. And the blue light that had mystified him since his awakening was gone. The two of them were not in a cupboard, they were somewhere else. They were in another world. The only thing was – they did not know which world.

'So what do we do?' asked Pim. Now he was really glad that Harry was with him.

'Let's try to feel our way around. But be careful, you could bump into just about anything. And hold my hand, we don't want to lose each other.'

They started to grope around cautiously in the dark. It was very unpleasant to extend your arm into the blackness knowing that you could touch 'just about anything'. Luckily, Pim thought of the flute in his pocket. Better flute than fingers, he thought. But as soon as he took out the flute, an eerie music began playing in the darkness.

'What's that?'

'I don't know,' said Harry. 'Just disregard it. This way.'

They were moving very slowly forward, feeling the ground with their feet. Harry extended his arms left and right, while Pim waved the flute before them. The violins that came from nowhere kept raising the pitch until Pim hit something, and a musical accent scared them both.

'I don't mind the darkness, but if they could just switch off the music!' said Harry.

'They?' Pim repeated, and there came another musical accent.

'It's a bottle,' said Harry groping. 'Two bottles, no, three … actually, there are many bottles. On a shelf, I think. Wait!' Pim could hear the friction of a cork being pulled out, a soft plop and Harry's nostrils inhaling air.

'Hey, it's rum!' Then there was the sound of two or three good gulps. 'And a damn fine rum at that!'

'Forget the rum! Let's just find the way out of here,' said Pim.

'Alright, alright, I am moving already – aargh!!!'

'What happened, are you alright?' said Pim.

'No, I'm not alright. I hit my big toe. There's a step here,' said Harry while the music took a comical turn, as if to spite him. 'No, wait, it's a staircase. I think we are in a basement of some sort. Let's go up.'

The steps were squeaking, Harry was cursing his big toe and the music followed them on the scale as they climbed up the stairs. They found a door at the top and opened it. The music stopped.

They entered a dim grimy room with a low ceiling and straw on the wooden floor. Before them were a few roughly hewn wooden benches and tables with remains of a dinner and a sooty fireplace with a big cauldron in the corner. The fire under the cauldron was about to go out. A woman with a bucket and a broom came in through a side door and said:

'Dinner's off, gentlemen, you are too late. The fire's out. It's past closing time. Are you staying for the night?'

'Would you happen to have two beds for two travellers?' said Harry.

'No, sir, I don't,' she said. 'But I have one bed that can take two travellers.'

Pim and Harry looked at each other wearily.

'That will be just fine,' they replied resigned to share a bed again and the landlady took them upstairs and showed them the room.

'Just one more thing,' said Harry as she was leaving a lit candle by the bed. 'What is the name of this fine establishment?'

'The Slimy Tentacle Inn.'

The Median lag took its toll. Pim and Harry fell asleep in the blink of an eye and woke up very late the next day. They almost missed the lunch – fish and turnips – as well. The Slimy Tentacle Inn turned out to be a low building made of massive granite stone, with fortress-like walls and gneiss slates on a roof overgrown with lichen. In the back the house leant against a tall cliff, while in the front the windows looked on to a small harbour.

'Sea View only available,' the landlady told them proudly, although the inn did not look like a place where guests came to require anything more particular than a straw bed. The whole landscape consisted of a small bay with the sea on one side and an inaccessible mountain on the other. The houses of the village barely squeezed in. Those exposed to the sun were bright white, while the less fortunate ones in the shadow were darker and mossy. The bay was just big enough to accommodate a shipyard next to the harbour where a brand new brig stood on the keel-block fully rigged, bedecked with colourful flags and ready for launch. The sun was high in the sky and there were few people outside apart from old fishermen repairing nets.

'I can't find this place in the Book of Gates,' said Harry as they were sitting on a bench in the harbour next to a somewhat unsettling plaque that read *Slimy-Tentacle-sur-Mer – twinned with Slimy-Tentacle-sous-Mer*. 'Either I am not reading it right or it's not in the book.'

'Let me see,' said Pim.

'Have a go,' Harry replied with an enigmatic smile and handed him the book.

'He cheated us!' Pim exclaimed when he opened the book. 'This is not the book we had yesterday. This book is in runic!'

'No, he did nothing of the sort,' said Harry. 'It's just that you did not bother to read further than the front page.'

'How could I assume that the rest was in runic? You didn't see that yesterday either, when you doled out all those thalers for that ridiculous price, did you?'

'Oh, does it really matter?' said Harry. 'I can read runic.'

'Oh, right then.'

'Well, a bit.'

'A bit? Harry, just how much is a bit? Can we use the book at all?'

'Of course we can! I can't read handwriting in runic, but I can certainly go about a simple tourist guide. That's what this is, a tourist guide. You find the place you look for and it tells you how to get out of there.'

'Handwritten runic? Runes were chiselled in stone or carved in wood. There's no such thing as handwritten runic!'

'Oh yes, there is. Lundonian trolls write in runes every day. Have you ever seen a Lundonian troll?'

'No.'

'When you have seen one, you will have seen why they need no chisels. Never shake hands with a Lundonian troll.'

'So why can't you find how to get out of here and go to Star Central?' Pim asked.

'There is no place that looks like this in the book,' replied Harry.

'Are you sure?'

'Completely!'

'And every world has at least one natural gate in and one gate out?'

'That's what I was given to understand.'

'Hmmm,' Pim said looking across the boats in the harbour gently rocking embraced by the breakwater. 'You know what that means?'

'No. What?'

'The gate is on the other side of the sea.'

There was a silence. Then Harry said, 'There must be some other way.'

'Look Harry, our landlady told me this morning in no uncertain terms that Slimy-Tentacle-sur-Mer has only two branches of economy: building ships and seeing them off. Many various beings have passed through Slimy-Tentacle-sur-Mer through the years, I was told, and there would always be a ship ready standing at the launch. And none of them came back. Ships only sail out from this harbour. The landlady also told me that a group of sailors arrived in Slimy-Tentacle-sur-Mer the day before yesterday. They were the last arrival before the Median Tunnels closed. They are the crew for the ship in the harbour. I am sure it can only mean one thing: there is a gate on the other shore.'

'Or in its twin borough!' Harry replied. 'Has it not occurred to you that the phrase "none of them came back" could have an altogether different meaning? There must be some other way.'

'Which other way?'

'I don't know. Another way.'

'Why?'

'I get seasick.'

'Great.'

The brig in the shipyard stood ready for launch. It seemed that not many exciting things had happened lately in Slimy-Tentacle-sur-Mer because the village came out in full force for the event – a few dozen people joined by the curious Pim and grumpy Harry. It was an elaborate affair. There were speeches recalling the glorious maritime tradition of Slimy Tentacle, extolling the workmanship of its shipbuilders and deploring the lack of interest in time-honoured crafts among the young. It was a hot afternoon and the speeches went on and on as the solitary champagne bottle suspended above the hull languished in the sun waiting to fall to its fate. Pim felt hot. He had unbuttoned just about every piece of clothing that was decent to unbutton when the flute fell out of his pocket.

As it hit the ground, it bounced once, twice, three times and began swelling and growing and, before Pim could even see what was happening, it transformed into a small orchestra.

'One, two, three, four!' a trumpet counted and the band hit off with a roaring tune which must have been written with nothing but ship launches in mind, because very soon the speaker finished the speech, the guests shouted 'Hoorah!' and the champagne bottle enthusiastically hurled itself into the hull. The Pride of Slimy Tentacle, now officially named, began the slow slide into the sea accompanied by much hat-throwing and a grandiose march from the band that had so fortuitously materialized out of Pim's pocket.

'What's all this?' Pim said to Harry.

'You should know, you brought him along, not me,' said Harry.

'I only brought a flute!'

'Whether it's a flute or a double bass or a tuba, it's Band. He is all his instruments and all his players. He is the Marching Band of Zandar.'

'A Band is a "he"?'

'No, he is Band. That's how he's called. It's his name, profession, hobby and probably father's name as well.'

'How monotonous his forms must look like.'

The orchestra finished playing and then shrunk into a small group of instruments which hurried back to Pim.

'My friend!' blew the trumpet. 'My saviour!' bellowed the bass-saxophone. 'If you hadn't shown mercy on me back in Fairybury, it would have been the end of me,' the violin fiddled and winked flirtatiously at Pim.

'Well, you were just a flute then – ' he tried to explain but they would have none of it.

'Nonsense! A good heart is a good heart. Flute or double bass makes no difference!' Band exclaimed with a rousing musical accent as the most direct way of showing his appreciation.

'If you are ever in trouble and need my help, just whistle this' – here the piccolo flute played five notes – 'and I will immediately come to your help!'

'Well, thank you, I don't know what to say,' said Pim.

'You don't really believe that, do you?' said Harry rolling his eyes in exasperation, but Pim decided to pay no attention to him: 'If I ever need a flute I promise I will call no other flute but you.'

'No, no, no, no!' more instruments popped out shaking their valves and strings in disapproval. 'You did not understand,' said the cello. 'I am one,' explained the timpani. 'I am not separate instruments,' added the French horn. 'I am Band, pleased to meet you,' the bassoon rounded it up.

'I will try to remember that,' said Pim.

'Anyway, are you joining the ship?' said Band. 'I hear it is to set sail with the evening tide. The ship is bound for Port Cockaigne in Dembeliland and the captain is keen to take on passengers.'

'We have other pressing business,' Harry replied to Band's great surprise.

'What business could possibly be more pressing than a visit to the legendary land of everlasting content and happiness where milk and honey flow in rivers and roast partridges darken the skies?'

'Our business is none of your business,' Harry replied curtly.

'Oh, well, suit yourselves then,' all the instruments replied in unison, turned on their spikes and left for the harbour.

'This was totally uncalled for,' Pim said to Harry when Band was gone.

'Oh yes, it was called for. We don't want every Tom, Dick and Harry to know we have the Book of Gates now that the Tunnels are down. Don't think that we are the only ones trying to make it to Star Central. The morphs, for one, would love to find a way there.'

'Alright, alright. But will you at least look for Dembeliland in the Book of Gates now?'

'I am looking, I am looking!' said Harry and spent the next five minutes shuffling the pages of the book. 'Well, who would have thought!'

'What? What?' Pim was impatient to know.

'According to this book, there are many gates in Dembeliland.'

'Good. Any of them leads to Star Central?'

'Many of them lead to Star Central.'

'So you changed your mind after all? You know, I knew all along that you'd come,' said Band when Pim hauled a still reluctant Harry to the dock. 'After all, who would want to miss out on roast partridges that take off only to fly straight into your mouth?'

'To be honest, sounds like a choking hazard to me,' said Pim. 'But that's not the most important thing right now.'

'We don't have the money to pay for the journey,' said Harry, secretly hoping that it may stave off the passage.

'Oh, that's alright,' said Band. 'I already spoke to Captain Bassalian. He's agreed to take all three of us on board. You gentlemen rescued me from Fairybury and it is only right that I repay you somehow.'

'How will you pay for the passage?' asked Harry.

'The captain asked me, and I gracefully agreed, to provide the musical accompaniment for the voyage.'

'Just when I thought that things could not get any worse ...'

And so Pim, Harry and Band boarded the ship in a single file over an old, worn-out stepping stone where many strange feet have trod through centuries on their way of no return. The anchor was raised precisely when the sound of Barisal guns came from the sea. The ship slowly drifted away from the dock lined up with well-wishers waving their handkerchiefs. The sails were unfurled and favourable wind took her to the open sea. Slimy Tentacle and its mountain, the last firm ground they knew, soon became just a dot astern. The ship slowly disappeared in the sunset, carrying a band playing sea shanties, a not-so-young young man who wanted to get home and a grumpy civil servant about to get sick.

The Academy of Obvious

Somewhere just off Horn Lane in West Acton, a suburb of London, in a terraced house not much different from all other terraced houses in all other suburbs of London, a long persistent bell rang at the door – for the third time. Comfortably lying on the floor of his room in the middle of discarded T-shirts, cables, consoles and pizza boxes, his eyes glued to the screen in front of him, Mehdi said to his younger sister Mia, also for the third time, 'Can't you see I'm busy playing? Go and open the door!' And for the third time Mia responded, 'Can't you see I'm busy watching you – I can't possibly!' Then their father's voice roared from his room for the first, but sufficient time, and Mehdi pushed his sister off the sofa with a well-practised nudge. 'Go open the door. It must be Andy and I really have to finish this.'

Things had not been going well for Mehdi ever since he returned from ACG without the place in the testing program that he coveted so much. Advanced Computers&Games, the company to which he had already devoted so much of his pocket money, was supposed to solve all his problems that morning – well, most of them: finding the officially recognized work experience for his final year, getting a chance to play computer games that not even his father could veto, showing his younger sister that, unlike her, he was a grownup, a *serious* person to be taken *seriously*, and most importantly, boosting his self-esteem just enough to face his friend Andy who was now leaning on his doorbell with all the gusto of the person who *did* get the place in that same ACG testing – yes, the testing from where Mehdi was sent away! Mehdi! The Player of Players!

Mia finally stood up and let out the deep sigh of the eternally oppressed classes – why me?! Of course, dodging anything that had to be done in and around the house in favour of her older brother was a pursuit that occupied most of her time. But, truth be told, she also genuinely enjoyed watching him play the games. He was so quick and so smart and just so deft at everything he did that simply sitting next to him and watching him play was probably the nicest pleasure she knew. He revealed so many new worlds that fascinated her, and slew so many monsters that scared her – that he was really her one true hero.

Of course, it would not do if he actually found that out. No. Never.

So Mia went to open the door and came back with a boy of Mehdi's age. He looked different from her brother in almost every respect – cooler, taller, more muscular, even his pimples were bigger than Mehdi's – except one: Mehdi and Andy both had a crop of unruly hair. But while Mehdi's hair looked impatient to jump off and run away from the top of his head, Andy had smothered his in layers and layers of thick gel reapplied many times over. Being in control was important to him, even if it meant that the world at large could perceive him in only two possible ways – 'Utterly ridiculous!' or 'Cool dude.' He was counting on cool.

While his pimples, frankly speaking, would have made anybody else shrink in embarrassment, his manners were, surprisingly, those of a pretty self-important person who always enjoyed being ahead of others. Mehdi was his best friend – and his favourite person to be ahead of.

Of course, Mehdi would never accept anything like it. Except that one thing – the one that really bothered him. It was the main reason why Mehdi was not overjoyed to see Andy today. He simply knew that Andy was going to find a way of bringing it up. He had done it every time they had a conversation in the past couple of weeks. You just had to wait.

Not for long, though. His own twelve-year old sister brought it on him: 'Andy, can you show me again that earpiece they gave you in ACG?' Mia said to Andy who was only too glad to oblige. He took a small earpiece from his pocket and started to explain to Mia how he was selected for the equipment testing in ACG – yes, the same testing for which her brother was not selected, aha. Yes, there were many candidates, but only a select few were chosen. He explained how they trained him for the experiment and how they gave him this earpiece to maintain contact at all times.

'But there was no experiment,' Mehdi said from the floor barely taking his eyes off the game. 'The lights went out before you could start, didn't they?'

'Yes, and we were all, like, plunged into darkness – '

'And you didn't get to maintain any contact through your earpiece,' Mehdi continued. 'There was no experiment and you didn't do any testing. They sent you home instead, didn't they?'

'Yes, but they told me that they'll call me as soon as all the systems are go again,' said Andy sensing that this conversation was leading nowhere. 'And you, have you find where you'll do your work experience?'

'I'll find a better place to do my work experience.'

'Aren't you just being jealous, Mehdi?' Mia said and looked at her brother, testing the limits of his endurance. Mehdi managed to remain silent, just barely.

Almost a full minute went by without mention of the ill-fated ACG selection procedure until a calculatedly wide-eyed Mia asked Andy to describe, just once more, how it came to be that he was selected for the testing.

Mehdi almost missed a monster when he heard that. She was doing this on purpose! Sometimes it really wasn't easy to decide who could be a bigger pain in the neck – best friends or little sisters?

On reflection, little sisters. Definitely little sisters.

'And the software crisis that struck the ACG systems on Monday was an unfortunate consequence of the violent thunderstorm that struck the city and in which many electricity-based facilities were stricken besides ACG. It was not in any way connected with routine experiments in … Wait, underline, in any way. No, wait, leave as it was, I don't want to sound panicky. Have you got that? Good. What? Twice struck, once stricken? What about it? So what if it's all in one sentence?'

Somewhere on the upper floors of the ACG skyscraper, not much below Mr. Furthermore's 360 degrees office, ACG Chief of Security Dabney McKitterick was dictating a memo. He was a big burly man, barely fitting into his office chair, with a thick moustache worthy of a Middle Eastern dictator that his secretary suspected he grew mostly to offset his mild, almost sheepish eyes. Dabney McKitterick thought of himself as a man of action, not words, and his memos often went through a laborious dictating process. He always knew very well, however, what he wanted to say. It was just putting it into words that bothered him. That is why a knock on the door came as a welcome distraction.

'Ah, just the man I wanted to see. Come on in. We'll finish this later, Gladys. You can go now.'

Gustav was shown into Dabney's office and the two men sat opposite each other. They looked and behaved very differently. Gustav sat upright, uncomfortable, looking at framed diplomas for various martial arts on the walls, most of which now had a distinct yellow faded look to them. Dabney was laid-back in his chair, chewing gum and shuffling papers on the desk. Gustav looked almost like a student, while Dabney's balding head and the stiff moustache, combined with his natural imperious style, could have been that of a headmaster.

'Well, young man, I am glad that I can inform you that the report is in and that our internal investigation has cleared you of any responsibility for the malfunctions during the testing you conducted as Research Director a few days ago in Laboratory 21.'

'Great. That's what I told you in the first place.'

'There was an electrical storm that day and a lot of equipment malfunctioned. It was not only your lab that was affected. Hey, not only labs, Personnel and Security, too, ran into problems on Monday. I tell you, it was one helluva storm. Nothing to do with you. In other words, you don't have to lose sleep over anything.'

'I am glad to hear that,' said Gustav. 'But did you find out what happened to that guy, Pim Pergamon, who was inside the lab when things started to go wrong?'

'Ah, what happened?' Dabney threw his arms theatrically into the air. 'The circuits must've malfunctioned and opened the door. So he got out. That's what happened. Everything else was his prank – relax.'

'But the door was hermetically sealed when I arrived,' said Gustav.

'You must be confused about that detail, that's all.'

'But I am telling you that I was the one who opened the doors.'

Dabney had spent almost all his working years in ACG, steadily rising through the ranks of the security service – which he was responsible for making a Directorate in the first place – and he never had a boss who did not think that McKitterick could not keep things under control. If things did go out of hand, Dabney made sure to proclaim that the security situation was intensifying. No memo of his with such heading was ever challenged.

He became impatient and waved a piece of paper in front of Gustav. 'Look, it's your word against my official investigation.'

'But I know what I saw – he disappeared behind closed doors.'

'Listen, Gustav. Anybody who wants to claim that somebody disappeared on my watch should better come up with some hard evidence – or,' Dabney waved another paper, 'think hard about their Performance Appraisal Report for this year.'

The two men looked at each other.

'The door was not closed. The guy walked away. End of story,' said Dabney. 'Look, Monday was pretty chaotic, lightning and everything. They say Lab 21 is going to be out of order for a long time. And we still haven't reactivated all the floors, this is a big building and we are just too busy. We had an official Security Situation. With a capital S – two in fact! Many people were just scared. Your guy is not the only one missing. Hey, nobody saw that motivational consultant they hired, Pingvarsson, ever since he arrived. But nobody's making a fuss about it.'

'That's because he observes the work process from the inside.'

'Yeah, whatever. Anyway, I see that you applied for a position in the X9 project.'

'That's correct,' said Gustav.

'Just between the two of us, that project also ran into troubles on Monday.' Dabney's face hardened. 'That's our biggest and most ambitious project so far. We need people there who share a common vision. Our common vision. Do you understand me?'

Gustav seemed to chew his lower lip but remained silent. After some time Dabney lost patience and pushed a piece of paper across the desk towards him. 'Your transfer to X9 is on hold. You'll be assigned to another department instead.'

'On hold? Until when?'

'Until such time when virtue is rewarded with love and honesty with fortune.'

'You mean to say – '

'I mean to say never. But if you soften up in your new department, you can always come back to me.'

'What new department?'

'You've been reassigned – to Customer Call Centre. I hear they are all very relaxed there,' Dabney said and turned away from Gustav with a theatrical lack of interest. As Gustav was leaving the office with his new assignment in hand, Dabney shouted after him, 'And remember: people don't disappear just like that! Not on my watch! Not in ACG!'

Barney burped. Very softly. But it was enough to awake Edna from her uneasy slumber in a forgotten storage room somewhere inside the ACG Tower.

She had spent the first night trembling in fear, afraid to fall asleep. For several hours she stood with her back against the door, right next to the hole which was supposed to be the emergency circuit-breaker for the door. All that time she was looking intently at the round yellow object in front of her and listening for voices in the corridor. At first she thought she would be quickly rescued from her unenviable situation. When it became clear that it was night and that nobody would be coming soon, Edna left her position at the door and climbed on a desk still covered in plastic, the one place in the storage room where her enemy could not reach her. But even there she could not fall asleep immediately because she was terrified that she might lose an arm or a leg if it dangled off the desk in the middle of the night.

When she was awoken by voices in the corridor, she jumped from the desk and banged on the door. But her banging awoke the yellow thing too. It moved towards her, so she quickly scrambled back to the desk screaming for help. Nobody came to open the door of the storage room. After that she spent all her waking hours in her sanctuary on the desk hoping for a janitor or somebody to come and rescue her.

After the first night which she spent awake, Edna had lost track of time. Without sunlight, under the perpetual light of a single fluorescent tube on the ceiling, she entered a counter-cycle and began to spend days asleep and nights awake. And so, when she listened, no matter how intently, she could hear no sounds in the corridor.

Throwing more printer toner to the yellow thing seemed to pacify it. When she was hungry, she would first throw some printer toner to the other side of the storage room. Then she would dare to get off the desk and pillage the boxes with supplies for ACG vending machines which she found after the first night. She lived on Coke and chocolate bars – and for once she did not feel guilty about it. But even the sound of opening a can of Coke would make her jolt.

It was during those lonely hours that Edna remembered how the staff in her department would secretly rejoice when she was away from the office. She always knew that they didn't like her and she didn't care about it, but now, for the first time, she wished they did like her. Or just cared for her. Or simply noticed her. Or anything! She was a human being, for goodness' sake, no different from her staff.

That was a novel thought.

When a burp woke her up, she decided that she had to do something. She threw more toner to the yellow thing and it dutifully moved to the other end of the room. Then she rummaged through the shelves until she found a piece of paper and a pencil. 'Help! I am locked in the storage room! Get me out!' she wrote in her craggy handwriting and slid the paper under the door. Then she quickly returned to the desk but couldn't help slumbering again. She didn't even notice that the yellow thing was not busy eating the toner. It was busy observing her.

Later that day, a cleaner with huge headphones over his ears came along pushing a floor-polishing machine and moving his body to the rhythm of the inaudible music. He picked up the paper absent-mindedly. Seeing that something was written on it, he decided not to throw it into the garbage. He pinned it to a nearby bulletin board instead – from which it must have fallen in the first place – and continued his round bathed in the never-ending led light that permeated the ACG Tower at all hours.

The bulletin board next to the storage room was full of various notices posted one on top of the other. There were administrative circulars, such as the one informing the staff about a new safety-security systems for doors being installed and asking for their understanding during the six-week installation period. There were Dilbert caricatures, almost brand new IKEA sofas for sale and hamster sanctuaries seeking volunteers for Thursday night shifts.

Edna's plea for help ended up right next to a plea for an exceptionally neat, tidy and clean roommate who didn't mind dog's hair. But before anybody could read it and figure out what to do, another notice was pinned right on top of it. It went like this:

ACG SECURITY DIRECTORATE
Office of the Director of Security
Extraordinary Security Circular no. 11/008
- strictly confidential -
From: the Desk of the Director of Security

To: All staff, all grades, contractors, visiting staff, interns, all
Cc: the Owners (by pneumatic post)
Re: Current Security Situation and Staff Attitudes in ACG

Dear all,

Despite the quick normalization of the situation in ACG, the unpleasant events of the past week have once again highlighted the need for utmost vigilance and a heightened circumspection among the ACG staff members, especially when responding to unsubstantiated hearsay. It is by now well established that the software crisis that spread through the ACG systems late on Monday evening was an unfortunate consequence of the violent thunderstorm that struck the city and disrupted many electricity-based facilities besides ACG. It was not in any way connected with routine experiments in any of our laboratories.

All staff are once again reminded that they are expected to act in a responsible and constructive way in the current sensitive security climate. All reports of missing persons within ACG have been thoroughly investigated and found to be false. Claims to the contrary are being spread by a handful of ill-disposed individuals intent on creating an atmosphere of apprehension and dubiety. Such individuals should be well aware that their attitude could hardly remain unregistered in their Performance Appraisal Report.

As you all know by now, the launch date of our new product, codenamed X9, is approaching fast. It will confirm this company's position at the cutting edge of information technology and ensure an unprecedented market share. I am sure that the great progress made so far is filling every ACG staff member with pride and enthusiasm, as per instruction 10/008.

Dabney McKitterick
Director of Security

The Pride of Slimy Tentacle swayed lazily in the calm. The wind had died towards dawn, as had Harry's nausea, and the sea was perfectly smooth. It was several days since they had left the port, but neither Pim nor Harry had adjusted to life at sea. True to his word, Harry had been seasick most of the time – and grumpier than ever –

while Pim had been annoyed to discover that the constant breaking of waves, tightening of ropes and grating of ship's timbers prevented him from having a good night's sleep.

Band on the other hand must have been born on a boat. Unlike the two sufferers below, he spent all his time on deck, to-ing and fro-ing from bow to stern, inspecting the rigging and asking a lot of questions about sails, ropes, clouds and winds. It had soon become obvious that none of the sailors was very talkative, but Band was undaunted. He found one person willing to engage in conversation, the bosun called Bangus McBroom. He was a charming character on the verge of complete toothlessness with a bushy, completely round white beard who had almost as many questions as Band. A friendly soul, he would answer every question of Band with a question of his own.

'I noticed that whenever we have a lot of sails on, there is a lot of wind. So why doesn't the captain always put on more sails to bring on more wind?' Band would stop Bangus McBroom on the forecastle.

'The skipper's command is my … er, command. But tell me, what's the best port in Dembeliland where a man can get some really good rum for his money?' Bangus McBroom would mumble through his round white beard.

'Wouldn't you get closer to rum faster if the captain adopted my proposal and put out all the sails?'

'Wouldn't you say that a good rum is worth waiting for?'

'Wouldn't you two stop your unduly persistent conversation so a man can have some peace now that the sea is finally calm?' a third voice could be heard from below. It was Harry, making his first visit to the deck since they set sail.

'The question at issue,' Band promptly informed him, 'is where can a man get some good fun for his money in Port Cockaigne?'

'You don't need any money to have good fun in Dembeliland. That's the whole point of this particular concept. But a man in my position has more important things on his mind than having fun in Dembeliland.'

'What position would that be, guv?' Bangus McBroom asked – as envisaged by Harry – and was met with the full recitation of Harry's titles, ending with the assertion that, 'In these troubled times, in the absence of both the Master and the Potentate-in Spe, the Bedel has a duty to place himself at the disposal of Zandar.'

'Somehow it doesn't look to me like the whole of Zandar is on the edge of their seats waiting for you to come to the rescue,' observed Band.

'How things look or don't look to you is, mercifully, entirely immaterial to Zandar,' retorted Harry just as Pim appeared on deck complaining that the heat below was unbearable.

'Believe me, that's nothing compared to this discussion.'

'Oh, the topic of our discussion does not entirely suit Sir Henry here,' said Band. 'What else could we be discussing?'

'Why don't you ask our young companion here to tell us something about himself. Such as, where he really came from. I am sure we would all be delighted to hear that,' said Harry looking at Pim.

'Yes, tell us about yourself – what's the best rum you ever had?' Bangus McBroom joined in.

'Better start by telling us where you come from,' said Band.

'Well, it's not so easy to explain,' Pim tried to extricate himself.

'Rubbish! Of course it's easy to explain,' Band would have none of it. 'Who is your father?'

'Oh, it's not that important,' said Pim.

'The heck it's not important,' said Band. 'My father was the Chief Pipe in Hamelin. I am not just anybody, you know.'

'I am so glad to hear that.'

'So why don't you tell us about your parents?' Band insisted. 'What's wrong with them? Are they dead?'

'Worse. They are dentists.'

'What is a dentist?' the bosun felt compelled to ask.

'Look, I am not that close to my parents,' Pim decided to give in to avoid further pestering. 'They are two very intelligent and very eloquent people, highly educated, capable of understanding everything – except each other. I grew up listening to their constant bickering and endless streams of witty put-downs and acrid one-ups. They kept changing jobs to keep up with the most lucrative markets. I was born in the Hague, but by the time I was fifteen I had lived in Aspen, Sydney, New Delhi, Prague and Dubai – follow the yellow tooth road, my father used to say. He thought it was funny. So as soon as I could, I went to live and work with Uncle Pohadka in London. I help him in his workshop in Brick Lane, where he makes and sells novelties and fireworks. We had a quarrel recently. I left him in anger and I very much want to go back to him.'

'Back? I say we should all be going forward, not backward in our lives,' said Band.

'Of course you do, you nitwit!' Harry roared at him. 'You are a marching band!'

'And I would like to go on with my life, but in my world – not here,' said Pim. 'This is not my world.'

'What is so special about your world?' asked Bangus McBroom.

'Oh, in my world, there are deep blue seas and high snow-capped mountains, and endless plains and turquoise lagoons, there are mountains and deserts, there are many forests and jungles, more animals than you can think of and – what I like most of all – my world is green when seen from close by, but blue when seen from afar!' Pim suddenly sparkled with the inexplicable passion people have only for things they've lost. 'We also have great bagels.'

'I don't know about the bagels, but the rest sounds like a thousand other places I know,' Band was unmoved by the description.

'Oh, if only it was like any other place you know, then I would be able to go back. But my world is what you here call Right World.'

'It is most certainly nothing of the kind!' Harry cut in. 'Your world may be one of the outer worlds, but it is certainly not beyond Hernia. Or the Dandiprat Grove. Or the Goblin Forest.'

'The outer worlds are unknown and dangerous,' Bangus McBroom said solemnly, obviously in awe before someone from the outer worlds.

'The true unknown has always lain beyond the outer worlds,' Harry conceded, 'but danger is now all around us. Haven't you heard what happened in Fairybury?'

'What?' Bangus McBroom replied with the innocence of the uninformed. When Harry began telling him about the attack on the Procession, he quickly stopped him. 'Wait. The skipper'd better hear this,' he said and went down to fetch the captain.

Pim looked over the vast expanse of the tranquil sea. How beautiful it looked now, so still and so immense.

Everybody on deck listened intently to the news about the attack on Fairybury. The captain kept stroking his black beard and drawing vigorous puffs from his pipe until his head was completely enveloped in a cloud of smoke, beard and all. When Harry was finished, the captain declared from inside the cloud that he did not like morphs. A murmur of approval could be heard from all hands on deck.

'Excuse my ignorance, but who exactly are morphs?' said Pim. 'I mean, Band here can also change his shape. Does that mean that you, too, are a morph?'

'How dare you!' Band roared over eight octaves. 'I have never been so offended in my life! Call me a morph! Why don't you look at yourself first? Remember how you looked like when you were born, ha? Well, you morphed quite a bit in the meantime.'

'Oh, stop it, it's a silly comparison,' said Harry.

'Not sillier than him calling me a morph just because I am the finest self-propelled orchestral piece in the whole of Zandar.'

'Morphs are different, very different,' the captain drew another puff and began to explain from the cloud that now seemed to perpetually occupy the space around his head. 'There are many beings in Left World who can change from their own shape into something else and back. Why, almost any wizard can do it. But morphs are the only ones who have no primordial shape of their own. They are always forced to be something or someone else and are unable to keep any shape permanently. They truly do not exist as themselves, only as others.

'Nobody knows the origins or history of this ancient race, led by one called Psalmanazar, except that they have been around since the beginning of Time and that the fearsome Psalmanazar is eternally old. They have a reputation for being hostile to all others, even other members of their race. They form no couples, have no families and cultivate no friendships.'

'And that's precisely why the attack on the Procession in Fairybury was so unusual,' said Harry. 'I have never heard of any such gathering of morphs ever before.'

'So, whoever organised them must be quite a persuader,' concluded Pim.

'Exactly,' said Harry. 'And I know of only one such powerful agent – fear.'

'Morphs afraid? Rubbish!' replied Band.

'Don't underestimate the power of fear. It happened before. Haven't they taught you about the Kaymak Betrayal? Instil fear in the heart of a great power, and it will shed all semblance of civilisation and start a merciless war.'

'That's true, I have seen it happen in my world,' said Pim. 'Then again, sometimes mere greed will suffice.'

'What I am saying,' said Harry, 'is that you have to bear in mind that morphs cannot, by their very nature, assume any permanent shape. That means that the option of settling down, as it were, was never open to them. They could never become "one of us". Regardless of how noble or how base their intentions might have been, they were always antagonised by all other races of Zandar whenever they would be found in their midst. It is no surprise, then, that morphs developed an unhealthy attitude towards others and became the most feared and the most universal enemy in all worlds.'

Harry's last words caused a small uproar on the deck.

'You are turning things upside down here, Harry!' said Band. 'You are confusing the victim and the attacker.'

'Morphs are not the most feared, the Hilalis are,' said the helmsman.

'Yes, but the Hilalis have no will of their own, while morphs know very well what they are doing,' replied Bangus McBroom amid murmurs of 'Nothing can excuse the attack on defenceless Fairybury! Nothing!'

'I am not excusing anything, I was just trying to explain things the way they are,' said Harry. 'Merely stating that we are the victims and they the attackers, although being factually correct, really serves no useful purpose – except making us feel good about ourselves. If we want to stop them, we have to understand them first,' he added and withdrew below deck.

'The attack on Fairybury is just a harbinger of far worse things to come,' declared the bosun.

'What things?' asked Pim.

'I prophesy the return of the Seven Ghost Ships commanded by the Seven Dead Captains!' Bangus McBroom announced in a dramatic voice. 'They have been moored in a secret bay since times immemorial, but they will soon weigh anchor and set sail to revenge the terrible curse that was so unjustly cast upon them!'

Everyone felt uncomfortable until Band asked, 'Are they moored in one bay or seven bays?' and brought about a chuckle on the deck.

'Morphs are a far more real threat,' Band went on to explain. 'They have already stricken once and they will certainly strike again. The only question is – where?'

'He is right,' said Pim. 'I think they had ample time to escape before the Tunnels were shut. They could be anywhere in Left World, biding their time. Literally anywhere.'

'Even on this ship,' whispered the captain, bringing on an uncomfortable silence to the deck of the Pride of Slimy Tentacle which was broken only by a 'Sail ho!' from the crow's nest. 'Off to starboard!'

Everybody moved to starboard straining their necks trying to get a better look. The sea was calm and the air clear and a small speck could be seen right on the perfectly sharp horizon.

'What is it?' Pim asked Captain Bassalian who was the only one looking through a telescope.

'It's hard to tell, but it doesn't look like a sail to me,' the captain answered and took another puff from his pipe. 'Here, take a look for yourself.'

Both Pim and Band took turns at the telescope but they could not see anything more than a slender, upright silhouette far away, barely protruding above the horizon.

'This telescope doesn't magnify at all!' Band whispered to Pim as soon as the captain was out of earshot.

'I think it's only function is to enable the captain to see out of his cloud of smoke,' observed Pim.

By the time Harry reappeared on the deck to take the telescope, the apparition had disappeared, inexplicably sailing away in dead calm.

'What was it?' Harry wanted to know, but the captain replied that it was too far to be identified with any certainty. Bangus McBroom, on the other hand, had an explanation ready, one which brought out a wave of superstitious murmur among the crew.

'It must be the Towers of Billbalirion. What else could it be?'

'Nonsense!' Harry scoffed at the suggestion. 'The Towers of Billbalirion do not exist. They are only part of the old folk phrase *When I see the Towers of Billbalirion* – which means never.'

But none of the sailors, captain included, was too convinced that the Towers of Billbalirion did not exist. True, nobody ever saw them, but still …

'The Towers of Billbalirion are the epitome of the unattainable and the symbol of the impossible,' Harry explained. 'They express our innermost yearning for that which we neither know, nor possess.'

'Now I am curious,' said Pim. 'I would surely like to see those Towers of Billbalirion.'

'It is very unwise to say such things,' declared Bangus McBroom. 'It can only bring bad luck.'

'Oh, come on – '

'It is true,' said the captain, 'that no one ever saw the Towers of Billbalirion, except as a fleeting apparition on the horizon.'

'Or at all,' interjected Harry.

'But the only unattainable thing about them is the great secret they carry within them,' said the captain.

'What secret?' asked Pim.

'That I don't know,' answered the captain.

'It wouldn't be a secret if we knew it, would it, now?' added Bangus McBroom, accompanied by general approval of on the deck.

'But it's got to be the secret of something,' Pim replied. 'The secret of untold riches? The secret of eternal youth? The secret of everlasting love? You've got to know what the object of the secret is, and then the secret part is how to get it. If everything is secret, it makes no sense. What is it the secret of?'

'That's also a secret,' the bosun replied unfazed.

'Ahh!' Harry cast a glance of understanding towards Pim meant to convey his untold suffering over the ignoble ignorance of the masses.

Band, however, was deeply impressed by the 'secret' secret. He said that he had heard somewhere about known unknowns and unknown unknowns, and the Towers of Billbalirion were very obviously a case of an unknown unknown – that much was clear to him.

He also had a secret. 'I have a secret fear of the Conducthorr.'

'But it's not a secret any more now that you said it, you cauliflower!' said Harry.

'What is a Conducthorr?' asked Bangus McBroom and Band was only too glad to explain.

'The Conducthorr is a mysterious and evil person set on conquering and enslaving me and all my kin. I haven't seen him, but I know that he is out there, roaming the outer worlds, and travelling the lands of Zandar looking for us. If he ever finds me, he will seize me, enslave me and – I shudder to even say it out loud – conduct me!'

'Oh, horror of horrors!' Pim reacted to this frightful prospect. 'An orchestra conducted! If I'd died yesterday, I would have died thinking it was perfectly obvious that a conductor would want to conduct an orchestra and, indeed, that an orchestra would want to be conducted.'

But Band was dead set against the concept. 'Obvious? Certainly not! I am deeply disappointed that you would even allow it, let alone believe that it was obvious – and to think that I agreed to play for you!'

'Captain Bassalian, tell him, isn't it obvious that conductors conduct and orchestras are conducted?'

As a matter of principle, the captain was not willing to get drawn into a dispute between passengers. 'I don't know,' he said without committing himself to either side. 'Perhaps this is a subject fit for the Academy.'

'What Academy?'

'The Academy of Obvious, obviously.'

'What on Earth is that?' Pim asked incredulously and Harry sensed another chance to expound on something.

'The Academy of Obvious,' he began, 'is the oldest scholarly institution of Zandar, devoted to the furtherance of research into the obvious.'

'Why would anybody want to research the obvious when there is so much unknown around us?' Pim interrupted him.

'Ah, precisely! Because any research of the unknown which failed to delineate the obvious first is simply not thorough enough!'

'Aha.'

'The Academy's approach is a comprehensive one. It was founded nearly 6000 years ago on a sound and solid basic premise: *What is – is, and what isn't – is not.*'

'It's a solid premise.'

'Millennia of intense philosophical efforts were invested into further research of the obvious until, some 2000 years ago, the Academics arrived at the second fundamental postulate which flows from the first part of the principal premise, What-is – is. And that is: *We are.*'

'We are?'

'*We are,*' Harry nodded weightily. 'But alas, as it so often happens that triumph is clouded by discord, the celebrations of the second postulate were not even finished before a clique of dissidents appeared within the body of the Academy. They claimed that the second postulate was incomplete in its present form and that it should be reformulated to read *We are, therefore we are.*'

'Therefore we are?'

'Precisely! The Thereforeists fought hard for their amendment to be officially adopted as the second postulate, but the rest of the Academics argued that the causal relationship between the *We are* and the *We are* which are connected through nothing more than a mere *therefore* was not sufficiently obvious to be considered obvious within the meaning of the Founding Articles of the Academy of Obvious! The body of the Academy bled and suffered as battles were fought over the amendment and when it became obvious that the future of the world (as they didn't know it) hung in balance, it was agreed that a vote would be held in Star Central to settle the issue of the second postulate once and for all.'

'I am on the edge of my seat,' Pim declared in a deadpan voice.

'The vote was in the Traditionalists' favour and the Thereforeists were defeated. But not all of them agreed to renounce their ideas and some went on fighting. One of them called Pimosthenes stood by his beliefs and threw himself into the Data River to demonstrate the absurdness of the opponents' postulate. He was never seen or heard again, but his foolish act rekindled the Therefore Debate. Ever since then, the body of the Academy has been divided into those who take his disappearance as a proof of their views, and those who consider it to be quite the opposite, i.e. the proof of *their* views.

'The majority of Academics refuses to adopt the new line of thinking to this day, but the Thereforeists are a stubborn and persistent gang and they appear every now and then. They are still trying to append *therefore we are* to any thesis brought before the Academy and especially to the second postulate itself which they deem to be woefully deficient.'

Harry would have been quite happy to further elaborate on the Academy of Obvious which he, obviously, held in high regard, if a breath of wind hadn't been felt on the deck. The first ripples on the still tranquil sea were the signal for the ship to burst alive. The bosun began issuing orders left and right, the helmsman started turning the wheel and the sailors were sent aloft to loose the topsails. The Pride of Slimy Tentacle soon began to move slowly across the surface of the sea.

And Harry became seasick again.

Satisfied that the ship was harnessing the breeze the best she could, the captain gave instructions to call him when the wind changed and invited the three passengers to his cabin. He filled four cups with rum from a small barrel.

'I have never told this to anyone, but I feel I must share it with you after what happened in Fairybury,' he said from the cloud of smoke around his head. 'My name is Captain Aral Bassalian. I have been a captain for many years now, but before I was a captain, just like any other skipper, I had begun my life on the sea up in the mast, loosing and dousing the sails, and scrubbing the deck when I was not aloft. Sometimes it was a hard life, especially the seven years with Captain

Vanderdecken. But sometimes it was everything a young man would want from the sea. I have only the best memories, for instance, of the time when I was the second mate of Captain Ahab. You wouldn't believe how different he was before he became obsessed with that whale. Incredible how a person can change …

'Anyway, I slowly but steadily worked my way down the mast and up the ranks and the day came when I assumed my first command on a barque in the Legends of the Malabar Coast. I was still young and I knew I was going to be promoted to a Legend myself if only I worked hard and did my job well.

'It was supposed to be an uneventful passage, just like this one, with a cargo of flax and a small group of passengers. When we were still on the mooring, a few hundred yards from the shore, a small boat approached us with one more passenger, an old man dressed in white. A sorcerer, I thought, and was glad to have another paying head in the poop, although it meant less comfort for the passengers who had already taken up their accommodation. You can easily guess that they didn't like it.

'Three days after we left port, a storm rose out of the blue sky and fell upon us with all its might. We reefed the sails and battened the hatches, and I set a half-hour watch at the helm, that's how fierce a storm it was. There was nothing more we could do. But then an elf among the passengers came to me and told me that the old man who was the last to join the ship was – a morph. I did not pay attention to this, I mean, how could anybody recognize a morph? But the storm grew mightier and mightier and it wasn't long before I heard a cry, "Elf overboard!" By the time I ordered hard to starboard, there was nothing we could do for him. I ordered the wheel back to port or she would have keeled over in the waves.

'But the word that there was a morph on board had already spread on deck, and now both the passengers and my crew blamed the old man for the hurricane gale. He caused the storm, they all told me, and demanded from me to do something. But what can you do with a morph on a ship? The only way to kill a morph is to burn him, and nobody would dare build a pyre on a wooden ship even if it was possible to do it in a storm. "Throw him overboard!" they said. What should I tell you? Back then I was still full of that vehemence that only possesses the young and this was my first command. I stood in front of all the passengers and crew and said that I would not allow any head overboard my ship, be it a morph or anybody else.

'But they wouldn't listen to me, and the crew easily overpowered me. They tied me below and together with the passengers took the old man to the deck. I could not see what happened then, but I felt the ship heave heavily as a series of colossal waves struck her abeam. I heard the wind roaring through the rigging and I felt my ship almost capsize as the waves rushed over the deck one after the other.'

Pim and Harry unwittingly exchanged uneasy glances but Captain Bassalian did not notice them. Swaddled comfortably by the smoke from his pipe, he continued the story from inside his cloud.

'The next thing I remember was the old man who came to slash my bonds. You are needed on deck, he told me and when I climbed from the poop I saw that no other living soul was left on the ship. The waves had washed them all overboard. All – but the old man.

'We steered the ship through the storm, the old man and I, and we reached the port the following day. The ship was battered and the rigging in tatters. We only just made it, but we made it.

'Before disembarking, the old man came to me and told me who he was. It was Psalmanazar, the ruler of morphs himself! He really did summon the storm! It was his way of "purging Left World of those not worthy to live among its many peoples", as he put it. He told me that he would spare my life, but only this one time, as I was the only one who did not try to cast him overboard.

'You can guess that my first voyage did not go down well on the Malabar Coast. Nobody would hire me any more there and I had time to think. I pondered over Psalmanazar's words, "those not worthy to live among Zandar's many tribes". I felt angry at him that he would take it upon himself to decide who was worthy of life and who was not. But I was glad at the same time that he thought me deserving and spared my life. I never saw him again.

'It was some time before I obtained another command, through Open Oceans IV. They gave me a second chance and I still get my work through them today.

'Gentlemen! Psalmanazar is out there again, deciding on who deserves to live and who does not. Only, judging by what you tell me, his yardstick is different now, and longer than ever before. There is no one in Zandar today who merits his mercy. It seems that we are all the morphs' prey now,' Captain Bassalian finished his story.

There was a long silence until Harry said, 'How long will the passage to Dembeliland take?'

'With this unseasonal weather?' Captain Bassalian kept stroking the cloud around his head while he contemplated the answer. 'It could be days, it could be weeks. But don't worry, your berths and your grub are covered for as long as it takes. We have enough provisions on board to last us to Port Cockaigne and back.'

'Oh, we won't be staying in Port Cockaigne, we're going straight back to Star Central,' Pim replied cheerfully. 'We have a –'

'No, we are not, and we don't!' Harry cut him off before he could mention their precious little book. 'It's just that I find the seasickness really unpleasant.'

When the Sun Was Over the Yardarm

Edna Edwards, Chief of Human Resources of Advanced Computers & Games Corporation, was in a sorry state. Locked in a storage room inside the ACG building that everybody forgot, she hadn't washed for days, her hair was a mess and her hands, face and clothes were encrusted with chocolate and Coca Cola. Nobody would recognize the Chief of Human Resources now, except for her majestic Cadillac-like glasses that represented her last vestige of dignity in an otherwise very ignominious situation. She had also lost all feeling of time and couldn't tell any more whether her regular periods awake lasted a couple of hours or the whole day or whether they were regular at all.

The yellow thing on the floor hadn't bothered her lately, and the past several days – or was it hours or weeks? – the two of them had spent in an uneasy truce. She made sure to throw him some toner whenever she woke up and he would mostly keep to himself when she darted towards one shelf or the other.

She didn't remember when the thought first occurred to her, but it quickly grew into an obsession – she became convinced that she was going to spend the rest of her life here, inside the storage room, this awful place with unpainted walls and a single fluorescent tube on the ceiling. No need to worry just now, though. She would live for a long, long time on chocolate and Coke and then, when she'd sense that her time was approaching, she would lie on the desk with her hands crossed, close her eyes and peacefully depart from this world. And that's how they would find her, serene, untroubled and dead – at peace with all the ACG departments.

She had always considered people who prepared their funerals in advance somewhat morbid but now she had a good reason to depart from her own rules, just like it happened with chocolate and Coke. Thorough that she was, she wanted to be ready for the inevitable, whenever it might come.

Until she realized, with some horror, just how dirty and unkempt she was. They were not supposed to find her like this, she had to scrub her face at least! There was water in the storage room, in a big plastic drum for the water coolers. It didn't take her long to decide that she would better use that water to bring some dignity to her visage, rather than prolonging her futile subsistence.

She created a safe passage with some printer toner as usual, but the horrible thing did not move from the back of the room. It just stayed there, as if it was observing her. The water barrel was so heavy, she barely lifted it from the shelf and it took a lot of effort to hold it. She'd made a few steps towards the desk when she lost the grip and the barrel slid out of her hands and smashed on the floor. She screamed and jumped back on the desk as the water spilled all over the floor and under the door. But the thing still didn't move. Nothing changed in the small world of the storage room, except now there was no more water and no more chance to wash. A new cycle of despair began and after some time Edna fell into slumber again.

From which she was awoken by muffled voices saying things such as 'slippery when wet' and 'Building Management Procedures for Leaks and Seepages'. Then she saw the doors of the storage room open and daylight flooded her dark abode. She darted towards the exit, screaming to everybody to run for their lives, run away from the monster!

Edna collapsed at the end of the corridor. Security guards quickly arrived with stretchers and gently laid her on as she kept on babbling.

'There, watch out, there! It will eat you. The monster will eat you up, just like he ate him! He almost ate me. Yes, me! Run, run!'

Nobody listened to Edna's babble, and nobody paid any attention to a round yellow box at the end of the storage room. Cleaners were called to bring the storage room in order, but then told to wait until the people from the insurance had had a look at it. Everybody professed to be aghast that somebody could be locked up in a room for so long, and the words 'hefty liability' kept popping up in every conversation in the building that day.

As soon as nobody was looking, the yellow round thing left the storage room and disappeared in the corridors of ACG.

'Oh, oh, oh, when the sun is, when the sun is, when the sun is over the yah-aard-arm!!'

The Pride of Slimy Tentacle was sailing under fair wind and the helmsman was singing along to Band's rendition of the popular sea shanty. The daily portion of rum was not supposed to be touched before the sun rose over the highest yard-arm on the main mast and this moment was duly celebrated in song. Even those sailors who could not sing to save their life would join enthusiastically in the refrain every time Band arrived at the three notes, 'Oh, oh, oh!'

'Oh, oh, oh, can't a man have some silence on deck!' Harry would demand in tune, which in turn made everybody sing the chorus even louder.

The winds had finally taken them in their favour and they were at last making good progress. Bolstered by the thought that the shore of Dembeliland was just a few days of good wind away, and having no other choice, really, Pim had undergone a thorough change. He had spent most of the past few days on deck, barefoot and with a tan to equal any Tentaclian sea dog. He liked helping around the deck and learning about the rigging from the bosun. He even overcame his initial fear and tried climbing the ratlines. He wasn't really a physical type so it wasn't easy at first, but once he climbed all the way to the crow's nest and was awarded with the best view on the ship, he began spending almost as much time up as on the deck.

The mysterious unidentified sail was spotted several more times on the horizon, always too far away to make anything out of it, and usually around the same time of day, when the sun was over the yard-arm. Pim saw it from the crow's nest but even from there it was little more than a speck on the horizon.

But then the winds died down again and an unusually long period of calm descended on the ocean. For three days and three nights, there was not a slightest breath of wind, and not a smallest ripple on the sea. The Pride of Slimy Tentacle lay in dead calm and there were no sails to unfurl and no ropes to tighten, nothing to do except to wait for the sun to rise over the yard-arm. After all the deck was thoroughly scrubbed, all the ropes neatly coiled and all the yarn expertly spun, the captain gave permission for the hammocks to be taken out on deck. But the sea was so quiet that the hammocks lay still, and the heat was unrelieved even by that slight motion of air that comes from swinging.

Now that the nausea was not his problem any more, Harry was languishing in the heat. Not even tying a wet gauze around his forehead could help him in his misery – it only made him look like an aging pirate, a fact that Band was sure to repeat at the most inopportune moments. In return, Harry repeatedly threatened to make Band walk the plank 'if the incessant cavalcade of mindless ditties did not stop this very instant!'

'So what kind of music would suit you, sir Henry?' Band replied after the latest insistence on walking the plank and, without waiting for an answer, switched from sea shanties to a slow tango. It hardly appeased Harry.

'Have you ever tried performing silence? You might discover you have a knack for it. Hey, it could change your life,' he paused and added, 'It would certainly change mine – for the better!'

'Come on, Harry, even you have to admit that this is beautiful music,' Pim said to Harry. 'It has something not only of your poise, but of your temperament, too, don't you think? Just close your eyes and listen. If I close my eyes I can almost see you on the dance floor. Yes, I see you gliding with Gertrude from one end to the other, giving her an expert turn on five, and then taking Gwendolyn for a number eight, before dancing away across the ballroom with Guinevere.'

'How dare you make fun of my aunts when we don't know what happened to them? I had to leave them in Fairybury because I made the foolish decision to come and pick you up. They could be dead for all we know.'

This finally killed the conversation and the music. Pim and Band withdrew to their hammocks.

Band, naturally, couldn't quite settle in. He kept tossing and turning around, complaining that the hammock was not swinging, that's how dead the dead calm was – and what's the point of lying in a hammock if it doesn't swing? Eventually, a French horn sprang out of the hammock and softly blew a note aside, just enough to give it a slight swing. That finally satisfied him so he nested himself comfortably inside the hammock and continued to blow a tone in regular intervals.

Before long, Harry was heard again protesting about the tones, but nobody else seemed to care about it – or about his complaints. The old Bedel still carped on, mostly for his own indulgence. When finally Band blew himself to sleep Harry didn't even notice, so absorbed he was in his grumble.

When a thin line of clouds appeared on the horizon nobody spotted it for a while. But when the captain came out on deck he immediately sent a lookout to the crow's nest. Try as he may, the sailor could only confirm what was visible from the deck, a thin line of dark clouds grouping far away off starboard to the north.

Captain Bassalian decided to have the topsails unfurled in the expectation of wind. The sailors scrambled along the ratlines and soon the two sails were hoisted and waiting for a wind to fill them.

Time passed without either wind or the clouds getting any nearer to the ship. Pim stole another look through the captain's telescope but could only see that the clouds were getting darker. They were still just a line hovering in the distance, slightly above the horizon.

Minutes passed, and then hours, with the sails still hanging emptily from the yard-arms, before a cry came from the lookout in the crow's nest:

'Weather off starboard!'

Everybody could now see that the clouds were not so thin any more. They were moving. The ship quickly awoke again. The captain sent more men aloft, ready to issue instructions the moment the first breath of wind reached the ship.

Pim and Harry could not hide their joy that the doldrums were over and that their journey back to Star Central was about to resume. They were ready to make shore as soon as it was possible to drop the anchor and lower the boat – even if it meant more seasickness, Harry heroically declared.

But Bangus McBroom was not so enthusiastic. 'Whatever wind is driving these clouds, not a puff of it is reaching our sails,' he declared. The captain looked through his cloud and said, 'Hmm, you are right. Those clouds only look like they are getting nearer, but they are not. They are not moving at all. They are just rising.'

'They must be pretty high if they are still that far away,' said Pim.

Harry announced that he had always considered clouds untrustworthy. Just when you decide to take seasickness like a man, they decide to stay away to spite you. Whoever heard of clouds spreading upwards instead of sideways anyway?

Bangus McBroom did. 'It's the Dead Man's Gale,' he said.

'What?' asked Pim.

'It's the most treacherous tempest of all seas,' Bangus McBroom replied with a pregnant cadence at the end of his sentence.

'Every other thing in maritime parlance is called after one dead man or another,' Harry felt compelled to add. 'On the other hand ...' The clouds were now a tremendous sight above the northern horizon, and still boiling upwards. Harry turned to the captain.

'Shouldn't we be doing something?'

'We can't do a thing without wind, sir Henry,' the captain replied. 'Anyway, the clouds are not coming our way. They are just piling on the horizon.'

'Oh, don't you worry for a minute,' said Harry. 'They'll start coming when they are done piling. They are not dark clouds for nothing. Just look at them! Shouldn't we maybe try to move away while we still can?

'Harry, we can't budge without wind,' said Pim.

'What about oars? Why don't we employ oars? Or is it deploy oars? Or oar oars? Or something!'

'Oars?!' roared Captain Bassalian. 'Oars?! This is a sailing ship! And a fine one at that. If this thing ever comes our way, we'll sail through it like an arrow through a leaf.'

'Ha! An arrow through a leaf!' Harry exclaimed and began a recitation of extra-thick and impenetrable leaves from various worlds he visited, some of which were cultivated specifically to be used as shields against arrows.

Pim for his part thought that any captain would know his job better than Harry. Especially one with such a tremendous draw from his pipe, he reassured himself. But the clouds were getting higher and higher and it was unsettling to think that they were just as far away as when they saw them first low above the horizon. They must be enormous by now, he thought.

When Harry exhausted all the thick leaves known to man, dwarf and elf, the clouds were towering menacingly at more than 45 degrees above the horizon. One whole side of the world was in darkness.

West Acton was all in darkness, as was the whole of London. It was the middle of the night and low hanging clouds seemed to want to smother the houses below them. Cold wind drove gust after gust of rain against rows of dark windows. In the whole of West Acton only one window remained lit up, just barely, on the upper floor of a terraced house in a street just off Horn Lane.

Behind that window, in a stuffy room full of things, surrounded by dirty socks, empty cola bottles and greasy old magazines, Mehdi was sitting on his bed. The only light in the room was coming from a bright blue screen right in front of him. He was trying to play a game but things weren't going his way. The moves just wouldn't come to him. He should have conquered an island and entered a secret cave long ago, but he couldn't even wade through the surf and make it to the shore. The waves kept pushing him back to sea instead of taking him on to the beach. He remained hovering around the island, looking for a way to land directly from the air but it seemed that Andy had been right when he told him that there was no way to access this particular island from the air.

Yep, it seemed that Andy was right. And that Mehdi was wrong – again.

Well, at least Mia was not here to see it. His sister was an expert in making his life even more miserable than it already was. It was hard to believe that that was possible but he was sure that if she was here now, she would have managed it just fine, unbearable as she was. All that energy and enthusiasm, and so ignorant of the woes of life!

On the other hand, Mia seemed happy while Mehdi definitely wasn't. What was the point in growing up if it meant that you stopped being like Mia and became like Mehdi? And further down the line, like their father. He was the least happy of the three. He was positively woebegone.

The word that he had recently heard in a class brought a feeble smile to his face. It sounded strange, like it was invented especially for his father.

When the sound of flushing toilet was heard through the door Mehdi quickly darkened the screen and covered the console in his lap with a pillow. Father was not supposed to find him playing a game so late at night.

As he sat in silence, listening to the rain charging against the window, it occurred to him that it was already too late. Father must have seen the light under the door when he passed by his room on the way to the toilet, before Mehdi heard the flush. Breakfast tomorrow would be unpleasant. Again.

The world would be a much better place if older people did not have to go to pee so often at night, Mehdi pondered in the dark. And exactly at the same moment, his father was thinking exactly the same thing. It was one of the rare instances when they thought alike, probably the only topic on which the two of them still agreed.

Lucky Mia, she agreed with father on most things – all things, come to think of it. Especially if they were related to Mehdi. Mia and father were very different, and yet the two of them liked to gang up against him. There were more and more instances of such unprincipled coalition lately.

But wait, in a few years Mia was going to be just as old as he was now – let's wait and see how much she'd agree with father then. Let's see if father would approve of her then! Well, maybe he would, her room was always tidy, but there was no way that they would agree on everything like they did now, thought Mehdi slumped on the bed.

And he, he was going to be an adult by then, which meant on a par with his father. How would that look like? Was he going to think like his father then? No. Never.

'Mehdi, are you still awake?' a voice came from behind the door. Mehdi kept his silence but father was not fooled. 'Switch that thing off and go to sleep. You have school tomorrow.' As if he didn't know.

Mehdi waited until he heard the door of father's bedroom close. He was about to log off from the game when he realized that he was not above that island with that secret cave any more. Damn! The pillow in his lap kept a button pressed all this time and he was now lost somewhere over the big blue sea. Woebegone, here I come!

He zoomed out to try to find a reference point or something before switching off the console, but there was absolutely nothing in the vast expanse of the ocean. He looked left and right and saw a small dot at the edge of the screen. He zoomed in – but the dot turned out to be a ship. This was no help because ships were obviously not fixed points of reference. Still, he zoomed in to take a closer look and saw a sailing ship with top sails unfurled and sailors sitting on yardarms. He zoomed in even more to try to read the name of the ship when something caught his attention.

The captain and the crew were all looking in one direction, at a weather front to the right. Standing among the crew on the deck, right next to the captain, was somebody who looked familiar. Mehdi couldn't get a good look from straight above, but he was sure that he knew that character from somewhere. He zoomed in a bit more. Now he could see him quite clearly.

Yes, there was no doubt about that. Mehdi had seen him before.

Wait, he had not only seen him before – he had met him before! In the lobby of the ACG building. He was the one standing right in front of him in the queue. He was the one that was accepted for the testing. He was the one who stole his internship from him!

He even knew his name. It was Pim Pergamon. And now this Pim was standing on the forecastle of a ship in Open Oceans IV! How –

'I said you have school tomorrow,' Mehdi's father entered the room, pulled the plug and left. The ship, the ocean and the internship thief all disappeared in the darkness that enveloped the room.

Now there wasn't a single lit up window left in West Acton.

Minutes ticked away on the deck of the Pride of Slimy Tentacle. All eyes were still fixed on the towering mass of dark clouds off starboard when it suddenly lit up from inside. For a split second, a huge lightning made it look as if a terrifying face was hidden among the clouds, the face of an old man with a long beard.

'Davy Jones!' shouted the sailors.

'Psalmanazar!' shouted Pim and Harry.

But the face disappeared with the lightning and only the seething clouds remained.

'They are coming!' the lookout shouted from the crow's nest, but nobody needed to be told that now. The whole colossal mass of clouds was starting to move towards the Pride of Slimy Tentacle.

'Davy Jones does not exist,' Harry reassured Pim. 'It's just sailors superstition.'

'Davy Jones or not, this does not look good,' Pim replied just as the first thunder reached the ship and shook her from keel to crow's nest, tossing Band out of his hammock.

'Steady on, lads! This is just what we've been expecting, fair wind and plenty of it,' the captain shouted from within his private cloud.

'Can he see anything through this? Maybe he should stop smoking,' Pim said to Harry. They both stared at the advancing wall of boiling clouds which continued to be pierced by enormous lightning bolts as they advanced. The sinister face wasn't there any more, but the storm that was approaching looked far more frightening than any face.

Just under the wall of clouds, right where they touched the sea, white crests of waves could already be seen coming their way. Above them the dark clouds stirred and boiled angrily while the lightning bolts kept writhing inside, as if prodding the clouds to advance faster towards the hapless ship which still lay motionless in their path.

'Shouldn't we at least batten down the hatches, sir?' the bosun addressed the captain.

'All in its good time, Mr. McBroom.'

'Here, take a look at it through your telescope, and tell me what you see,' Harry handed the telescope to Captain Bassalian. When he saw the approaching storm through the telescope, the expression on the captain's face somewhat changed.

'By my pipe!' he said. 'The optics does make it look a tad more unpleasant. Lay aloft, you scoundrels! Douse the topsails! Set the storm jib and trysail.'

'The hatches, sir?'

'And batten down the hatches!'

The sailors scuttled up the ratlines and set about unfurling the storm sails, but the ship still could not move. She lay helpless before the advancing storm.

'No sails are going to help us face this thing. We have to escape it,' said Harry.

A sense of alarm spread among the sailors as they frantically worked to execute the captain's orders and lay alow before the storm reached the ship. The only person on deck seemingly unaffected by the commotion was Band. He had just reinstalled himself inside his hammock and had once more began swinging when a shout from Pim flipped him out of it again.

'You!!! Hey, you there! Get here! Get here at once!'

Band picked himself from the deck and walked up to Pim, fully intending to protest this tone of voice when Pim said, 'How many horns can you blow at once?'

'I am outraged to see music discussed in the face of doom!' Harry declared but Band immediately understood what Pim was aiming at.

'Oh, I can pull quite a number of horns at once. But the horns will not do. We need something bigger.'

'Go there,' Pim gestured towards the stern, 'and give us the best you've got.'

And soon the twelve largest sousaphones that ever blew double b-flat lined the poop deck facing astern.

'And what, pray tell, have you selected for tonight's programme?' Harry said oozing with irony. 'Capsizing Concerto? Sinking Symphony? Rhapsody in Canoe?

'Ready?' the twelve sousaphones looked at Pim.

'Ready when you are.'

Band blew one single low but powerful note – and the ship lurched forward. Another note, and the ship began moving.

'Hooray!' shouted everybody on deck.

'Let's give it to him, lads!' shouted Bangus McBroom and the sailors responded with an encouraging Heave-ho! to help Band keep the rhythm in b-flat.

'Keep her up to her course!' ordered Captain Bassalian.

'Keep her up, sir,' answered the helmsman and swung the wheel. The ship slowly turned and began to edge away from the storm under the sway of the sousaphones, still without a breath of wind in her sails!

'World's first Sousaphone Propulsion System – music to my ears!' said Harry as the sailors quickened the rhythm and Band blew more and more eagerly. The Pride of Slimy Tentacle was underway once again.

But the storm that they were trying to leave behind kept advancing towards them. Moments of lightning more brilliant than the sun itself alternated with deep darkness that threatened to overtake and enclose them. The sea around them lost its deep blue colour. It was now dark green, almost black. Huge waves could now be seen competing with one another under the wall of clouds.

'We need to go faster,' Harry declared and joined Band on the poop deck. He began cheering and encouraging him, even puffing up his cheeks to help him, playing coach and cheerleader at the same time. Band quickened the rhythm and kept building up the tune until he outpaced the sailors' heave-ho. Soon he was competing for loudness with the thunder with the most energetic bass line ever produced in Left or Right World.

'Do I know this gusty shanty?' mused Bangus McBroom on the poop as a breeze began to ruffle Captain Bassalian's cloud.

'The Sousaphone Propulsion Rhapsody! Just the repertoire to save us!' Pim shouted out loud.

'Go, go, go, go, go!' Harry was rousing Band even as the chip log in the bosun's hands showed that never had a brig gone this fast. Right behind the stern lightning bolt after lightning bolt lit up the threatening clouds from inside as they covered more and more of the sky, but the sousaphones blew harder and harder, driving the ship like a twelve-pistoned engine.

When the captain ordered Bangus McBroom to double-check the hatches, Harry sneered at his lack of nerve. But the storm was getting nearer and nearer and Band who had to face it from the stern began to panic. 'We're never going to make it,' one sousaphone paused to exclaim, disrupting the rhythm. Harry would have none of it – like a harsh coach he kept prodding Band to go on. Band blew more frantically than ever but his cocksure, even arrogant self now gave way to pure mania. 'It seems that deep under all the jazzy swagger lies a little neurotic,' Pim said to Harry but Harry ignored him.

'That's it, let's go! We can make it! Blow, Band blow!' he shouted at the sousaphones, and then at the captain who tried ordering him below deck. 'None of your business, I say! We are going to make it!'

The sun was still shining far in front of the bow, but the light was fading fast. The topmost clouds overtook them just as the captain ordered the last sailor below deck. The storm finally reached the ship and the first heave of the sea pushed her forward and raised the stern. All the sousaphones slid off the poop in a cacophony of sounds and tumbled on the main deck together with Harry.

'We didn't make it, you lousy instrumentalist!' he shouted as the sousaphones swept him off the poop.

Then the winds caught up with the ship, howled through the rigging and filled the storm sails.

'Every cello for himself! Violins and piccolos first!' could be heard on the main deck.

The wind blew away the cloud of smoke around captain's head, giving him for the first time a good, if terror-stricken, look at the weather that he was so confident of sailing through. Finally, the waves caught up with them and the tempest engulfed the Pride of Slimy Tentacle.

The ship pitched heavily as the masts groaned in heavy gusts that drove a thick spray across the deck. The bow kept rising high in the air and sinking deep into the troughs of waves that grew bigger and bigger. The brig became a dot amid a rising seascape that threatened to devour her.

Harry had great problems standing up on deck and untangling himself from Band. The ferocious wind kept knocking him off, but that did not prevent him from shouting at the mess of all imaginable instruments strewn around the deck and still playing.

'Go on, blow Band, blow! We need to get out of here!' Harry prodded Band but the Sousaphone Propulsion Rhapsody had given way to a blustering symphonic piece that kept rising in a perpetual climax, in tune with the raging elements. Disheartened by his failure and compulsive as he was, Band continued playing the accompaniment to the storm despite the waves that washed over the deck. It was impossible to call him to senses and Pim had to enlist the help of a couple of sailors to drag the angry Harry away into the relative safety of the cabin below.

The only living souls that remained on the deck were Band and the hapless helmsman who was promised a replacement 'as soon as practicably possible'. He could be heard between the waves cursing and promising himself never to work for Open Oceans IV again. The clouds had in the meantime travelled across the whole sky and closed on the other side of the horizon, enveloping the ocean around them in an oppressive darkness. The ship was tossed by immense waves and driven by hurricane winds but Band kept playing on, completely oblivious of the forces of nature raging around him. For the poor helmsman, it was difficult to decide what was more frightening: the moments of brilliant lightning which revealed colossal waves towering over the highest mast of the Pride of Slimy Tentacle, or the spray driven from the crests which prevented him from seeing the threatening waves – or yet the cataclysmic music from Band in which every note seemed to indicate the imminent sinking of the ship and all the souls on her.

The situation was not much better below deck. Harry was not any more the only one affected by the seasickness. Some sailors lay in wildly swinging hammocks, unable to rise or do anything to improve their situation. The movements of waves felt inside the ship like a gigantic roller-coaster in the dark. Pim and Harry were trying to sit down around a faint lamp in the captain's cabin, but the heavy roll made even sitting in one place impossible. They were spared the terrible sight that the lightning revealed outside, but the thunder sounded even more frightening inside the confined space. The scariest sound below deck, however, was the eerie grating of the ship's timbers under the pounding of the heavy seas.

'Where is the storm taking us?' Pim asked Captain Bassalian.

'For that you have to ask the storm,' the captain answered. 'It came from north-northwest and is carrying us 120 degrees off course. And pretty fast, from what I saw when I was out on deck the last time.'

'What lies at 120 degrees?'

'I don't know. Open Oceans IV only gave me the map for the planned course,' said the captain and showed Pim a piece of paper with a perfect blue square on it. Slimy Tentacle Island and Port

Cockaigne were written in small letters in two opposite corners. There was nothing but the blue sea in between, or anywhere else on the map. 'It is the Endless Ocean after all, you know,' Captain Bassalian said by way of explanation.

'But there could be some other land out there and we could be riding the waves towards her rocks,' Harry interrupted a long nauseated silence to share this thought.

'Oh, there are many worlds which look on to the Endless Ocean,' said the captain.

'Of what kind?' said Harry.

'Of both kinds.'

'Both kinds of worlds?' Pim was intrigued to hear.

'Yes, island and shore.'

'Aha.'

Harry wanted to say something else but had to abandon the attempt when he was overcome by a new bout of seasickness. The ship's timbers groaned loudly as another wave struck the hull. It nearly knocked over Captain Bassalian together with his pipe.

'The seas used to be less stormy when I was young,' he said when he regained his balance.

'How long do these weather fronts normally last here?' Pim asked him.

'What weather fronts?'

'You know, the places where high and low air pressure meet and cause bad weather.'

'Bad weather is not caused by air pressure, young man, but by a spread of irresponsible behaviour among younger generations,' Captain Bassalian declared. 'Instead of sailing the old way, young captains nowadays use wind ropes.'

'Wind ropes?'

'They are pieces of rope on which a witch has made three knots. Things like that sell for good money in small shops behind the docks on the Tortuga Islands. People buy them more and more, but I just don't like it. You see, at first everything is alright when you use the first and the second knot.'

'And the third knot?'

'That's the problem, the third knot. The first knot, when untied, gives a steady breeze, the second a strong wind. The third knot, however, should only be used exceptionally – because it gives a storm.'

'So why do they ever untie it, why don't they just use the first two knots and then buy a new wind rope?'

'People get careless and don't count carefully. A minority even gets addicted to knots so that they simply can't resist untying the third knot although they know that a storm will come. That's why I never use wind ropes. In my time nobody used wind ropes. I still only use natural wind.'

'There's your natural wind,' said Harry after another piece of rigging was heard snapping on the deck, followed by a musical accent. 'If we'd had a wind rope, we would already be lying on a beach in Dembeliland with sushi flying into our mouths.'

'I think wind ropes should be banned,' said Captain Bassalian and decided to send a replacement on the deck to relieve the helmsman. Pim went after him to see Band. But when he climbed on the deck, he decided to go no further.

Outside the storm raged unabated. The storm sails were now in tatters, but the rigging still held and the masts were mercifully undamaged. Band was still on deck playing with full force amid waves, apart from an odd gargle of a tuba or a horn when the deck was washed over. You could certainly not recognize the easy-going jazzer from earlier that day in the frenzied symphonic orchestra spread all over the main deck.

When the wind tore a yard-arm on the mizzen mast the music did not miss a beat. The instruments just moved slightly aside to let the yard-arm fall and produced a masterful musical accent in the process. Band played on, undeterred and unperturbed.

The new helmsman behind the wheel decided to tie himself to the poop to avoid being washed away. The wheel was becoming more and more difficult to control and the ship rolled heavier and heavier.

Then Harry suddenly burst on the deck from below. He staggered among the instruments, his hand on the mouth, looking for a place to throw up.

'Harry, come back!' shouted Pim, but a loud thunder drowned his words. Harry barely kept balance on the heaving deck, looking left and right among the instruments to find a way to either side of the ship. Pim went after him, despite the helmsman calling out to him.

He only made a few steps when Harry started to jerk forward in spasm. He could no longer control his stomach. He kicked a fat cello aside, reached the ship's fence and threw up into the sea.

But in that instant the ship heaved heavily and the cello slid all the way to the edge and fell overboard.

'Get that cello!' Pim shouted as the whole body of the orchestra swept across the deck following the cello, as if gripped by an invisible force. Pim tried to avoid one of the four double basses coming towards him, but the spray blinded him and he jumped too late. The double bass rammed into him and carried him across the whole deck. They broke through the fence and flew overboard together.

Harry didn't notice that Pim and Band fell off the ship because he was too busy vomiting. When he saw the instruments in the sea, he was first surprised to hear them still playing. The music was still dramatic, but in a gargly way, which made it funny. Or it would have been funny to Harry had it not been for a freak wave which shook the ship and tipped him into the sea as well.

'Man overboard!' the helmsman cried.

Pim kept swimming and shouting at Band to stop playing, spray flying in his face. It took several shouts and a couple of good shakes of a fat cello to bring Band back to his senses. As soon as he stopped playing, Band folded into one single double bass and Pim clung to it, shouting to Harry to swim towards them.

'Orchestra overboard!' shouted Bangus McBroom from the deck.

The captain rushed to the deck and ordered the wheel hard to port. The ship heaved heavily as the wheel turned.

The sailors scuttled across the deck and quickly cast a rope towards the three passengers in the foamy waters. But the rope fell short. Both Pim and Harry clung to the double bass and could not risk swimming out to the rope. The captain ordered another rope to be cast, and another, but none of them came any closer.

Pim and Harry held on to the double bass. They were being carried away from the ship, tossed by the huge waves which alternately pulled them deep into a trough or lifted them high up, sometimes higher than the ship's masts. Whenever the lightning struck they could clearly see Captain Bassalian and the sailors on the deck, still throwing ropes but unable to help them as the distance between them and the Pride of Slimy Tentacle increased.

Soon they were just a silhouette against the background of the raging seas lit by the lightning. They were last seen clinging on to the double bass high on a crest of a rising wave. When the next lightning struck, they had disappeared in the trough and the ship lost sight of them forever.

How to Resuscitate a Double Bass

'Hey, Reg, what's up, mate?'

'Greg! At long last on a shift with you! Oh, if I'd known, I would've brought the photos I told you about.'

'You *are* bringing them to the club meeting next week, aren't you?'

'Hundred percent so!'

The late night security shift in the ACG building on the Isle of Dogs in London was about to begin. Reg and Greg were two security officers with more than twenty years on the beat shared between them in the corridors of various London office blocks. They had many things in common, not least that they both parted their hair the same way and were both lifelong bachelors. They had recently been hired within a week of each other to join the Security Directorate of ACG, the biggest and most magnificent of all office buildings on the Isle of Dogs.

Reg and Greg had been assigned to the basement tonight and told to be on the lookout for anything unusual. The Chief of Security was getting more and more worried about possible industrial espionage. He wanted a report on any suspicious activity inside the building outside normal working hours.

The two of them enjoyed every minute of their shift together. They were both in their forties and both tall and thin, but their similarities went further than that. They had one great shared passion – UFOs. The photos Reg was so enthusiastic about were taken during his recent trip to a small town called Roswell in New Mexico. There were also many other new developments in the field of UFO sightings that needed to be examined and, as always, the final proof of the Roswell incident was just around the corner. But this time it was different. The chairman of their UFO Club was about to publish his life-long research into the classified government laundry logs for all the personnel working in Area 51 at the time of the crash. And that should finally convince all those cynical disbelievers out there who just could not accept that there was more to this world than met the eye.

'Much, much more, Greg. Much, much more.'

'Quite so. But you have to keep your eyes open.'

'Definitely.'

They entered a long corridor. They could see the lights go on at the opposite end. There was something on the floor, moving towards them.

Almost immediately after Edna had escaped and he left the storage room, Barney entered a lift. Trying to get out of it, he got lost inside the ventilation system. He soon discovered that the system of ventilation ducts in the ACG building was bigger and more labyrinthine than anything he saw before. There were literally miles of it to explore. Barney set out to survey his new habitat with the meticulous tenacity that had historically enabled pacmans to prosper and flourish in mazes.

The first strange thing about Barney's new maze was that it was completely empty. There was no one else besides him in there. Everybody else seemed to be in another maze, very close to his, but always separated by a grille or a grating. And that maze consisted of corridors which corresponded to his ducts but were separate from them. He could clearly see the beings in that world but he could not get to them. Barney finally concluded that there must exist a complete parallel universe to his ventilation world. A universe that had to be investigated as soon as he found a safe way to cross into it.

Then one night Barney found a ventilation opening with a loose cover. After some effort he managed to swing it aside far enough to cross through the slot and into the other world. The multiverse theory so confirmed, he crawled out into one of the side corridors and quickly found his way to the main corridor. The lights switched on as he began cautiously moving along the corridor wall. Then lights went on at the other end of the corridor and two armed security guards appeared there. Barney did not know that they had been instructed to be on the lookout for anything unusual, but his instincts told him that they might not be well disposed towards him if they noticed him.

He turned left and right, but there were no open doors in the corridor close to him and no place to hide. Barney slowed down but kept moving forward. The two guards seemed engrossed in conversation.

'That's exactly what the Club Protocol is here for – to safeguard the integrity of the UFO research!'

'Well, yes, but what if it means you never get to prove the aliens are still in Roswell, mate? You know they are there, I know they are there, but what about everybody else? They have the right to know it, too!'

'Good point, Greg, good point.'

The two guards were approaching Barney who slowed down even more. The tension was rising inside him. He began emitting a low growl. He closely followed every movement of the two human figures coming towards him, flexing his jaw in a succession of microscopic sharp movements. The jaw opened and closed almost imperceptibly, readying for a deadly snap. Neither of the two guards in the narrow corridor noticed it.

'Besides that, Reg, just think of the technology they've got and we need.'

'Right, but that's an old point.'

'Of course it's an old point. What I am talking about here is that the transfer of technology will have to go through someone. Somebody will get rich on the UFO technology. Fantastically rich!'

Reg's face suddenly lit up with a big smile. 'I see your point now. The first one to establish the contact with the aliens will be the first one to reap the benefits.'

'Exactly!'

The two guards barely noticed the presence of the round yellow thing moving on the floor. They were both engrossed in Greg's take on the commercial aspects of extra-terrestrial technology. Reg stepped behind Greg to let the humming thing pass and went on to explain his understanding of the idea. 'You're right, mate. Just think of the guy who owns the patent for automated floor-cleaning machines like this,' he said gesturing behind him. 'He must be rich! And that's nothing compared to the technology the aliens have! Nothing, I am telling you, nothing!'

The two worlds were not fated to meet that evening.

When the sun rose on the Endless Ocean there was not a trace of clouds in the sky as far as the eye could see. Apart from a light breeze coming from the south, the weather was calm again. The breeze raised very small waves, barely perceptible on the surface, which lazily followed one another in an endless march towards the sun poised high over the ocean. The sea was deep blue again and there was not a trace of the last night's terrible storm.

Except for a small, insignificant dot lost in the vast expanse of the ocean which, on closer inspection, revealed itself to be a battered double bass with two lifeless bodies stretched across. It was full of water and barely floating, only just enough to prevent the two figures from sliding off and disappearing in the enticing blueness below. The warm sea gently lapped at their feet as if inviting them to awake, but it took a long time before one of them slowly opened his eyes.

The bright piercing light at first made Pim's salt-encrusted eyelids recoil in pain. He washed his face. When he finally fully opened his eyes he was surprised to find himself in the middle of a sea – and on a double bass. He could not remember at all how he got there. He was even more surprised to find another comatose individual spread over the bridge of the double bass, gargling with every breath. He looked at him and his sharp moustache, now encrusted in salt, and thought how it must have been quite a proud and pointy specimen in its heyday.

And then the events of the recent past slowly started coming back. His descent into a strange world where he ploughed into somebody called a Bedel. How he was attacked at that weird Procession. How he came to be on a ship that was caught in a terrible storm. How he ended up fighting for his life amid colossal waves that seemed higher than mountains.

When Pim finally sat up to look around him, he promptly lost balance and tumbled straight into the sea.

'Help! Bedel, help!' he shouted once or twice until he caught the edge of the double bass again, but the Bedel did not react. Pim managed to climb back with some difficulty. The difficulty was mainly in trying not to dislodge the Bedel from his position on the double bass.

'Harry!' he remembered the name, 'Harry, wake up!'

There was no reaction from the lifeless body.

'Harry, it's me, Pim!' he shook the old Bedel gently, very gently, so as not to push him off the vessel. 'Wake up, *sir Henry*!'

Harry's body shook up in a series of convulsions. A muffled cough came from deep within his chest, culminating in a small spout of sea water coming out of his nostrils. A familiar grunt followed. Pim's face lightened up.

'Harry, you're alive!'

Another series of coughs brought the old Bedel to life. He coughed out some sea water, spat out some sea weed and opened his eyes. A faint smile appeared on his face when he saw Pim awkwardly bent over him, looking worried.

'Harry, it's me, Pim. Oh, thank goodness you're alive!'

But as soon as Pim uttered those words, Harry's eyes opened wide in horror. Then he lost consciousness again.

'Harry, Harry! Don't leave me! Stay with me! Harry!' Pim shouted at the listless body in his arms. 'Damn it, Harry, wake up. Wake up!'

Pim didn't know what to do. He remembered that people usually pumped water out of the drowned by applying pressure on the chest. But he couldn't pump anything out of Harry in their precarious position on the double bass. So instead he sprinkled some water on his friend's face.

Harry shook again, emitting another grunt, and opened his eyes again. 'Enough water in my face, I say,' was the first thing the reawakened Bedel had to say to his rescuer. He squinted at Pim and was about to say something when his eyes again opened wide despite the intense sunlight, his face convulsed in disbelief.

'What is it Harry? What's wrong?' Pim asked full of apprehension. 'Are you alright?'

Harry remained speechless. He stared at Pim. He tried to point at something behind Pim's back when suddenly a huge shadow moved across them both. When Pim turned around he had to raise his eyes higher and higher trying to take in the whole immense edifice that had appeared before them.

It was bigger than a supertanker and taller than an oil rig. Its enormous base hovered just above the surface of the sea. Two towers, dozens of floors high, rose on each side festooned with a multitude of bigger and smaller turrets. It was as if the two towers blossomed into an unlikely baroque thicket as they grew upwards, ending in two tall steeples so high up that they were barely visible from Pim and Harry's Lilliputian perspective on the surface of the sea.

In their everlasting lonely voyage, the Towers of Billbalirion had stopped right in front of Pim and Harry.

Harry was the first to recover from the surprise. He began paddling towards the Towers and Pim quickly followed his example. As they came closer, the enormous Towers looked like a forbidding mountain. There was not a sound to be heard on this mountain – but anything was better than clinging to a half-submerged double bass.

They approached the mess of flotsam and jetsam that got ensnared at the base during the storm. The Towers would have normally been inaccessible from the surface of the sea, even for somebody standing on a double bass, if something like that were possible. Now, however, splintered timbers, worn-out ropes, sea weed and even some barrels were entangled in a mess which enabled them to climb over it.

The feeling they experienced when they reached the base was different from being on any ship. Neither movements of waves nor the heave of the sea could be felt on the Towers. They both remained standing in silence just to enjoy the firm ground under their feet.

'There is no flotsam on the other side of the base,' said Pim.

'That must be the side that faced the storm,' concluded Harry looking around them. 'But look at all this clutter here. This must have been a mast, just look at the shreds of the sails still attached to it. And this looks like a whole forecastle of a schooner.'

'And that thing there – hey, where's Band?'

'Troglodytes of Hernia!' Harry exclaimed and they both turned back. A thoroughly miserable-looking double bass was gently swaying in the sea below.

'Band! He's floating away!'

They both scrambled down and managed to grab hold of the battered instrument just in time. They quickly turned it over and emptied it of water. It took some effort to pull it up on to the base.

'Band! Band!' Harry kept saying to the double bass which looked no different from any other soggy wooden instrument. 'How do you reanimate a double bass?

'Shake him?'

'Band, Band, wake up!' Harry turned to shaking the lifeless instrument but without much success. 'Pim, where are you?'

'Stop shaking him or you'll break him,' Pim responded from the bottom of the heap.

'You told me to shake him! Come back here at once!' said Harry. 'What are you doing down there anyway?'

'I am trying to find … Aha, here it is!' Pim replied and proudly raised something high in his hand.

'What is it?'

Pim did not respond until he returned with – a bow.

He slid the bow across the strings. Out of the double bass came terrible creaking noise.

'Pull him upright,' he commanded Harry. 'I'll stand next to you.' He then took the proper grip of the instrument. This time he gave it a less forceful slide.

'Again,' said Harry. Pim slid the bow three or four more times until the first sound came out of it, rough and hesitant.

'That's it! Keep it going,' Harry said enthusiastically to a series of indistinguishable tones. To Pim they sounded very much like a double bass coughing. After the last cough, the instrument shook from spike to scroll and began to make tones.

'Listen! He can sustain a melody now,' Harry exclaimed.

'You call this a melody?' a voice, still rough, came out of Band. 'I call it sawing,' he declared with a gargle, 'but don't stop. It feels good.'

Pim continued to slide the bow and a slow, exhausted music continued. Harry stepped aside and began checking all his pockets. He patted himself at almost every centimetre of his body before triumphally producing the Book of Gates, which in the shade of one of the Towers now seemed surrounded by a halo of bluish light.

'I was worried you'd lost it,' said Pim.

'I never lose things,' Harry replied. 'I only ever misplace them.'

'So is there a gate here?'

Harry looked at the index and then said: 'A gate? No.'

'I thought this book contained all the gates in Left World.'

'It does. The only hitch is that we happen to be in the middle of a sea called the Endless Ocean, and on a mythical object that was not supposed to exist.'

'I thought everything imaginable existed in Zandar.'

'Well, it doesn't. Or at least not for everybody. And if for Arne Saknussemm, who knew all the gates, the Towers did not exist it means that there's no gate here.'

'How will we ever reach Star Central from here? How will I ever find that taxi? How will I find my gate?' said Pim.

'Never mind your taxi, what will happen to Zandar if I don't get to Star Central soon?' said Harry.

By now Band had recovered enough to pop out three curious horns. They stopped playing and were keenly listening to the conversation between Pim and Harry. 'What is it exactly that you two are talking about?'

Harry immediately returned the book to the pocket. 'We were talking about the secret of the Towers. Isn't that so, Pim?'

'Ahem.'

'The secret, of course!' Band suddenly remembered. 'Now that we are here we have to find the secret of the Towers of Billbalirion.'

'No, we don't!' said Harry.

'Yes, we do!' Band replied passionately. 'This secret has been sought by generations of sailors on the Endless Ocean. They were willing to give away their keel and cargo for it. They could not have all been wrong.'

'But the Towers are empty! There's nobody here,' said Harry pointing at the Towers with his moustache.

'Yes, but what if he's right, in a sense?' said Pim. 'Maybe there is something to be found here. Something that could help us.'

Harry emitted a long 'Hmmm' before answering. 'It seems there's not much else that we can do here anyway. Alright. Let's rest and then devise a plan.'

'There is just one small hitch with this plan, too,' said Band.

'What?'

'I am afraid of the secret.'

'What?' said Harry.

'Why?' said Pim.

'Because it's a secret secret.'

'Right, then you stay here and take a look around the base. Harry and I will climb the towers.'

Harry looked at Pim. 'You mean *climb* the Towers?'

'Yes.'

'You mean climb *up*?'

'Aha. You wanted to devise a plan: so choose a tower. That will be your plan.' But Harry did not look convinced.

'Look, secret or no secret, we did not come here to sunbathe.' said Pim. 'We have to find a way to get off this thing. We can only do it when it comes close to land. And that we can see only from the top.'

'That's a plan,' conceded Harry. 'But it's impossible to do it in a day,' he said looking up at the two immense ornate towers before them.

'Then do it in two. If night falls before you're back, lie down and sleep. That's what I'll do anyway,' concluded Pim.

An hour later, the plan had not been devised yet – that is, Harry had not made up his mind about which of the two towers to choose. More precisely, he kept changing his choice. After he changed his mind for the umpteenth time, Pim stood up impatiently.

'That's it. I am going. You just plan to go to the other tower from the one I take,' he said and left for the left tower.

'That's exactly what I was planning to do,' Harry said after him and then set out towards the right tower, leaving Band lying in the sun and stretching his strings one by one.

Pim decided to walk around the base of his tower first. It took several minutes and revealed only one entrance. It was really only an opening, just big enough to pass through. When his eyes got accustomed to the darkness inside, he saw a hall more spacious than any cathedral, mosque or warehouse that he had ever seen, even in a Taschen book. The hall was completely empty. Its walls were smooth and arched upwards to form a high ceiling with a large opening in the middle. When Pim stood right below it he could see that it ended in a long open tube which provided the only light inside the hall, apart from the minuscule trail of sun coming from the door he used to enter.

There was a staircase on the opposite wall. It was made of slabs sticking out of the wall and it stopped abruptly half-way up. There was no fence and Pim had to make sure he kept close to the wall as he went up. The hall seemed even bigger from the top of the stairs and at the bottom the door through which he came in looked small and distant. There was a short passage through the wall on top of the stairs leading to another big hall, not much different from the first one.

I wonder if the Towers were ever inhabited, Pim thought as he climbed the stairs in the second hall. They must have been made by somebody or something, and for some purpose. But it was not at all obvious what that could have been. Maybe that's the secret, he thought for a moment and then decided against it.

The staircase went straight through a wall, came out on the other side and continued on the outside wall of the tower. It was an unpleasant feeling because there was no fence and nothing to separate him from the drop below. When he carefully went down on all fours to peek over the edge he could only see the sea below him.

The climb around the outside wall did not last long and Pim soon ended up in a chamber that looked exactly like the others, only it was smaller than the two previous halls. The ceiling curved into a vertical tube just like before, but there were three exits out of it. Pim went to check all three and they all led to similar chambers which differed only in size.

He returned to the outside stairs to see which exits led to turrets and which exit would lead him higher up. It wasn't immediately obvious which passage to take, but Pim was satisfied with his decision when the path he chose led him higher and higher, through a succession of chambers and terraces.

He was not particularly afraid of heights but the feeling of standing at the edge of a terrace and looking straight down was not a pleasant one. In the end he overcame any fear he might have had by thinking that he only needed to see a trace of land somewhere on the horizon. As soon as he could determine the direction of land, he would go down and tell his two companions about it.

How to get to that land was another matter, but Pim preferred not to think about it for the moment – in films they always build a raft or something. They would surely be able to find something among the jetsam and flotsam at the base. The main thing now was to find the direction of the closest land. Pim decided to convince himself that he would not be afraid to take to the sea on a simple raft if he knew that land was close.

After all, the storm may have pushed them closer to Dembeliland, he thought. The full circle has 360 degrees, and at least some of them must lead to land. Then again, others don't. But that's exactly why all this climbing is worth it, Pim repeated to himself.

And as for the secret, he didn't terribly mind if they didn't find it. What they needed was one sole sighting of land, any land on the horizon.

The Towers were huge and it took quite some time before Pim concluded that he had maybe climbed one fourth of the way up. There were more branches with turrets now and it wasn't always a straightforward thing to choose the right staircase on a terrace or in a chamber. More than once he climbed several flights of stairs only to end up in a beautifully ornamented turret with no way out except the way he came.

But there was one good thing about turrets and that was their sturdy balcony walls. There, he did not have to edge slowly on all four towards the emptiness beyond an open ledge. He could stand and walk along the balcony wall to look all around. The view was different from every turret. From turrets on the inner side of the tower he could regularly see Band on the base, a smaller and smaller dot fidgeting deep below. Every now and then he scanned the opposite tower for any sight of Harry, but he didn't see him.

Pim was now so high that he could not guess any more how far the horizon was. He looked at the endless lines of waves sporting a white crest here and there, slowly disappearing in the distance. The view is not all that bad, he thought, although there is pretty much nothing to see. But still, the higher I go, the nicer it is. Well, at least as long as I have the strength to climb.

When he came to what he thought was about one half of the total height of the tower, he ran out of steam and made a break. He sat on a terrace, not too close to the edge, and looked out at the sea, still breathing heavily.

'I know what the secret of the Towers is,' he said aloud. 'The secret is that there is no secret. That's what it is. There is absolutely nothing remotely interesting on these towers and that's what they tried to keep secret. Bloody stairs! There's more of them here than in the Petronas Towers. Oh, if I could only go there again, and take one of their elevators.'

Then he stopped talking to save his breath and continued the internal monologue. It's nonsense, this secret. Only because nobody ever set foot on the Towers before, people think that there must be something here. Something unknown, and of course, fantastically desirable. Stairs, stairs and more stairs, that's the famed secret of the Towers. Let's face it: there is no secret and there never was. OK, alright, maybe we don't know who built them and what they are all about, but that's just something we don't know. It's a mystery – not a secret, he finished, satisfied with this conclusion and then spent the next twenty minutes lying on his back and looking into the blue sky.

The climbing continued for the better part of the day. Pim could not quite say what rule he was following, but he became quite adept at choosing the right passages. He did not have to go back down and choose another staircase so often.

Then as he came out on a terrace and looked up, he realized that there were less turrets at this height. That is why it was easier to find the way up. Good, he said to himself, I'll rest when I climb to the top. No more breaks – this was the final push.

But it still took a couple of hours before he stood at the base of the central spire of the tower which rose over all other turrets, spikes and steeples. The spire was empty and there was a narrow spiral staircase inside leading up. Pim covered the last few dozens of steps easily, knowing that there were no more to come. He came out inside a plump little turret that stood at the very top of the Towers of Billbalirion in a curious contrast to the elongated spire whose tip it was supposed to embellish. It was the highest and the loneliest turret on the Towers.

There was no fence, just a wide circular ledge on the outside. Pim walked all around to take in the view.

There was a similar turret on top of the opposite tower, but it was too far away to see if Harry had managed to climb that far. The base and Band could not be seen because of the turrets below. The sea extended in all directions as far as the eye could see. There was no hint of land anywhere on the horizon. 'Well, that's the Endless Ocean for you,' he said thinking of Captain Bassalian's map.

Pim still spent some time looking towards the sun, hoping that maybe a sight of land was lost somewhere in the silvery reflections of the waves below. He again went down on all fours and then carefully edged towards the edge of the terrace. At first he lay prone and looked into the distance in front of him but then, little by little, he sat up, felt more courageous and, in the end, even let his feet dangle below the edge. He felt strangely attracted by the sight in front of him.

The vast immeasurable expanse of the ocean extended as far as the eye could see. Pim sat facing the sun which was by now only slightly above the distant horizon. Never before has anybody seen a sunset from such an amazing perspective, he thought. All imaginable shades of red, orange and yellow filled the view as the sun slowly sank behind the only cloud in the sky that just happened to be spread low above the horizon. It was no more than a thin veil over the sky, but it was this veil that was responsible for all the magnificent colours of the sky and sea.

An unexpected feeling of well-being suddenly filled Pim from the inside. He was overcome by the pure splendour of the sight before him. The beauty of the dying sun which spread its golden mantle over the ocean was amplified by the sheer scale of this spectacle seen from the very top of the Towers of Billbalirion. Now I know, when they speak of a once-in-a-lifetime experience, that this is what they mean, Pim said to himself.

There are not many people who can say that they have seen a sunset from this perspective, he thought. Others spend a fortune going to the farthest corners of the Earth to witness something not nearly as beautiful as this. Just look at it! It's as if some giant goldsmith kept engraving waves on an infinite sea of solid gold, nudging them gently towards the oblivion of the setting sun.

I don't really know how it came to be that I found myself here, Pim thought, and to be honest, I don't even know if I am ever going to return home. But when I look at this glorious sight, it is as if everything I did so far in my life had only one purpose – to bring me here and make me experience the most dazzling splendour that nature dares to divulge to mortals.

A breath of warm air tickled him on the chest as if to increase his feeling of oneness with the spectacle slowly playing out around him. He enjoyed the wind in his hair and on his closed eyes. A soft pleasant breeze rose from the sea, playing around the Towers of Billbalirion, seeking a way into its cavernous bowels. The wind came in short gusts, feeling the turrets and tubes that led all the way to their chambers, looking for a chance resonance to get inside. And when it finally found the way in, one clear loud tone emanated from the Towers over the ocean. Another followed it soon, and another, and the Towers of Billbalirion began to sing.

A melancholic melody in perfect tune with the sunset rose from the Towers and travelled over the ocean. Pim was overwhelmed by the multitude of tones that all the chambers and all the halls could produce together. He was sitting on the greatest organ of both worlds as it performed its piece to an ocean devoid of any audience. As the last remnant of the sun sank into the sea far away, Pim Pergamon was completely overtaken by the spectacular experience. All of a sudden he felt happy that he was part of the magnificent show that Left World played for him.

'So that must be the famed secret of the Towers of Billbalirion,' he said, mesmerized by the perfection of the tones which reached crescendo together with the beauty of the last moments of daylight on the sea. The secret is the beauty itself, he thought.

Great secret, tremendous secret! But not of much use right now.

Far away on an outpost on a distant shore, a guard walked on his solitary patrol in darkness. The sun had already set there and only a very faint glow of day remained on the horizon. The ramparts were long and deserted. The long evening heave of the sea breaking below was the only sound on his lonely rounds. It was a moonless night and the sea merged with the starry skies somewhere far away in the growing darkness before him.

The guard stopped and turned, listening intently to the darkness above the sea. A faint tone came from across the ocean and was heard for a moment above the waves. And then, in the few moments when the sea below silently retreated before being embraced by the next wave, there came a brief respite. The guard heard the wind carrying a clear sequence of tones from far away. He listened intently until the next wave came crushing on the rocks below and drowned the sounds coming across the sea. When the wave withdrew again there was only silence on the ramparts.

The guard shrugged, stretched his wings and continued his lonely round.

The Duty Cloud

Pim thought he must have overslept because when he opened his eyes the next day in the topmost turret of the left Billbalirion Tower, he awoke with a gloomy feeling of a rainy afternoon. The weather outside was dull and sunless and he did not feel at all like springing into action. But his bones ached from sleeping on the hard floor and he forced himself to get up and stretch.

Things did not look good outside. There was a thick fog and he could not see even the end of the ledge in front of him, let alone the sea. Yesterday's sunset was spectacular but sunsets were not the best time for observations and Pim had intended to scour the horizon once again under the morning sun.

But waiting for turn in the weather could take very long indeed, he thought as he paced around outside the turret. Hardly had he made a full circle when he heard a giggle. He stopped and looked around.

'Anybody there?' he said. The giggle stopped. He returned inside and looked at the staircase which led from below. 'Band? Harry?'

Just as he was about to go down, bright sunlight flooded the turret. All of a sudden, blue sky could be seen through all the windows, as if there were no clouds outside. He turned back.

When he came out on the ledge of the turret there was not a trace of the fog. What was just a moment ago an overcast leaden sky now looked like a bright sunny morning. The visibility was excellent, far better than yesterday and he could see far, far away.

He walked around the ledge of the turret slowly taking in the full circle of the horizon. To his great disappointment, the Towers were still surrounded by nothing else but an infinite expanse of the ocean. There was not a trace of land in sight.

This was not good news.

He looked inside the turret as he pondered his options and was surprised to see a cloud through the opposite window on the other side where there were no clouds just a few moments ago. The weather here could change very quickly indeed!

But when he came to the other side, the sky there was crystally clear. A cloud could now be seen through the windows on the opposite side, exactly where he had just come from.

Pim now walked slowly around the ledge, keeping an eye on the cloud. There was no mistake – just as he was making a circle on one side, the cloud was doing the same on the other side. When Pim walked slowly, the cloud moved slowly and when Pim paced up, the cloud did the same. Not once, but in three full circles, almost as if it did not want to be seen. Whoever heard of clouds playing hide and seek!

OK, if he wants to play, I know how to play, Pim said to himself. He darted inside the turret and appeared on the opposite window. 'Aha!'

A small cloudlet stood right in front of him not far from the turret.

At first nothing happened. Then the cloud said, 'Hello'.

'Hello,' Pim replied and came out from the turret.

'Who are you?' said the cloudlet.

'My name is Pim Pergamon. And who are you?'

'I am Dapertutto. I am a cloud. And you?'

'I am a human.'

They looked at each other in silence for a while. What on earth do you say to a cloud?

'It's nice to meet you, Dapertutto,' was the best thing Pim could come up with. 'And very unexpected.'

'I didn't expect to find anybody here on the Towers either,' Dapertutto replied. 'I was really frightened when I felt somebody tickling me from inside. I am very ticklish as we clouds go.'

'I didn't mean to tickle you. I was walking around the turret, trying to see through the fog.'

'A fog? It was no fog, it was me. And I am a cloud,' the cloudlet firmly declared.

'I didn't mean to offend you.'

'Oh, I have nothing against fogs. It's just that I am a cloud.'

'I know that. But hasn't anyone ever told you that from inside you look just like a fog?'

'What? Me? No, nobody ever told me that. Oh, well …' Dapertutto sounded a bit crestfallen. 'I guess that's because nobody ever saw me from inside. I was told already that I am too airy and that I talk too much. But I didn't know that I was a fog inside! I guess I don't know myself very well. A fog, you say …' The cloud's sadness was almost palpable. All his droplets had lost their sparkle.

'Don't take it too much to your heart,' Pim tried to back-pedal looking at Dapertutto's hung face. 'All clouds are foggy on the inside.'

'Oh!' Dapertutto's world was crumbling before his eyes.

'There's nothing wrong about a fog,' Pim hastened to add. 'And trust me, inside you've got one of the best fogs I've ever seen. Thick, firm and very hazy. Really. Totally hazy. I've seen fogs and fogs and yours is, mmm, positively foggy.'

'Really? You know fogs?'

'Oh, yeah. Sure. Fogs are my speciality. I am into fogs – very much into fogs,' Pim repeated a couple of times before switching to another topic. 'But listen, tell me something. You see, I was trying to look for land when I inadvertently tickled you – for which I am really sorry, and – '

'Oh, I like tickling, I just didn't expect to be tickled on the Towers – of all places. I come here whenever I have an itch and I've never come across anybody else before.'

It occurred to Pim that this could also be the famous secret of the Towers, a scratching place for meteorological phenomena. But he chased this thought away to concentrate on more important things.

'Do you know where land is?'

'Of course. That way,' Dapertutto made a puffy gesture showing somewhere far away.

'How far is it?'

'Oh, I don't know. Far away.'

'Are you sure it's that way?'

'Of course. Look for yourself. The Towers of Billbalirion are always aligned parallel to land. That means that the direction of land is perpendicular to the line between the two towers.'

'Always?'

'Always.'

Finally a secret that is useful!

'What's so special about land?' asked Dapertutto.

'I can walk on it, for one,' said Pim. 'And there are no waves and no storms on land.'

'That's not true, there are storms on land.'

'Yes, but they simply don't compare to storms on sea. Take last night's storm for instance, it was the most terrible storm I have ever seen.'

'The night before last you mean.'

'Yes – wait, how do you know? Were you involved?'

'Of course I was involved. We were all involved.'

'What came over you people?' Pim shouted at the cloud. 'It was terrible! I almost drowned!'

'You see, normally we clouds just play by blowing to and fro. Sometimes we get carried away and, before you know it, there is a storm. But – '

'Carried away! You got carried away? Is that the best explanation you can think of?!'

'No, no, I am telling you – two days ago a powerful wizard named Talambas appeared on the ocean and summoned all the winds and all the clouds of the sky into a storm.

'Aha, so you were invited to a storm. Is that your excuse? Did you bring Mrs. Dapertutto as well? Was the buffet to your liking?'

'You have to understand, Pim Pergamon, that there is no answering back when Talambas orders you to do something. He rules over the Ocean and we are all in his thrall.'

'Yeah, but what about all other people at sea? Not everybody can fly above the waves, you know! In fact, nobody I know can fly. We keep to ships and we are not invited to storms – they come to us, uninvited!'

'You mean you were not here on the Towers during the storm?'

'No. I was on the Pride of Slimy Tentacle.'

'Oh.'

'Oh? *Oh??* It was the most frightening experience of my life! I was this close to dying! It was horrible! I thought I would never make it! I almost drowned!'

Dapertutto looked down in embarrassment while Pim paced left and right until his fury subsided. Summoned to a storm! What a concept! And what a callous disregard for others!

It took some time before Dapertutto dared open his mouth again. 'I am sorry for the storm. Do you still want to talk to me?'

'Harrumph.'

'I have never before had a chance to talk to someone like you,' said Dapertutto. 'I only get to talk to other clouds. And lightning bolts. But you can't have a meaningful conversation with a lightning bolt. It's over before it began. That's why I really want to talk to someone like you.'

'What's so special about me?'

'You've got a body, and arms and legs! And I am so curious about how it feels to run and jump.'

'Well, now that you mention it,' Pim softened up, 'I was always curious about clouds and rainbows and sunsets.'

'Oh, I was the duty cloud for yesterday's sunset. Did you see it?'

'It was you?'

'Did you like it?'

'Did I like it? It was the most awesome sunset I have ever seen!' exclaimed Pim.

'You know, proper cloudage is very important for a good sunset. Not too little and not too much. You've got to stretch almost into a veil, but not go as far as haze.'

And so it transpired that Pim and Dapertutto had many things in common. They were both curious and they both liked explaining things. Dapertutto wanted to impart to Pim everything they taught him at the Cloud Conservatory while Pim tried to teach Dapertutto how to jump.

If somebody had watched the Towers of Billbalirion now, they would have been intrigued by a small cloud which kept fluttering around the highest turret like a balloon in a wind. But there was no wind. The cloud flapped about on his own as he explained meteorology the way clouds see it to Pim, who had two questions for every answer.

They talked for hours, and would have talked for days if Dapertutto at one point hadn't insisted on showing Pim just how strong clouds were. His demonstration consisted mostly of a tremendous inhaling of air. He kept huffing and puffing, getting bigger and bigger with every breath – until he simply couldn't hold it any more. When he proudly tried to say 'See?' all that he managed to say was 'Sss...' before exhaling with such a colossal force that he was blown off the Towers and far into the distance.

When Dapertutto was no more than a dot in the sky and it became clear that coming back would be more difficult than going there, Pim remembered that Harry and Band were waiting for him at the base of the Towers.

Somewhere in London a doorbell rang.

Nothing happened.

It rang again.

Nothing.

And again.

Finally Mehdi appeared in the corridor even more tousled up than usual, tossed a cushion back at someone, and opened the door. It was raining in West Acton.

'Hey, how's things, how's it going?' Andy greeted him full of cool. Mehdi did not say a thing, but took him by the arm to his room instead. When he closed the door, he grabbed him by the shoulders.

'I've seen that guy again – in Open Oceans IV!'

'Who? What guy?'

'Remember the guy that I told you about, the one who was standing right in front of me in the queue when they were doing the testing in ACG? The one who was accepted for the program?'

'Yeah, and like, what?'

'I saw him again – only inside a game! He was on the sea in Open Oceans IV.'

'What?'

'You know how sometimes if you do not calculate your bearings correctly, or something happens, you end up in some part of the ocean that's completely empty? Well, that's what happened to me yesterday. And when I was about to give up and just switch it off, I saw a ship on the ocean below and I was curious. So I zoomed in to get a better view, and there he was!'

'Who?'

'The guy who was standing in front of me in the queue on the Isle of Dogs was standing on the deck of a ship in Open Oceans IV!'

'You mean the real guy from in front of you?'

'Yes!'

'Listen, it must have been something like one of those morphing characters from – '

'I can recognize a morph when I see one, thank you!' Andy rejected the ludicrous proposition outright. 'I'm telling you, it was him, I had a good look, it was, like, totally him.'

'But that doesn't make any sense,' Andy replied dismissively. 'Why would anybody want to play as himself and not through an avatar? I mean, like, it's the whole point, dude! To be someone else, someone cooler than your real self! Get it?'

'I'm telling you I saw him there.'

'I don't believe you.'

'Well, I'll show you! I calculated the approximate coordinates.'

Mehdi switched on the computer. 'You'll see, it's him. Now everything makes sense – remember the storm that morning? Remember how they called it a freak show of nature? Well, it definitely wasn't nature.'

Andy didn't even respond to the last suggestion. He just puffed impatiently at a lock on his forehead that somehow avoided the gel onslaught that befell the rest of the hair. When the console finally finished waking up Mehdi quickly keyed in the position he visited earlier. The picture rotated and then zoomed in on a quadrant of sea. But the sea was empty.

'And?' said Andy.

'Wait, I'll move it around a bit,' Mehdi replied and began to circle above the waves. They waited as he made wider and wider circles but all the sea they could see was empty. 'I think I have to increase the elevation.'

There was still nothing on the screen. No ship, just the blue expanse of the ocean. Mehdi kept working the joystick in wider and wider circles, his eyes glued to the screen looking for any sign of life on the sea below.

'Say, have you seen my earpiece?' said Andy. 'The one from ACG. I can't find it anywhere.'

'No, I haven't,' Mehdi replied, his eyes glued to the screen.

'I've got to have it when they call me again to the testing, you know.'

'If they call you again.'

'Maybe I lost it here. Can I look around for it?'

'Sure,' said Mehdi and reluctantly paused the game.

Searching for anything in Mehdi's room was a lost cause from the outset. The mess in his room had a life of its own. Sometimes it would produce long-lost objects so that they were all of a sudden noticed at the most conspicuous places – but there was no such luck today.

'I don't think it's here,' Mehdi said after a while.

'Can you ask your sister if she saw it?'

Mehdi opened the door only to find Mia standing right behind it. 'What is it that you wanted to ask me about?' she said.

'Have you maybe seen my ACG earpiece? I think I lost it,' said Andy.

'No, I am sure you took it with you when you left.'

'Then I definitely lost it,' Andy said glumly.

'Oh, they'll give you another one when the testing resumes,' Mehdi wanted to reassure his friend.

'Yeah, but I won't have it until then. I wanted to show it to Michelle.'

'And just what makes you think that she would want to see it?'

'She asked me to show it to her. But then I couldn't find it. I told her I'd bring it as soon as I found it.'

It didn't pass unnoticed by Mehdi that his best friend had apparently chatted up the most attractive girl in the school with a story about the ACG testing – so he felt depressed all over again for not making it to the testing. He certainly wouldn't have lost the most important piece of the story as his fool of a friend did! He would be showing the titillating Michelle the earpiece even as they spoke.

'I think I'll be going now,' said Andy. 'And listen, if that thing in Open Oceans IV bugs you again, you should call the helpdesk. I can't help you, I don't play that game any more, it's like, sooo last month.'

'Well, I am not into it that much anyway,' Mehdi quickly said. 'It's just that I saw that guy there, and I was curious about how that could be. You think there's a way to play as yourself? That'd be cool.'

'Naah, it wouldn't,' Andy said and left.

Mehdi went to his room and closed the door. He planned to turn the room upside down. He was sure the earpiece was somewhere inside and he fully intended to find it.

When Band woke up on the base of the Towers of Billbalirion, the sun had already passed through the meridian and begun its slow descent towards the horizon. After a long session of stretching which would have looked like an orchestra roll call to an unknowing bystander, Band walked slowly back to the place where they had agreed to meet, the same place where they climbed on to the Towers. For most of the way, the base was just a wide empty space overlooked by the two immense towers looking from above.

Although he had the least to explore, somehow Band was the last to come back and he found Pim and Harry already sitting on the ground.

'A fire! We should light a great fire to attract passing ships,' Harry was explaining to Pim. 'That's what everybody does in this kind of situation. It always works.'

'I think that we have to consider the likelihood that we might have to be self-sustainable on the Towers for some time,' Pim was explaining to Harry. 'For instance, we might have to grow our own vegetables.'

'Grow vegetables?' Harry looked at Pim with enough incredulity to bring down a whole system of philosophy.

'It could be fun.'

'It could be fun? Have you ever grown your own vegetables before?'

'No, but it's a good thing to grow your own vegetables. Practically everybody says so.'

'Really? I'd like to meet "practically everybody" some time. I think I might learn a lot. Tell me, from what do you intend to grow these vegetables?'

'Hmm, you have a point. In actual fact, we don't even have something to set fire to, let alone grow vegetables,' Pim said accompanied by a long, wistful sound of hunger from his belly. 'I say we might have a problem.'

'I say we are doomed,' said Harry.

'What a fine outfit you two are,' Band spoke in b-flat after listening patiently through the better part of the discourse. 'Sir Henry Grenfell-Moresby, Royal Bedelmator Plen*im*potentiary! And with him, a representative of nothing less than Right World, and you can't muster enough wisdom between the two of you to fill your empty stomachs,' said Band. 'What's the use of having the Book of Gates if you can't solve such a simple problem?'

'We don't have any such book,' Harry replied vehemently.

'Of course not. I have it,' said Band and produced a small booklet. 'I went through your pockets when you were resuscitating me. But I am giving it back to you.'

'You impudent fiddler!' Harry grabbed the book from Band.

'Harry, you don't seem to realize that we are in it together – '

'Don't you call me Harry!'

' – whatever that *it* is and wherever it might bring us,' Band finished the sentence and turned to Pim.

'Alright, we are headed for Star Central,' Pim said to Band. 'And you?'

'Sounds good enough to me,' Band replied. 'Although maybe a bit optimistic looking from here.'

'The more of us working for the same goal, the more reasons to be optimistic,' said Pim and turned to Harry.

Harry looked at Band and then slowly said: 'First of all, I am not a Bedelmator. I am Sir Henry Grenfell-Moresby, Royal Bedel and Proclamator Extraordinary *and* Plenipotentiary – '

'A Bedel! A Royal Bedel!' Band interrupted him. 'You live in a bygone age, man. Bedel used to mean something, maybe even used to be something, but times have changed. Your title is just – just an administrative ornament now! A part of folklore at best! You should get a real job, man.'

'What, and incessant fiddling around with no constant abode I suppose *is* a real job, ha!'

'Our temperaments differ significantly. So do our jobs, Sir Henry,' Band gleefully enunciated the last two words.

'Don't you call me Sir Henry!' came the roaring reply. Pim felt it was high time he stepped in.

'Look, it's easy for you two to sneer at each other's meaningful contribution to society – '

'Don't side with him!' shouted Harry.

' – but what will you do when you get hungry?'

'Oh, that? Follow me,' Band said nonchalantly.

He walked towards the edge of the base and started to descend down the slope. 'What are you waiting for?' he waved. 'Come on.' Pim and Harry reluctantly followed.

'This!' Band said when they came to the edge of the massive mess of the flotsam and jetsam at the bottom of the base. 'This is where I would look if I were hungry,' he stepped off the Base and on to the flotsam.

A long entangled mess of ropes, timbers and sea weed extended left and right from them. 'If I am not mistaken,' said Band, 'everything that could be found on sea can be found here. We just have to look.'

'Look for what?' said Harry.

'This for instance!' Pim pointed towards a chest covered with sea weed that he discovered below.

The three of them disentangled the chest from the rest of the flotsam and Pim impatiently opened it. Its contents were soaked in sea water. Pim took something that looked like a leaflet out of it.

'"The best winds – the calmest seas – a great benefits package",' he read out aloud. 'What's this? "Human, elf or spirit – all are wanted by Open Oceans IV for superb maritime operations positions. Knowledge of knots and coarse language an asset. Apply to Cmrd. Krivonossoff at Open Oceans IV." I think the box is full of them,' he ended on a less enthusiastic tone.

'We just have to look further,' Harry responded suddenly full of enthusiasm as if it was his idea. 'Let's go this way. Let's see what we can find around the base.'

'Listen to the man, the man is right,' said Band as if there had never been a shred of discord between him and Harry. So the three companions spread over the face of the flotsam and began to work their way forward. The heap consisted mostly of timber, some of it still obviously in its former sea-faring form, the rest mangled beyond recognition and wrapped in ropes and seaweed. Every now and then they would come across a mast sticking out of the tangle of flotsam and jetsam, battered and broken, but sometimes still pointing upwards. There were many sails, shredded or wrapped around unrecognisable lumps of material.

'There,' Band said after some time. He was pointing at a bleached sail that looked like it was wrapped around a giant bunch of grapes. 'Let's look there.'

When they rolled up the sail they came across a heap of barrels. All three of them descended at the first barrel at hand and struggled to open it. It turned out it was full of sauerkraut.

'Iyyahh!' Band said at this discovery.

'There is nothing wrong with a good sauerkraut,' said Harry and pulled Band away from the barrel.

'My thoughts exactly,' Pim joined in at the sight of the first food in days.

They also found a barrel of beer and another filled with salted beef. 'This is it guys, these are our vegetables for now,' said Band. All three of them settled wherever they found themselves and eagerly began to eat, despite occasional demands coming from Harry's full mouth that a proper table be set.

It was some time before anybody could pause long enough to say anything. Harry was the first one who managed to make up a sentence between bites: 'By the way – I found – the Secret – of the Towers ...'

'You did?' Band and Pim answered, surprised. Harry was chewing a hefty chunk of salted beef so he only said, 'Ahamm.'

'Well, tell us about it,' demanded Band.

'Yes,' said Harry and took one more bite to last him through the explanation. 'Yes, I found the secret inside the topmost turret on the tallest spire of my tower. The tower itself was empty – I passed through many chambers on the way up but I haven't found anything in any of them. And then, inside the highest turret, on a pedestal, I saw the last thing one would expect to find on a tower in the middle of the sea,' he said and paused as if expecting Pim and Band to guess what.

'What?' they said instead.

'It was a beautiful stone flower,' replied Harry. 'It was the most amazing and delicate thing made of stone that I ever saw. It would have looked like a real flower if it wasn't for the green colour of the malachite from which it was made. Nothing else that I have seen comes close to the magnificence of that stone flower. It was beautiful and priceless.'

'A flower. A stone flower,' Pim said to Harry's story. 'What's so special about a stone flower that it would constitute the legendary secret of the Towers?'

'Malachite is only found inside mountains, as far from any sea as it could possibly be,' said Harry impatiently. 'Don't you see? Malachite is not the stuff of seagulls. It is the favourite working stone of dwarves high up in the mountains. The flower I saw does not belong here. It belongs to someone who doesn't know that it is here. And that is the secret of the Towers of Billbalirion.'

'Maybe,' said Pim. 'And then again, maybe not.'

'What do you mean?' said Band.

'I discovered another secret. And I think that it is the right secret of the Towers.'

'We have another nomination for the secret of the towers,' Band announced to a displeased Harry.

'I also climbed a tower yesterday,' Pim started to explain while Harry's moustache began to twitch on one side. 'And I passed through many chambers of various sizes on the way up. And I noticed that all of them had a tube leading out and upwards. Yesterday evening, when I was on the topmost turret watching the sunset, I felt the wind when it came and entered the tubular bowels of my tower. And when the wind reached the chambers below, the whole edifice became a gigantic organ and began to sing. Didn't you hear it? It was the most beautiful melody I have ever heard.'

'Yes, we heard it. And you are right, it was magnificent,' Band replied. 'But what's so secret about it? It must have been heard for miles and miles around.'

'On the contrary,' Pim said. 'Nobody ever heard it.'

'How can you know that?' Harry said impatiently as the moustache twitch moved from left to right. 'Have you asked everybody on the ocean?'

'Sometimes you don't need to ask everybody to know something about them. Just think: everybody on this ocean keeps talking about the Towers of Billbalirion, but nobody ever mentioned that the Towers made music. Surely something so unusual and so fantastic would have been the first thing to mention when explaining the Towers to somebody.' The moustache under Harry's nose stopped twitching. 'And yet nobody on the Pride of Slimy Tentacle said anything about the most magnificent organ that ever existed in Left or Right World. Why? They just haven't heard it. Nobody ever heard the Towers of Billbalirion. Nobody knows that they sing. And something that nobody knows is a secret. This happens to be the secret of the Towers – just as Bangus McBroom described it.'

'We are the first ever to hear the music of the Towers? Wow, that's quite something,' Band looked excited by the thought. 'Quite impressive – but not impressive enough.'

'Oh, yeah?' said Pim.

'Oh, yeah.'

'Does this mean that you have also discovered a secret?' Harry asked Band full of suspicion and his moustache began twitching again.

'I think it does, Harry,' Pim said and turned to Band. 'Come on, tell us your nomination for the Secret of the Towers of Billbalirion.'

'I don't have to nominate anything,' Band replied in a-flat. 'I will show it to you. Come.'

As it turned out, there was a narrow trench in the middle of the base of the Towers gently leading down into a narrow passage. The path they took brought them to a small platform under the base of the Towers. It took some time before their eyes got accustomed to the darkness below. They stood on the platform suspended just above the sea. The Towers of Billbalirion formed a vast low ceiling above them spreading far in every direction. As far as they could see, the water below the base was as calm as oil. The only light there was the knife-like ray of light shining vertically through the cut in the base and the thin circular sliver of sky on all sides that encircled them like a bright but distant ring at the ends of the base.

'Lie down here,' Band gestured towards the edge of the platform, 'and listen closely to the sea.'

'Do we have to lie down?' asked Harry.

'You have to bring your ear just above the surface, almost touch it.'

'And then what?' said Pim.

'And then you'll hear the secret.'

Harry did not look like he was about to lie today. He stood upright, with his arms crossed, and no intention of playing along. So it was left to Pim to lie down at the edge of the platform. The dark deep blue of the sea was just centimetres away. The feeling of his head being the closest point of the whole Towers of Billbalirion to the sea was somewhat unsettling for Pim. But Band prodded him on and he turned his head and lowered his ear to the sea.

Suddenly he heard a multitude of sounds. Wind, shouts and waves, seagulls, singing and whispering, grating of ship's timbers mixed with friction of ropes, and many restless voices could be heard coming from all sides. Pim saw Band saying something but could not hear him as long as he was immersed in the cacophony around him. He lifted his head, just a bit, and all the sounds went away.

'We are exactly between the two Towers and at the centre of the base,' Band declared with great satisfaction. 'This is the place where all the sounds from all over the ocean meet. What you can hear here is everything that is happening on the ocean now. If you listen carefully, you will hear every word uttered on the sea, you will know every secret. And this, put simply, is the great Secret of the Towers of Billbalirion. Yours were fine, but my secret comes with a capital S,' he finished beaming with satisfaction.

Pim lowered his head again into the ocean of sounds. He could hear quarrels mixed with crying out of fish prices, and orders to fasten the sails interspersed with orders to launch boats. There was a constant background of waves and wind and it was hard to understand the words that came in squalls from everywhere around him. He heard songs and avowals of love followed by promises to come back. He heard thunder and rain and children splashing on beaches somewhere far away.

Harry was by now sufficiently intrigued by the expressions on Pim's face as much as with the fact that Pim showed no signs that he was about to stop what he was doing. So he slowly kneeled, crouched and finally lay down – face up.

'You can't hear anything like that,' Band told him.

'I am more comfortable this way,' Harry replied and pretended to feel around for the most suitable position before finally clumsily turning over. His face changed when he immersed his head into the sea of sounds. He listened for awhile and then turned to Band: 'But it's impossible to discern anything. There is too much to be heard.'

'You just have to try and concentrate. Listen carefully. Don't you know how to listen?' replied Band. Then he too lied down.

By the time the three companions had enough of the sounds of the sea, nobody among them had any idea how long they were listening. First they looked at each other in silence. Then Harry spoke.

'I think this is the real secret of the Towers. The place to hear everything – if only I could hear anything.'

'I think your sarcasm is misplaced. Even if we don't hear everything, the third secret is certainly the most impressive secret so far,' said Pim.

'What sarcasm? I agree with you. It *is* the real secret!' Harry loudly protested. 'Why do you have to bend everything I say?'

'So we are all agreed that this is the secret of the Towers?' said Band.

'Yes,' answered Pim.

'Harry?'

'Though it pains me to do so, no Grenfell-Moresby has ever shrunk from truth, and so shan't I,' Harry declared with great magnanimity – and great tragedy in his voice.

'A simple yes will suffice, thank you,' said Band.

'Having said that,' Harry hastened to add, 'I could hardly understand anything, except one constant sound in the background, something like *Ing Ping, Ing Ping, Ing Ping*.'

'I heard that, too,' said Band.

'I only managed to catch one name, and that only because it was repeated so many times.'

'Which name?'

'Psalmanazar.'

'That's strange,' said Pim. 'I didn't hear that name at all, although I also heard the thing you heard, *Ing Ping, Ing Ping, Ing Ping*. Just like you, I also couldn't understand most of the words coming from the ocean, what with all the waves and thunder and ingingpinging in the distance, but I clearly heard one thing, and more than once – the Villain of the Deepest Dye.'

'No, I didn't hear anything like that,' Band resolutely declared. 'I heard something else. Something very frightening.'

'What? What was it?' Harry and Pim were quick to ask. Band paused for the dramatic effect before answering: 'The words that I heard were Rector Cinerum.'

'And that's supposed to be frightening?' Harry scoffed loudly.

'I didn't hear anything like that,' said Pim. 'Did you, Harry?'

'Absolutely not.'

'Well, I know what I heard,' Band stood his ground. Each of them continued to murmur what they heard and trying to make some sense out of it, but to no avail.

When the three of them returned to the base, Band was acting like the undisputed champion of the secret of the Towers. The particular way that he chose to rub it into the noses of Pim and Harry was to keep speaking highly about their respective discoveries, basking in the knowledge that everything positive he could possibly say about their secrets applied to a far greater degree to his own secret.

But Harry could only take it so far. 'The problem with all three secrets is that they are completely useless,' he declared at one moment.

'What do you mean useless? If we listen more, we may still hear something really important,' Band defended his secret. They were standing on the flotsam at the side of the base where Band and Pim continued to rummage for anything useful.

'The flower, the music, and even the sounds of the sea are not going to help us leave the Towers and find the gate to Star Central,' said Harry. 'And that's why they are useless.'

'I guess you are right,' Band agreed, but without much enthusiasm.

Pim cleared his throat. 'Well, actually, there is another secret that I found out about. And that one might turn out to be useful. It is the fourth secret of the Towers.'

'Secret number four, ladies and gentlemen. Secret number four,' Band announced as if calling the number on a TV show.

'What is the fourth secret?' Harry asked.

'It is the direction of land. Wherever they are on the sea, the two towers of Billbalirion are always aligned parallel to land.'

'That could be useful indeed,' said Band, 'if we could find a way to sail away from the towers.'

'What else are we to do? That is our only chance,' Pim declared in a resolute voice. 'Or we will stay here forever.'

'And what is it that you propose we do?' asked Band.

'Pim is right,' said Harry. 'We have to leave the Towers.'

'But how?'

'We have to build a raft,' said Pim. 'Look at all this stuff here, all the planks and timbers, and sails and ropes. That's our ticket out of this place.'

'I have a better ticket,' Harry declared.

'Ticket for a VIP lodge, I assume?' said Pim.

'Compared to your proposal, it certainly is. I propose a sousaphone-powered double bass.'

'I'll choke,' said Band. 'I can't blow so close to the waves.'

'Then a double bass with a sail,' said Harry. 'Hey, we'll fix a mast on you.'

'I am adamantly against anything being nailed into me,' said Band.

'We'll tie it up with a rope then. Or how about you simply hold it? Or just hold the sail? Listen, we just need a way to go forward,' Harry explained and was about to proceed into the details of double bass naval technology when a shout interrupted him. Pim had slipped on the edge of the flotsam and fallen into the sea.

Harry and Band quickly scrambled down looking for a rope that they could toss to Pim. But when they saw him, they stopped abruptly. Pim wasn't in the sea. He was on the sea, more precisely sitting on it and rubbing his posterior.

'Troglodytes of Hernia!' said Harry.

'What are you doing?' said Band.

'I am not doing anything,' Pim said sitting on the surface of the sea. 'I fell and hit the ground pretty hard. Only it's not the ground, it's the sea that's hard here.'

He slowly rose on his feet while Band and Harry watched on. Pim was standing on water, right in front of them.

'How can it be?' said Band.

'It's like standing on soft sand,' Pim said and made a few unsure steps. 'My feet are sunk just a little bit.'

'You are walking on sea!' said Harry.

'Why don't you try it too?'

Band and Harry slowly approached the edge of the flotsam looking for a good spot to step down. Band was the first to leave the firm ground behind and Harry followed him hesitantly. Soon all three of them stood on the surface of the sea, still unable to comprehend what happened.

'Gentlemen,' Harry said solemnly looking at his feet in the water. 'The ancient mystery of the Towers of Billbalirion turns out to be the innermost wish and the deepest desire of every being on any shore. It is revealed only to those fortunate few who ever set foot on the Towers. Today it is revealed to us. The secret of the Towers is – the gift of walking on sea.'

'And all our problems are solved,' Band replied sarcastically.

'Well, at least one,' said Pim, full of optimism.

The Bottom of Darkness

No amount of flowers around the office could offset the feeling of gloom in the Human Resources Department of the ACG. It was Monday morning, Edna's first day at work after her enforced recuperation at the tactfully named Institute for the Executive Fatigue. A small delegation of her uneager staff led by Staff Administration Officer Kingsley Err had been waiting for 45 minutes in front of a huge bouquet that came from the upper floors. Their own flowers, bought with the money from the office kitty, looked positively forlorn in front of it. A tastefully printed notice attached to the bouquet stated that this and similar items could be ordered at www.evenmoreflowers.com. On the back of the card was printed the name of Alexander Benjamin Lawrence Furthermore, with 'Larry' written below in hand.

Edna Edwards entered looking very much the same she always used to look in the morning: stern expression on her face but full of energy and already dispatching instructions – before she stopped and noticed the delegation and the flowers.

'Welcome back,' they said more or less together.

'Oh, my goodness, how very nice of you,' the stern expression on her face melted away on the sight of her staff and their flowers. Nobody had expected this. Edna even seemed moved by the gesture. 'Thank you very much. I didn't expect it.'

'We are all very pleased that you are back with us ...' Kingsley Err began. He had been chosen very much against his will for the head of the delegation, and now couldn't remember what else he had meant to say.

'And I am so glad to see you all again,' Edna said smiling and looking in earnest at her staff.

'We often thought of you while you were away. Did you receive our card?' Kingsley Err remembered to say.

'Yes, all of them,' Edna interrupted, leaving him visibly puzzled. 'Thank you all so much!'

'Knock, knock!' a voice was heard from the corridor. 'May I come in?' Lawrence Furthermore, the CEO of ACG himself, appeared at the door. 'How very nice it is to see you again, Edna! I am so glad to have you back on board.'

'Thank you, Larry, how nice of you to have come down,' said Edna.

'What are lifts for?' Mr. Furthermore winked at Edna and they both laughed. The staff around them willingly dissipated and Edna showed Mr. Furthermore into her office.

'Really Edna, I don't want to see you overworked any more,' Mr. Furthermore said when he sat down. 'Your health is very important to all of us here. How have you been feeling lately?'

'Fine, very fine, thank you.'

'We are about to embark on some very interesting projects. I had a very important meeting a few days ago and I tell you, our business is about to flourish! I hope you don't go through the same thing again, Edna, I sure need to have you aboard,' Mr. Furthermore said without elaborating further, although the whole building knew about the hallucinations of the poor Chief of Human Resources.

'I am back at work, Larry, I have things in control,' Edna said and switched her computer on, eager to prove her words. 'Look, I have here the report I was doing on the day I fell ill. I didn't finish it, but I'll give you just the charts, they are worth looking at.'

'Sure, I'll be expecting your email.'

'It's much better if I print it out and you arrange the charts on a desk. I'll show you,' said Edna and walked across the office. But there were no charts to pick up because there was no printer.

'Things can change even during a short absence, eh? My printer used to be here, but it seems they moved it while I was away,' Edna said and looked around her office. 'I'll ask Jennifer.'

'Yes, changes, Edna,' Mr. Furthermore followed her to her secretary's office nodding enthusiastically. 'We've had quite a few changes lately. As you know, we managed to get the Shelwood-Iberd-Tubston&Eaglestone on board. They are the crème de la crème of consultancy – they work with Ingvar Pingvarsson! I expect there are going to be more changes. They are the top cats in their field and they brought their top people for the job – for the top dollar they charge, heh, heh – '

'Jennifer, I just printed something. Do you know to which printer it was sent?'

'Oh, you sent it to the right printer, but the printer is not here. Some maintenance must be underway because my printer is missing too. Shall I call the helpdesk?'

'Just my luck! Of all printers, my printer is on maintenance today.'

'It's not just ours, half of the printers around are missing,' said Jennifer.

'That cannot be,' said Mr. Furthermore. 'Which idiot scheduled this maintenance?'

'What kind of maintenance is it where they simply cut off the cables instead of unplugging them? Look!' Edna said pointing at where her printer used to be and where now only a couple of clean-severed cables hung from the wall.

'I see a lot of explaining coming my way,' Mr. Furthermore got up and left Edna's office. Then a bewildered girl ran into him in the corridor and asked to show him something in her office. 'Get me the shift leader in Helpdesk,' he said to Edna and followed the girl to the office.

Her printer was not missing – it was neatly cut in half.

'How is Helpdesk going to explain this?' Mr. Furthermore said when the sound of the lift stopping on their floor announced that the help was on its way. But instead of a bunch of helpdesk people with their shift leader, it was a group of uniformed security officers led by the Chief of Security.

'Good that you came, there is hardly a printer left on the floor, Dabney. We are undoubtedly facing an organized ring of thieves, possibly an inside job,' Mr. Furthermore said.

'This could be more than a case of simple theft,' Dabney replied in his very serious voice.

'Are you sure?'

'If I was ever sure, I'd be a judge,' replied Dabney. 'I operate on hunches and conjectures. And I have a hunch that our competitors know that this is a very important time for us.'

'You might be right – the dastardly competition!' Mr. Furthermore pressed his fingers into a fist.

'They've been green with envy ever since you took the helm of ACG, but once X9 takes off the ground, they will really have a lot to fear,' said Dabney, furiously nodding.

'Dabney,' Mr. Furthermore declared, 'the future of our project and the future of this whole company depends on our ability to keep our ideas for us until they are in a billable form.'

'I know that very well.'

'We can't afford any spies or saboteurs in our midst – not now. I want you to clear up this mess and give me the initial risk evaluation by lunchtime.'

'Of course Larry, don't worry, I'll nab them. Spies and saboteurs are my bread and butter,' Dabney said with deep conviction. After a few short instructions, his men scattered all over the floor.

When everybody left, a deep muffled burp was heard from an air duct.

The rain was getting heavier – or it just seemed so to Pim. He was walking in the middle of the sea with nothing to provide shelter from the elements anywhere around him. Pim, Harry and Band had been walking for several days, alone on the Endless Ocean.

The weather had been fine if hot at first, but when they woke up this morning there was a mist on the ocean which soon turned into a light but persistent drizzle. Both Pim and Band welcomed the change in the weather after days spent walking in scorching sun. Harry, on the other hand, would have preferred the sun. The clouds weighed too heavy and too low on him. Besides, no drop in temperature would have ever been tolerated anyway if it was up to Harry.

All three of them walked loaded with the proviant scavenged among the flotsam, as much as each of them could carry. Pim felt a bit awkward because it turned out that both Band and the old Bedel could take more than he could. Harry was fortunate because he had found a pair of sturdy leather saddle bags and managed to fill them and hang them around his neck. Tall and hunched, he pressed on in silence, resembling an inmate of a penal colony drudging along. Band was in the marching mode and each instrument carried a small sack or a barrel. Pim was the only one carrying just two bags. His plan to find a backpack in the flotsam proved to be just wishful thinking. But he had found a compass.

They did not stay long on the Towers of Billbalirion after they had discovered the true secret of the Towers. First they scoured the flotsam for anything useful and then, after a hasty packing, climbed down the heap and once more stood on the surface of the sea. They set out in the direction Dapertutto pointed. When after a while Pim turned to see the Towers behind him they were again just a silhouette on the horizon.

'Look,' he said to Harry and Band and they all stopped and turned. The Towers once more looked as distant and unattainable as they would forever remain for the seafarers of Zandar. The three companions were again just three dots on the surface of the vast expanse of the ocean.

The first night Harry feared that he would not be able to sleep properly without some kind of shelter above his head. But once he closed his eyes, a gentle heave soon cradled him to sleep. He slept long and sound and only opened his eyes after the sun tickled them in the morning. No sooner had he raised his head than he bumped into something hard and heavy.

He found out that he had awoken next to a massive piano leg. And the hard and heavy thing above him was a grand concert piano. Just as he was about to shout at Band he remembered that it was him who complained about not being able to sleep under open skies. Band must have chosen to spend the night in this shape to give Pim and him some shelter. He vigorously rubbed the bump on his head and kept quiet. When evening came again he was glad that Band again transformed into a piano and invited them to crawl under him.

The day which had started with a drizzle turned out to be particularly tiring. The temperature was on the rise and the rain was getting heavier and heavier until in the end they found themselves under a real tropical downpour. Heavy raindrops falling straight down undisturbed by any breath of wind joined the surface of the sea in a myriad of small kisses on the water all around them. Nothing else could be seen in any direction but a heavy rain falling down.

'If this goes on, we soon won't be able to tell the difference between above and under the sea,' observed Band.

'Let's stop and wait it out,' proposed Pim, so Harry and him again took shelter under a grand concert piano in the middle of the ocean. They sat in silence watching the rain which showed no signs of letting up.

'I feel a bit under the weather,' Band said and laughed at his own joke to cheer them up.

'I didn't have a chance to ask you yet, but what was that thing that I heard under the Towers, the Villain of the Deepest Dye?' said Pim. 'Does it mean something?'

Harry and Band began the explanation – by immediately disagreeing about it. At issue was whether the Villain of the Deepest Dye was something real or imaginary.

'He is as real as any Master of Zandar, he only hasn't been seen for a long time,' said Harry.

'Or ever,' said Band.

'Yes, but what is he?' Pim wanted to know.

'Let me explain,' Harry volunteered. 'You should first know that the Master of Zandar is the only one in Left World with the power to summon the Hilalis.'

'Who are the Hilalis?'

'It is more a question of what than who. They are fierce mechanical tribes which destroy everything in their path as they advance across a landscape. They are the most frightening weapon of destruction because they leave pure void behind them. Not even empty space remains in the wake of the Hilalis. Pan Kratohvil once told me that the technical name for this was void in the Median Continuum, I think – anyway, no Master in recorded memory has ever availed himself of the terrible power of the Hilalis because, once unleashed, the Hilalis are not easily held back.

'But it is also said that there is a counterpart to the Master of Zandar. The Villain of the Deepest Dye is said to be evil as much as the Master is good, callous as much as the Master is compassionate and vile as much as the Master is just. The problem is that just as the Master can summon the Hilalis, so can the Villain of the Deepest Dye.'

'He seems to be a rather introvert villain since he hasn't tried to do it since the Beginning of Time,' Band observed. 'What is he waiting for?'

'Nobody knows where he is or whether he still exists. But during the Interregnum, when Zandar awaits the coming of a new Master, the Villain of the Deepest Dye is said to be on the lookout for a chance to summon the Hilalis and unleash them on Left World.'

'Aha,' Band confirmed, 'except the guy never existed.'

'Oh, he most certainly existed,' Harry replied. 'His name was Corradus van Morthorr and he called himself the Great Morthorr.'

'Anybody who managed to pronounce his name was in for a bit of evil,' said Band.

'And he almost certainly still exists. Because, even today, the worlds of Zandar are replete with small and seemingly insignificant occurrences which can only be explained by the existence of a malignant force that permeates the whole of Left World.'

'Such as bread falling buttered side down – surely the work of a malignant force.'

'Do not think for a moment that the Great Morthorr is a fiction. Lest you forget, the greatest things in universe can never be seen directly, they can only be gleaned from a plethora of small ones.'

'Like dark matter?' said Pim.

'The Great Morthorr was defeated by the first Master of Zandar in a fierce battle at the beginning of Time when many worlds collapsed into oblivion leaving no trace behind. That is why no Master has ever summoned the Hilalis since then, not even in the direst of needs. They are not really a weapon, they are the end of the world. The Villain of the Deepest Dye, on the other hand, will not seek to conquer the world if he ever reappears. He will seek to end it. The Great Morthorr has been looking for a battle to depose the Master ever since he was forced to retreat to the bottom of darkness,' Harry finished his explanation.

The three of them sat quietly for a long time listening to the rain bobbing on the grand piano. Everyone was in their own thoughts but they all converged towards one place – Star Central. Harry thought about his friend Otokarr Gnüss and the Crisis Staff that was trying to protect Star Central from the same fate as Fairybury. What if they have already failed? Pim thought about the portable computer that somehow found its way from ACG to Star Central and the gate that was waiting there to take him back to ACG, back to London, back to Uncle Pohadka.

Then the light faded and they knew that the sun was about to set. In the dying light of the day, the Book of Gates in Harry's hands definitely seemed to have an aura of blue light around it, thought Pim. But, aura or no aura, it was of no use in the middle of the ocean.

They went to sleep without supper, trying to make themselves as comfortable as they could in their wet clothes. Before he fell asleep, Pim thought about the last words he heard.

The bottom of darkness.

In the days that followed, the sky was cloudless again and the sun was shining mercilessly on the three small beings lost in the vastness of the Endless Ocean. At one point they had to take a couple of small sacks each from Band who declared that he was too spread out for this heat and asked if he could walk in a smaller formation. They took some of his load. He shrunk to a six-piece ensemble and, to his credit, did not complain any more.

When the weather changed and a breeze brought a respite from the heat, Harry was the first to complain. It was the first time since they had left the Towers that the wind picked up sufficiently to make waves and the sloping surface heaving up and down beneath their feet was becoming somewhat of a problem.

Or quite a big problem if you were Harry. It took less than five minutes for him to vividly experience the reason why sea sickness was not called boat sickness or ship sickness. Being on the undulating surface of the sea was quite enough. The nausea was back.

It soon became too difficult to keep the balance standing and they sat down and let the waves thrust them up and down. The sky was clear but a stiff wind had picked up strength and was now blowing in their back.

'This is not good,' said Harry and turned to vomiting.

'At least the wind is carrying us forward,' Pim said trying to sound positive looking at his compass.

'What is forward on this ocean?' Band replied despondently as they rolled on the waves listening to Harry's misery, but unable to help him. It was obvious that the waves were gaining in strength and size.

Pim decided that the easiest thing to do was to lie down, use a sack under the chest to prop himself and let the waves slide him forward. He sank in troughs and was raised to crests several times before he suddenly said, 'Look! Harry, look!'

Some distance in front of them and to the left there was a cliff rising from the sea. 'Land! We have to make land! Get up!'

'Harry, get up!' Band helped pull Harry on his wobbly feet but even if Harry was able to walk on his own the waves simply would not let him stand. They sat again.

'We've got to move! Look Harry, there's land,' Pim said to Harry. 'If we don't move now, we are going to miss the cliff. And if we miss the cliff now, it's going to be even more difficult to walk back against the wind and the waves.

'Harry, can you move at all?' said Band.

Harry was in a truly sorry shape and yet he managed to pull himself together and start crawling towards the cliff. But the advance was not fast enough. When they slid forward from the crest of a wave, the trough would push them back as it rose.

The darndest thing about the sea is that you have nothing to hold on to, Pim said to himself trying to prevent the backslide to every trough, mostly unsuccessfully.

'Now, Harry! If we don't move now, we are not going to make it,' Pim said to his tortured friend when they came close to the cliff. The old Bedel was by now too exhausted to do anything. He gestured them to go and leave him behind. A single look between Pim and Band was enough to dispense with this suggestion.

'We are in this together, I said, and I am not going to repeat it every time the going gets tough,' Band told Harry as he helped pull him up.

'We won't make it to the cliff with these waves,' Pim said between a crest and a trough. 'It's just too far away.'

'Yes, but let's push in the direction of the cliff. The more we advance now, the less we will have to cover going back,' Band said and gave Harry's rubbery body another pull just as the wind pushed them past the cliff.

It was only when the lone cliff was behind them that Pim and Band heard a new sound coming from in front of them. It was the sound of breaking waves. They both looked up at the same time and saw a narrow strip of beach and behind it – a low mountain.

'Land! This is true land!' Pim shouted to Band. 'Forget about that cliff!'

'This is more than land, this is a continent,' Band shouted back enthusiastically when he saw that the mountain extended left and right as far as the eye could see. The waves carried them forward faster and faster and they could see the point after which the waves began to roll towards the beach.

'Don't lie down when we come to the roll or you'll be crushed!' Pim shouted. 'Band! Help me get Harry on his feet. Harry! You've got to stand up or these rocks will be the end of us.'

'Rocks? What rocks?' Harry responded feebly.

'Land! We found land!'

'Land?' Harry said and managed to stand up just as they were jolted forward by a roll.

'Jump with me! On my sign ...' Pim firmly held Harry's hand. 'Now!'

The wave carried them all the way up the narrow beach and to the rocks behind it. Pim and Band jumped forward from the wave holding Harry between them. All three fell clumsily on the rocks and shouted in pain but there was no time to lose. Pim and Band quickly stood up and helped Harry on his feet before the next wave could catch up with them.

'Land! Land at last!' the old Bedel kept repeating as they helped him get away from the roaring sea. 'A firm ground under my feet.'

'Yes! A firm ground under our feet,' Pim said when they reached the foot of a tall rocky escarpment that rose above the beach. Only then did they breathe a collective sigh of relief.

Standing on firm ground and looking at the waves that had just brought them to the shore, Pim realized that his perspective of the sea changed profoundly. Viewed from the shore, the sea now looked like something uninviting and inaccessible. The waves breaking around the lonely cliff that they luckily missed seemed dangerous. The ocean looked foreign and forbidding again.

They had hardly had time to rest when Band pointed up with a bow. There was a dot in the sky and it was moving. Harry sat on the ground still feeling sick, but Pim and Band kept looking up until the dot came right above them.

'What do you think?' Band turned to Pim.

'At least we are on land again,' said Pim. 'We are not so exposed now. It's easier to find shelter or escape on land than it was at sea, if it comes to that.'

'Where do you see a shelter here?' said Band looking around. 'Or an escape for that matter?'

Band was right. They were on a narrow strip of beach at the bottom of a tall cliff which enclosed it on both sides. The rocks there seemed impassable, and the cliff above them was practically vertical. Pim was compelled to admit that the land they reached was not exactly the land they dreamt of while they were at sea.

'Look!' Band nudged Pim to look up again.

The dot in the sky was getting bigger and bigger. Something was descending from the skies and coming towards them very fast.

'Where's that shelter that's easy to find?' Band barely managed to say before a terrifying dragon swooped down on them and discharged a huge ball of fire.

Incredibly quickly, Band folded into a mouth harmonica and jumped inside Pim's breast pocket, escaping the singe in the last moment. Pim raised his hands to protect the face, but did not save the top of his eyebrows from the heat of the fire around him. He could feel the smell of burnt hair.

The dragon then exhaled a succession of smaller fireballs which danced in a semicircle around them. Pim felt Harry pulling the sleeve of his trousers, signalling him to help him up. The dragon belched fire again, this time above their heads, as Pim helped Harry stand up.

We are doomed, Pim thought. What can Harry possibly do against a dragon? He is not a warrior, nor a wizard, he is just a Bedel. Harry straightened his jacket and took a step forward to which the dragon reacted by spewing a tongue of fire directly at him, but just enough to miss him.

'My name is Sir Henry Grenfell-Moresby and I am the Bedel of Zandar, Proclamator Extraordinary and Plenipotentiary, Bringer of Royal News and Warrants and …'

'Harry, now is not the time!' Pim hissed at him but then an extraordinary thing happened. The dragon stopped spewing fire, sat down – and spoke in plain English.

'I am Wing Lieutenant Danko of the Dragonland Coastguard. You are under arrest for illegally entering Dragonland.'

'As I said, I am the Proclamator Extraordinary and Plenipotentiary …' Harry was about to resume the recitation of his titles but the dragon interrupted him.

'I understand you very well, sir, but my orders are clear. Any and all persons entering Dragonland from the sea must be detained and escorted to the authorities in the capital.'

'He really *is* a Bedel,' Pim tried to bolster Harry's credentials but the Coast Guard dragon was unyielding.

'Sir, you have to understand that, ever since the morph attack on Fairybury, the whole of Dragonland is in a state of heightened alert. We are on the lookout for a possible morph attack, as well as closely following the unrest in the northern provinces.'

'What does it have to do with us?'

'Sir, with all due respect, you happen to be standing in the middle of a beach in a northern province.'

'I understand you fully, Wing Lieutenant,' Harry replied. 'You see, we made an emergency landing here as a matter of urgency, as it were. Can you tell me how far from Dembeliland are we? That was our intended destination but factors beyond our control brought us here after many days at sea.'

'Dembeliland?'

'Yes.'

'I have never heard of such a place,' the dragon replied. 'You are in Dragonland now, and there is only the Endless Ocean on one side and the Boundless Mountains on the other. In any event, I have to escort you to the capital where you will be able to remonstrate with the appropriate authorities.'

'Don't worry, everybody knows me in Dragonborg,' Harry turned to Pim to reassure him.

'Everybody?'

'Everybody who is somebody,' Harry corrected himself and turned to the dragon. 'We shall be pleased to accompany you to the capital. How do you propose to transport us there?'

Without a further word, the dragon took them in his claws as if they were feathers and took off. In several powerful beats of dragon's wings they soared into the sky and flew high above Dragonland.

To their left lay the snow-capped peaks of the Boundless Mountains, to the right the vast expanse of the Endless Ocean. The sun was low in the sky and another sunset was in the making. It promised to be even more magnificent, seen from this height, undoubtedly greater than the Towers of Billbalirion. Except that there was not a cloud in the western sky, thought Pim. Who knows where on the ocean Dapertutto is the duty cloud today?

'It is good that we ended up in Dragonland,' said Harry holding tight on to the dragon's claws as the breeze played with his moustache.

'Things look pretty scary to me right now,' said Pim.

'That's nothing, my friend. There are far worse places. You should see the dwarves of the Barren Marshes, or the Troglodytes of Hernia – Dragonland I call civilisation.'

'Harry, my eyebrows are burnt. I do not normally associate deliberate burnings with hallmarks of civilisation.'

'But my dear boy!' Harry exclaimed. 'Dragons speak with fire! He didn't do it to singe your eyebrows, he was reading you your rights in Flameish!'

'Oh, if it is the standard procedure, consider my eyebrows unsinged. How do you know that he wasn't just spewing fire at us?'

'What a question! Pim, I am the Bedel! Not only do I perfectly understand Flameish, but I happen to be Zandar's foremost authority on Flameish grammar. It's a very interesting language with 12 declensions, but the basics are very simple: nouns are balls of fire and verbs are tongues of fire. Amazing how much you can express with fire! Did you know that dragon actually means fire in Flameish, only they pronounce it drhghnnh?'

'I never suspected it.'

'They also have 47 other words for fire. It is an element present in all aspects of traditional dragon life – while smoke is considered terribly impolite. No properly brought-up dragon would be caught dead discharging fire with smoke in front of other dragons. They can be sticklers for the etiquette, the dragons.'

'Why are we here if they are so keen on etiquette?' Pim said looking through the claws at the ocean below.

'Oh, have some understanding, Pim. These are very difficult times for the whole of Zandar. Besides, caution is the mother of vigilance. Young Wing Lieutenant here is simply charged with the duty to protect his homeland from the dangers coming from the sea. The Coast Guard should be proud of officers like him. Don't worry, I enjoy diplomatic immunity and all this will be quickly resolved when we come to Dragonborg.'

'Yeah, right!' was heard from Pim's breast pocket – but Harry continued to boast about his social connections undeterred.

'I have had the honour of attending several sessions of the Dhrghrleet, the Royal Dragon Fleet, which is also the supreme assembly of Dragonland,' he declared. 'Not only am I exceptionally well acquainted with most of the nobility of dragon lands, but the King himself is a close personal friend of mine. His Majesty often calls on my advice. He holds me in deepest confidence.' Pim could feel that Band was about to say something, so he pushed him deeper into the pocket.

'I will further have you know,' Harry went on, 'that dragons are exceptionally civilised beings. By and large, they prefer to keep to Dragonland when they are not called on business throughout Left

World. They are affectionate creatures who live in big families and spend long periods of time in deep sleep, a hibernation of sorts. They have high regard for arts and are especially attuned to poetry.' Here Harry lowered his voice and continued.

'They have only been cursed by one misfortune, and that is the schism among them to which here they refer as the "unrest in the northern provinces". Dragons are divided into two bitterly opposing groups, each calling the other "the black dragons". The origins of the dispute are rooted in an ancient battle fought long ago in Dragonland, but regrettably the divisions haven't healed and only seem to deepen with the passing of time and the ascension of every new king on the throne of Dragonland. The royal family has its roots in the southern nobility. The northern provinces have never formally declared loyalty to King Ragnagnoknorr, the current king of Dragonland. His Majesty and I would not at all put it past them if they were to try and gain some advantage in these turbulent times since the attack on Fairybury.'

Pim was about to say something when the astounding view of Dragonborg opened before them as they cleared a summit close to the city. Hundreds of dragons could be seen swirling in the air between majestic buildings and palaces while many more were milling through the incredible maze of cobbled streets below.

The city was nested between the mountains and the sea and encircled by walls and watchtowers. The ramparts on the sea side formed the Corniche, a popular promenade which was now full of dragons on their evening walk. 'It is a custom of life in Dragonborg to put down the apron and leave the workshop at the end of the day, and hurry to the Corniche to enjoy a long leisurely stroll in the fresh air coming from the sea,' explained Harry. Further inland the city rose to a series of small hills dominated by a magnificent castle perched atop a cliff above all of them.

'The fact that the Royal Standard is not flying from the highest turret of the King's castle signifies the fact that the King is currently asleep,' said Harry but that detail was lost on Pim. He looked in amazement at the hustle and bustle below him. There were no skyscrapers here like in Star Central. The buildings of the city looked old-fashioned, built from slabs of stone. As far as the eye could see there was hardly a building without a turret or a spire. Most were covered in dark slate quarried high up in the Boundless Mountains.

As the sunset slowly faded away and the night started to fall on Dragonborg, the blue light of street lamps was beginning to compete with the orange and red fires of conversations in the streets. It seemed as if the whole population had left their homes and congregated in the streets. Pim was reminded of small Mediterranean towns which in summer linger lifelessly through the day, only to burst alive in the evening and continue with excitement long into the night.

Wing Lieutenant Danko softly landed them in front of a big official-looking building not far from the ramparts and overlooking the sea. There were many brightly lit windows on the building and dragons could be seen inside, hurrying left and right through its long corridors. Danko asked them to follow him inside. They found themselves in a big hall with many busy-looking dragons coming and going from all sides. It gave all the appearances of a government building, probably a police station, which worried Pim. Harry, on the other hand, couldn't care less.

'One thing I still don't understand about dragons and Dragonland is the architecture,' he said. 'You would think that the place would be full of landing pads on tops of buildings – but no! Instead of building landing pads on the roofs, they still indulge in old-fashioned spires and turrets. So buildings can only be accessed through winding staircases – and the staircases don't even start in the street, oh no! The staircases are always in the courtyards, called traboules, which connect all the buildings in a block. Dragonborg is full of them – Ha, what did I tell you!' said Harry as they were led out the back into a traboule and then up a staircase. 'What's the point of being able to fly if you then have to climb the stairs like everybody else. I mean, really!'

As a disciplined Coastguard officer, Dragon Danko had been reluctant to enter into a discussion with his detainees, but now he could not resist: 'Sir, what you call turrets are in actual fact chimney-pots whose function is to relieve the interiors of buildings of the heat of conversational fires. That's why it is not possible to use them to enter and exit the buildings.'

They were led into a spacious well-lit room on the second floor and told to wait there. Danko told them that it was a public holiday in Dragonland today and that it might not be easy to find somebody to take charge of them. He was going to do his best to assist them, he said, but they might have to wait some time.

'You absolutely must find a person of appropriate rank that I could address,' Harry said to Danko. 'One-headed dragons are below my station.'

Pim was still surprised by everything he saw in the capital of dragons, but he was sure of one thing: snubbing one-headed dragons in front of the one-headed dragon who had just offered to help them was unbelievably rude.

Harry obviously did not share his view. 'Young man, I insist to speak to none less than the Secretary of State,' he shouted imperiously after Danko as he left the room.

'Things are not looking good,' Pim said to himself.

'You mean things are not looking good again,' said somebody inside Pim's breast pocket.

A State Visit to Dragonland

Pim and Harry waited in the room where Danko had left them. Harry was dozing in a chair while Pim stood at the window taking in his new surroundings. On one side he could only see the darkness of the sea and feel the cool breeze over the ocean. On the other side he could see the brightly lit streets made even brighter by dragons' conversations. Flameish required fire in all imaginable shapes, not just balls and tongues, and Pim found it fascinating to watch dragons speak. Some of them exuded slow stately red fire, probably talking about times past, while others spewed many complicated shapes in quick succession. Pim noticed that the more excited conversations often involved sending small orbs of fire which then changed the shape of the other dragon's fire and presumably the meaning of other dragon's words. Heated debates could be recognized by the constant sparring, where every flame was quickly reciprocated by another. Older dragons were more likely to acknowledge each other which resulted in their fires intertwining to form a flame of concord. Pim wondered how a declaration of love would look like in Flameish.

At last, steps were heard in the corridor and Danko opened the door and let an expensively dressed elderly five-headed dragon into the room. He wore five sumptuous white wigs. His five faces were powdered white while his lips were carefully delineated with red pencil. He looked as if he fell right out of an eighteenth-century French novel, except that he was a five-headed dragon.

'Mr. Secretary of State!' Harry stirred on seeing the bewigged gentleman before him.

'Sir Henry! I am so pleased to see you!' the elderly dragon amicably replied raising five pairs of bushy eyebrows in five delighted smiles – to the obvious surprise of both Pim and Danko.

'Please accept a thousand apologies from the Kingdom der Dragonlanden for this unfortunate incident and for the most undiplomatic way in which you were brought to Dragonborg,' the Secretary of State even genuflected to Harry! 'I hope the flight, at least, was not uncomfortable.'

Pim could hardly believe his eyes and ears.

'Your heartfelt apologies are most sincerely accepted,' Harry effortlessly reverted to the role of top diplomat, injured but full of understanding. 'You understand, however, that the nature of my office is such that I am seldom allowed to be my private self. It was a wise predecessor of mine who once said that the high office of Bedel must not only be respected, but seen to be respected as well.'

'I couldn't agree more!' was now heard from Pim's pocket.

'Of course, of course,' a somewhat confused Secretary of State kept nodding with all his five wigs to those words. 'My apologies to your esteemed companion as well.'

Before Pim could say anything, Band jumped out of his breast pocket and actively joined in accepting the apologies offered on behalf of the Kingdom der Dragonlanden.

'What brings you to our lands in these difficult times?' the Secretary of State asked Harry and his two friends after apologies had been professed and accepted in sufficient quantities.

'Difficult times indeed,' said Harry. 'Zandar without the Master and the Potentate-in-Spe! The young gentleman here, Pim Pergamon, is a representative of an important world joining me on a clandestine mission of utmost importance. We have been trying to reach the Crisis Staff of Star Central ever since the Tunnels closed. And this is our footman,' he gestured nonchalantly towards Band.

'I fully understand your position, Sir Henry,' said the elderly dragon. 'The situation has been very tense here in Dragonland, too, ever since the attack on Fairybury. The Median Tunnels are still closed and you are the first visitors from other worlds that I have seen in weeks. We are in a state of a heightened alert because of the unrest in the northern provinces. The Black Dragons are sure to be plotting against the King even as we speak – and His Majesty is still in hibernation, alas.'

'Have there been any sightings of morphs in Dragonland lately?' Harry asked.

'No, none. But I consider a valiant dragon a match for any morph.'

'Certainly, Mr. Secretary, certainly – some of them, anyway.'

'The closure of Median Tunnels has hit us very hard,' the Secretary of State said. 'Nobody knows how long it is going to last and our economy is already suffering from the lack of access to our traditional markets.'

'What are your traditional markets, Mr. Secretary?' Pim interrupted him.

'Oh, there are many things for which us dragons are simply indispensable, such as kidnapping maidens and swallowing suns to cause eclipses – services sector mainly. Yet kidnappings and eclipses are essential for resolving important issues like the outcomes of battles and inheritances of thrones. And that has all stopped with the closure of Median Tunnels. I shudder to think of what things must be like out there – we have had no news from any outside world since the last dragon arrived in Dragonborg just before the Median Tunnels were shut down.'

'Unfortunately we are unable to tell you more than you obviously know already,' Harry said to the Secretary of State. 'We were in Fairybury when the attack happened and we were lucky to have survived it. But we have not been able to get in contact with Star Central ever since then. And we only came to Dragonland because we were thrown off course during a storm at sea,' Harry said and paused for a theatrical yawn. 'Frankly, Mr. Secretary, right now we need to rest.'

'Of course, of course, it is very late indeed,' the five-headed dragon pulled up a grandfather's clock out of his pocket. The clock hung on a gold chain that could weigh anchors. 'Sir Henry, do not think for a moment that I would acquiesce in anything less than treating this as an official state visit. You and your companion are our guests for as long as you choose to stay in our lands,' said the Secretary of State. Then he summoned an aide and ordered him to ensure that the Presidential Suite in the Grand Dragon Hotel was prepared without delay to receive a state visit to Dragonland.

'Wing Lieutenant Zmayski?'

'Yes, sir?' Danko stood to attention.

'Wing Lieutenant Zmayski, you will temporarily relinquish your duties in the Coastguard. I hereby assign you as the adjutant to Sir

Henry and his party during their visit to Dragonland. I am sure you will see to it that their stay here is agreeable in every aspect.'

'Certainly, sir,' Danko replied and turned to his charges. 'At your service, gentlemen. If you would follow me this way.'

Pim and Band quickly exchanged glances as they were ceremoniously led out of the room and down the same staircase that they climbed as prisoners not an hour ago.

The Grand Dragon Hotel was a big old building in a secluded square in the centre of Dragonborg and a definitive statement of understated opulence. It stood on a small square – but dominated it. It had only two turrets – but six gargoyles, portraits of the six generations of owners. Its main entrance was low, but wide and crowned with a magnificent Dragonland coat of arms – a ring of fire with two fiery dragons inside, locking fires over yet another fire. It must be said in defence of this coat of arms that all the fires were very exquisitely forged in solid gold, down to the smallest flamelet.

The ceiling of the big lobby of the hotel looked almost higher inside than its turrets were outside. It was tastefully lit by many carbuncles that bathed the lobby in deep red light. In addition to the precious fixtures, about a dozen of lantern-dragons stood in a semi-circle around the reception and when Pim, Harry, Band and Danko entered the lobby, the manager gave a discreet signal. The lantern-dragons moved closer to the guests.

'Your Excellency, the Grand Dragon Hotel and its staff are delighted to welcome you again in our humble establishment,' the manager said with the well-oiled reverence of the staff of luxury hotels.

'I know this establishment to be of the highest excellence,' Harry replied to match the tone. 'And I am certain that I can expect this tradition to continue.'

'We shall do our utmost not to disappoint you, Your Excellency.'

The manager waved his hand and a group of young dragons with gilded caps quickly appeared around them.

'May I ask your manservant to instruct our pages about your luggage?' he turned to Band.

'We are travelling light,' replied Band, trying to tune into the tone of the occasion, 'and we shall only be requiring your assistance in acquiring a change of attire.'

'Most certainly,' the manager nodded and turned to Pim.

'Forthwith – ' was the most appropriate thing Pim could come up with.

'My staff will take your manservant to his accommodation. Meanwhile, allow me to show you to your suite,' said the manager.

'Actually,' Harry replied after a vicious stab by a clarinet, 'we Grenfell-Moresbys are used at having our domestics close at hand. I hope you will find a way to accommodate him in the suite.'

'I am sure I will, Your Excellency.'

They walked past the row of the hotel staff reverently assembled along the path to the lift. Every dragon piccolo, cook and chambermaid bowed to the two distinguished guests and their manservant as they passed. Harry graced them with the slightest of nods. Band kept bowing back, rather inappropriately for a servant, while Pim just walked along in slight embarrassment.

'Stick with me and you'll get used to this,' Harry whispered to Pim as they left the lift on the top floor. Two dragon pages at the end of the corridor bowed and slowly opened the magnificent double door of the Presidential Suite in perfect synchronicity with their walk down the corridor.

'I'll call you the minute I can't open a door myself,' Pim whispered to Harry while smiling to the pages.

The suite was the size of a small church. The expensive furniture in dark green leather finish contrasted the golden lustre of almost every surface in the room that could possibly be gilded. A sequoia log burned in the fireplace. Long heavy curtains at the back of the room illustrated the scenes from the most famous moments of dragon history. The manager pulled a switch and the curtains parted to reveal a glass door which led to a wide balcony overlooking the square. He would have proceeded to show them all the rooms and bathrooms of the suite, but Pim interrupted him.

'We are most thankful for your assistance, but I think we would most of all like to rest now.'

'Certainly, sir. Should you desire anything else, do not hesitate to send a message down the pneumatic post. All the chambers in the suite are equipped,' said the manager and then he and the pages withdrew with greatest politeness.

'I hope you are not disappointed, young man, that you have been taken away from the active service in northern provinces and assigned to our little group,' Harry said to Danko.

'Not at all, Sir Henry. It will allow me to spend more time with my family here in Dragonborg,' Danko politely replied looking at the state prisoners turned distinguished state visitors. Then he smiled at them and said, 'Thank you.'

It was obvious that Pim, Band and even Harry were very much impressed by their newly acquired status and the luxury surroundings to which it brought them. It was also obvious that each of them was trying to hide their excitement – with various degrees of success.

Harry was most adept in playing a state visitor. He immediately had room service hard at work catering to his requests. First, Danko was sent to the kitchens to announce Harry's special wishes for the dinner (*œufs bombaste*, pork *Trendafiloff* and, of course, the legendary speciality of the Grand Dragon Hotel, *crème bien brûlée*). Then chambermaids were asked to redo Harry's bed in the master bedroom and a pneumatic message was sent down requesting silk linen. Finally, the concierge was tasked with finding a set of fine grooming scissors suitable for bringing Harry's sadly neglected moustache back in order.

Harry himself was meanwhile busy trying out every brocaded sofa and leather armchair in the drawing room of the suite until he found one which afforded him the most stately position from which to observe Band.

Band had never before been in a place like this. He could not hide his excitement at all. He tried every bed in the suite, opened every wardrobe, checked the view from every window, and ended up messing up the curtains mechanism so that a maintenance dragon had to be called in to repair it.

Only Pim pestered Harry to open the Book of Gates. Harry at first responded by signalling him to keep quiet about the book in front of Danko and the hotel staff who kept coming and going on various errands for the Royal Bedel. When all the linen was changed, all broken mechanisms repaired and the most expensive titanium grooming set available in Dragonborg presented to Harry – compliments of the Secretary of State – Harry declared that he needed to rest first.

'We are not leaving anywhere tonight anyway,' he said. 'I think we all deserve to relax a bit after what we have been through.'

'Yes, but that's no reason not to make plans!' Pim replied thinking of the Star Central taxi with letters H8 on its registration plate and the gate to ACG that existed somewhere in that city.

'Don't be so demanding,' Band said coming out from the bathroom in a heavy red velvety bathrobe, large dragon size, monogrammed all over in golden thread with letters GDH. 'Harry is in no state to concentrate on finding Dragonborg in the Book of Gates after what we have been through today. He needs to rest. Say, how do I look in this?'

'You are absolutely right, I need a respite,' said Harry. 'You know, the robe really becomes you – gives you a kind of grandeur. Just pull in the saxophones – yes, that's it! A perfect you. A good cigar would fit in nicely. Shall I call the room service?'

'Oh … what do you think, Pim?' Band couldn't make up his mind.

'Are you two trying to set a room service record?' Pim retorted impatiently and went to the bathroom, leaving the alliance of spoiled convenience behind him. He could not stop thinking about the gate in Star Central.

The bathroom was spacious, as was to be expected in any dragon hotel. But the bathroom in the Grand Dragon Hotel was claw-carved and polished from a single slab of dark basalt. Or rather inside the slab, as Pim found out when he realized that the walls and the ceiling were an unbroken continuation of the same piece of dark stone. All the taps were, unsurprisingly, made of gold and Pim grumpily observed that there were separate taps for hot and cold water. For a moment he longed to be back in civilisation where they had mixer taps and travelling did not entail walking across oceans, even if not everything was cast in gold there. Plastic is just as good, Pim was thinking when he opened a tap.

But instead of water, fire shot out of the tap, curved back along the beautifully polished sink and burned Pim's right hand before he could close the tap. Harry and Band burst into the bathroom drawn by his cry.

'What happened?'

'I burned myself! Close the tap!'

'Are you alright?'

'No, I am not alright! Look at my hand!'

'Oh!' Harry saw the red skin on Pim's hand beginning to blister in front of his eyes. 'Call the reception, quick! We need to put something on this.'

'We don't have the time for the pneumatic post,' Band replied. 'Danko!'

The adjutant cautiously opened the door of the suite.

'Do you have anything for burns?' Band asked him.

'Burns?' Danko was puzzled. 'No, I don't. We don't have burns in Dragonland. Why?'

Band took him to the bathroom where Pim was heroically suppressing screams as the pain was spreading to his arm. 'What did you do?' Danko asked him when he saw a nasty red burn on his hand.

'It's this tap! It lets out fire instead of water!'

'But so it says here – hot. It means fire. Cold is water. Don't you know the four elements?' he said and opened the cold tap. 'Put your hand under the water, keep it in the flow.'

'That might not be enough,' said Harry. 'He needs something for the blisters.'

'I'll get help,' Danko said, stormed out to the balcony and from there deftly took to the air, contrary to the manners of a well-brought up young member of the Coastguard Fleet.

'Wait, who are you going to call?' the surprised Harry wanted to say but Danko was already out of the earshot. 'I am not at all sure that a local doctor will know much about burns. They probably heal with fire, too.'

'You are right, he'll bring a pyrorinolaryngologist,' said Band. 'I was once playing at a water-sprites parade and I fell in the river. I got cold and had terrible shivers. Luckily, there was an aqualogist at hand, the water-sprites told me. So the guy came and just wanted to pour more water down my tubes! I was gargling for weeks! It's never a good idea to call a doctor outside your own kind.'

'Your kind? You mean there's more of you?' Pim tried to deflect his attention from the growing blister on his hand.

'Of course! I am related to all the magic flutes and all the magic bells. Not to mention the Hamlin pipes. Then there is Uncle Hydraulus, the water organ. He is married to Aeolian Harp. Yeah, there's a quite a number of us. Some even say I am related to the Emergency Carnival.'

'You don't say,' said Pim trying to think away his pain.

'Pyrophones and steam organs also belong to my kind. I once dated a chick called Calliope, a steam organ. Boy, was she hot! In the end it didn't work out, she was under such a high pressure all the time,' Band continued to reminiscence while Pim continued to stoically bear the pain in his right hand.

Then Danko reappeared with a plump three-headed dragoness. She was dressed in several home knitted loosely fitting garments, each in different colour. 'This is my aunt, Tetka Savka,' he said.

'Is she a doctor?' Harry asked suspiciously.

'No, but I know how to help,' Tetka Savka replied.

'Yes, she knows how to help,' Danko earnestly tried to reassure them.

Tetka Savka looked at Pim's injured hand. 'Yes. Just as I suspected. This is a burn.'

'At least we know where we are,' Harry said despite Band's scolding looks directed at him. Tetka Savka took out a small bottle with some sort of a tonic and started to clean the burn with it. 'You know, I used to travel a lot when I was younger,' her other head said to Harry. 'I have seen it happen before. No matter how careful you are, if you travel outside Dragonland, you are bound to burn someone or something sooner or later. So I learned how to deal with it. Let me see,' the head bent down to examine the wound.

'But tell me, where do you come from?' another head continued to talk. 'I have been to places in my time. I've hitchhiked down more Median Tunnels than they'll teach you about in school. Meadowland, Bou Regreg, the Kingdom of Castles, Arachnodar, Zhaloprrdian Empire, I've even passed through Via Mala once. I was anorexic then. After that I lived in Venta Quemada for a while, but nobody there knew about it! You could say the only place I haven't been to is the Thirtieth Empire, he, he!'

'I've been to Venta Quemada once, I was at a brass festival,' said Band.

'Oh, the brass festivals at Venta Quemada! I remember, I would spend the whole weekend by the window, listening to the music outside, but I could not go out. I was there incognito.'

'A dragoness travelling incognito?' Pim looked at her, trying to imagine the bulk of Tetka Savka in all her brightly coloured knitwear blending into the crowd.

'Why not? I lived with a centaur under a false name once – but that's another story,' Tetka Savka said. 'I can't talk too much about it in front of my young nephew. He is such a well-brought up young man.'

'Danko is the pride of the family,' another head began to explain, 'so dear and so smart and so good-looking. And already in active service! Oh, you should see him in uniform, he's so elegant. Danko, why don't you wear the uniform now that you're on duty in Dragonborg? Everybody could see you then, not only the family, but the Azhdayskis too.'

'The Azhdayskis are my neighbours,' another head interjected for the benefit of others present. 'Oh, they'd truly croak if they saw you! You have to come home with me when I'm finished.'

'Tetka Savka, I'm on duty!'

"Exactly! I bet you can even wear your pageant uniform now that you're an adjutant! Oh, I am so worried for him,' she said to Pim, 'he just doesn't know how to make it in this world.'

'He was so cute as a young boy,' another head remembered fondly. 'You should see his photos when was an egg! So plump and so cuddly.'

'Tetka Savka – ' Danko began when another head cut in, 'And so good in school. Everybody said this boy would grow up to be quite something.'

'You know, he grew up faster than other dragons. When he lost his parents, he acquired a certain seriousness that never really left him. He became wiser than boys his age, didn't you Danko?'

'Yes, he is an upright young man. And don't think that girls haven't noticed it. Danko here could get a wife like this' – a claw snapped a centimetre away from Pim's face – 'if only he cared more about all the dragonettes that look his way. Or any one of them. There's many a good catch out there, Danko – '

'He just wouldn't make up his mind,' another head interjected before the first head continued: 'I am telling you, I am so worried for him, times are different now.'

'I know, Tetka Savka – '

'Life was simpler in my time, you could just go after your heart and do the things you wanted – '

'Which I did!' another head added on behalf of the whole of Tetka Savka.

'You didn't have to think about black dragons, and morphs, and who knows what else is going to befall us.'

'But I choose not to dwell on these things, you know,' another head continued the monologue. 'The Zmayski family name has survived two Draken Wars – not that nowadays anybody remembers drakens at all, thank you – because we Zmayskis always stick together. And there are Zmayskis in every walk of public life, not only here in Dragonborg but in the provinces as well! The late Uncle Bitanga was the governor of the mines on the Emerald Mountain. Just between you and me, we trace our lineage to the Royal Family.'

'Don't exaggerate, Tetka Savka,' said Danko. 'We are not related to the Royal Family.'

'Uncle Tchitcha would never let you say something like that! I am not exaggerating! My great-great-grandfather's uncle's sister's husband's … no, she was the wife's sister's, … oh, it's difficult to explain. I don't know the proper kinship terms in English. Really, everyone is just cousin in English! It's impossible to keep track of one's family in that uncouth language, I'll say it in Flameish. She was – ' and a beautifully shaped genealogical tree of fire with many intricate branches appeared before Pim to symbolize the connection between the great-great-grandfather's uncle's wife's sister and the Royal Lineage. 'You understand?'

'Looks beautiful but complicated,' said Pim.

'I never said it was not complicated to explain. But it counts, you know, to every true Zmayski, doesn't it Danko?'

'If you say so, Tetka Savka – ' Danko replied signalling an unending helplessness behind her back.

'The Zmayskis took part in both Goulash Rebellions. And there was not a valid sitting of the Royal Dragon Fleet since then without a Zmayski among its constituents! Of course, we never took part in the invalid sittings.'

'What were the invalid sittings?' asked Pim.

'They were the sittings which were invalidated at the valid sittings,' Tetka Savka firmly asserted.

'Left behind at the scrapheap of history!' added another head supplemented by the third one which rose from the wound for a moment to observe, 'That's the choice of Zmayskis. We know of no other history – and that's what counts.'

'Anyway, so young and already a Wing Lieutenant, our Danko!' another head swerved the conversation back to its proper course. 'I am telling you, he's a premium marriage material. Top drawer!'

'Here you are, young man, I hope you feel better now,' the last head to rise from Pim's hand smiled at him. Pim looked down and saw that the blister was gone. Not only that, he did not feel any pain. In fact, the burn had healed completely.

'Tetka Savka! How did you do it? It's gone! As if it hadn't been there at all. Thank you!'

'I told you, a Zmayski knows how to deal with things,' Tetka Savka gave a triple wink and stood up. 'It was very nice meeting you all, gentlemen. I wish you all the best in the future,' she said with a triple bow on the door of the suite. 'Not that you need much more while you're in the Presidential Suite at the Royal Dragon,' a head reappeared to say just before the doors closed.

'I am so sorry, gentlemen, for the improper behaviour of my aunt,' the embarrassed Danko began to say.

'There is nothing improper about healing a burn!' responded Pim.

Harry examined Pim's hand with silent wonder. As he retired to his bedroom, Pim could hear him talking to himself. 'Troglodytes of Hernia! She knew what she was doing. What was her name again?'

A soft plop was heard at the writing desk. Danko took out a cylinder out of the pneumatic post and unrolled a miniature message.

'It's from the Secretary of State.'

'Can't it wait until morning?' said Pim.

'He is inviting Sir Henry and you to attend the Raivaru Festival tonight as guests of the crown.'

'It most positively can't wait,' Harry returned from his bedroom. 'You can reply that we shall be most pleased to join in the festivities.'

'What festivities? Harry, I am tired, I spent most of the day climbing the waves. And you spent most of the day throwing up.'

'Now, now, I may have been indisposed at times, but that's no reason to offend our gracious hosts. The Raivaru Festival is a very important event in the social calendar. It is celebrated on the anniversary of a battle in which the first Dragonking defeated an individual named George. It would be an inexcusable snub to decline the invitation of the person who put us up in the Presidential Suite.'

'What about Band?' Pim gestured towards the door where a soft snore in f-minor could be heard.

'Oh, let him rest. His absence is too small to be noticed. His notice is largely absent.'

The streets of Dragonborg were alight in a wonderful mixture of blue, orange and red flames from street lights, ordinary dragon conversations and occasional exclamations such as, 'What, your nephew appointed the Keeper of the Royal Forges? And you only tell me now!' with another head simultaneously saying to another dragon in another conversation, 'No, really, I lead such a healthy life ever since we bought the house on the pyrolake, it was such a great investment!'

Pim quickly realized that dragons lived to know what other dragons were up to. Tonight, the last evening of the Raivaru Holiday, nobody wanted to remain indoors. Now he was glad that he came along. Nowhere else would he have the chance to witness the spectacle of so many dragons in such a good mood. 'Who would have thought? Not a zilch of what they taught me in Right World about dragons,' he said to Harry.

'I told you that dragons of Dragonborg are among the most civilised creatures I know. A bit odd sometimes – just look at the architecture – but otherwise very refined,' Harry replied as they walked past a wide street that lay exactly in the direction of a distant hill crowned by an imposing fortress that looked down on the turrets of Dragonborg.

'Danko, what fine establishment is situated in that exquisite fortress?' said Harry.

'It belongs to the Royal Household. It is the famous Baibok Prison.'

'Who would want to have a prison in their household?' Pim couldn't help noticing to which Danko responded, 'Oh, but it's regularly emptied according to the custom.'

Many of the elegant buildings around them on Karabatack Boulevard looked like they had roots in the ground, and branched upwards into stylish turrets. Harry was right, some of the turrets were absurdly tall and thin, while others were bedecked with ornaments and elaborate insignia of the noble merchant houses of Dragonborg. Even for the smallest dragons it was impossible to land or take off anywhere in that forest of turrets, except on squares and wider streets. And the doors on most of the buildings looked rather narrow for dragons, but they wiggled their hips so skilfully through the doors that it appeared that they shrunk on one side, only to grow again on the other side.

There were many dragon children strolling with their parents and grandparents. They all seemed well-behaved, answering to countless queries about their age and the progress of their fire-making abilities.

'Dragons begin their education while they are still in the egg, where they spend three years. When they hatch, they are not babies any more,' said Harry.

Karabatack Boulevard ended at a wide square built around a massive fountain in the shape of a big seven-headed dragon. Each head spewed a different shape of intricately woven flames.

'This is Ragnagnoknorr Square,' Danko said as they stopped to admire the view of the square. 'The Ragnagnoknorr Fountain represents King Ragnagnoknorr reciting the first seven lines of the national anthem of Dragonland.'

'Wow, Harry can you read it?' said Pim. 'Or is it hear it? What does it say?'

'Which line is of particular interest to you?'

'Oh, any line. Say, the first and the last line.'

Harry looked carefully at the fires before answering. '*Grace and kindness, unity and harmony, dragon heart is big,* goes the first line. And the seventh line says, *Slash and shatter, crush and ruin, dragon heart is fierce.* It's an amazing transformation in only seven lines.'

'It's nothing unusual. Have you ever bothered to listen to words of any other national anthem for more than the first line or two?' said Pim. 'You'll discover many don't last longer than three lines before they begin to smash and burn for the greater glory of someone or other.'

'Speak for your world,' Harry replied as they left the fountain and the square behind them. At the end of a short street filled with slowly moving dragons stood a magnificent building called the Ragnagnoknorr Hall. Danko signalled the two dragon guards in heavy brocade uniforms who immediately made space by pushing away the dragons who did not know better than to stand in the way of the distinguished state visit to Dragonland. Pim briefly saw the many flaming turrets on the imposing walls of the Ragnagnoknorr Hall before they were whisked inside and led to their seats in the open-air auditorium.

'Sir Henry!' Harry was immediately recognized by the VIPs of Dragonland, most of them many-headed, all of their faces powdered beyond recognition.

'Most esteemed Royal Counsellor! And Mrs. Counsellor. Your Firishness, I am delighted to see you tonight! I have always looked forward to meeting you outside the working session of the committee.'

'Likewise, sir Henry, likewise. It seems such a long time since we met at the Incantations Regulations Deliberations.'

'Sir Henry, I am so surprised to see you here!'

'You oughtn't be, Governor. I consider it my duty as the Bedel of Zandar to attend Dragonland celebrations even when my dear friend King Ragnagnoknorr is asleep in his Royal Slumber. It's as if it was yesterday that I had a chance to entertain His Highness with a most amusing game of cards just before he withdrew to the Royal Hibernation Chamber.'

'That is so gallant of you, Sir Henry, to be here again after exactly 99 years, and with the Median Tunnels closed. How did you do it?'

'How long has it been? Ninety-nine years already? Are you sure?'

'Of course I am sure, Sir Henry. This is why this Raivaru Festival is so special this year, it coincides with His Slumbering Majesty's Royal Awakening. Today's public holiday is meant to mark the end of the ninety-nine years that King Ragnagnoknorr has been asleep. His Royal Awakening will be the finale of the Raivaru Festival tonight.'

'Really? How time flies!' said Harry and his moustache twitched. 'Pim, are you still tired?'

'No, I am fine, I am excited to see the festival,' Pim politely replied to the great approval of the Royal Chamberlain.

'Well, I don't really feel in top shape tonight,' Harry suddenly announced. 'Maybe it would be better if I returned to the hotel after all.'

'I am so sorry to hear that,' said the Governor.

'It's nothing really, but I have a headache. It has been a long day and we woke up so early this morning and it's so late now and I am so tired and my eyes are so sensitive to smoke ...'

A number of dragon heads turned toward Harry on overhearing the suggestion that there could be smoke among the present company. Some dignitaries were not at all amused to hear such an insinuation and they did not hesitate to show it. Harry's embarrassment was mercifully cut short by the beginning of the program.

A very talkative three-headed master of ceremonies walked on to the open-air stage and gave an excited speech of many fires. Although it looked at first sight that all three heads were talking at the same time, Pim soon realized that the heads actually took turns in uttering a few words each, but their quick and skilful exchange made it into a string of seamless fire.

Then the first performer appeared on stage. This dragon produced fire of many shapes and hues for about a minute after which he withdrew accompanied by a warm applause. The master of ceremonies then introduced another dragon who did more or less the same, or so it seemed to Pim. After a couple of other dragons came to the stage also spewing fire in various patterns, Pim turned to Harry.

'This Raivaru Festival? What kind of festival is it?'

'What a question! Can't you see the beauty expressed in those fires? Aren't you taken by the joyful play of flames?'

'A festival of fire?'

'No, silly you! It's a festival of poetry! These are not just flames, they are words. This is not just fire, this is joy and sorrow, penance and exaltation! Dragons are among the greatest poets in Left World. Everybody writes poems in Dragonland, and wants to be acknowledged for them. Every dragon, no matter how big or small, rich or poor, wants to forge a poem by which they will be remembered. And every year the recitations at the Raivaru Festival in this auditorium bring out the best poetry of the past year – look!'

It was the Secretary of State who took the podium now. There was a respectful wait until the elderly gentleman found the head with his reading glasses.

'What is he saying?' Pim asked when Mr. Secretary produced the first flame.

'Shall I compare Thee to a smokeless flame?' Harry interpreted as many dragons in attendance nodded a higher than usual share of their heads in approval. 'Beautiful comparison, isn't it?'

'Yes, but I've heard something along these lines before – well, I guess sooner or later a guy starts thinking about his girl in metaphors, and then some of them actually write it down.'

'Yes, but dragon poetry is more than just pretty words. It is about making shapes pleasant for the eye, hissing pleasant for the ear and words pleasant for the soul – and all at the same time! That's why it is one of the highest art forms in Zandar, it is a visual and dramatic art in one.'

A resolute young dragon came out on the stage and gave a steadfast blow of fires in many colours.

'*Oh, the firishness of those fiery firers of my firen firedom*,' Harry interpreted,

That fired up the firelings of my fireless fireplace
Into the firely fireballs,
Like the Firebird who was fire-fanged from a fire-cross
Until it was –
Fire!

'He is one of the favourites to win,' Harry declared while the audience around them rose in standing ovation, clapping the claws and shouting fire in collective acclaim.

'They tend to be a tad partial to fire,' said Pim.

'Ah, did you see how he called his youth his firedom? What depth, what beauty!' Harry was just as carried away as everyone else.

The young poet kept bowing and saying thank you in a blue self-conscious flame.

The audience, taken by the regaling young poet, responded louder and warmer to the poems that followed. Despite the boldly functional design of the arcades of the Ragnagnoknorr Hall intended for quick conduction of heat from thousands of spectators, it was becoming very hot in the stalls. The circle of clear sky visible above the stage seemed distant and insufficient to provide respite from the heat. Every now and then a well-received poem would make Pim feel he was in a blast furnace. Everybody was sweating a lot but the enthusiasm continued, as if spurred by the sweat.

When it was the turn of Yulka, the dragon king's seven-headed daughter, Harry nudged Pim to look at Danko. The young Wing Lieutenant sighed deeply as the lovely dragon princess with seven exquisitely slender necks, wearing seven designer sunglasses, said something about, 'Alone, the flame of love only burns stronger.'

'Nobody with so many heads can truly know loneliness,' Pim said as bizarre pyropoetic recitations continued. Or was it Harry's translations that were bizarre?

Pim was still waiting for a poem that did not mention fire when a hush descended on the auditorium, which also meant that it became much darker. The recitations were finished and it was time for the best poets of the Raivaru to receive their laurels. But this time the protocol was changed and ornately dressed royal pages first wheeled in a giant four poster bed. A majestic seven-headed dragon enrobed in a red and golden velvet pyjama was asleep in it.

The silence in the Ragnagnoknorr Hall was now complete. For a minute nothing happened. And then the sleeping dragon stirred from heads to toes. The seven heads one by one let out seven yawns and seven pairs of eyes slowly opened. King Ragnagnoknorr looked around. He could see dragons sitting in excited anticipation all around him. His first head let out a small flame. Three pages ran up and carefully powdered the face. The second head gave a bigger one. The pages repeated the powdering. The third and the fourth head spewed out more serious fire, while the fifth and the sixth blasted a whole conflagration. They were all powdered in their turn. The dragon king then stood on all four legs and raised his seventh head high above the stage, roaring a giant red sword of fire high into the skies of Dragonborg.

It was the signal for all who saw it to stand up and start spewing fire in unison. And not only in Ragnagnoknorr Hall, but wherever the fire of Dragonking's awakening was seen, dragons rose and discharged tremendous blasts, from the squares of Dragonborg to the villages in the mountains overlooking the city.

'Stand up, it's the national anthem,' Harry nudged Pim and they both stood up.

As the anthem was carried away from the king's initial roar at the sky, a Mexican wave engulfed the land, a semi-circle of fire spreading through the night from the capital into the hinterland. At the same time, Pim saw the Royal Standard slowly rising on top of the highest turret of the Royal Castle overlooking the city. It reached the top of the flagpole exactly when the anthem ended and gave way to fires of jubilation. Those assembled in the big auditorium of Ragnagnoknorr Hall, however, had to refrain from further exaltations as the ceremony was not over. The Secretary of State now approached His Fiery Majesty and proceeded to crown the seven perfectly powdered heads with the seven crowns that the pages handed him on seven velvet pillows, each of them covered in silk and woven with golden threads forming the royal coat of arms.

The audience continued with ovations while Harry turned to Pim and said, 'Well, that's it, then. It's time to return to the hotel for our well-deserved rest.' But the space around them was full of dragons who came forward trying to catch a glimpse of the newly awakened Dragonking.

The most important dignitaries had already lined up, waiting for the king to descend from the stage. After the pages helped him ease out of his red and golden velvet hibernation pyjama and into his red and golden velvet royal cloak, he approached them accompanied by the Secretary of State. He shook claws and exchanged a few words with each of the dragons assembled to greet him. Dragons did not have the custom of kissing the royal claw, but shaking claws with the Dragon King as soon as possible after his awakening was considered a particularly good omen for the whole family.

Pim and Harry were trying to find their way out through the throng of excited dragons, but it wasn't easy. Harry had to stop frequently to exchange a few words with the dragon dignitaries who recognized him. More and more dragons were arriving from all directions to greet the king, pushing them towards the stage. At the same time, the thick circle around the king kept moving forward, squeezing them between two dragon fronts.

'We shouldn't be here, it's time to blend away,' Harry said somewhat tersely. His moustache had begun to twitch.

'I can't go against the current, and especially not this one. It's either go with the flow or be squeezed,' Pim said pointing at the excited dragons who kept pushing against them in greater and greater numbers. 'Let's try the other way out closer to the stage.'

Pim and Harry turned back only to see an over-excited Tetka Savka coming towards them and cutting off their exit. 'Oh, the King, gentlemen, the King! Ah!' she kept panting at the two of them while squeezing them closer and closer to the king and his entourage. Harry was becoming more and more jittery as the entourage approached them.

'What's the matter with you? Stand still until they pass or we'll end up under a stampede,' Pim said when Harry tried to use him as a wedge to pass by Tetka Savka who was all besides herself in Oohs! and Aahs! Harry then produced something from under his jacket. 'Here, you hold it – just in case.' It was the Book of Gates.

'But what am I – ' Pim began to say when the crowd of dragons opened. Pim and Harry stood in front of the Dragonking. Harry quickly slid the book back under his belt. 'Your Royal Majesty,' the Secretary of State announced, 'allow me to present the Bedel of Zandar, Proclamator Extraordinary and Plenipotentiary, Sir Henry Grenfell– '

'You!!!' the king roared at Harry. 'You!'

'Your Fiery Majesty?' Harry responded feebly.

'Arrest this man at once!'

'I beg your pardon, Your Majesty?' the Secretary of State strained his bushy eyebrows to understand what was going on. 'Surely you don't mean the Proclamator Extraordinary and Ple – '

'I know who he is! How dare you show yourself in front of me?' the King shouted at Harry. 'I'd known your face if I'd slept nine thousand and ninety-nine years!'

'Your Majesty, let's be reasonable,' Harry tried to deflect the royal wrath, but Dragonking was so furious that all the seven heads belched out clouds of smoke in anger while everybody around pretended not to notice the soot falling on their white powdered faces.

'Tell them who you really are – if you dare!'

'I know you are a bit grumpy, Your Majesty, you've just awoken. It happens to me every morning, after only one night of sleep, so I can imagine how it must be after ninety-nine years of the Royal Slumber. In a word, Your Majesty – this is no time for rash decisions.'

The king turned to the Secretary of State and said, 'The last time we met he cheated me in cards! Arrest him!'

'Your Majesty, have mercy on me!' Harry pleaded once again, but was cut short. He was immediately put in chains amid general uproar and disbelief in the auditorium. Not even the oldest dragons remembered something like this ever happening at the Raivaru Festival.

'Let this be a warning to everyone,' the King proclaimed in a loud voice that echoed around the Ragnagnoknorr Hall. 'Take him to Baibok Prison – and behead him according to the custom.'

Harry shouted something to Pim as he was led away, but Pim could not hear him. A moment later the guards seized him too. They escorted him out through the crowd that was looking at him with a hushed dislike. He was taken straight to the nearest gate and very unceremoniously thrown out of the city.

Extra Muros Draconensis

Whistling Band's five notes for help in distress had yielded nothing. Pim gave up on finding him – ever again – and decided instead to get as far as possible from Dragonborg. He hadn't heard everything very well in the commotion when they were throwing him out of the city, but he distinctly remembered hearing the words *dawn* and *death*.

Now it was the middle of the night and Pim was walking guided only by the waning moonlight. He had left the lights of Dragonborg and the coastal road behind him, following any path that took him higher into the mountains. Whenever he felt tired he thought about what he heard from Dragonking: 'Behead him according to the custom.'

But when his whole body began to ache from all the exertions of that endless day, Pim realized that he should stop soon. He looked around at the monotonous rocky landscape under the moonlight. None of the rocks looked more comfortable to sleep on than any other. Then he saw a faint light in a hollow at some distance from the path. Overcome with fatigue, he left the footpath and carefully approached the light.

When he came closer he saw that it was a remnant of a camp fire. Only a few logs remained aglow. Right next to the fire someone was asleep. Not a dragon, but someone reddish in face and with white beard, curled around a small barrel with an outsized homburg hat on top of it. Maybe a dwarf.

Pim called out to him.

The sleeper awoke with a jolt and pushed the barrel away. 'I've got nothing to do with it, it's not even mine!' he shouted before he fully opened his eyes. He was a human, not a dwarf, but quite short and chubby. 'Oh, you are not a dragon?'

'No, I am not a dragon and I am trying to avoid meeting one if at all humanly possible,' replied Pim.

'Then you are in a like-minded company,' the portly man said picking his homburg hat and brushing it off. When he was finished he put it back atop the barrel.

Pim sat down by the fire. 'My name is Pim Pergamon. I am very tired and I am looking for a shelter. I was expelled from Dragonborg and threatened with death if I am still in Dragonland after dawn.'

'This is a strange direction to take if you want to leave Dragonland. You will only go deeper into it if you follow this path,' the man explained. 'I am Dr. Ernst Theodor Amadeus Schlosen-Bosen, merchant of dragonsweats and pixie dusts, the sole proprietor of Supranatural Supplies of Star Central. I know the country around here, I am coming down from the mountains and I can tell you that these mountains are not a way to leave Dragonland.'

'It's nice to meet you, Dr. Schlosen-Bosen. I was really lucky to find you. And I really only want to sleep by your fire, if you don't mind. I am very, very tired.'

'Of course, of course,' Dr. Schlosen-Bosen said and gave Pim one of his sacks as a pillow.

'I won't bother you tomorrow, I just need to get some sleep,' Pim said and nested his head in the rough sack which felt like a finest pillow for his tired neck.

But Dr. Schlosen-Bosen was by now fully awake and too excited to fall asleep any time soon. He was delighted to see a human face after quite a spell in the Boundless Mountains of Dragonland, he said. He had come to Dragonland a few weeks ago with all his savings to buy dragonsweat and, just between the two of them, he did well. He was sitting on a barrel of cross crude!

'A barrel of what?' Pim said half-asleep.

'A barrel of crude, unrefined dragonsweat, and a fine one at that. They are willing to pay a fortune for it in any of the witchworlds.'

'Why?'

'It's a basic ingredient in so many spells and potions. And this is not just any dragonsweat, it's a cross crude.'

'A what?'

'A cross crude. The quality of the dragonsweat depends on the mood of the dragon from which it is harvested,' Dr. Schlosen-Bosen kept explaining, oblivious to the fact that Pim was almost asleep. 'You have sulking crude, resentful crude, annoyed crude, displeased crude, cross crude, angry crude, furious crude and irate crude. True, I had hoped to get at least the furious crude, but it's just impossible to get high quality stuff these days. It's been years since I last traded in furious crude,' he said with nostalgia in his voice.

'Isn't it forbidden?'

'I normally buy from a middle man, I know it's forbidden to take dragonsweat out of Dragonland. But these are hard times for us magic merchants. You can't get dragonsweat any more through a reputable wholesaler. They say Talambas bought out every last drop for some of his concoctions – well, he didn't buy it from me. And yet, apart from dragonsweat my warehouse is full, but the wares just won't shift! I've got everything: invisible cloaks, magic broomsticks, grow-your-own-poisonous-apple kits, seven-miles boots, flying carpets, magic lamps – come to think of it, I had a batch returned recently because the lamps only lit up and nothing else, the customer did not accept that it was magic enough simply on the account that there was no oil in the lamp,' Dr. Schlosen-Bosen sighed, but did not stop. 'I've got magic wands and camping pumpkins – they turn into trailers at midnight, very convenient – I've got love potions, dark concoctions, pixie dusts, magical swords – I can even get swords in stones on special order! I've got best incantations and magical thrones, and even Havliček's plot thickeners – '

'Havl – what?'

'Plot thickener. Havliček from Žižkovo once took it out at an inopportune moment and it made him sneeze right into a king's face. His plot thereby greatly thickened. But people still buy it on the strength of the Havliček brand.'

'Hmm-mmm.'

'Except they don't really buy it any more,' Dr. Schlosen-Bosen went on undeterred by the lack of interest in his story. 'At least not from me. Everybody shops at Weaponics.com nowadays. The times have come when people prefer a gadget to an honest potion or pixie dust. Not even spells sell as they used to – people lease spells nowadays! But things are going to change for me with this baby,' Dr. Schlosen-Bosen gestured at his precious barrel. 'Next time a mighty wizard like Talambas needs dragonsweat, he'll have to knock on my door.' The prospect of a much-feared wizard among his loyal customers animated Dr. Schlosen-Bosen so he continued to talk.

'I came here as a tourist and a pilgrim and I managed to pass undetected so far. I have to do this sort of business in the mountains where dragons are less principled and the eyes of the authorities are not as omnipresent as in the coastal towns. Although, truth be told, – I'd much rather deal with the authorities than with Black Dragons. I'll be glad when I'm back in civilisation, I don't think I could've pushed my luck any more. I expect to reach Dragonborg tomorrow. And as soon as I step out of the Median Tunnel in Star Central, I will be a rich man.'

'Median Tunnels are closed,' Pim mumbled from his sleep but Dr. Schlosen-Bosen was too much taken with his visions of better tomorrow to pay any attention to him. He continued talking about what a barrel like this could fetch in outer witchworlds.

'Just don't be counting on returning to Star Central soon,' Pim said before he finally turned to sleep. 'Maybe even ever.'

When Pim slowly opened his eyes the next morning, the sun was already high up and the stout merchant of dragonsweats had already packed most of his camp. He was rarely away from home for so long nowadays, he said. He certainly shouldn't have left his daughter to manage the shop alone all the time that he was away.

'There is always so much to do, even when the business is slow. New stock keeps coming in and has to be filed in the right drawers or I won't know where it is when I want to sell it,' Dr. Schlosen-Bosen explained. 'We don't have as many staff as we used to have, but there's still lots of work around the shop. My daughter had to go out on a delivery to Fairybury the day I left. Pnishl, our delivery gnome, had an attack of gout and I simply couldn't do it all myself.'

The mention of Fairybury finally awoke Pim. 'When did she travel to Fairybury?'

'On the morning of the Procession.'

Pim stood up and told Dr. Schlosen-Bosen to sit down. 'I was in Fairybury for the Procession. Things did not go well there.'

'Why? What happened?'

Pim quickly explained to a dumbstruck Schlosen-Bosen what happened at the Procession. 'I am sorry to tell you that many died that day in Fairybury. It was a morph attack. The Mamluks were helpless,' he concluded his story.

'*Aechterla Slechterla*!' Dr. Schlosen-Bosen said and fell silent.

'There is also this other thing that I think I mentioned yesterday,' added Pim. 'Median Tunnels were closed shortly after the attack on the Procession. The idea was to prevent the morphs from striking again somewhere else, particularly in Star Central. But ever since the Tunnels were closed, there has been no communication between worlds. I have not heard any news from Fairybury or Star Central ever since the Fair of Zandar – they are both completely cut off.'

'My daughter was supposed to return immediately to Star Central to tend to the shop. But if she wanted to see the Procession, of course, who could blame her? It would have been a perfectly normal thing to do for someone who hasn't seen many other worlds, her first Procession.'

'In short, you will not get out of Dragonland through Dragonborg,' Pim said matter-of-factly. 'The Median Tunnels are closed. And the last person in both worlds who could help us – well, I'd rather not go into details. Last night he met a gruesome end,' he said with a deep sigh.

'What will I do now? What is going to happen to my daughter if I don't return?' Dr. Schlosen-Bosen sat on a rock overwhelmed by everything he heard from Pim. 'It wasn't easy to raise her on my own. And I had to wait for her for so long before she was born. When she was a baby, a terrible bird of prey almost snatched her from the cradle. And then growing up in Supranatural Supplies, I admit it was not the best place to raise a child, among boxes of magic seaweed and lamps and jars with all sorts of jinni. They didn't have security caps back then, any child could open a jinni bottle. But my daughter knew better and she grew up to be a very good shopkeeper,' he said on the verge of tears. 'We only ever had each other, you could almost not tell us apart. Oh, will I ever see her again?'

'Listen, not everybody in Fairybury was killed in the attack. I survived, for instance – although I was cut in two! And I was not the only one to come out of Fairybury,' Pim felt he had to say something, moved by the fatherly love for a creature in all probability even rotunder than Dr. Schlosen-Bosen himself.

'Yes, but we are here and she is there. And we are stuck. Without the tunnels, we are absolutely stuck,' Dr. Schlosen-Bosen stood up and kicked his barrel away. 'And this is worthless.'

Pim went to pick up the object which until just a moment ago was treated with so much affection. The barrel was heavy and it bore a strange inscription. The more Pim looked at it, the more he thought that it wasn't so strange. It looked familiar. It looked similar to something else that he had seen. It was a runic character.

'Dr. Schlosen-Bosen, can you read runes?'

'Can I read runes? I wouldn't last longer than a magpie's breath in this business if I didn't read runes. Or Alphabet of the Magi. Or Grantha. Or Thaana. I am a merchant of strange potions and I have the largest collection of magic recipes and incantations in Star Central – of course I can read runic!'

'I thought only dwarves knew runic,' said Pim. 'But now I think I have an idea.'

'I am a dwarf on my grandmother's uncle's cousin-in-law side,' Dr. Schlosen-Bosen replied unfazed. 'What idea?'

'Well, somewhere in Baibok Prison in Dragonborg there is a book in runic that might just tell us how to get out of Dragonland and get back to Star Central. If we find it, that is.'

When Chief of Security Dabney McKitterick had revoked Gustav's clearance to work as Research Director in the ACG testing program and assigned him to the Call Centre, Gustav already had a pretty good idea of what was coming to him. The Call Centre bore the stigma of the most boring department in the whole of Advanced Computers&Games. And it had managed to live up to its reputation from day one. But, as the unfortunate Gustav was destined to find out today, there was one thing even more boring in this life than answering the calls in the ACG Call Centre.

And that was attending the Strategic Workshop on Answering the Calls in the Call Centre.

If the first weeks had seemed simply boring with their endless stream of helpless callers, the Strategic Workshop was mind-numbingly tedious. In the Call Centre, even with all the reassigning of serial numbers and helping to unpack consoles over the phone, every now and then there would be a nice caller on the other end of the line with an intriguing technical problem that Gustav could solve for him.

The Strategic Workshop, however, had no such redeeming feature. It entailed a lot of Power Point presentations in a windowless room in the basement. They were mostly demonstrations of such deeply thought-out concepts as facilitating the initial phase of a limited affirmative affinity with the customer. Gustav was trying to concentrate as much as he could, but it was only towards the end of the morning that he realized that what they meant by this was answering the call! The workshop facilitator commended him for understanding and chided him for using the old inadequate term.

In school I could have at least been saved by the bell – but this thing here never ends, Gustav thought as project-wide proximities followed policy-oriented synergies no end. Nobody around him seemed to be the least disturbed by the fact that getting the complaining customer off the line in as short time as possible – the golden rule of all call centres around the world – now had to be called expedited inception of the auto-supportive phase of product experience.

The past few weeks in ACG did not look at all the way he had envisaged his career in the company. All his work in Laboratory 21 was a distant past and he had to devote himself to advice on faulty chargers and improperly inserted cartridges. So after the consultants from Shelwood, Iberd, Tubston & Eaglestone had announced a whole plethora of seminars, workshops, courses and curricula, he volunteered for a Strategic Workshop thinking that it would help him get out of the Call Centre – closer to his goal of joining the team on the far more interesting X9 project. But when he appeared in the designated office, he found out that the Staff Administration had for once taken less than an eternity to process a post replacement and had already assigned him in accordance with his current position: Strategic Workshop on Call Centres it was for him.

Not to mention that his former assistant Lia was already working in X9. His thoughts kept wandering away from facilitated synergies to the as yet unfacilitated ones. Ah, lovely Lia ...

And then, just before lunch, all of a sudden the Strategic Workshop was interrupted. The workshop facilitator had just nipped out to her office to bring the props for the afternoon role-playing session. She soon returned empty-handed, but very agitated. The props were missing – as did a half of her office.

'Everything is cleaned down to the sockets! Gone! And not just my office. Mr. Shelwood's office too, and Mr. Iberd's and Mr. Tubston's and Ms. Eaglestone's! Right here in the ACG. Outrageous! What kind of place this is, where open theft occurs in broad daylight?'

The workshop facilitator terminated the workshop to everybody's great relief. She was still fuming when she picked up her laptop and left. 'That the workshop now has to be suspended is entirely ACG's fault,' she could be heard from the corridor. 'They should not expect any rebate in billable hours!'

The sun was high in the sky above the mountains of Dragonland and it was hot. The dark red rocky landscape around Pim and Dr. Schlosen-Bosen seemed to absorb the rays of the sun only to radiate them as heat that penetrated through the soles of their shoes as they walked. Pim still hasn't quite got accustomed to the idea of returning to Dragonborg where he could very well be beheaded according to custom – but he could see no way of ever finding a way out of Dragonland without finding the Book of Gates first. Dr. Schlosen-Bosen's stories about the recent upsurge of sightings of the mysterious Black Dragons outside their native Northern Provinces only served to reinforce this conclusion. On the other hand, as Dr. Schlosen-Bosen was at pains to point out – as if it needed pointing – returning to Dragonborg was not without its dangers.

'We should not take any risks. King Ragnagnoknorr can be very moody when he wakes up from the Royal Slumber. Dragons who displeased the king have been known to find themselves a head or two shorter. Or even five. And you only have one.'

'I know,' Pim said gloomily.

'The king is notorious for his changing moods. Between you and me, I think he is bipolar – his mother was a complete schizo. And after the hibernation, he is always depressed, brooding over his dreams – and you can imagine that there are plenty of dreams to go through after ninety-nine years of sleep!'

Pim was not very interested in Dragonking's mental states. 'I hope that Boundless Mountains is only a name, and not a fact of physical geography. How are we going to get to the gate once we find where it is? How big is Dragonland?'

'Well, it's pretty big.'

'I should have known it.'

'Vast, to be honest. I have never been more than a week's travel away from the coast,' Dr. Schlosen-Bosen replied, 'and I don't know anybody who spent more than a month in the mountains and actually lived to come back and tell about it – but I am speaking only about humans and elves. There are dragons high up in the mountains who own the mines there – malachite, emeralds, carbuncles – the higher you go the more precious stones you will find. But as I said, I don't know of anybody who went higher than the emerald mines and returned. There are dwarves there who work in the mines, of course, but they never come down from the mountains. You need to be able to *fly* to really move about the Boundless Mountains – and fly better than the Black Dragons.'

'I know a dragon who can maybe fly us to the gate if it turns out it is far away.'

'How well do you know him?'

'Not very well,' Pim admitted, 'but it's better than nothing. He is a Wing Lieutenant in the Coastguard, his name is Danko.'

'Ah, young Wing Lieutenant Danko!' Dr. Schlosen-Bosen smiled mischievously. 'Yes, he just might agree to take us to the gate if we ask him nicely.'

'You know him too?'

'No, I don't know him, but I know a thing or two about him,' Dr. Schlosen-Bosen replied. 'In my business it is not so much knowing dragons that is important. It is knowing about them that really counts. Anybody can ask a dragon for a favour, but not anybody can ask them a favour they can't refuse.'

'You mean you get your dragonsweat through blackmail?!'

'Let's not get into too many details. Suffice it to say that I have my methods and that they just might work on the young Wing Lieutenant.'

'I think there are better ways of getting him on our side than blackmail,' said Pim.

'What could be better than threatening to expose his love affair?'

'Danko is too proud to buy into that,' Pim dismissed the very idea of blackmailing the dragon that had always treated him fairly and friendly, even when he had arrested him. 'Tell me instead, how will we move about Dragonborg? Where will we hide?'

'Hide? I normally don't say this, but – you worry too much,' said Dr. Schlosen-Bosen.

'Oh, only about the structural integrity of my neck,' said Pim.

'The same unpleasant fate would have befallen me long ago had I not become an expert in avoiding it.'

'So what's your plan?'

Dr. Schlosen-Bosen stopped and turned to Pim. 'The key word is – disguise.'

Later that day, two strange characters appeared out of a small hidden door in the ramparts of Dragonborg. One was short and wore a tall homburg hat and black cape over a highly-poised hunchback. He looked around the empty street and gave a sign to the other one who sported an inordinately long black moustache, more commonly found on Spanish painters. When he stepped out and closed the hidden door behind him, the wall again looked as impenetrable as a dragon stronghold should be.

The moustache was more nervous than the hunchback – his eyes anxiously darted left and right, and when he saw a dragon approaching them in the narrow street, he froze. The hunchback noticed it, came back to nudge him and they both slowly continued walking. The dragon came and passed by without paying any attention to them.

'Pim, we are not the only non-dragons in town,' the hunchback said to the moustache. 'Nothing is going to happen to us unless we get accosted by the authorities. Act normally.'

'I know, I know, I am sorry.'

'Now let me see, Baibok Prison, that must be this way. But it will be better if we avoid Karabatack Boulevard and use the side alleys. Follow me.' The hunchback opened a door and led the moustache into a dark hallway which led to a courtyard.

Just as Harry had described it, several buildings overlooked the traboule, squeezed next to each other, and each of them had its own staircase on the outside. Washing lines were strung between windows with dragon underwear hanging heavily in the sun. Smells of spices wafted through the open windows, along with clinks of forks and plates and conversations around tables in dragon homes.

The scene aroused pleasant memories in Pim. He thought of summer vacations when he was a kid, but Dr. Schlosen-Bosen soon led him out on the other side of the traboule and into another narrow street. 'This way,' he said.

The two of them walked through a maze of cobbled streets. Dr. Schlosen-Bosen led the way. Luckily the streets were mostly empty in the lunchtime.

'What love affair?' Pim suddenly exclaimed the question that had been bothering him.

'Oh, just the love affair between young Wing Lieutenant Danko and Yulka, the Dragonking's only daughter,' Dr. Schlosen-Bosen replied.

'What? Who told you that?' said Pim.

'They have enjoyed secretly seeing each other during the last ninety-nine years while her father was asleep, but things are not looking very well for them now. Old King Ragnagnoknorr has very old-fashioned ideas about his daughter's suitors. And needless to mention it, he would produce some top-quality furious crude if he were to find out about Danko – '

'You are not going to betray them just to get your dragonsweat!' Pim stood up.

'No, but I will use what I know if it will get me out of Dragonland – hey, I didn't come here to unmask the illicit love affair of your friend. But I also wasn't the one who closed Median Tunnels!'

'He is not exactly a friend,' Pim grudgingly admitted. 'More of an acquaintance, but – '

'Shhh!' said Dr. Schlosen-Bosen. There was music coming from a side street. A strange kind of music. Pim cautiously looked around the corner. What he saw was an unusual contraption moving steadily along the pavement. The music was coming from the flames shot through a set of glass tubes of various calibres. Each tube produced a different note and together they made a simple, but fiery marching melody. And then it occurred to Pim – it was the best possible disguise one could have in Dragonland!

'Band! Hey, Band it's me,' he called after the fiery instrument in the street. 'Band!'

There was no reaction and Pim walked towards the instrument when suddenly a long hook shot out of a doorway and violently pulled him inside. 'Band! Help!' he barely managed to say before another hook appeared around his mouth and one more around his waist. He struggled to escape but the hooks kept pulling him deeper and deeper into the traboule until he heard someone say, 'Silence!' There, in a dark corner below a staircase, the hooks released him and retracted into trombones.

'I am Band, you fool,' the trombones said. 'That guy in the street is Pyrophone. He is a cousin of mine.'

'Band! I thought I would never see you again!'

'The same here. You know, I am glad I've spotted you before you ran into that snotty cousin of mine – he thinks anything to do with fire is inherently nobler than the rest. That's why he lives in Dragonborg, what an idiot. But tell me, what are you doing in Dragonborg, and with that silly disguise? Danko told me that you were thrown out of the city and that your life was not worth a starter flame if they found you here.'

'At least I am still alive. Did you hear what happened to Harry?'

'Yes. It is a most unwelcome complication – ' Band began to say when the door of the traboule creaked. All the remaining trombones promptly turned into an accordion and jumped on Pim almost knocking him off. 'If they ask, pretend you're a busker,' the accordion whispered and immediately spread into a popular melody.

A red face crowned by a homburg hat, full of trepidation, appeared from behind the door, just above the door-knob. It was Dr. Schlosen-Bosen. When he had seen Pim disappearing into the traboule, he had gathered all his courage and entered, determined to find out what happened to him.

He found Pim playing chardash.

As soon as he realized that they were not in danger, Pim threw the accordion on the floor and shouted at it. 'What? An unwelcome complication? You heartless bastard!' The accordion clanked in pain on the floor. 'You callous egoist! OK, you didn't have to like him – but to describe his death as nothing more than an unwelcome complication!!'

'Shhh,' Dr. Schlosen-Bosen tried to calm Pim down. 'What's going on? Why are you shouting at an accordion?'

'That's not an accordion. That's the Marching Band of Zandar – and the most uncaring, insensitive, thick-skinned being in all of Left World!'

'How do you do? I am Dr. Schlosen-Bosen of Supranatural Supplies, merchant in fine dragonsweats and pixie dusts.'

'Don't fraternize with him!'

'Why not?'

'Why not?! There were three of us trying to reach Star Central. Harry, the Bedel of Zandar, Band here and me. Heaven knows that Harry was not always the easiest person to be with. But yesterday, we were at the reawakening of King Ragnagnoknorr and when the king saw Harry, he had him arrested because of some old dispute. And then, in front of my eyes, he ordered him beheaded – that's the custom in Dragonland. And Band does not have the common decency to show respect for a dead friend. He was my friend, you know!' Pim looked angrily at Band.

'Mine too,' Band said, massaging his various instruments. 'And in case you are interested ...'

'What are you talking about?' Dr. Schlosen-Bosen turned to Pim. 'The custom in Dragonland is to behead only on the night of the new moon. The king would never allow any break with the tradition, least of all in such an important thing like beheading. Nobody could have been beheaded yesterday.'

Pim looked into the sky. And there, conspicuously white against the pallid blue of the afternoon sky, was a thin crescent of the waning moon.

'As I was saying,' said Band, 'in case you are interested, Harry is alive.'

Baibok Prison stood on top of Baibok Hill, one of the seven principal hills of Dragonborg. It was a gloomy fortress with a thick circular wall. A single row of deep barred windows high above the ground looked out on a narrow street which ran along the circumference of the fort. On the other side of the street stood a row of warders' houses. Even if it were possible for someone to saw off the inside bars, crawl through the narrow window that resembled a gun-hole, saw off the outside bars and rappel down the wall, any such escape would inevitably unfold right in front of the warders' windows, and unavoidably end in front of their doors.

A marching band appeared in the street, still breathing heavily from the climb up Baibok Hill. It paused at the gate of the prison, catching its breath and regrouping the instruments. Two men joined it. One of them, the shorter one with a hunchback, said, 'If you ask me, this is absurd.' The other one, the taller one with a moustache, said, 'But it's worth trying. Just repeat after me. Ready? *Oh, oh, oh!*

'*Oh, oh, oh!* the shorter one repeated half-heartedly and the orchestra began playing a simple tune marching along the street. A dragon or two looked through the windows of the warders houses but the reaction was mostly to shut the shades and withdraw inside. It was a hot afternoon and definitely the time for dragon siesta.

The marching band advanced alongside the prison wall playing the short melody over and over again. The two men were looking up, towards the windows of the prison and singing, '*Oh, oh, oh, when the sun is, when the sun is, when the sun is over the yah-aard-arm!!*

'Silence!' a muffled shout was suddenly heard from inside of one of the windows. 'Can a man not have some peace even in the last days of the waning moon!'

'It's him! He is alive!' Pim said to Dr. Schlosen-Bosen.

'Harry, it's me!' Band shouted towards the window.

'Of course it's you – who else would risk their life just to torment me with frivolous euphonies!' came the reply through the bars on the gun-hole.

'Shhh!' Band hissed towards the window, but nobody on the other side of the street seemed to have paid any attention to it.

'Band, I owe you an apology,' said Pim. 'I was convinced that I was never going to see Harry again. And when it seemed like you did not care about him – '

'You were very wrong, Pim. Danko came to warn me and he told me that Harry was taken to prison with just days to live,' said Band. 'How could you think that I did not care about – '

'Enough with sentimentalities!' said the voice from above. 'What are you going to do about my situation?'

'Well, strike that from the record,' Band said to Pim.

'What do you suggest we do?' Pim shouted towards the window.

'I suggest you get me out of this place. And soon!'

'But how?'

There was a long pause. 'I don't know.'

'We need a plan,' said Pim.

'You know, he can always ask the King for clemency,' said Dr. Schlosen-Bosen.

'I don't think that plan would quite work,' said Band.

'Who's that?' asked Harry, hearing an unfamiliar voice.

'Dr. Schlosen-Bosen of Supranatural Supplies of Star Central, merchant in fine dragonsweats and pixie dusts. Pleased to meet you, Sir Henry,' Dr. Schlosen-Bosen shouted and then slapped himself across the mouth when he realized that he had uttered the word dragonsweat.

'How do you do, Dr. Schlosen-Bosen? I am Sir Henry Grenfell-Moresby, the Royal Bedel of Zandar, Bringer of Royal News and Warrants, Proclamator Extraordinary and – '

The rest of Harry's title was drowned in the sound of snare drums. Both Pim and Dr. Schlosen-Bosen looked towards Band. 'It's not me!' he said before Pim gave the sign to everybody to be quiet.

Then three dragon City Guards with silver snare drums appeared around the prison wall and stopped right in front of them. Dr. Schlosen-Bosen quickly adjusted his cloak, Pim furtively pressed his moustache firmly against his upper lip and Band pretended that he had to polish his trumpets this very moment. But the dragon guards turned away from them and towards the houses across the street where the windows began to open. By the time the drums fell silent and one of the guards unrolled a huge roll, all the windows were full of dragon heads in expectation of some important news. The City Guards read the following proclamation:

'His Royal Highness King Ragnagnoknorr wishes the following announcement to be made throughout the Kingdom der Dragonlanden: His Royal Highness King Ragnagnoknorr has recently dreamt that His Late Royal Queen Mother wept in front of the Stone Flower that had been stolen from the Copper Mountain by the evil wizard Talambas. His Royal Highness King Ragnagnoknorr wishes to know the true and authentic meaning of this dream. He who can interpret the Royal Dream about the Stone Flower shall receive a Royal Reward.' A moment of pregnant silence ensued. 'And he who cannot – shall not.'

'I told you he was obsessed with dreams,' said Dr. Schlosen-Bosen.

'I can interpret the Royal Dream!' Pim exclaimed. 'And I will get the Royal Reward!'

The Revenge of Slevski

The square in front of the Royal Palace in Dragonborg was always a busy place, swarming with dragons, most of whom went about on palace business. The upkeep of the Royal Household required a constant stream of cooks, servants, artisans and other workmen in and out of the palace gates. Among them mingled the officials and the Dhrghrleet officers who came about the state affairs, petitioners before the king who hoped to obtain a royal favour or the redress of some injustice, and sellers of all sorts of wares. All of them were frequently dispersed by the palace guards to make way for a particularly high dignitary arriving for an audience with the king. But as soon as gilded carriages cleared the palace gates, the dragons in the service of the Royal Household resumed their hurried routines. It was an impressive sight, especially considering that the Royal Dragon Household consisted of only two members – the king and his daughter.

The towers and turrets of the Royal Castle stood high above the square and the crowd jostling around the palace gates. Somewhere inside, among the multitude of halls and chambers, the king was receiving dragons in the first royal audience after ninety-nine years of sleep. Present today in the Royal Chamber was Her Royal Highness Princess Yulka. It was the first time that she attended a royal audience. Last night, after the festivities, her father had summoned her to his chambers. As the pages took off his big powdered wigs one by one, he told her that the time had come for her to take part in the duties of the reigning dragonarch. 'My daughter, I am not very old and I hope to live long,' Dragonking said while Princess Yulka stood before him still in her stiff ceremonial dress, 'but I feel that I have neglected your education in Royal Matters. If anything happened to me, you would have to be ready to take over the duties of the ruler of the Kingdom der Dragonlanden. And the best way to learn what it entails is to spend time by my side while I work.'

When Pim, Band and Dr. Schlosen-Bosen arrived at the palace gates, Dr. Schlosen-Bosen was still trying to come up with a better way of doing what they were about to do. Pim brushed his objections aside and told him to hand over his waistcoat and homburg hat which Pim then put on. He firmly pressed his false moustache once again and then walked away, leaving Band and Dr. Schlosen-Bosen behind to wait. 'If I don't return within an hour, switch to Plan B,' he said.

'What's Plan B?' Band and Dr. Schlosen-Bosen asked together.

'I don't know. Work on it!' replied Pim and walked to the gate.

The gates of the Royal Castle were huge and, in keeping with the grandeur of the place, ornamented with no less than nine hundred and ninety-nine flames and fires in solid gold. In front of the gates stood two fearsome dragons bedecked in golden armour and armed with long halberds. It was an intimidating sight for anybody not raised in Dragonland.

The first reaction of the guards to the diminutive creature with a moustache who presented himself and demanded to see the king was to laugh at him and turn away. For a brief moment, Pim thought that his plan was bound to end up in failure and he almost gave up and walked away. Then he remembered Harry. What would Harry say? How would he win the favour of the guards?

'You impudent dogs!' the next instant Pim heard himself shouting at the two heavily armed dragons at the gate. 'I am a famous Arcanist Plenipotentor, a Magical-Astrological Diviner and Grand Revelator of Dreams! What is King Ragnagnoknorr going to do with your heads once he finds out that you turned away the one person in the whole of the Kingdom der Dragonlanden who can interpret the troublesome Royal Dream?'

The guards jolted and turned back on hearing those words. They looked at each other for a moment and then pushed the massive gates open. 'Revelator of Dreams to see the King!' one of them shouted and several chamberlains immediately appeared and took Pim inside the palace. He briefly turned back and saw Band and Dr. Schlosen-Bosen standing in the square.

Pim was taken deep into the castle and conveyed to the king's chamber without delay. The Lord Chamberlain of the Royal Household waited for him there.

'Whom should I announce, sir?' he asked just before the door opened.

'No need to announce me, I shall announce myself,' Pim replied loftily, took a deep breath and entered the king's chamber. The next instant he was standing in a magnificent oval marble hall lined with pillars of black basalt. Between the two central pillars stood the throne and on it sat Ragnagnoknorr, King der Dragonlanden, surrounded by a suite of bewigged royal counsellors, state ministers, illustrious fire-keepers and distinguished chamberlains, all of their faces powdered pallid white. There wasn't a dragon with less than three heads in the room – and all their eyes were on Pim.

'Your Majesty,' he said as pompously as he could, 'I am Professor Doktor Doktor Dapsul von Zabelthau, Dominus Doctorus Aureolus, Bombaster Grandiloquent, Engineer of Whipped Creams and Revelator of Dreams, Doctor of Chemistry and Iatrochemistry For Whom No Secret of Animate and Inanimate World is Unimpregnable, holder of many somniferous titles, by fortuitous coincidence presently travelling through the lands of dragons and thus able to prostrate myself at King Ragnagnoknorr's disposal in the disconcerting matter of the royal somniation of which the kingdom was recently informed.'

One by one, the seven heads of the Dragonking rose from the seven headrests of the royal throne as the incredible declamation went on. Both the king and Princess Yulka were taken by surprise. Truth be told, they did not understand half of the words. All the royal counsellors and the royal chamberlains looked perplexed at the haughty newcomer who stood before the throne. Professor Dapsul von Zabelthau now had their undivided attention.

'Your Majesty, the somniatory implications of your dream are quite clear to me. Indeed, to a somnomancer of my calibre, they are manifestly blatant. If you permit me, I should like to proceed with the somniative elucidation.'

'You want to do what?' said Yulka on behalf of everybody in the room, taking off seven sunglasses one by one.

'Should Your Highness be so inclined, I propose to reveal to all those assembled here the true and genuine meaning of the dream that so troubles His Flamatious Majesty.'

'Oh, by all means,' said the king.

'Your Majesty,' said Doctor Dapsul von Zabelthau and then made a short pause to heighten the suspense. 'Your late Queen Mother, may she rest in flames, shall not stop weeping until the Stone Flower is restored to its proper place on the Copper Mountain and your daughter, Princess Yulka, is given in marriage to whoever brings back the Flower.'

A chuckle spread from head to head of the king and then spread to everybody else in the room.

'And if you bring back the flower, you want to marry my daughter?' said king Ragnagnoknorr, redoubling the chuckle among others present.

'I would not dream of such a thing, Your Majesty. Such honour should certainly be reserved for the valiant dragon who brings back the flower. I will, however, request that you grant me one wish the moment the Stone Flower is returned to Dragonland: I ask you to release and hand over to me one Henry Grenfell-Moresby who is currently – quite deservedly, I hasten to add – awaiting execution in Baibok Prison.'

The mood in the room suddenly changed. It was obvious that the king was not amused by this request and the audience chamber fell silent. No royal counsellor and no royal chamberlain dared guess what the king's reaction would be to such an audacious demand. Try as they might, they could not read what was going on in any of the king's heads.

But Princess Yulka sensed that the strange doctor's proposal was her only chance, however slim, that she would be married to her secret love. Just as the king was about to speak, she stood up, coughed significantly seven times and said, 'Doctor Dapsul von Zabelthau is a wise and noble man.' She sat down again and the apprehensive silence in the audience chamber continued.

The king looked at his daughter and then at the somnomancer in front of him. 'Doctor Dapsul von Zabelthau, you will get your reward, but only if the Stone Flower is brought back to Dragonborg before the new moon – and not a minute later.'

'Your Flamatious Majesty!' Pim was frantically trying to think of what else to say, but the Dragonking rose from the throne and everybody in the room stood up.

'Let there be an announcement made throughout the kingdom,' said the king, 'that the dragon who returns the Stone Flower to its rightful place on the Copper Mountain shall receive the claw of my daughter in marriage. The Royal Audiences are adjourned for the day,' he declared and left the room followed by Princess Yulka and a trail of counsellors and chamberlains.

The sky over Dragonland began to fill with dragons in search of the legendary Stone Flower even before the City Guards could make the first official announcement of the new royal proclamation. The news had spread through the palace like a wildfire. Every royal counsellor, cook and chamberlain had a young eligible dragon in the family who deserved to hear the news before anyone else. Soon the traboules of Dragonborg were brimming with excitement as young dragons bade farewell to their parents promising to find the Flower, win the claw of the Princess and bring the royal favour on the household.

The news travelled fast to the provinces as well, spreading first along the coastal road and then into the mountains. The inexorable attraction that every young dragon felt for the incredible combination of the greater glory of Dragonland and the hormonal bliss at the mere sight of the seven heads of the Dragonking's daughter meant that there was no shortage of volunteers for the improbable mission. In every house, a father had something to say on the probable location of the Stone Flower and a mother on how to behave in front of the Princess once it is found. From every house a young dragon was sent to try his luck in the chance of a lifetime.

Barely fitting into her small turret in Dragonborg, Tetka Savka looked at the sky, watching all the potential suitors taking off and trying to spot Danko among them. She had not been able to find him when she heard the news from a friend in the palace. Now everyone knew that the king was looking for someone to find the Stone Flower and marry his daughter, even those who were in no way related to the Royal Family. This made her upset. She could not bear if it came to it that the royal blood were to be mixed with some riff-raff!

During her morning workout in her Private Royal Gym Princess Yulka too could hardly think about anything else. Her thoughts were fixed on Danko as she beat her wings inside a wind tunnel, the dragons' most popular exercise machine. What if he didn't find the Flower?

Soon countless dragons spread across the skies of Dragonland, even in the restive northern provinces, each of them with an idea of where to look for the Stone Flower that was stolen from the Copper Mountain by the evil wizard Talambas. But only one dragon set out to fly across the sea.

Cradled in his arms were Pim Pergamon, Dr. Schlosen-Bosen and a mouth harmonica.

In the ACG Call Centre, Gustav was not assigned many shifts that coincided with the lunch hour of most of the ACG staff that worked, like the rest of London, from nine to five. So when his Strategic Workshop was unexpectedly cancelled, he finally had the opportunity to visit the canteen when all his friends were there having lunch. He found the place abuzz with stories about disappearances of printers and other strange happenings in the building. At first it was only printers and only during the night, but lately all sorts of office equipment were found missing or damaged, often in a bizarre way. The most common was a clear cut in half, with one half of the machine missing and the other half neatly left open as if it was some sort of didactic tool for easier understanding of the workings of printers and photocopiers.

He took his tray to the table where he saw lovely Lia in company of other laboratory technicians. They were discussing the latest office rumours.

'It's all the fault of those people in the Procurement and the cheap equipment they buy for us. Things are just not as well-built as they used to be. Now, when I first came to work here back in – ' one of them wanted to explain but was booed off by the others.

'Not built well enough? My foot! I saw the armchair in an office sawn right in half and I tell you that that armchair was solid as a dreadnought!' one of them said.

'This company is going down the drain, and that's what I've been telling you all along. This is just the beginning, and the end is near,' another one declared.

'Repent! The end is nigh!' Gustav announced to the general laughter as he sat down among them. 'So what is it that's worrying you guys? A couple of printers goes missing and you are all worked up about it – if only you knew what I am up against in the Call Centre!'

'It's not just a couple of printers, Gustav,' said Lia. 'Something really strange is going on in the building. Things disappear, or just bits of them are left and it's all happening in broad daylight. My father told me that not even the upper floors are safe any more. And nobody knows who is doing it or why.'

The mention of Lia's father and the upper floors of the ACG building made an impression on everybody at the table. Mr. Liu was the Chief of the Research and Development Division of the ACG and Gustav's personal hero. His abode among the top management was a place that none of them could access. It was not easy to understand how somebody could get into this sequestered area reserved for ACG's top brass – and then get away with printers, photocopiers and what not.

'Alright, listen, I was at a workshop seminar this morning with some highly-placed people from Shelwood-Iberd-Tubston &Eaglestone and I'll tell you what I heard there,' said a chubby girl in a red sweater sitting next to Lia. Her name was Nina Sylph and she worked in Staff Administration. 'But it's strictly confidential and it does not leave this table. Understood?'

Everybody nodded solemnly so that they could hear the secret.

'Prepare to be afraid – remember Slevski from Plot&Context who was fired last year after that altercation with Edna?'

Everybody nodded again and Nina Sylph continued in dead serious voice.

'Not everybody knows it, but Slevski went mad shortly after he was fired. One night he came back to ACG and managed somehow to get past the security and to the upper floors. He broke into the CEO's office, smashed one of its glass walls and jumped out. It all got hushed up but, just before he jumped, he swore to return to ACG and exact his revenge. What we are witnessing now is the revenge of Slevski. It is his ghost that is stalking the corridors at midnight and wrecking our office equipment in a Luddite revenge on his former work environment. And Slevski himself will return on the first night of full moon after the anniversary of his summary dismissal. That's what I heard and you'd better believe it.'

There was silence around the table for a while, until Gustav managed to formulate the thought that was nagging them all: 'You don't really believe all this crap, do you?'

Nina Sylph stood up, took her tray and left the table mumbling, 'You'll see, I'm telling you, you'll see.'

'I think it's those people from Shelwood-Iberd-Tubston &Eaglestone who are responsible for all this,' somebody said to break the silence. 'They are so greedy that they'll stop at nothing.'

'That theory is far more plausible than the last one we heard, but I think it's still incorrect,' Fred McMurray from Finance replied. Fred was Gustav's friend and he liked to think he was informed. 'Word has it that the Shelwood-Iberd-Tubston&Eaglestone top brass have taken up their offices on the upper floors.'

'Yes, that's what I heard too,' the conversation immediately got livelier. 'Shelwood himself, and Iberd, too, are working in the building.'

'Yeah, and Tubston and Eaglestone.'

'They normally never leave their headquarters – '

' – although they have offices ready and waiting for them wherever they've got contracts.'

'But apparently they came to ACG!'

'I know, I saw Ms. Eaglestone in front of the lift this morning.'

'And I saw Mr. Iberd. He's actually quite handsome in real life, you know.'

'Enough about consultant celebrities!' said Gustav. 'Tell me about X9. I know that almost all of you have been reassigned to work on X9 and that's far more interesting than some glorified accountants. I want to work on that project too, and you should help me to get in on it.'

Again there was an awkward silence around the table. 'What, what'd I say?' Gustav tried to break the silence.

'Well, you see,' Lia began to explain, 'the X9 project is indeed very interesting, but the thing is, we are not really supposed to talk about it to the external personnel.'

'What? External personnel? What is it now? What am I, a subcontractor? A caterer? Do you see me selling sandwiches around here?'

'No, no, that's not what she meant,' said Priyanka, one of Lia's friends at the table. 'She just meant personnel external to the X9 project.'

'Yes, that's what it said in the undertaking we all had to sign when we were assigned to X9,' Lia explained. 'The bosses are rather touchy about it, what with the missing printers and everything. You should really try to understand. My father says that the future of the company depends on the X9 project and that's why everybody on the upper floors is at the same time so nervous and so secretive about it. We should really try to change the subject and talk about something else.'

'Yeah, have you heard that the Chief of Personnel took up knitting while she was in the Institute for the Executive Fatigue?' somebody said.

'What! Edna Edwards? No way!'

Dragon Danko had spent the whole night in the air with Pim, Band and Dr. Schlosen-Bosen nested in his arms but the young Wing Lieutenant showed no signs of fatigue. On the contrary, he kept talking the whole night, helping everybody else to stay awake. He told them about the rigorous entrance examination for the Coastguard service where no dragon unable to stay in the air continuously for at least seven days and seven nights can hope to even begin with the theoretical part of the exam. He also revealed that he had been trailing Pim, Harry and Band walking on the sea for days before he arrested them on the beach.

He spoke of his duties as a Coastguard officer with pride. It wasn't a particularly exciting life, he told them, because there were not many of those who managed to cross the Endless Ocean and arrive to Dragonland by sea. His job consisted for the most part in helping dragons who found themselves in trouble anywhere along the coast, mostly careless picnickers, and keeping dragonsweat smugglers in check. He told them little about his private life, mostly about growing with Tetka Savka and her antics. He would not say anything about his parents or the Dragonking's daughter, no matter how much Band probed him.

Every now and then Pim looked at the sickle of the moon and it seemed to him that it was becoming thinner and thinner right before his eyes. When the moon disappeared below the horizon, he lost his most precious measure of time. He shouldn't have agreed to the Dragonking's terms, he thought, he should have gained more time. But then, how do you bargain with a seven-headed dragon, even if you are a Bombaster Grandiloquent? And now the Towers of Billbalirion were nowhere in sight. He was worried.

Dr. Schlosen-Bosen was worried too. What seemed like a great opportunity to get out of Dragonland and back to his shop turned into a daring rescue mission to find a stone flower, of all things, and help somebody who didn't know better than to cheat the Dragonking in cards. He had tied up his homburg hat under the chin, but the wind kept blowing his cloak off and threatening to uncover the barrel on his back.

'You seem very worried about that barrel,' Danko suddenly said. 'Why didn't you leave it in Dragonborg?'

'Who, me? Oh, well, I didn't want to delay our departure, seeing how important it was that we leave at once,' Dr. Schlosen-Bosen answered all the while trying to adjust the cape over his barrel.

'You are right, it's good that we left early,' Danko agreed. 'Say, you look familiar. Do you come often to Dragonland?'

'Who, me? No, no, I never looked familiar in my life!'

'We are never going to find the Towers like this,' Band said to interrupt the conversation that caused poor Dr. Schlosen-Bosen's face to go beyond red. 'This is the Endless Ocean, after all. Nobody ever managed to find the Towers of Billbalirion before. The more I think about the whole plan, to tell you the truth, the more worried I am.'

The only one on the flight not worried was Danko. 'There is an old dragon proverb,' he said. '*Worrying is for before taking to the air.* Now that we have come this far, we only have two options: looking for the Towers where the Stone Flower is, or turning back. I am in charge of this flight and I say we are not going back. This narrows it down to one option for the rest of you.'

If he was expecting an enthusiastic reaction to his words, it did not materialize. His three passengers kept gloomily looking at the immense and empty ocean all around them. The sea below looked perfectly smooth and unchanging in all directions, mirroring the cloudless sky.

'How did you find the Towers the first time?' Danko asked.

'We didn't really find them,' said Pim. 'They came to us.'

'What did you do that they came to you? You should try doing it again.'

'We didn't do anything. They just appeared out of nowhere.'

'Wait!' said Band. 'I have an idea!' He fidgeted left and right until he pulled out a long horn. And then he began to play a slow melancholic melody.

'Yes!' Pim said when he recognized the tune.

'Yes what?' asked Dr. Schlosen-Bosen.

'This is the melody that the Towers produce when wind blows through their tubes. We heard it the evening we spent on the Towers. That's exactly how it sounded, only deeper.'

'And?'

'Well, keep looking at the horizon. Nobody else except us ever heard this melody. Maybe the Towers will appear when they hear it.'

Dr. Schlosen-Bosen wanted to say something about the notion that a tower was supposed to decide on a course of action upon hearing some music familiar to it, but he kept it for himself. Danko slowed down the beats of his wings and they glided high above the sea in perfect synchronicity with the Billbalirion sunset melody.

Pim concentrated on the horizon far away, searching for even a smallest irregularity in its flawless straight line. Band played the whole melody, exactly as they heard it that evening. When he came to the end, he continued from the beginning.

'I've never heard it played in this key. But I have to say it's maybe even better than the original version,' somebody said.

'Shhh, keep looking,' Pim replied, his eyes glued to the horizon.

'Looking for what?'

'The Towers of Billbalirion, what else!'

'But they are not here,' came the reply.

'Are you pulling my leg? Who said that?' Pim looked at his three companions, but they looked equally puzzled.

'I am not pulling anybody's leg but I could try if you want me to,' the same voice was heard again. 'It's just that the Towers are nowhere near here.'

Band, Dr. Schlosen-Bosen and even Danko shrugged their shoulders in bewilderment.

'Who's that talking? Show yourself!' Pim said, more irritated than frightened.

'Pim? Is that you?'

'Yes. And who are you?'

'Up, look up!' Everybody looked up. There was a cloud exactly above them, trailing them along as they flew.

'Dapertutto!' Pim exclaimed at the sight of his foggy friend.

'Hey, Pim! You are not on the Towers any more.'

'As a matter of fact, I am looking for them.'

'Oh, I can take you to the Towers if you want.'

A wave of jubilation overcame the dragon and its passengers.

'On one condition, though,' added the cloud.

'Oh,' the jubilation deflated suddenly.

'I have this terrible itch here, just below this puff. Could you guys scratch me a bit?'

'Danko?' Pim looked at his dragon friend.

'Sure. Hold on everybody!' Danko replied and made a wide turn.

'Are you sure it's safe to fly into clouds?' Dr. Schlosen-Bosen asked anxiously, but before anybody bothered to reassure him they flew straight into Dapertutto and a giggle was heard all around them. The next instant they flew out on the other side.

'A bit higher,' Dapertutto said when he saw them again and Danko made a tight U-turn.

'Higher and to the left!' came the next instruction while they were still inside the cloud and Danko immediately executed the terrifying turn. The panic-stricken Dr. Schlosen-Bosen clung to Pim for his dear life, almost dislocating an equally frightened but furious mouth harmonica out of Pim's pocket in the process.

'No, no, to the side,' said the cloud and Danko obliged him. 'Yes, here! That's it! Do it again!'

They spent the next couple of minutes executing hair-raising aerial bravuras inside the cloud while he kept saying, 'Oh, I've never had a scratching this good before. Oh, this is so-ooh good! More, more!'

When Dapertutto was finally scratched to his heart's content, Pim introduced him to the others. 'Gentlemen, meet my friend Dapertutto. He is the person that will take us to the Towers of Billbalirion.'

'How?' Dr. Schlosen-Bosen asked.

'Just follow me,' Dapertutto said and a breath of wind appeared out of nowhere and carried him away. Danko beat his wings faster and faster and in a few moments they were under way.

The flight was long but it felt easier now that they knew where they were going. The moon was still below the horizon, yet Pim was more confident that they were going to make it on time. He relaxed a bit and spent most of the time looking enviously at Dapertutto. The big blue skies were his home and he could go wherever he wanted whenever he wanted it.

'How is it that there's always some wind to take you where you want to go?' he asked him.

'How else would I go around if I couldn't muster some wind?' Dapertutto replied.

'Muster some wind?' said Dr. Schlosen-Bosen. 'I thought you clouds were just carried along by the wind.'

'No, no, what an absurd idea!' Dapertutto could hardly hide his astonishment. 'It is us clouds who make the wind so that we would get where we want to go. What a miserable existence it would be if I had to float around and wait for a random breath of wind to move me. Uh, I shudder to even think about it.'

'I would like to see a cloud shudder,' said Band when Danko shouted, 'Look!'

The silhouette of the Towers of Billbalirion was visible against the rising sun on the horizon far in front of them.

'The fire safety of the building has been reassessed and given the highest possible mark for the sixth consecutive year. Safety at the workplace here at Advanced Computers&Games conforms to all national and international standards,' Chief of Security Dabney McKitterick paused to take a sip of water in a meeting room on the 66th floor of the ACG building. 'Further on, my informants among the staff, most of whom are ISO9001-certified, inform me that the staff morale is at a satisfactory, even enviable level. I can report that the esprit de corps is among the highest in the industry. In short – '

'In short, Dabney, we still don't know who is behind the sabotage in the building,' ACG CEO Mr. Furthermore cut short the briefing on the security situation. Had it been up to the Chief of Security, the briefing would have gone on and on about the outstanding successes of the Security Division.

'Err, no, not yet,' said Dabney McKitterick. 'But we have some very good leads.'

'Such as?'

'The pattern of the damage.'

'What pattern? The bloody things are cut in half.'

'No, I mean the pattern of the damage inside the building. If you look at the times and places of the damage occurring to the equipment, there can be only one conclusion – it is an inside job. No day visitor or contractor could have done it. Which leads us to a suspect.'

'Oh?' Mr. Furthermore was suddenly all ears. 'Who?'

'Look at it this way. The suspect must be someone who has an unfettered access to all areas of ACG. And I know of somebody who was given just such a level of access immediately before the troubles began. Somebody who has not only the ability to get wherever he wants, but also to leave whenever he wants. Somebody who hasn't been seen since he came and yet, we know that he is around.'

'Yes?'

'Ingvar Pingvarsson.'

'*Pingvarsson*? Impossible!'

'Impossible? I don't think so.'

'No way. Absolutely out of the question. It can't be him. Just think, a man of his calibre, of his standing. Of his *net worth*! No, it has to be somebody else,' said Mr. Furthermore.

'Larry, I have a method of work of my own,' Dabney began to explain. 'And it goes like this: when I exclude everything impossible, whatever remains – however improbable! – must be the answer.'

'It's not your method, Dabney, it's a cliché from Sherlock Holmes,' Mr. Furthermore replied.

'It's been weeks since Pingvarsson came here to ACG and we haven't heard anything from him or about him – all this while paying him quite handsomely, I understand. I find this suspicious.'

'Handsomely? More like gorgeously, Dabney. But that doesn't matter. He comes on the highest possible recommendation from our close strategic partners, the Abenteuer Kapitalisten Fondsen of Schaffhausen. Ingvar Pingvarsson is famous for his methods. He has been known to carry our his internal research for months before resurfacing with ideas worth millions in cost cuts. Let him be, Dabney. And, to get back to 'your' method, you haven't excluded one very impossible thing from your reasoning.'

'Which one?'

'You think Ingvar Pingvarsson is capable of personally sawing anything in half?'

'You may have a point there,' Dabney reluctantly admitted stroking his moustache. He was not among the people who readily warmed up to the idea of consulting with anybody about anything – least of all about how to do their job – and he certainly thought that no consultant would be capable of doing anything as hands-on as sawing a printer in half. 'I will have to increase the surveillance of staff.'

'Do it. In the meantime, what can you report on the IT problems?'

'What IT problems?'

'The missing and damaged equipment in the building is only a half of the problem – the visible half,' said Mr. Furthermore. 'Quite apart from the mechanical damage, we had a series of computer malfunctions throughout the building,' said Mr. Furthermore.

'But surely that's all gone by now, the storm was weeks ago.'

'I am not talking about the storm – that was in the past. I am talking about the present. Have you seen the IT helpdesk numbers for the past week? Sure, it's mostly software, but one thing is clear to me

– something is interfering with our computers. And our computers are our bread and butter, Dabney.'

'But surely, the IT people are on top of this. I don't see any immediate link to security here,' said Dabney but Mr. Furthermore became impatient.

'This is a very sensitive time for this company, Dabney.'

'I know, I know – '

'Dabney, I've already instructed the IT people to find out what is causing the software problems. What I want you to do is to find out who is causing them!'

The conference on the 59th floor of the ACG skyscraper with the people from Shelwood-Iberd-Tubston&Eaglestone had been going on for some time. The consultants were by now in full swing in ACG and the time had come for the pendulum to touch Edna's department too. All the senior staff of the Human Resources were there, listening to the consultants proposals for increasing efficiency of their work and dutifully noting them down. There was not a thing in the Human Resources Department of the ACG that was to be left unchanged, not a section that could not be reorganized.

Edna had been silent throughout the meeting, merely nodding and aheming at regular intervals to show the appreciation for all the work that Shelwood-Iberd-Tubston&Eaglestone did to increase her efficiency. Kingsley Err, Head of Staff Administration, and others from her department sitting to her left and right had already noticed that she was not as active as usual in this sort of meeting. Before, when consultants had visited ACG, she would have enthusiastically supported and embraced their proposals, regardless – or precisely because – of their inanity. (The opinions were divided on this.) But now she looked indisposed. She must've eaten something that didn't agree with her, Kingsley Err thought.

'Finally, it has been decided to rename your department to better reflect the multi-disciplinary delivery as well as formative and summative assessment of its prerequisite competencies,' said Mr. Tubston. 'The Human Resources Department will from now on be called Human Assets Division.'

Everybody nodded and began to note down the new name when Edna cleared her throat and said, 'Is it really necessary?'

The consultants were taken aback that someone would ask such a question. The managers of Edna's department were taken aback that

Edna of all people would ask such a question. Mr. Tubston gave the floor to one of his more junior and more fervent partners to explain why the name change was necessary. The explanation was long and involved a lot of unit-specific inter-dependencies, integrated asset visibilities and time-based collaborative strategies. When he was finished, the senior partner again took the floor, summarized the explanation in a few acronyms and emphasized that the substance of their function would remain unchanged.

'But if we all just continue to do our work, and we do it well, what's in a name?' said Edna. The consultants were again taken aback – the concept thus defined was unfamiliar to them. They murmured among themselves for a while, some of them questioning the efficacy of treatments offered at the Institute for the Executive Fatigue.

'It's alright, I was just asking,' Edna said and took a bundle of knitting from under the table. Undaunted by the looks around her, she found the stitch where she had stopped earlier and proceeded to knit in full view of everybody while the meeting continued.

She was knitting something big.

Dragon Danko had dropped his passengers off on the ledge of the topmost turret before making a turn and coming in to land on the Towers of Billbalirion. Pim, Band and Dr. Schlosen-Bosen were safely inside when the big dragon somehow came to rest on the narrow ledge amid much flapping of wings. But once on the turret, he had no trouble getting inside although the doors seemed incredibly small compared with the size of his trunk.

Inside the topmost turret stood a beautiful flower carved out of a single piece of dark green malachite. As they stood in front of it, it became clear to Pim and Band why this flower had so impressed Harry when he saw it. Although it was all in one colour, there were myriads of shades and nuances in the green malachite of the Flower. The veins in the stone perfectly corresponded to the curves of the leaves making the stone almost alive. The petals were so thin that light could pass through them, revealing a structure of fine lifelike veins. It seemed impossible that they could be mere mineral lines in a dead stone. The whole flower was carved so exquisitely that it seemed that the slightest breath of wind could ruffle its petals.

And the most amazing thing, the one which Harry did not mention that morning on the base of the Towers, was the fact that the flower – smelled of flowers. It smelled like a thousand of other flowers put together, as if every other scent known to nature had been woven into the amazing fragrance that filled the topmost turret of the Towers of Billbalirion and enchanted all those in it.

'We found the Stone Flower,' said a wide-eyed Danko, still in awe before the precious green flower, 'and it is beautiful. And I am going to be the dragon who brings it back to Dragonland where it rightfully belongs.'

'Who made it?' asked Pim.

'That is not known. The Stone Flower had stood on the Copper Mountain long before dragons came to those lands and claimed them as their own, which means that it is very old indeed. Some dragons, like Tetka Savka for instance, think that the Flower had been there even before the Boundless Mountains rose from the Endless Ocean and that it was merely lifted from the bottom of the sea where it had lain from before the beginning of Time. The dwarves who work in the malachite mines on the Copper Mountain are capable of carving anything out of malachite, but even they do not claim it as the work of their hands. Ask any dwarf and they will tell you that every hundred years a stonemason is born blessed with such extraordinary abilities that he would be capable of carving a stone flower – if only he could find the perfect piece of malachite. Because the true secret of the Stone Flower of the Copper Mountain is in the stone from which it was carved. Nobody has ever been able to find a lode of malachite that would yield a stone with such perfect unbroken veins.'

'Well, if this doesn't save Harry, nothing will,' said Band. 'Let's see what we can do about bringing the Flower back.'

They helped Danko to carefully slide the Stone Flower from the pedestal and move it outside the turret. When the Flower was removed, Pim discovered that it had been covering a round hole in the pedestal and that the hole was filled to the brim with a milky-white fog.

Band and Dr. Schlosen-Bosen were outside discussing the safety of various seating arrangements for the flight back. Danko had told them that now that he had to carry the Stone Flower in his claws, they would all have to travel on his back. Dr. Schlosen-Bosen was telling Band that he was not a morph, that he could not travel in anybody's pocket and should therefore have a priority in choosing his place. Band could be heard trying to explain that there was no such thing as boarding priority on dragons.

Meanwhile inside the turret, Pim felt a great curiosity for the hole filled with the fog. First he put his hand inside and felt a pleasant warmth. Then he thought that he could hear voices coming from the fog, so he leant over the edge and immersed his head into the hole. The fog cleared immediately and he discovered that he could see a beautiful scenery below. Gently rolling hills covered in green forest could be seen forming a tame and inviting landscape of a whole new world. Farms and cottages were scattered among the trees, all of them neat and whitewashed, surrounded with vegetable gardens and small meadows. Narrow country lanes could be seen winding in and out of the woods, with stone bridges crossing the gurgling forest streams below.

In front of every house children were playing in the grass and Pim could hear their laughter and merriment from above. He was taken by a sudden desire to join them. He forgot about everything else. The children noticed him and gathered right below him, smiling at him and stretching their little arms trying to reach him. He extended his hands as far as he could, but it was not enough to touch their little fingers. The children all stood on their toes trying to reach his outstretched arms, but it was still not enough. Pim felt that if only he climbed over the edge of the hole, he could touch their hands. Their faces, dirty around the mouth but smiling and inviting, made him bend and lean deeper and deeper towards them. Their fingers almost touched when suddenly somebody pulled him back.

'What has come over you!'

Pim lay on the floor inside the turret while Band stood over him with a worried face. 'We've got to go, we have no time to lose.'

'Yes, yes, I know. It's just that this looks like a gate. You know, a gate into another world.'

'Is that world Star Central? Is Harry waiting for us there with his head still on?'

'Well, no, of course not ...'

'Well, then! Besides, Dapertutto just returned with news. Looks like there's going to be another storm.'

'Another storm?'

'Yes,' Dapertutto could be heard from the outside as fog enveloped the turret. 'I just came to scratch once more on the Towers. Then I have to go, the clouds are being summoned to a storm again.'

'Not to worry,' Danko could be heard from outside. 'I can fly above any weather.'

'Dapertutto, we have to get going,' Band shouted through the window. 'Could you please move away, I don't want to catch anything from you.'

'Yeah, yeah, just a minute, I am going,' said Dapertutto. Pim and Band came out of the turret and found Dr. Schlosen-Bosen already waiting, straddled on Danko's back just behind the shoulders. 'Your seat is right behind me,' he said to Pim, looking somewhat worried.

Dapertutto then moved away from the Towers and the top turret basked in the sun again. 'They say it's gonna be pretty big, this one,' he said. 'I wish you luck. Dragonland is in that direction. Straight on,' he pointed somewhere towards the horizon where big clouds could already be seen rolling towards the Towers of Billbalirion.

'Danko, are you sure this is going to work?' Pim said as he took his place on the Wing Lieutenant's back.

'I used to fly my younger cousins like that. We did it a thousand times,' Danko reassured him.

'Yeah, but they were dragons,' replied Pim.

'Aha, but you have no other option.'

They took to the air with a few powerful beats of dragon's wings. Just before he disappeared inside Pim's breast pocket, Band had one final piece of advice for Dapertutto: 'You ought to see someone about this itch, you know. I wouldn't wait a day if I were you,' he said. Then a gust of wind came and carried the cloud away.

'Left World!' Pim said to himself. 'Where else can you hear what a trombone would do if he were a cloud.'

Hand, Head and Flower

The moon was out again – or what remained of it. Only a tiny sliver could be seen in the sky above the clouds and it was obvious that this was the last day of the old cycle. The new moon was only hours away while a tremendous mass of clouds still stood between Danko and Dragonland, somewhere far away in front of him.

They had already spent many hours flying above the churning weather below. The weight of the Stone Flower and the three passengers required greater than usual physical effort from Danko. Added to that was the fact that they had to remain above the menacing clouds. It wasn't Dapertutto with his itchings any more, it was a big storm boiling with lightning bolts. They could not afford to rise much higher, so they flew close to the top of the clouds. To Pim it looked as if they were sailing on a giant bowl of beaten egg whites – except that they could hear the storm below. There were moments when the thunder rose so high that they could not hear each other talk. Danko had stopped talking to them shortly after they took off from the Towers and concentrated his whole body and mind on flying. There was only one thing on his mind – his beloved Yulka.

Sitting behind deeply worried Dr. Schlosen-Bosen on Danko's back, Pim had more than one thing on his mind. He was not sure any more they were going to make it on time. In fact, he was not even sure whether the moon seen from Dragonborg was the same as seen from here. They had no way of knowing how far from land they were. What if there was a geographical difference in the phases of moon? What if the new moon was already visible in Dragonborg? What if Harry was already dead and he had put Band, Dr. Schlosen-Bosen and Danko in jeopardy for no good reason and without a chance of success? What if all this was for nothing?

What if that empty-headed Dapertutto gave them a wrong direction and they were flying out into the Endless Ocean?

'What if you're wrong and everything's gonna be fine?' a mouth harmonica was heard from his pocket.

'Band? Can you read thoughts?' said Pim.

'Anybody who can see your face right now could read your thoughts,' the mouth harmonica replied looking from the pocket. 'And I can feel the beat of your heart. All this tells me that you are one worried knot of nerves right now.'

'Yes, I am. I am beginning to realize that I should not have brought you all in this situation.'

'Then stop this realizing right away,' Band replied sharply. 'Number one, nobody here had to come. You only proposed it – we all came of our own will. I wish I had come up with your plan – but I didn't. I wish I acted like you more often – but I don't,' he said in a deadpan voice. 'And number two, far more important, is that you pulled all this off in order to save your friend. That's what counts and that's why we all came along. Well, that and certain hormonal urges on the part of young Wing Lieutenant here, which you skilfully wove into your plan.'

Pim thought about this for some time, trying to convince himself that Band's words were true, but without much success. Then he tried to divert his thoughts to some other topic.

'Have you ever been in love, Band?' Pim asked him.

'Sure – and more than my fair share. You?'

Pim waited before answering. 'Well, I thought I was at the time. Every time. But now that I think back about it, I am not sure it was love. I think it was just … longing.'

'Aha! So you didn't actually – '

'Look out!' shouted Danko. A big white protuberance of clouds rose in front of them, taking the shape of a giant arm coming from below and moving towards them. 'Hold on tight!' he shouted and swerved to avoid the cloud.

'What on earth was this?' said Pim as the arm of clouds closed in on empty space behind them.

'Look out, there's another one!' said Dr. Schlosen-Bosen. Another bulge in the clouds below suddenly rose right in front of Danko, trying to take hold of them.

'Don't fly into that cloud!' Pim shouted and Danko again veered sharply to fly around it.

'Higher, you've got to fly higher!' Dr. Schlosen-Bosen was also shouting but Danko replied that he was already flying as high as he could with the Flower and the three of them weighing him down.

'Drop the Flower!' Dr. Schlosen-Bosen said when another arm of clouds rose towards them.

'Drop the Stone Flower into the ocean? Never! I'd sooner plunge down myself than give up Yulka!' shouted Danko.

'Hormonal urges have their downsides,' was heard from Pim's pocket. Then an arm of clouds appeared from the right side. Danko veered to the left but could not avoid it altogether and the cloud slammed into them sideways. Pim and Dr. Schlosen-Bosen were almost knocked off by the turbulence and Danko barely managed to keep the heavy Flower in his claws.

'What's with these clouds?' shouted Dr. Schlosen-Bosen. 'If we get hit again, we're doomed!'

'Dapertutto! Dapertutto! Help!' Pim shouted to the clouds, but no answer could be heard in the thunder.

After a few minutes it became obvious that the storm below them was gaining strength. Danko kept forcefully beating his wings and both Pim and Dr. Schlosen-Bosen could feel his muscles struggling to keep them above the boiling mass of clouds. It was becoming harder and harder for him to manoeuvre between the protruding clouds as there were more and more arms rising and trying to bring them down. Quick manoeuvres were difficult to execute with the Stone Flower in his claws. Danko kept swerving left and right, but every swerve meant less and less control over their course, exposing them more and more to the next cloud that tried to take hold of them. When another arm of clouds shot out from below trying to ensnare them, they almost ended up right in its clutches. It touched them only slightly, but the turbulence pushed them downwards.

'The clouds are closing in on us! We're goners!' said Pim.

'Aechterla Slechterla! Nobody can save us now! I will never see my daughter again!' Dr. Schlosen-Bosen cried and resigned to his fate.

At exactly the same moment in Right World – in London, in West Acton, to be more precise – there happened another resigning to fate. Full of sombre thoughts, Mehdi came to realise that he was never again going to find Pim Pergamon in Open Oceans IV. He gave up on the search and let the console drop to the floor with a big sigh.

Ever since Andy left that afternoon when he could not find his earpiece, Mehdi had spent all of his free time – and some school time to be honest – trying to find Pim Pergamon again. It was obvious that Andy was not at all convinced that Mehdi had ever spotted Pim Pergamon in Open Oceans IV. He needed to be convinced. So Mehdi scanned all the islands and all the ships that he could find, he scanned all the quadrants of all the seas that he knew of – but with no success. He could find no trace of the ship with the passenger who looked like Pim Pergamon. As time went on, he became more and more despondent. He even began to doubt what he saw.

Now, after so much searching without success, the whole thing did not make any more sense. How could he have seen inside a computer game somebody that he'd met just days ago in the lobby of ACG? It hadn't made much sense in the first place, he admitted to himself. Andy was right – nobody would play as themselves. It was a ridiculous thought. It sounded like one of Otto's stories.

Otto was a mutual friend who always had the most incredible excuses for his various mishaps, often connected to preparation or consumption of food. 'I lost the game cartridge you lent me the other day,' he had once announced to an unpleasantly surprised Andy. 'Well, what I mean is, I didn't really lose it,' he tried to explain seeing that his friend was upset. 'It's just that I was frying some wienerschnitzels and your game just sort of fell into the pan. I tried getting it out really quickly, but by the time I managed, the plastic was already melting. I tried playing it after, but it wouldn't work,' concluded Otto. 'Ruined the schnitzels, too.'

From that time on, Andy stopped calling him Fatso and called him the Schnitzelmaster, in front of everybody in the school. Mehdi noticed that Otto was hurt when some people laughed too loud, so he didn't repeat it in front of him. But it was still funny – the Schnitzelmaster! Andy was capable of being very funny, if sometimes cruel.

Mehdi could now see a mean nickname coming his way, too, for thinking that he saw a real person in a video game. Serves me right, it was such a stupid idea, no wonder Andy didn't believe me, nobody in their right senses would believe me, thought Mehdi.

'Oh, I believe you,' Mia said sitting next to him. 'Of course I know what you are thinking about, it's all over your face,' she added when she saw his surprised face. 'And don't be so worried about what Andy thinks.'

Mehdi looked suspiciously at his little sister. He wasn't prepared to trust her just like that. Surely there was something behind this sudden compassion of hers. Still, he decided to overcome his reluctance and to respond to kindness with kindness. It was probably the one thing where he agreed with his father.

'You are very sweet, little sister. What you wouldn't say to make your big brother feel better,' Mehdi said, testing the waters.

'There's only four years difference between us,' Mia replied matter-of-factly looking up from a book she was reading. 'Plus, I *really* believe you.'

'Believe me what?'

'I believe you when you say that you saw that guy in Open Oceans IV.'

'Have you seen him, too?'

'No, I haven't.'

'There you go.'

'But I heard him.'

'Yeah, right.'

'Remember that earpiece that Andy brought with him the first time he came to visit after the testing? The one that he lost? Well, he didn't exactly lose it. I actually kept it.'

'What?'

'Well, it wasn't really his in the first place, was it? It belongs to ACG,' Mia said and stood up. 'Anyway, I've been listening to it almost every evening, in bed under the covers, as soon as father thought I was asleep. Sometimes I heard nothing and sometimes I could hear voices and music and stuff. And every time I heard something, I always also heard this name – Pim Pergamon.'

'Get outta here!' Mehdi roared with excitement at his newly found ally – his sister, of all people, would you believe it! 'Mia, where's that earpiece?'

The whole day the clouds were restless in the skies above the sea off Dragonborg. A huge mass of clouds was piled right up to the coast. But in the city itself, it was a sunny day because the clouds never reached the shore. Cumulodistantus was a well-known phenomenon in Dragonland. A storm would come from the sea, stopping just short of the land. The clouds would then writhe and boil at some distance over the sea, as if trying to escape the lightning bolts which pierced them incessantly, but they never made it to the shore. Half of the sky would be engulfed in a storm while the other half continued to bathe in the sun, the two halves magically divided by the shoreline.

When cumulodistantus appeared, dragons would flock to the shore to enjoy the sight of it. In Dragonborg, it meant that the Corniche, the promenade which covered the top of the ramparts where they faced the sea, was always crowded. Dragons came to the Corniche to bask in the sun while enjoying the refreshing breeze which invariably reached the sea-walls as a spill-over from the storm. Those were always enjoyable moments, watching the tempest that was so close while standing safely on the Corniche.

There were several learned explanations for this natural phenomenon, ranging from the evildoings of Talambas, the ever-scheming evil wizard, to an ancient curse bestowed on the great-great-grandfather of King Ragnagnoknorr who had once swallowed a whole sea after a particularly heavy lunch and was punished for it by half-weather.

However, none of the explanations was so ludicrous as the recently aired theory of the Secretary of State – who liked to think of himself as something of an amateur weatherman – suggesting that the whole cumulodistantus phenomenon had something to do with evaporation, precipitation and the Boundless Mountains acting as some sort of a barrier for the moisture-laden air coming from the sea. 'I mean, really!' was often heard on the Corniche during the current cumulodistantus as the more learned among dragons kept retelling the latest fancy of the Secretary of State, shaking their heads in disapproval. 'Moisture-laden-what? – Air? – Preposterous!'

Meanwhile, in Baibok Prison, it was busier than usual. It was the day of the new moon. But due to the fact that the King, the only beheading authority in Dragonborg, had spent the past ninety-nine years asleep, the number of prisoners awaiting execution was smaller than the norm – only one. And it was Sir Henry Grenfell-Moresby, the Bedel of Zandar.

In keeping with Harry's favourite saying that the high office of the Bedel must not only be respected, but seen to be respected, the King had ordered that none less than the Head of Beheadment was to take care of Harry during his last moments. It was an ugly hunchback dragon with an ill-fitting badly powdered wig and rumours abounded in the prison that he had not actually beheaded anyone ever since he took up the managerial post.

When he came to personally escort Harry out of the cell, Harry's head was full of the stories of various beheadment mishaps told to him by prison guards. Once they cut off a wrong head first, and the correct one only later, the other time the axe kept slipping so in the end they used a saw and so on. None of the incidents quoted ended happily for the beheadee, and many turned out to be rather more unpleasant than the swift and simple act Harry had come to expect. It all meant that Harry was even less pleased to see his executioner than would normally be the case – if that was at all possible. As a result, he conducted himself even more grandiosely than he normally would – if that was at all possible either.

An imposing chopping block was being prepared in the prison courtyard. Its seven grooves were scarred with many indentations of countless axe-falls on the nights of the new moon. Tonight, however, only one groove was being prepared for its impending use. The spectator stalls looked emptier than it would be expected for the first beheadment after ninety-nine years of hiatus, partly because there were no dragons on the programme tonight, but mostly because the social life of Dragonborg had moved to the Corniche on the occasion of the cumulodistantus.

King Ragnagnoknorr, however, was not at the Corniche. Shortly before the sunset, he arrived from the Royal Castle and entered the courtyard of Baibok Prison dressed in a sumptuous red and golden velvet justice robe. Accompanied by the Secretary of State and a handful of Royal Counsellors, he took up his position overlooking the place of the execution. When the King was comfortably seated, Harry was brought into the prison courtyard. Full of pride, he scornfully looked at the King, stealing a furtive glance towards the moon which had almost disappeared from the sky.

The King asked him if he had anything to say before he was beheaded. Harry was ready for that.

'The only authority empowered to sit in judgement on the Bedel of Zandar is the Master of Zandar. This judgement is therefore invalid and illegal.'

The King looked at the Secretary of State. He stood up, took a deep sigh, adjusted three of his five powdered wigs and finally said, 'The necessary authority was delegated to the King of Dragonland by the Treaty of Dragonborg. His Majesty King Ragnagnoknorr was in his full rights when he passed the judgement on you.' It was obvious that the elderly dragon did not relish this moment.

'Yes, but while Zandar is without a Master, all judgements have to be held in abeyance, including those based on delegated authority.'

The King looked at his Secretary of State again. It seemed that he could not think of what to say to this. 'This is a point of dispute,' he finally said.

'I am the King of the Kingdom der Dragonlanden and I resolve disputes here!' King Ragnagnoknorr said impatiently. 'And I decide that this dispute is resolved in favour of the King.'

'Why all this pomp and circumstance, all the semblance of legality, if you can just decide whatever you like?' Harry challenged the King in a firm voice.

'I am the King and I do what I like. It's a pretty basic thing about being a king, don't you know?'

The Head of Beheadment took the still-protesting Harry to the execution block where his hands were tied behind his back by one of the executioner's assistants. He was then made to turn away from the King. When they tried to blindfold him, Harry defiantly shook his head.

The Secretary of State nervously took out his grandfather's clock out of the pocket. He looked at the King who looked the other way. The Secretary of State dropped the clock and left it to swing slowly on the heavy chain in sync with its own pendulum.

All eyes turned to the sky where the last remnant of the old moon was slowly but inexorably disappearing. When the sickle was not visible any more, the King nodded seven times with seven heads and Harry was made to kneel.

'I can still see it,' Harry protested. 'There's not much of it left, but it's still there! It's not the time yet!'

The King nodded again and Harry was pushed down on the block again shouting, 'If you can't see it, it doesn't mean there aren't others who can, Your Pompous Short-Sightedness!'

The assistants took the Great Baibok Axe and handed it to the Head of Beheadment.

'It's so crude not to use astronomical tables anyway!' Harry was still shouting. 'I've always considered Dragonland to be one of the most backward and uncivilised places in Left World! Bloody primitives, you lot!!!'

The Head of Beheadment looked at the King. The King nodded again, impatiently, this time more than once with some of his heads, when a faint music was heard from a distance.

The Head of Beheadment lifted the axe. Harry's neck was exactly under the blade.

The music became louder. The Head of Beheadment took a deep breath and tightly grasped the axe whitening the knuckles of his claws.

The music could now be clearly heard. It was a silly oompah-oompah tune, exactly the kind Harry could not stand. But a smile appeared on his face.

A great commotion was heard outside the prison. The Head of Beheadment hesitated. He looked at the King.

In that moment a dragon appeared in the sky above Baibok Prison. A colossal trumpet was on his back, effortlessly blowing away the remnants of clouds around him. Two men could be seen sitting behind the trumpet, cheering the dragon in the beat of the music. One of them was waving a homburg hat. Right below them, in the dragon's claws, was the Stone Flower.

Everybody in the prison courtyard stood up in amazement, their eyes fixed on the malachite flower in the sky.

The axe was slowly lowered and left to rest by the chopping block.

That evening, the whole Dragonborg was whistling the melody that brought the long-lost Stone Flower back to dragons. When Danko had appeared in the sky above the Corniche with the malachite flower in his claws, celebrations immediately spread across the city and all the other searchers were promptly forgotten. In fact, the patriotic euphoria seized even those dragons who failed themselves to find the flower and win the Princess.

No official festivities were scheduled before tomorrow, but celebrations in Dragonborg were already under way. Everybody, dragon and non-dragon alike, celebrated in improvised street parties across the city. The festive mood spread outside the city too and the whole hinterland behind Dragonborg was aglow with fires of jubilation. Soon there was hardly a dragon who did not hear about the return of the Stone Flower and messengers were quickly dispatched to the Copper Mountain with instructions to repair the old pedestal on top of the mountain.

Tonight everyone simply wanted to be happy and have fun. The morph attack in Fairybury, the Black Dragons, the unrest in the northern provinces and other ominous incidents of the recent past were temporarily cast aside and forgotten. Strangers embraced each other in the streets and the traboules of Dragonborg were brimming with a feeling of elation and happiness.

When King Ragnagnoknorr returned from his early evening nap and informed everybody how he dreamt that his late Queen Mother stopped weeping, Pim thought it was safe enough to tear off his false moustache and declare who he really was. The King took it magnanimously and squeezed him in a warm embrace.

'You and your friends have brought the Stone Flower back to Dragonland and comforted my late mother! How could I hold anything against you?' the King said and turned to Harry. 'Sir Henry, I forgive you everything. If it wasn't for you, Pim Pergamon would never have arrived in Dragonland and rescued the Stone Flower. Next time, however,' he added, 'I'll keep fourteen eyes on your fingers at the card table.'

'There will be no need for that. I have learned my lesson, Your Majesty,' Harry responded in the voice of a penitent, quite uncharacteristically for him.

The King then turned to the Secretary of State. 'I want the best among the Grace & Favour Quarters in the Royal Palace given to Pim Pergamon, so that in the future, he may have a place to stay whenever he visits Dragonland.'

'Certainly, Your Majesty,' the old gentleman responded, moved to tears by the King's grace. He already loved the brave human who came up with the plan to give the Stone Flower back to dragons. And also to save the life of his old diplomat friend Sir Harry, the Bedel of Zandar, when it seemed that nobody could help him any more. 'The distinguished guests are also invited to the festivities tomorrow,' added the Secretary of State.

'What festivities?' asked Pim.

'The wedding of my daughter, of course!' replied the King.

A hastily proclaimed public holiday was to be held tomorrow to mark the wedding of Yulka, the King's daughter, and the brave dragon Danko, and to celebrate the beginning of the long journey of the Stone Flower back to the Copper Mountain along an ancient pilgrim route through the mountains.

But tonight, every dragon's wish was to be on the list of invitees for the Grand Dragon Ball taking place in the Royal Castle to honour the five saviours of the Stone Flower.

All the turrets and all the windows on the Royal Palace were brightly lit and the Royal Standard was proudly flying from the highest mast. The Grand Dragon Hall of the castle was brimming with the *soot de la soot* of Dragonborg while many more would-be-guests crowded the square outside the gates of the palace before the crossed halberds of the unflinching palace guards.

After a small commotion and a short, but heated discussion, one latecomer managed to win the right to enter. The halberds opened to let Tetka Savka pass. Her delay was regrettable, but well worth it – she managed to fit into her best dress after all. When the page announced her entrance into the Great Dragon Hall, she felt that all that she could have possibly wished for had come true. Nothing could diminish this happiness, not even if the Villain of the Deepest Dye sprang up at her right here and right now. But it wasn't the Villain of the Deepest Dye who was waiting inside. It was King Ragnagnoknorr himself, in a lavishly grand robe made of, yes, red and golden velvet. He greeted her and exchanged more than a few pleasantries – he even remembered Uncle Bitanga!

Seated at the other end of the hall was her nephew, the apple of her eye, bewigged and duly powdered for the first time in his life – and in a more splendid uniform than a doorman at the Grand Dragon Hotel! Right next to him was Her Highness Princess Yulka, soon to be a close relation of Tetka Savka. From now on, it was going to be so much simpler to explain the connection between her and the Royal family!

Tetka Savka looked around the sumptuously appointed Grand Dragon Hall and instantly felt at home. The lights were bright, the guests were distinguished and the buffet was unlimited.

It was the best of all possible worlds.

Pim, Harry, and Dr. Schlosen-Bosen were the three guests of honour, seated next to the King in the Royal Loggia overlooking the vast hall filled with swirling dragons in expensive evening wear. The fourth guest of honour, Band, chose to be on duty on the stage opposite the Royal Loggia, and was making the dragons swirl in the most elaborate orchestral setup that Pim had seen from him so far. His all-brass rendition of Puttin' on the Ritz was an instant success among the dancing dragons and he would have to repeat it twice before the evening was over.

The Royal Tailor had surpassed himself and had in no time outfitted Pim, Harry and Dr. Schlosen-Bosen with three elegant single-neck tuxedos. The three of them did not dance much but they looked absolutely spiffing sitting in the Royal Loggia, especially Dr. Schlosen-Bosen who was finally wearing something matching his homburg hat. The atmosphere was very different from any other moment since the beginning of their journey. They were relaxed. Dr. Schlosen-Bosen even let himself be persuaded to leave his precious barrel behind in his room. Also, the mood between them had improved. Harry, for one, did not hesitate to show that he was thankful – he went as far as admitting that Band could be a pain in the neck, but that he was a great fellow and without doubt the best instrument he had ever met.

'One has to admit one thing about Band – if it's about music, he's never tired,' he said. 'It is really a nice gesture that he offered to play tonight.'

'I thought they'd asked him to play,' said Pim.

'Oh, no. If he hadn't stepped in we would be bored to death now with the pyrostrings.'

'With what?'

'It's a traditional dragon folk instrument,' Dr. Schlosen-Bosen explained. 'It's basically a strung vibrating copper wire that changes pitch with temperature, depending on the flames directed at it. Its tone is a bit melancholic, though.'

'Suitable for suicides and funerals only,' clarified Harry.

'It is better that Band took over,' Dr. Schlosen-Bosen concurred. Pim had been somewhat worried at first about how Harry was going to react to the company of an ordinary tradesman, but it turned out that he had heard of the very best reputation of Dr. Ernst Theodor Amadeus Schlosen-Bosen and the Supranatural Supplies of Star Central. The two of them quickly struck a rapport on the issue of the importance of premium quality magic in these times of disintegrating values.

Meanwhile Band was busy showing the cosseted dragon youth assembled in the Grand Dragon Hall what delights lay beyond a single vibrating copper wire. He went from one fiery dancing number to another. Everybody enjoyed the music immensely and before the evening was out he had earned a nickname – Big Band.

The five daughters of the Secretary of State were immersed in dance. They had all shed a tear or five when the wedding of the handsome Danko was announced at the beginning of the ball, but had by now redoubled their attentions to other young dragons – and the Grand Dragon Hall tonight was full of eligible young bachelors. All the best families of Dragonborg were represented at the ball.

Even Mr. and Mrs. Secretary of State danced tonight, a grand total of ten heads gently pressing against each other, their feet moving in the beat twice as slow as the rest of the ball. Tetka Savka was overwhelmed by invitations to dance from ministers and admirals. She must have danced with just about everybody, except the King who was not much of a dancer. But whenever she caught a glimpse of Danko and Yulka together, she got all emotional and would have to sit down – many tuxedos and admiral's uniforms tonight ended up soaked with her tears of happiness and her face had to be repowdered many times over.

The newly promoted Wing Commander Danko Zmayski – nothing less than the rank of Wing Commander would befit the King's son-in-law – hardly had eyes for anybody else in the Grand Dragon Hall but his beloved Yulka. He still could not quite believe that the King accepted their marriage and it was only Yulka's firm seven-fold embrace in front of everybody that anchored him in the new reality. For her part, Yulka's chest could not stop swelling at the thought of all the dangers that Danko defied to get her hand in marriage. What a hero! Oh, and there was the matter of Harry's head. Oh, yes, and the Stone Flower! Hand, head and flower – three in one go!

The two of them glided effortlessly across the dance floor followed by many curious eyes. Not only was it exciting to see a one-headed commoner engaged to a seven-headed high-born – and of royal blood at that! – but the way Danko proficiently pressed his head against each of Yulka's seven heads in turn caught attention of many fellow dancers. It was not long before other daring couples of different social ranking started to imitate them. A new dance style was being born in Dragonland tonight, and with it a new egalitarian etiquette.

'As long as the King is oblivious to the fact that the two of them are not improvising, everything is going to be fine,' Harry leaned over to Pim. They were both enjoying a cocktail personally recommended by the Secretary of State. It was a mysterious concoction prepared especially for Pim according to the old gentleman's instructions. 'Mr.

Secretary of State promised to give me the recipe before we leave Dragonborg tomorrow,' said Harry.

'What? We are leaving tomorrow?'

'Of course we are leaving, we have a quest to finish,' said Harry.

'But where are we going?' said Dr. Schlosen-Bosen.

'You don't think I was just sitting on that Book of Gates while I whittled my days away in Baibok Prison, do you?'

'Well, I wouldn't be surprised if you did,' stated Pim.

'I found a gate. And I have some good news and some very good news. Which one do you want to hear first?'

'Hit me with the good news first,' replied a suspicious Pim.

'The gate is practically around the corner – on Ragnagnoknorr Square to be precise.'

'And?'

'And it leads to Star Central.'

'Star Central?'

'Straight, non-stop, direct gate to Star Central. This time tomorrow we'll all be home.'

The announcement was followed by silence.

Star Central – the destination that they had been trying to reach for so long, the city that was so much on their mind. All three of them continued to watch the dragons swirling through the Grand Dragon Ball, each one immersed in his own thoughts.

Have the morphs found the way to Star Central and attacked it – or is it still safe to go there, thought Harry. Will I get to the gate to Right World before it shifts again, thought Pim. Is my daughter alive and well? And if she is, will she be waiting with dinner ready, thought Dr. Schlosen-Bosen.

end of Part 1

Part 2: The Varieties of Administrative Experience
already available in Right World

For A. who made it possible.

Printed in Great Britain
by Amazon